PHANTOM

WHISPERS

JESSICA HAWKE

Mighty Fine Books, LLC

PO Box 956

Evans, GA 30809

Editing by Rainy Kaye

Cover Design by Clarissa Yeo

Book Design by Jessica Hawke

ISBN: 978-1-944142-16-2

First Edition: February 2017

Second Edition: April 2018

10 9 8 7 6 5 4 3 2

ALSO BY JESSICA HAWKE

Phantoms Series

Phantom Touch

Phantom Traces

Phantom Whispers

Visit www.jessicahawke.com to download

your <u>free</u> prequel novella, *Phantom Light*.

For those who walk this world with the shadow of loss.

CHAPTER ONE

I LEFT SCHOOL ON MONDAY with a stack of homework and a talkative spirit on my heels. While I had to weave through the flood of students pouring through the open doors to freedom, my spectral best friend and Guardian, Kale, passed through them like air. Even when the entire boys lacrosse team barreled through him on the way to the gym, it didn't interrupt his story.

"She had one of those silver things and was puffing on it in the lounge," he said. It was too bad that no one without the dubious honor of seeing the dead and otherwise non-corporeal could see him. Kale was a first-class hottie, with dark tousled hair and dreamy blue eyes. I wouldn't have minded if my classmates saw him walking next to me. He was even more gorgeous than my human crush Michael, although Michael had the advantage of a heartbeat.

After checking over my shoulder to make sure no one was looking right at me, I whispered, "An e-cigarette?"

"An e-cigarette," he murmured. "I'm starting to think you'll put *e* in front of anything."

I ignored him as I approached a cluster of girls blocking the hallway. Crammed shoulder to shoulder near the custodial closet on the science hall, they all looked down at someone's phone held between them. One of them screamed, while the other two laughed at her.

"Not funny, you guys!" she protested.

"Now you should go try it," the phone's owner said as she tucked the phone into her pocket. "I dare you."

My science teacher, Mrs. England, shooed them along. "Ladies, let's get moving. You don't have to go home, but you can't stay here." With a chorus of sighs, the girls spread out three across and sauntered down the hallway.

I darted around the girls and hurried outside to the bus loading area. Bus engines roared, echoing off the metal awning. Dodging a couple of boys beatboxing while a third filmed on his phone, I headed for the sidewalk that ran parallel to the front of the school.

I'd gone back to Mrs. England's classroom for an extra copy of the homework, putting me at the opposite end of the school from the parking lot. But the extra walk didn't bother me. It was a chance to let my guard down and quit pretending I didn't hear Kale chatting. After more than two years of dealing with ghosts, I had a great poker face.

"Yes, they're called e-cigarettes," I told Kale when I got past the crowd. I pulled out my phone and held it close to my mouth like I was voice-texting, not talking to myself. "It just means electronic. I'm just confused about why you think the electronic part is more interesting than the fact that the German teacher is smoking in the bathroom between classes. I'm pretty sure that's not allowed."

"She was," he said. "At least three times today."

"You watched her all day?"

"I got interested. I would smoke too if I had some of her students. So rude," he said. Then his brow furrowed. "I did other things, too. It's not like I float around your school all day looking for gossip."

"Well you should. Speaking of gossip, I found out that Brady Thomas waxes his chest," I told him. Kale's eyebrows shot up. "Yeah, as in hot wax, then rip!" I pantomimed on my chest. He winced.

As always, Kale wore light clothing that could have been linen if it was real and not just some aspect of his ghostly nature. I envied his ability to not get cold or hot, which would have been a much more useful superpower here in Georgia, where we would go from winter to summer and back again in the course of a week. Today, there was a sharp chill in the air, though the sun shone bright in a crystal clear sky.

Just minutes after the last bell, the student parking lot was already half empty. Bumper-to-bumper traffic crawled between the rows of parking spots. It was easy to spot Emily's yellow Volkswagen in her assigned spot. The loud music blaring from inside her car reached me four rows away.

As we approached Emily's car, Kale waved. "I'll leave you two to catch up. See you when you get home."

"I'm meeting with Detective Fulbright today," I said. "So after that."

He nodded. "Right. Be careful."

"Always."

With a wry smile, he faded away to wherever cute Guardians went when they weren't checking on their wayward charges or snooping on nicotine-addicted German teachers. Unlike most spirits, Kale didn't expect me to solve his problems and send him into the light. He was my Guardian, although he was annoyingly vague about what that meant. And while he had a 'gorgeous boy in white' thing going on, he wasn't an angel. After years of asking questions, I accepted that Kale was Kale, and that was all I knew. But our friendship had its limits, and he had long grown tired of my best friend Emily's taste in music and her relentless attention to detail when it came to discussing gossip and fashion.

Loud music bombarded me as I opened the passenger door. I had to move a heap of jackets and scarves into the backseat, where there was already enough clothing to outfit the entire junior class.

Emily turned down the stereo for me, which was a sure sign that we were best friends. "Hi, honey," she said. Her most recent hair overhaul had left her with dark roots that faded into dark purple ends. Blue glitter eyeshadow sparkled in the afternoon light as she turned to acknowledge me.

"Hi, darling," I replied.

She glanced over her shoulder to inspect the back seat, then looked at me with wide, dark-lined eyes. "Are we alone?"

"Just the two of us." I'd kept my ability a secret for two years, but I'd finally told Emily about it a few months ago.

Back in November, I'd helped an angry spirit named Natalie find the sicko who killed her. Natalie had been a senior at my school who had run away from home in the past, so people thought she'd taken off again. But when I encountered Natalie's enraged spirit in my bedroom, I knew better. The killer had kidnapped Emily before the police converged on him and scared him out of town. Once she was safe, I confided in her about my abilities. It had taken her some time to get used to the new development, but she was open-minded about it now. It was nice to have someone else in my life—someone with a heartbeat—who knew what I could do.

"I want you to watch this video," she said, trying to maneuver the phone with one hand while she backed up the car. She stomped the brake as a horn blared behind us. A red Jeep was inches from the back of Emily's car. "Whoops."

"Here." With my heart leaping into my throat, I grabbed her phone. She wasn't the greatest driver to begin with, and I wanted to get home in one piece.

Cursing under her breath, she twisted around in her seat to check for cars, then backed out slowly to merge into traffic. Once we stopped again, she took the phone back and swiped through her apps. "This. Tell me what you think."

When she handed me the phone again, it was displaying a paused video in YouTube. The caption read *Uno Bros Tres: Dead Eyes Challenge.* "What is it?"

"Everyone was talking about it in gym today," she said. "It made me think of you."

That wasn't an answer, but I pressed *play* anyway. A slick animated intro spelled out *Uno Bros Tres* in glowing letters. Then the screen appeared to shatter like exploding glass before fading onto a dark shot of trees and what looked like tombstones.

The camera bounced, following two figures with flashlights. A male voice narrated. "This is Uno Bros Tres bringing you the Dead Eyes Challenge. We were tagged by our buddy Darkstar, so we're heading out to the cemetery tonight."

The video cut to three figures with flashlights. The camera had stabilized, like it had been put onto a tripod. Now it was clear that they were surrounded by tombstones, rising like teeth against the dark backdrop of night.

One of the figures, a boy with shaggy blond hair, stood in front of the camera. "Here we go." They sat in an arc around a large headstone. The blond boy took a folded piece of paper out of his pocket and read from it, "Restless spirit, come to me. Tell me what your dead eyes see. Unbroken and unfettered be; from your ancient graves be free!"

I shivered. They were just a bunch of dumb high school boys, but the thought of calling out to spirits in a graveyard was stupid no matter who you were.

Silence fell as the three boys stared at each other, then looked around frantically. The blond boy looked off camera and whispered, "Did you hear that?"

A shadow passed in front of the camera. One of the boys shouted, then the camera fell over. The audio was all pops and static, with the occasional muffled shouting breaking through. On screen was a blurry dance of black and gray, as the camera bounced along without focusing.

The video cut to a shot of the three boys sitting at a yellow plastic table that could have only been a Waffle House. All three boys were still, eyes wide and faces pale.

"So what did you see?" one of them asked. Dead leaves stuck out of his messy, dark hair.

"I didn't see it, but I felt it," the blond boy said.

The third boy snickered, apparently unshaken by what had happened. "That's what she said."

But the others didn't laugh.

The boy with leaves in his hair shook his head. "There was definitely something out there."

"You think it was real?"

They continued like that for another few minutes, but they just kept repeating that they were sure something was there without giving any details.

Finally, the video cut back to the blond boy alone in front of a white background. "Have you taken the Dead Eyes challenge? Let me know what you thought of this video in the comments, and tune in next Thursday for a new video."

The video cut to credits with embedded animations of his other videos over techno music. The two featured videos were *Home Depot Toilet Prank* and the *Sriracha Challenge*. Not exactly high art.

"So?" Emily said. When I looked up from the screen, we were on the road toward my house, with the winter-bare trees blurring by the windows.

"I don't know," I said. "It seems like some douchebags trying to get YouTube-famous."

"But was there something there?"

I frowned at her. "I don't know. I don't see anything."

"Oh." Her expression fell. "Well, it seemed like your kind of thing."

I handed her the phone back and shrugged. "Sorry, I didn't mean to ruin your surprise."

She rolled her eyes. "Girl, please. I have plenty. Let me tell you about what Eliza Jane told me in gym today."

I half-listened to her story about two junior girls getting busted for sexting. Despite my initial disbelief, my mind drifted back to the video. Could the invocation have worked? I had called out to spirits and stirred them up, but I was different.

About two years ago, I was in a car accident that killed my older sister Valerie and left me injured. They had to do surgery on my leg, and a bad reaction to anesthesia made my heart stop for a few seconds. According to Kale, I came back as a new and improved version of myself, one that wasn't completely in the world of the living. That was when my ability had started. But these boys weren't like me, as far as I knew.

Emily elbowed me, sending a sharp pain down my arm. "Ow!" I complained.

"You totally checked out on me," Emily said.

"I'm sorry, I was thinking about that video."

But instead of rolling her eyes in annoyance, her glossy lips curved into a wide smile. "I knew it was something!"

"I'm not saying it's definitely a ghost thing," I said. "But I'll try to find out more about it."

When Emily drove up to my house, a sleek police cruiser sat in the driveway. "What the...what did you get into now?"

"It's okay." I said. In case it wasn't already obvious that my life was weird, the sight of the police cruiser in the driveway didn't faze me. The car belonged to Detective Fulbright, who I'd been in contact with several times over the last few months. After my most recent adventure with the life-impaired, Fulbright had decided he wanted to check in on me every few weeks. Today was our first meeting. "He just wants to check in with me once in a while."

"You are so weird," Emily said. "And I love it."

"Thanks."

"Skype me later if you get bored."

"Got it. Bye!" Grabbing my heavy backpack from the floorboard, I got out of the car and waved goodbye to her.

Fulbright was fiddling with a file in his lap and looked up in surprise when I knocked on the window. With my heart thumping in anticipation, I dropped into the seat. Though he wore a normal plaid button down and jeans, his close-cropped salt-and-pepper hair and craggy face gave him an aura of authority.

"Hey kiddo," he said. His gravelly voice sounded like he was trying for warm and friendly, but considering the situation, it came off a little awkward. "You ready to go?"

It probably said something about me that I was hanging out with a detective instead of a cute boy—one with a heartbeat—but I'd long learned to accept the sheer weirdness of my life. "Let's go."

CHAPTER TWO

MY NOT-DATE WITH THE DETECTIVE took us to Lovely Ice, a frozen yogurt and bubble tea shop near Target. He started to make small talk about my day at school, but got interrupted by a call from the station, which saved us both from some awkwardness. I couldn't help eavesdropping, but it seemed to be an issue with paperwork one of his coworkers had filed that morning. Boring.

He was still on the phone when he parked at Lovely Ice. The store was at the opposite end of the Target shopping center where Mom dragged my brother and me every Sunday after church. Three girls wearing matching school hoodies sat at one of the outdoor tables.

Before we got out, Fulbright pulled down the sun visor, dropping a folded bundle of papers into his lap. He shuffled them together and tucked them into his jacket pocket, and then got out of the car. As I followed suit, the three girls looked my way. I ignored them and followed him inside.

Inside, the shop was crowded and warm. Teal vinyl dots scattered across the neon green walls. Cheerful K-pop music played over the speakers.

Fulbright let me order first, and then paid for both of our drinks. As we waited at the end of the counter for our drinks, I scoped the crowded shop for an open table and for any unexpected guests.

Ever since I'd started seeing the lingering dead, I scanned crowds for ghosts the way my mom checked her scalp for gray hair. I had a choice to block them out. Kale had taken a necklace that belonged to Valerie and imbued it with a protective power that kept me from seeing the spirits. But it made me feel disconnected, and it didn't prevent spirits from seeing me or touching me. It was just a set of blinders to let me concentrate. I usually only bothered with it if I was having trouble focusing at school, or if I was out in public with Mom and couldn't deal with the stress of maintaining my poker face.

Near the front window, a pair of blonde women sat on the same side of a four-person table. Their curly hair and high cheekbones were similar enough that they could have been sisters. They both sipped lavender-tinted drinks mounded with fluffy whipped cream. An older woman sat across the table from them, but she had no drink. I frowned. The two younger women didn't acknowledge her presence, although I wouldn't make the quick jump to *ghost* immediately. Still, my pulse quickened, and I made a note to keep an eye on her.

"Tom?" someone called. "And Bridget?"

I startled from my creepy staring to see an older woman in a neon green apron pushing two pastel-colored drinks across the counter. Fulbright picked them both up and handed me the pink one.

The barista beamed. "You are the spitting image of your dad."

"Thanks," I said. I didn't bother correcting her that Fulbright and I weren't related.

"You know, most kids would get embarrassed about that," Fulbright said as we walked over to the side of the bar to get napkins.

I shrugged. "I didn't want to make her feel awkward."

The only open table was a two-seater near the front of the store, right next to the trash can. Fulbright pulled out my chair and waited for me to sit down. As I considered the table, I glanced over at the maybe-sisters. They still weren't looking at the older woman.

I ignored the seat Fulbright had pulled out and sat on the opposite side. He gave me a quizzical look. "Air vent," I lied. Really, I wanted a clear view of the three women, and the seat he'd offered me put my back to them.

We sat down at the table, and he slid the folded papers to me like we were spies in a movie. After taking a sip of my sweet strawberry drink, I unfolded the papers and smoothed out the creases. The papers were copies of police reports. I skimmed over them. "What am I looking at?"

"I think they're called papers," he said.

"You can't dad-joke me," I said. "We're not taking the act that far."

We'd first met a few months earlier when I helped Natalie Fullmer solve her own murder. Despite Kale's insistence that I was dangerously reckless, I tried to be safe. With some detective work and assistance from Natalie, I'd found where her killer, dubbed the Runaway Killer, buried his victims.

Once I found the burial ground, which was hard evidence instead of my crazy-sounding claim of seeing her ghost, I called the cops like any intelligent person would do. But Emily got taken before they caught him. Then I'd summoned his other victims to help me find her. When I got a location, Fulbright wouldn't take my tip seriously, so I took it into my own hands. Considering he'd killed dozens of supposed runaways from all over the state, the case had made national news. Thankfully, being a minor meant my name stayed out of the news, and both Emily's mom and mine had denied any media requests.

Then right before Christmas break, two local kids disappeared after leaving school. I'd seen a post about it on Facebook. While they had been gone for less than a day, I couldn't shake a bad feeling about it. I'd mobilized spirits all over town to search, eventually discovering they'd gotten lost in the woods. This time, Fulbright had listened, but his single patrol out to the sprawling state park hadn't been anywhere close to finding the missing kids in time.

After escorting the kids out of the woods, Fulbright finally realized I wasn't just getting lucky. A few days after that, he'd asked if we could meet periodically to check in. He'd even called my mother, telling her he wanted to make sure I was recovering from the traumatic experience of encountering Emily's killer. My cover story had been that he texted me from Emily's phone to lure me to his lair, which made sense except for making me look like a victim instead of the one who'd busted him. Mom had been thrilled about Fulbright's suggestion, and I'd managed to surprise the words right out of her mouth when I agreed to meet him.

"I know this is kind of weird," he said. "It's just...well, you've been right on two cases. And it keeps me up at night to think about what could have happened if you hadn't intervened. So I want you to feel comfortable talking to me if you know something. I thought you could look at this and tell me if you..." He trailed off and pinched the bridge of his nose. "This is ridiculous."

"It's okay," I said. "Let me see."

I flipped to the second page of the police report, which was covered with blue sticky notes with notes in Fulbright's neat cursive. A quick scan revealed that it was a report on several home invasions in the same neighborhood. It wasn't my usual sort of thing.

"Are you...uh, getting anything?" he asked.

I suppressed a laugh. He seemed to think I was psychic. "Is there anything the houses all have in common?"

His brow furrowed in surprise. "You think like a detective."

"I watch a lot of TV." And another of my ghostly companions was a local cop who'd been killed in the line of duty. Sal liked to watch *Law and Order* reruns with my mom from the corner and comment on the inaccuracies. Though he thought I didn't listen, I'd learned a lot from him.

"As far as we can tell so far, nothing in common," Fulbright said. "A couple had security systems, a couple didn't."

Behind him, the two women were clearing their table. Still sitting, the older woman looked wistful. As they walked out the door, her gaze followed them, until her eyes fell on mine. My breath caught in my throat, though it wasn't from the usual embarrassment of being caught staring.

Her head tilted slightly, like a dog hearing a high pitch. Her eyes widened, and pointed at her chest, as if to say *are you looking at me?*

There was no obvious sign of her death. Except for the fact that no one acknowledged her, she looked normal. I gave her a little wave. Her sad expression lifted, and her lips curved into a faint smile.

Fulbright glanced over his shoulder. "Who are you waving at?"

My cheeks flushed, and I lowered my hand. "I thought I knew someone over there." I cleared my throat and took a sip of my tea as I looked back to the reports. "So how do you know all these robberies are connected?"

Fulbright was digging for one of the bubbles with his straw. He looked up sheepishly. "Well, I don't for sure. They've all been in the same neighborhood. MO is similar. They tend to ignore the big stuff and take game systems and tablets. Smaller stuff that's easy to carry and easy to fence."

Over the edge of the paper, I saw the older woman inching toward me. I ignored her and looked back at the paper, skimming the words without really reading them. How was I going to help with a bunch of robberies? Could I enlist my ghost friends to be an undead neighborhood watch?

Fulbright suddenly reached out and covered the paper with his callused hand, lowering it to the table. "This is nuts. I don't know what I'm doing here."

"Last I checked, you asked for my help," I said, trying to move the paper back.

As she got closer, the old woman moved faster, until she had closed the distance between us. Her presence bathed me in a rush of cold air. My left side was warm with the residual heat of the sun through the plate glass window, but my right felt like I was standing in the doorway of a walk-in freezer.

He shook his head. "You're a sixteen year old kid."

"Seventeen," I said, using all my self-control not to react to the sudden presence of the ghost and her accompanying chill. "And I think we both know I'm not like other kids." Her fingers grazed my shoulder, sending a needle of ice down my arm. Even as my blood seemed to freeze, I smiled to hide my shock.

"But you should be. I shouldn't be putting this crap on you."

I gently took the paper away. "Fulbright," I said. "This crap is out there whether you tell me about it or not." The old woman touched my cheek. I flinched. "I'll have to deal with it sooner or later. And I'd rather not do it *later*." Judging by the glacial chill still engulfing my right side, the ghost wasn't getting my hint.

He sighed. If he noticed my efforts to stave off the old lady's roaming hands, he didn't let on. "I guess you're right. But promise me you'll honor our deal. You don't run off half-cocked if you find something. You let the professionals handle it."

"Yes, sir." The woman's hand ran over my hair, sending a prickling chill over my scalp. I shivered. "Can I borrow your pen?"

He took a ballpoint pen out of his jacket pocket and handed it over. "So I try not to ask, but what do you really do? How does this whole thing work?"

I covered the police report with my arm and scrawled across the top edge.

231 Shadowbrook Lane <u>COME SEE ME LATER</u>

After underlining *later* several times for emphasis, I held the paper up like I was reading it over. With one finger, I traced the line under the word *later* for my touchy-feely ghost friend to see. "Funny how you said you tried not to ask and then asked anyway," I said mildly. "If my end of the bargain is letting you handle the police work, then your end is to not ask me that question."

"Why?"

"Because you'll think I'm crazy," I said. "And it doesn't matter."

My right side went warm again. I flicked my eyes over my shoulder. The old woman had disappeared, leaving no sign that she'd ever been there. I hoped she wouldn't show up that night, because I had a lot of homework to do and doing therapy for another ghost didn't fit into the schedule for the night.

My phone buzzed in my pocket. I took it out to see a new message from my mom glaring at me from the lock screen.

Mom: OMW home. Make sure you have your stuff together for class

What class? I mentally reviewed the last few days, but my memory was a blur of school and ghosts and the occasional attempt at sleep.

"Shoot," I said. "I need to get home." And at home awaited Mom, who had some mysterious class in store, and yet another ghost that wanted my attention. Peachy.

CHAPTER THREE

I BREATHED A SIGH OF RELIEF when we arrived at my house. The driveway was still empty, which meant I had a few minutes before diving back into the never-ending struggle of life with my mother. After promising Fulbright for the third time that I wouldn't go all vigilante Batman-style if I found anything about his home invasions, I said my goodbyes and trudged up the front sidewalk.

The house was quiet and still. I heard the muffled sound of my brother talking upstairs, probably playing a game on his computer with his friends. The only other sign of life was an open bag of Doritos on the kitchen counter. I dropped my backpack, then went to put the chips away so Colin didn't get in trouble when Mom got home. We'd moved after my sister Valerie's death two years earlier, and Mom insisted on keeping the new house so spotless that it could have been the "after" on one of those house-flipping shows she liked. It looked nice, but it was cold and devoid of the warm touches that made the old house feel like home.

Anyway, I owed Colin. I'd snuck out of the house to find Diana and Corey, the two kids who went missing in the woods. When I crept back into the house just before sunrise, half-frozen and exhausted, Colin had busted me. After watching the news the next day, he'd figured out I was responsible for the rescue, but not exactly how I'd done it. To my surprise, he didn't rat me out to Mom, so I'd been trying to go easier on him ever since.

I grabbed a handful of chips before rolling the top of the bag closed and stuffing it back into the cabinet.

"How was your date?"

I whirled to find Kale standing in the open doorway of the kitchen.

"Fine," I mumbled around a mouthful of nacho cheese-flavored crumbs. "And it's not a date. That sounds gross. He's old enough to be my dad."

I hoped my breath wasn't atrocious, because Doritos were hell on your oral hygiene. Then again, Kale didn't technically breathe, so maybe he couldn't smell my breath. One could hope.

"What did he have for you?"

"Some home invasion case," I said. "I told him I'd peek at it, but it's not really my thing."

"Let's remind ourselves. You're not—"

"I already promised Fulbright." I put up my hand like I was taking an oath. "I will not run off to solve the case myself."

"Good."

It wasn't like I enjoyed putting myself in danger. Well, that wasn't entirely true. Mixed in with the terror, there was always this electric streak of exhilaration, like the first drop on a death-defying roller coaster. And what was I supposed to do, anyway? Sit back and let innocent people get hurt or worse because the adults in my life didn't take me seriously? Maybe meeting with Fulbright would change things. When the next mysterious case presented itself—as I was sure that it would—I hoped he would call in the cavalry instead of "taking it under advisement" yet again.

"I also met another spirit. Kind of." I told him about the older woman and her total lack of respect for my personal space.

"And she didn't talk to you?"

"No," I said. "She seemed shocked that I could see her. I wrote down my address for her."

"I'll stick around in case she shows up tonight."

"Okay. If you want to," I said casually, but my heart did a tap dance complete with jazz hands at the thought of Kale staying around. He came and went as he pleased, usually leaving me alone at night unless I was on the job. If I was dealing with a spirit face-to-face, he lived up to his title and acted as a guardian to prevent spirits from harming me.

Kale had first appeared to me not long after my ability developed. I'd seen Valerie a few weeks after her death, making me question my sanity. Then Kale had come along a few weeks later, helping me communicate with Val and gradually teaching me about my ability. According to him, it was his job as my Guardian to protect me and guide me as I grew older.

It was weird to have a crush on a ghost, but I didn't have to be anyone but myself around Kale. No lying about my ability, no pretending to pay attention while a ghost yammered away in my ear. Except for the occasional butterflies at the thought of his soft lips and graceful hands, his presence brought a sense of peace that was so rare in my life.

"Hey, I have a question for you," I said. "Emily showed me this video after school. She thought it was weird, but I wasn't sure."

"Can you show me?"

I dug my phone out of my pocket and texted Emily.

Hey, will you send me that graveyard video? I want to show Kale

The typing animation danced across the screen. Before she had sent her response, a car door slammed outside.

"I'll be upstairs," Kale said. He disappeared in a rush of cool air as Mom opened the front door. She couldn't see him, but I couldn't talk to him with her around.

"Bridget?" she called. "Colin?"

I stuck my head out of the kitchen door. "I'm home."

Mom jumped, pressing one hand to her chest. "You scared me. I thought you'd be in your room."

"I'm full of surprises, I guess."

"Colin!" she yelled. "You need to get your stuff together. We have to leave by 5:40 to make it on time."

I frowned. "Make it where?"

She sighed and peeled off her pink monogrammed scrub jacket as she walked through the living room. Her foot caught on my backpack strap, making her stumble. "Son of a...Bridget, don't leave your things out."

"But I—" I cast a glare back at the pantry, which had interrupted my mission to put my backpack out of sight in a Mom-approved location. So much for helping Colin. No good deed goes unpunished. "Sorry."

She kicked off her shoes, then bent to pick them up. "You guys start your classes at the community center tonight."

"Classes?"

She gave me an exasperated look. "It's on the calendar."

Hanging on the refrigerator was a dry-erase calendar covered in Mom's tight handwriting. Considering I was usually paying attention to needy ghosts or my growling stomach, I had about zero chance of noticing updates to the calendar. "Can you give me a reminder?"

"I reminded you last night and you said okay. I suppose this answers the question of whether you were really listening." Her thin eyebrows furrowed as her tone sharpened.

"Mom, maybe you could just answer me instead of reminding me of how much I suck." My temper flared. Sometimes I wondered if she spent her entire commute home gearing up to fight with me.

"SAT prep," she snapped. "Remember? I signed you up for the May test so we can get a head start on your college admissions. Donna signed both of her kids up for it, and they improved their scores by three hundred points."

I sighed. "Yay. More school." With a stack of homework and ghost business to discuss with Kale, that was the last thing I needed.

"This is for your future. And it's non-negotiable. Make sure you have pencils and a notebook." She glanced at her watch. "We have fifteen minutes." She yelled again for Colin, then ran upstairs to remind him.

I didn't even bother unpacking my backpack. Instead, I sat on the couch and waited for Mom to come back downstairs and go to her room. Once I heard the quiet click of Mom's bedroom door, I whispered, "Kale!"

Though a living human wouldn't have heard me all the way upstairs, the connection between us made it easy to contact him. He could hear me from miles away, although he promised he couldn't read my mind. Thank God for that, or things would get awkward fast. He reappeared downstairs a few seconds later, wrapped in a cool breeze that smelled of green, growing things.

"Watch this real quick," I said. While I opened Emily's reply and cued up the video, he materialized next to me on the couch. Though he appeared to be sitting next to me, there was no solidity or weight that shifted the cushion like a human being would have. Leaning the phone against a candle on the coffee table, I pressed *play*.

As the boys recited the "dead eyes" poem again, Kale's eyes narrowed. Throughout the video, his nostrils flared and his lips pursed in annoyance. "Is this what passes for entertainment?"

"Is there really something there?"

He regarded me. "It's difficult to say. You know technology is unpredictable with spirits," he said. "I don't see anything."

"So could it have—"

Mom's door opened, and she called out, "Bridget! Colin! Get down here, we have to go!"

"We'll discuss when you get home," Kale said. "Have fun."

I rolled my eyes at him, holding back my verbal response so Mom didn't hear me. She emerged from her bedroom wearing exercise clothes. She'd exchanged her black work scrubs for a pair of loose black capris and a bright blue tank top. Her short copper hair was pulled up in a tiny, bouncy ponytail. That was a new look.

She yelled again for Colin, who came thundering down the stairs in a pair of loose white pants and a faded green t-shirt. He had a folded strip of white fabric in one hand. "I don't know how to tie the belt, Mom."

"They'll teach you," Mom said, grabbing her keys from the counter. "Come on. I don't want to be late."

"Wait," I said as we walked out the door. "I have to do math and he gets to do karate?"

"I wanted to do programming," Colin complained, as if he could sympathize with my plight.

"Well, let's trade," I said. "He can go to SAT class."

"Programming was already full, Colin," she said. "And he's not trying to get into college yet. You are." Wait. When was it decided that I was headed for college? "Quit complaining. It'll be good for both of you."

When we arrived at the Coral Park community center, the parking lot was nearly full. Women with gym bags and spandex pants hurried inside, followed by kids in karate uniforms. A bright blue banner hung over the double doors, welcoming us to the *Winter Activities Kickoff*.

I tried to fix a Mom-approved, sass-free expression on my face as Mom got directions to our classes from the receptionist. After sending Colin on his way toward the karate room, Mom walked with me toward my class.

She stopped halfway down the hall and gave me a stern look. "Please take this seriously. You need to be thinking about your future now. We can't wait until next year to start thinking about college."

We were here, and it wasn't worth arguing now. "Got it," I said flatly. She just gave me a nod before going into the Zumba room, where a flock of women in bright tanktops were chatting amidst the noisy din of Latin music. I couldn't picture my mother loosening up enough to shake her bon-bon for Zumba. Maybe we could trade.

It was January of my junior year, and I hadn't given college much thought beyond the mandatory guidance counselor visits. In ninth grade, I'd been on track for a totally normal, maybe even awesome, high school experience. Then my sister Valerie died, and I became a certified freak. Seeing the dead had a way of shaking up my priorities. Suddenly, school, college, and everything else about my future had faded.

Now, I couldn't even picture the future. When the guidance counselor said, "Where do you see yourself in five years?" I didn't have an answer. It wasn't like I didn't want to be alive or something, but my future was a question mark in pencil.

I trudged into the classroom at the end of the hall. About half of the seats were taken, all with high school kids. A middle-aged woman in a Mount Sharon High School sweatshirt was setting up a projector. She glanced at me and said, "Hi, sweetie. Grab a card and put your name on it."

After making my nametag, I chose a seat in the middle of the room and sat down. As always, I scanned the room for spirits so I wouldn't be caught by surprise. Everyone looked lively and healthy, if a little bored. Out of habit, I reached for my blue spiral notebook, which contained pages of research on spirits and cases. But focusing more on ghosts than school had tanked my GPA, and I had been trying to fix that to get Mom off my back. Good habits had to start somewhere. Fighting the urge, I made a point of zipping my backpack and laying out a pencil and a highlighter in the groove in the front of the desk.

A few minutes later, the teacher cleared her throat. "Okay, folks, let's get started. I'm Mrs. Zapruder, and I teach geometry at Mount Sharon High."

She prattled on through an introduction that emphasized how important the SAT was, and how proud she was that we were investing in our future. While she talked, I examined my classmates. About half of them looked eager and ready to learn, while the other half looked like they would have rather been in karate class. The ones staring at her with blank eyes and pursed lips were probably in the "Mom Made Me" club like me. We weren't investing into crap.

"The SAT is now in three sections," she said. While she talked, she passed out a set of workbooks. When mine thumped on the table in front of me, I jumped a little.

I wanted to walk out and tell Mom where she could stick her SAT book. If I couldn't handle high school, I didn't have a chance at college. Besides, even if I could make it through college, what kind of future did I have? Maybe I'd start a business as a psychic or something. Emily had suggested a reality show when she first found out what I could do, but I wasn't a big fan of cameras.

Once upon a time, I'd believed I could get rid of my ability with an arcane ritual. But that had just been an elaborate story Kale concocted as "motivation," which the rest of the world called "lying." He'd done it to force me to accept Valerie's death and help her move on, but I'd always resented him a little for dangling false hope in front of me. Now I had to grieve the loss of a normal life as much as my dead sister.

But Mom didn't know any of that. She thought I was being difficult and rebellious. Maybe I was, but not for the reasons she thought. Kale thought I should tell her, but I enjoyed not being locked up in a mental institution if at all possible. I tried to tell her once, not long after I first saw Valerie. Convinced I was having a nervous breakdown, she homeschooled me for the rest of the year so I could have regular therapy sessions and go to support groups for grieving teenagers. I wouldn't make the same mistake again.

Mrs. Zapruder returned to the podium. "Okay, guys, we're going to do some practice questions so you can get a feel for it. Did you bring calculators?"

I looked around. Sophie and a few other kids pulled graphing calculators out of their bags. The rest of us in the Mom Made Me club shrugged.

"No worries," Mrs. Zapruder said. "I'll trust you with your phones. If you go to this website, it's got a great free app you can use in a pinch."

She grabbed a dry erase marker and wrote the website on the board. Underneath, she wrote *Questions 1 – 20, page 18 – 31.*

I sighed and opened the book to page eighteen, then set my phone on the desk next to it. To my credit, I did open the website, bringing up a neat little coordinate grid. My intentions were good, but my willpower was weak. After checking that my sound was off, I opened the YouTube app and searched for "dead eyes."

The search returned over thirty thousand hits. Holy crap. Most of them had *#deadeyeschallenge* in the title. I wasn't big on social media trends, but how had I missed this one? An endless stream of graveyards blurred past as I scrolled through the top results.

It was just a stupid social media trick, but I didn't like the idea of people trying to get famous by goofing around on people's graves. It was disrespectful to their families and the spirits who might have lingered. And plus, it was creepy.

But creepy didn't mean I had to focus on it right now. I tried to push it out of my brain by swiping back to the calculator app. While I stared at the first problem, my mind drifted again, this time to the case Fulbright had brought me. If I could come up with a map, I could find a number of friendly spirits in the area and ask them to keep an eye out. Spirits could travel quickly, and unlike me, they were in no danger of being seen or caught somewhere they didn't belong.

No, I scolded myself. With a deep breath, I forced my attention back to the first question, mouthing the words silently to keep myself on track.

Mrs. Zapruder meandered through the quiet classroom, pausing to inspect work as she went. I skimmed the question, then jotted down the measurements to calculate the volume of a swimming pool. As I used my phone to calculate the volume, my phone buzzed with a text from Emily.

Emily: what did kale think?

Floral perfume tickled my nose as Mrs. Zapruder paused next to me. With her shadow darkening my paper, I made a show of labeling my units, then tapping my pencil on each option in the workbook before writing the correct answer. The shadow moved on, and I returned to my text.

Can't talk right now. Mom put me in SAT class. Home soon.
Emily: Gross

Emily: Skype when u get home. Found another one you should watch, they go to Marymount

OK

Marymount High School wasn't far from my school, which meant they had probably done the video close by. Where would they have gone? I shook myself and gripped my pencil tightly to focus. *Not now.*

I made it through the second problem without interruption, and was reading over the third when the familiar cool breeze of Kale's arrival blew over me. I sighed and looked up, raising my eyebrows at him.

He put up his hands apologetically. "Just thought you should know, there's a spirit at your house. I told her to come back later, so she's sitting in your driveway."

I sighed and wrote *OK* on my paper next to my scratch work. Couldn't a girl get a break once in a while?

CHAPTER FOUR

IT WAS ALMOST EIGHT O'CLOCK by the time we got home, after a brief detour to pick up pizza for dinner. Despite Kale's warning, there was no spirit in the driveway. Relief washed over me. Maybe she'd gotten tired of waiting.

Mom hit the remote to open the garage door. As it rose, a familiar spirit in a faded green sweater appeared. She stared intently at the storage bins of Christmas decorations that hadn't been organized yet. I was annoyed at first, but I only had myself to blame. I had given her an actual handwritten invitation to visit me at home.

Colin grabbed the pizzas and bounded into the house. Mom shouted after him. "Wash your hands before you touch that pizza!"

I took my time walking up the driveway. The interior of the garage was even colder than outside thanks to the ghost's presence. As Mom stepped around a coiled pile of Christmas lights, she shivered. She paused and looked over her shoulder. "Is it cold in here?"

I shrugged. "You do have on a tank top."

She was still wearing her gym clothes, with a heart-shaped sweat pattern on her back. But it was much colder than it should have been. My living grandma left a cloud of powdery-smelling perfume in her wake; this ghostly granny brought an Arctic wind. While it took an ability like mine to actually communicate with ghosts, normal people like my mom could still feel their cold aura.

"Yeah, that must be it." Mom frowned as she rubbed her bare arms.

After more than two years of hanging out with the life-challenged, I was used to the rapidly swinging temperatures. Mom was always searching for the draft, fussing at us to make sure our windows were completely closed while she was spending good money to run the heat. But at least we didn't have to run the air conditioning as much. Fortunately, Mom couldn't smell the spirit like I could. Some spirits had a distinct odor which worsened the longer they stayed. A faint rotten smell lay under the weird blend of motor oil and cleaning products.

Deep lines creased the corners of her mouth as the spirit smiled. There was something nice about people—even dead ones—being excited to see you. I gave Granny Ghost a once-over. Most spirits I met had milky white eyes, but hers were still warm brown. As far as I knew, there was no science to it, but I had noticed that the longer a spirit lingered, the more their eyes clouded over. They would also begin to show signs of their death over time. If the spirit had died violently, it might take no time at all for their eyes to turn or the signs to show. Based on Granny Ghost's appearance, she probably hadn't been dead long, and her death hadn't been ugly. Maybe this would be a little less stressful than my usual encounters with the dead.

"Bridget?" Mom said. "What are you doing?"

I shook myself. "Huh?"

"You're standing there staring into space and I can't close the door." Her hand was poised over the button.

I averted my eyes from the spirit and followed Mom into the house. The cold breeze nipping my neck told me that Granny was close behind me.

Colin had already turned on Netflix and was sitting on the couch with a plate of pizza. "Oh, no, sir," Mom said. She reached over him and grabbed the remote. "We're having a family dinner." As she walked into the kitchen, she turned her forceful stare on me, and I froze with my hand inside the pizza box. "You, too."

"I have a ton of homework," I said, releasing the warm crust.

"And you're more than welcome to do it after dinner," Mom said.

A prickling sensation spread up my arm. Granny Ghost was running her translucent fingers down my forearm. The tiny hairs stood straight up, and I shivered involuntarily. Ghosts had no respect for the personal bubble.

"But—"

"This is not a discussion." Mom opened the fridge and took out a pitcher of tea. "Do you want water or tea?"

"You decide," I said. "Since my opinion clearly doesn't matter."

She shot me a glare. "I do not need your sass, young lady."

I sucked in a sharp breath through my nose. The sarcastic response lingered in my mind, pressurizing like an impending sneeze. Granny touching my hair again didn't improve my mood. "Water, please," I said in my sweetest voice.

Mom regarded me warily, then turned back to get a glass of ice from the fridge dispenser. While her back was to me, I whirled to face Granny and pointed upward emphatically, trying to send her a hint to go upstairs.

I lowered my hand as Colin came into the kitchen. He gave me a sidelong glance, then helped himself to a Coke from the fridge.

"It's after eight," Mom said. "No soda."

"Mom…" Colin complained. She responded with a steely stare, and he returned the can to the fridge without protest. She got down a glass for him and he filled it with orange juice instead.

"Orange juice has just as much sugar as soda," I said mildly. "I learned that in health class. See? I pay attention in school."

"Don't be a smartass." Mom took our two glasses of ice water and set them at the dinner table. Once we had both gotten our pizza, we sat down at the table and joined hands. "God, we thank you for the food we're about to receive. I thank you for another day with my family, and for bringing them both home safe to me again. I ask that you would help us make good choices and be the people You made us to be. Amen."

"Amen," I murmured.

I wondered what Mom would react if I told her the person I was made to be was a borderline psychic ghost whisperer. Granny Ghost was still lingering in the kitchen, watching me intently. Did inviting strange spirits into our house qualify as making good choices?

"So how was the karate class?" Mom asked.

"It was pretty cool," Colin said. "I learned how to count in Japanese. *Ichi, ni, san...*" He hesitated. "And how to punch properly."

"Which is how?" Mom asked around a mouthful of pizza.

I tuned them out and tried to send the spirit a message. *Go upstairs.* I tilted my head away from my family, letting my long hair hang down one side of my face. Using it as a curtain, I pointed up again. Granny tilted her head.

"What are you doing?" Colin asked.

"Scratching my ear," I snapped. "Mind your own business."

"Don't be rude," Mom said. "And elbows off the table, please. How was your class?"

"Thrilling."

"Bridget."

"It was wonderful," I said. "I learned so much."

Mom sighed and rolled her eyes. "Sarcasm doesn't suit you."

"Neither does an SAT class, so I guess we're both making bad choices." As soon the words spilled over my lips, I regretted them.

Her nostrils flared. Colin squirmed in his seat, like he'd sensed the change in the winds.

"What's gotten into you tonight?" Mom asked.

I shivered as Grandma approached. Her presence was like a cold vent blowing on the back of my neck. Couldn't she take a freaking hint? I had two choices to deal with Mom. I could unleash the explosive anger boiling inside me, which would feel good for about five seconds—at least until Mom started lecturing—or I could suck it up and apologize.

It shouldn't have been an overly difficult decision, but it took me several seconds of hard thinking to finally commit. I might have been a friend to the restless dead, but I was no saint.

"I'm sorry." I tried to keep my tone respectful to defuse the situation. "It's just that I go to school all day, and I'm trying really hard to improve my grades. So I don't really want to do another three hours of extra class every week now."

"Well, you want to get into a good school, don't you?"

I shrugged. "How come Colin gets to take karate while I have to do extra schoolwork?"

"He's in seventh grade," Mom said. "And he already got a good score on the PSAT. He doesn't need any help right now." Colin beamed. I rolled my eyes. He'd been picked out of his school's gifted program to take the PSAT early, because he needed that much more confirmation that he was smart. "And you didn't answer me. Don't you want to go to a good college?"

"I did answer you."

Mom mimicked my shrug. "This is not an answer. Use your words."

"You get on my case when I use my words." I finished my last bite of pizza and pushed the plate with the crusts over to Colin. He'd been eyeing my plate since I finished my first piece. He took the crusts silently. "May I be excused?"

Mom set her jaw and stared at me. It was her Stern Mother Stare, which might have been intimidating if I didn't spend so much time around dead people. I mean, there was literally a dead old lady watching us eat. Mom didn't even register on the spectrum of scary, and I only minded my tongue as much as I did so she wouldn't ground me or take my phone.

"You're the one who wants me to get better grades." I managed to keep my tone neutral. "I want to go to my room and do my homework."

Mom sighed and put up her hand dismissively. "Fine."

I made a point of rinsing my plate and putting it in the dishwasher so she wouldn't have anything else to gripe at me about. On my way up the stairs, Mom's disapproval hung thick in the air like a cloying air freshener. Cold air rushed around me as the spirit followed me up the stairs. The glass in the picture frames on the wall fogged over.

"Kale?" I said. I closed my bedroom door quietly.

Painted in a soothing shade of lavender, my room was the smallest one in the house, but I couldn't blame that on Mom. We'd gotten to pick our own rooms, and I liked the big window that overlooked the back yard. Colin's room was bigger but he had a winning view of the neighbor's chimney.

The spirit paused in the center of the rug, looking around in wonder. I plopped back on my bed and kicked off my shoes. "Can you speak?"

Granny Ghost frowned, then appeared to inhale. In reality, she didn't take a breath, but she imitated the motion. Many spirits mimicked the gestures they would have made while alive, like breathing, or moving around physical objects instead of straight through. I appreciated it, because it was incredibly disconcerting when they didn't.

Granny hesitated, mouth hanging open like she'd forgotten what to do. No sound came from her mouth, but the room grew colder as she tried to talk.

I closed my eyes and pictured Kale. This time I put a little more force into my tone. "Kale, I need you here."

Another cool breeze blew through my room as Kale faded into sight at the window. He was a shimmery blue-white human shape at first, then gradually solidified into himself. "I see you found your guest."

Granny stared back at Kale, her white eyebrows raised high.

"This is my friend Kale. Before we go any further, I'd like you to recognize that I'm being very responsible by calling you here."

"That would be a first," he said.

"Hey. More recognizing. Less sass."

"I'm sorry. You have shown a modicum of responsibility and forethought. I'm so proud," he said. A faint smile teased at his lips. Even with the sarcastic expression, he was obnoxiously cute.

"Okay, Mr. Sarcastic-pants," I said. "I want to give her a little jolt so she can talk, but considering how it went last time, I wanted you here." Weaker spirits had a difficult time talking and putting together their thoughts. Making contact with me transferred some of my energy to them, like recharging their batteries.

Kale moved closer to me. Compared to the hint of decay emanating from Granny Ghost, Kale's clean smell was reassuring. In my late-night search for Diana and Corey, I had gotten a little too close to the spirit of a dead hiker who almost sucked the life out of me. I didn't care to repeat the experience, so Kale would watch and intervene if Granny Ghost got hooked and wouldn't let go.

I extended my hand to Granny Ghost. She hesitated, then brushed her fingers over my palm. At first, it felt like submerging my hand in cold water. "Now focus," I told her.

A healthy pink glow bloomed in the tips of her fingers, spreading up the back of her hand and into her arm. The exposed skin transformed from a watercolor of muted gray to vibrant, healthy tan. Her eyes widened.

As warmth spread into her, icy cold bit into me. When my chest tightened, making it hard to get a full breath, I gently pulled my hand away. "That's enough."

Her jaw dropped as she stared at her hand, turning it back and forth to examine it from all angles. "How?" she said. Then she stopped, mouth hanging open in surprise. "I can speak now. How?"

"I'm a wizard," I said. A shiver shook me from head to toe. I grabbed a fuzzy gray blanket from my bed and threw it around my shoulders.

She tilted her head. "Really?"

"No," Kale said, shooting me an irritated look. "She's a sensitive. She can communicate with spirits. Like you and me."

The ability to interact physically with spirits was still new. Until Natalie, I'd seen only the spirits of the wrongfully dead, like victims of accidents and murders. No spirit had touched me before. Furthermore, I couldn't communicate with them directly, but had to use electronics as a conduit. Except for Kale and my sister, I'd had to use anything from a laptop to a police radio to understand the spirits. It was like I only saw the spirit world through a peephole in a locked door.

Natalie's anguish over her death had made her strong enough to reach through and affect me directly. When I'd been desperate for answers to save Emily, I used a ritual to throw the door open to the rest of the spirit world. After that, Natalie and Kale had been able to touch me, but it was me that had changed, not them. Kale told me later that I wasn't entirely in this world anymore, like part of me was overlapping into the spirit world.

"I'm dead," she murmured.

"I hope that's not a surprise," I said mildly.

She stared at her hands. Her right hand was bright and looked almost alive. Her left was still translucent and tinted gray. "No. I know I am."

"What's your name?"

"Shirley."

"It's nice to meet you. My name is Bridget," I said. "Can I help you with something?"

"What do you mean, dear?" Shirley said.

There was no polite way to ask *why are you here when you shouldn't be*, so I had to phrase it carefully. "Well, most spirits that linger after death have something they're worried about."

Her brow furrowed as she nodded slowly. "My daughter. She's having a baby."

"Oh, that's nice," I said. "Was she one of the ladies at Lovely Ice?"

Shirley shook her head. "Those were my other daughters. They were getting ready to go check on her at home. She's a high-risk pregnancy, and the doctor has her on bedrest. She's already lost one pregnancy."

I nodded. "That must be hard."

"I knew I probably wouldn't be around to meet the baby, but I had hoped," Shirley said, her expression wistful.

"Would it help you to see the new baby?"

"Oh, yes," Shirley said. "But it's hard to stay here. Sometimes I close my eyes and whole days seem to fly by."

That was because she wasn't supposed to be here. The boost of energy I gave her would help her for a while, but she would fade again if she didn't move on. Lingering too long would cause a spirit to lose all of who they once were. And while I'd never seen it, I wondered if there was a point of no return, where a spirit like Shirley was stuck forever regardless of someone like me trying to help. I didn't want to take that risk.

"If you want to come back and see me, I can try to help you stay here a little longer. But you can't stay forever."

"No, of course," she said. "I just want to make sure she's all right. I know you're too young to understand, but a mother would do anything for her children."

I swallowed hard. "Okay," I said. "Come back and see me when you start to feel weak, and I'll do what I can."

Shirley reached out like she was going to touch my cheek. Instinctively, I recoiled. She flinched, letting her hand fall. My chest ached at her wounded expression.

"Sorry, I didn't mean to," I said, offering my hand again.

With that sad expression still pulling at her lips, she brushed her hand across mine. Cold surged into my veins like ice water. The tension in her face eased. When dizziness churned my head into a whirling mess, I pulled away.

"I can't do much more right now, but I promise I'll help you, okay?" I said.

A faint smile pulled at her pale lips. "You're very kind. Thank you."

With that, she disappeared.

"Don't overdo it," Kale warned.

"I won't," I said automatically. "Hey, so what did you think of that video?"

"I thought it was stupid."

"Eyes," I said.

Kale turned to the window and dutifully covered his eyes while I peeled off my school clothes and changed into a t-shirt and a pair of yoga pants that had never seen a single *Namaste.*

"I'm done." I plopped onto my bed and looked up at him as he turned around. "I agree that it's stupid. But could it have been real? Could they be contacting real spirits?"

Before he could answer, my phone buzzed. I checked it to see another text from Emily.

Emily: U home yet? Skype me

I grabbed my laptop and opened it on my bed. I started Skype and opened a video call with Emily. We often used video chats while we did homework. It was a lot faster than typing.

"Hey B," she said. "What took so long?"

The tattered Galactic Bite concert tee shirt and glasses told me she was getting ready for bed. In the background, her walls were plastered with band posters.

"Mom signed me up for an SAT class," I said. "It was awesome."

"Gross," Emily said. "So check this video out. They go to our school."

She sent a URL in the text window. I clicked the link, and it brought up another YouTube video. This one was by someone named *MakeItRaina*, and like the others I'd seen in my search, it had *#deadeyeschallenge* in the title. It was made by a guy and girl who introduced themselves as Raina and Justin.

The pair appeared in a graveyard like in the first video. They recited the same words, but they didn't react or run away. A digital clock superimposed on the corner of the video showed the time lapse as they sped up the video, but nothing happened. At midnight, the video went back to normal speed.

Raina approached the camera, casting an eerie blue glow from the bottom of her face. "Sorry guys, this one's lame. No evil spirits out here! Give it a try, if you're brave enough to do the Dead Eyes Challenge," she said. But the video didn't end there. The next shot showed the girl in a bedroom with bright blue walls and twinkling white lights in the background. "Okay, update. I didn't think anything happened, but I swear I woke up and there was a person standing in my room. Turned on the lights, and they were gone." She went on for a few minutes about how scary it was, but didn't add any more details. I minimized the screen, and went back to my chat with Emily.

"So what do you think?"

"It just seems so fake," I said. "Unless she's like me, she wouldn't have seen anything."

She shook her head. "But they said they felt something. I mean, all that stuff they were chanting...is that real?"

"It's only words," I said. I glanced back at Kale, who was frowning over my shoulder. "What do you think?"

"Who's there?" Emily asked. "Is it Kale?"

"Tell her I said hi," he said. "And that I like her new hair."

I raised an eyebrow at him, then turned back. "Kale says hi, and that he likes your new hair."

She'd never met Kale, but she'd heard plenty of my gushing about his dreaminess when he wasn't around to eavesdrop. "Thanks," she said, one hand drifting to twist a purple-tipped curl around her finger. "What does he think? Of the videos, I mean?"

"It could be real," he said. "What would they gain by pretending?"

"Well, their video won't be popular if they sit there and say 'well damn, nothing happened.'"

"Why do they want it to be popular?"

"That's a whole different discussion," I said. "So could a spirit have showed up?"

"Theoretically, yes," he said. "It's not so different than when you ask them to come to you."

"That's all it takes? Even without an ability like mine?"

"Bridget, give me an update here." With her brow furrowed in confusion, Emily was looking back and forth between me and the seemingly empty space next to me.

"Hold on a sec," I told her. "Is it something I need to check out?"

Kale frowned. "I'll look into it. I don't think it's anything you need to worry about."

"He says there's nothing to worry about," I told Emily.

"That's not what I said," he said. "I said you don't need to personally worry about it, because I know you and you'll get yourself into trouble."

"Nothing to worry about," I repeated. "Okay, babe, I have a bunch of chemistry. I have to go."

After a few minutes of commiserating, we said goodnight, and I turned my attention to my homework. While I searched for my chemistry worksheet and the notes from class, my mind kept circling back to the videos like a dog who'd found an irresistible scent. I tried to push the thoughts out of my head as I slapped the worksheet down on my desk. The sea of equations looked like a foreign language.

I started to work on the first problem, then hesitated. "Kale, would that dumb poem actually work? It sounds like something out of a bad horror movie."

He shrugged. "The words don't matter. It's more about the intent. If they really believed they could summon something, then maybe. And if there was a spirit lingering nearby, then maybe. And if that spirit was strong enough to interact physically, maybe."

"That's a whole lot of ifs and maybes."

"It is. I doubt they experienced anything."

"Yeah," I murmured. "They probably just freaked themselves out. Or faked it to make it more entertaining."

"I do not understand your generation at all," Kale said.

"That makes two of us." With a sigh, I planted my elbows on the desk and glared down at the worksheet. "I have to do this." I painstakingly copied the problem to a sheet of notebook paper, then looked up again. "What if I contact the girl who made that one? Emily said she goes to our school."

"Would that get it off your mind?"

"Yes. Maybe."

"Then do it. And then let it go."

"Okay." With that, I slammed down my pen and fished my ghost notebook out of my backpack. Flipping to a new page, I carefully wrote *Dead Eyes Challenge*. I switched windows again to read the description of her video. The text included links to her Facebook fan page and Instagram account. I wrote down both names, then added a neat bullet point on my paper.

-*Message Raina about video*

Kale laughed quietly.

"What?" I said.

"You know it's going to bother you, and you're going to keep asking me about it all night. Do it now and get it off your mind."

Without argument, I grabbed my phone and opened Facebook. I found the fan page associated with her channel, then carefully typed a message. I didn't want to sound crazy.

Hi Raina! I'm a big fan of your channel. Just watched your Dead Eyes video and it was awesome. I'm really interested in ghosts so I was wondering if I could ask you more about it. Thanks!

I read it aloud to Kale. "Does it sound weird?"

"Yes."

"Kale, you're supposed to be supportive."

"I'm not going to lie to be supportive. Just send it."

I sighed and hit send, then returned to my homework. There. I'd done something concrete to solve this problem. So why didn't I feel any better?

Chapter Five

MY SIX O'CLOCK ALARM was unwelcome, to completely understate it. After two hours of battling with unbalanced equations last night, I'd still had three chapters of A Tale of Two Cities to read for class. Considering I woke up with a badly creased paperback on the floor, my reading didn't go well. And I had no response from Raina. Damn.

By the time I got downstairs, Mom was already up and puttering around the kitchen. "You look tired," she said. "Did you stay up late?"

"I told you I had homework." Which would have been a lot easier if I didn't have to take a stupid SAT class.

"Well, I don't like you staying up so late," she said.

"And I don't like you signing me up for class," I muttered under my breath.

"What?"

"I said I needed a break from class," I lied. "It's fine. That's what caffeine is for."

"Bridget, what's going on with you?"

A honk sounded outside.

"Emily's here," I said. "Gotta go."

Mom sighed. "Okay. Love you."

There was something automatic, and almost forced in the way she said it. I was too tired to argue with her, or to placate her. Instead, I grabbed my backpack and headed out the door.

It was still dark and bitterly cold outside as I hurried to the car. A long trail of exhaust puffed from Emily's Volkswagen in the driveway. When I opened the door, the rich smell of coffee greeted me. There were two white cups in the cup holders.

"You are the patron saint of caffeine," I said. "Thank you."

"Peppermint latte. You're welcome." She glanced over at me. "What's wrong? You look exhausted."

I didn't take it as an insult. "I'm super tired and my mom is about to drive me insane."

"I feel you."

"I don't get it," I said as I pulled down the mirror to check my appearance. Wincing at my dark-ringed eyes, I picked up Emily's purse from the floorboard and dug a tube of concealer out of her makeup bag. I dotted the thick cream under my eyes and tried to rub it in. "She wants me to get better grades, so she puts me in extra class? I already can't get my work done, so how am I going to get it done with even less time?"

Emily shook her head. "I know."

"And it's not like I'm not trying," I said. "I really am."

We arrived at school a few minutes early. Kids were already trickling into the school from the parking lot, but we sat in the car to finish our coffee, so our homeroom teachers wouldn't make us throw it out.

As we got out of the car a few minutes later, the tail end of the shrill homeroom bell finished.

"Crap," I muttered. I had three minutes to get to homeroom to avoid a tardy. We hurried into the building, said our goodbyes, and I headed down the hall to my locker.

Homeroom passed without incident. I had to fake a nice conversation with Allie Williams, one of my least favorite people in the universe. We'd been best friends in middle school, but that had ended in ninth grade when my sister died. When Mom pulled me out of school, Allie told everyone I was having a breakdown. My therapist had told me that punching her wasn't a healthy response, but it sure had felt like good medicine. Thanks to our end-of-the-alphabet names, we'd shared a homeroom for three years, which had been awkward once I came back to school. Since I'd become slightly cool after my involvement with Emily's abduction, Allie had re-inserted herself into my life. I wanted her around about as much as a case of herpes, but I didn't have the spine to tell her off.

Fortunately, Allie had first period on the opposite end of the school, so we headed our separate ways after the bell. As I was walking down the science hall to chemistry class, I scanned the hall for spirits. No sign of the life-challenged today.

The tardy bell rang right as I reached the science classroom. Mrs. England started to close the door, but I stuck my foot into the opening and slid in. She frowned at me.

"Next time it's a tardy," she warned. I mumbled an apology and hurried inside.

Mrs. England's room was cramped, with rows of desks squeezed into the small open area between the lab tables that surrounded the perimeter of the room. The air had a faint chemical smell that reminded me of a hospital.

As I headed for my normal seat in the back, I paused. I'd gotten in a habit of choosing back seats so I could get away with peeking at my ghost notes during class, but that needed to change. I followed Mrs. England to her desk. "Mrs. England? Do you think I could switch seats and sit closer to the front? I'm having a hard time following along back there."

She looked up at me quizzically. "I don't see why not," she said. She looked up, then gestured to Jaquira Williams, a pretty girl with elaborate braids twisted on her head in a bun. "You can sit next to Jaquira."

I hurried to the vacant desk. As I sat down, Bryce Holloway turned around. He was in my US History class, though I didn't know much else about him. He had a big build that made me think he played football, but I didn't pay close enough attention to school sports to know for sure. His shaggy brown hair flipped over his pocked forehead. He eyed me as I took out my notebook and dug out my worksheet. "You do the homework?"

"I tried," I said.

Without asking, he swiped my paper, then wrote something on his own paper.

Wait, was he copying? My stomach fluttered. I didn't want to get in trouble, but I also didn't want to make a fuss.

"Please put your homework on your desk so I can check it off," Mrs. England said.

"Shit," Bryce muttered. He waited for Mrs. England to turn around, then slipped the paper back onto my desk.

Once he was looking ahead again, I secured the paper in my binder and rested the notebook against the edge of the desk to shield it. Thankfully, she was only checking that we'd completed it, and not that we'd actually gotten any right. She gave my paper a cursory glance and made a note in her gradebook.

"Bryce, is there a reason you only did half?" she said as she got to his desk.

"I had track practice," he said.

"That's not an excuse," she said. "Academics take priority."

As she walked away, he muttered, "bitch" under his breath. I ignored him and made a mental note to keep my papers covered until it was time to turn them in from here on out.

Once she put up the answers on the projector, I wasn't surprised to find out that I had gotten most of them wrong. My usual response would have been to tune out and tell myself I'd learn it later, but I made an effort to focus on her explanations and ask questions.

When Mrs. England went to change the Powerpoint to today's topic, my mind started to drift. How was Shirley? What could I do about Fulbright's robberies? And what was Kale doing?

As Mrs. England said, "Moving on," I looked up and noticed there was already a slide up, and it wasn't the usual cutesy title slide with a science comic strip.

"Crap," I muttered, frantically trying to catch up.

She was already raising her arm with the remote to change the slide. I used as many abbreviations as I could, but I only got halfway down the slide before she moved on.

I'd gotten so used to coasting through school that I couldn't keep up anymore. By the time she finished giving notes and passed out our assignment, I was nearly in tears with frustration. I had only gotten to the third problem when the bell rang for second period.

"Okay, guys," Mrs. England said over the rustle and roar of packing up. "You need to finish the rest for homework. You'll have a homework quiz tomorrow. Open notes, so get it done."

I let out a sigh and shoved the packet into my backpack. It was even longer than last night's homework, and I was still clueless.

Well, at least next period was gym. I could manage an A in the class simply by putting on my gym shorts and following instructions. Even Bridget the Easily Distracted could handle that.

Shouts and laughter echoed off the gym walls, punctuated by basketballs slamming against the wood floor. My friend and human crush, Michael, also had gym this period. He was the only other person who knew about my ability. He was the brother of Natalie Fullmer, and he'd helped me investigate her disappearance, though he hadn't known at the time that she was already dead.

Since then, we'd gotten to be friends, largely because we shared the unfortunate experience of having lost our older sisters. He'd also helped me search for the two missing kids at Christmas. It seemed to help him focus his energy on something positive after what happened to Natalie. And I wouldn't say no to spending time with a cute senior boy.

As I headed into the locker room to change, I found myself face to face with Allie. "Hey Bridge," she sang out. I shuddered. I hated that nickname. "Girl, I love that top!"

I looked down at the plain blue shirt, which I'd bought at Target with tag that read *basic tee*. There was nothing distinctive about it, which confirmed what a fake Allie was. Her bright, toothy smile reminded me of a hungry shark.

Once upon a time, I was just average. Not particularly cool, but not a loser either. After Valerie died, I'd been the subject of morbid curiosity, if not actual concern. But when I hadn't recovered quickly enough, largely because I was literally seeing dead people, I was deemed a total downer. Most of my friends disappeared, and I was about as low on the popularity scale as a girl could get for the better part of two years.

Then the pendulum swung back again a few months ago. When I helped find Natalie Fullmer's killer, I became cool again, or at least interesting. I wasn't stupid; I saw right through it. The people who were suddenly interested in me were the same ones who'd shunned me after Valerie's death, like Allie, and it was only a matter of time until it swung back the other way.

"We should hang out soon and catch up! Me and some of the girls are going to Sephora to have our makeup done this weekend," she said. "You should come!"

What I wouldn't have given for Kale to show up and go full poltergeist on the locker room. "I have plans. Sorry."

"Oh," Allie said, undeterred. I couldn't tell if she didn't pick up on my dislike, or if she just didn't care. "Maybe another time."

When hell freezes over.

After changing, I hurried past Allie and into the cluster of girls gathering around the volleyball net for attendance. The boys were gathering on the other side for basketball.

Allie ended up as a captain for volleyball, and made a point of picking me to be on her team. It was social strategy, not athletic, considering my only notable skill was managing to not trip over my own feet. I hung back as she designated her starting players.

Across the gym, the boys divided into teams for basketball, and I saw Michael's familiar frame among them. He had lost most of his football tan over the winter, and his handsome face looked tired, with a faint scruff dusting his jawline. His gaze was far away while his teammates joked and laughed.

I sidled over to the half-court line and waved at him. His smile woke up the herd of butterflies in my stomach. He jogged toward me and said, "How's it going?"

"Good," I lied. "Well, kinda busy. But pretty good."

"Anything exciting going on?"

"If chemistry homework is exciting," I said.

"Yuck. I meant...you know." He leaned in and whispered, "I've been doing some research on cold cases. Do you want to look at them with me?"

"Fullmer!" Coach Hargrove shouted. He gestured for Michael.

"Sure," I said. The last thing I needed was to pile my plate even higher, but I couldn't bring myself to turn down the chance to spend time with him like a normal person.

"Gotta go," Michael said. "Meet me at the senior parking lot after school."

He grinned at me and jogged back over to the coach. Though he'd quit football when Natalie disappeared, he still had the broad frame and chiseled muscles of nearly four years of hard training. And he had a pulse, which was the only thing that made him even more attractive than Kale.

I looked back to see one of my teammates, Kayla Ferguson, staring at me with an incredulous expression. She crossed my path as I walked back to the bleachers and said, "Are you guys, like, a thing?"

"We're just friends."

"He's super hot," Kayla said.

Well, duh. "He's also not interested in dating."

She looked me over, her heavily shadowed eyes fluttering. "You know, you're kinda pretty in your own way."

My eyes went wide at the backhanded compliment. I kind of missed the days when people ignored me. "Well, I'm sure you're pleasant in your own way." With my cheeks burning, I walked over to the other side of the court to where Allie was barking orders at the other girls.

"Bridget, you're in!" Allie said. "Get off, Courtney."

The redhead cleared the court, and I took her place. My heart thumped with anxiety as a girl on the other team served the ball. Kayla sent it over the net, and Sanaia Morris on the other team hit it back toward me. My feet shuffled in a little dance as I tried to get under it. *Thwack!* The ball smacked into my arms, and I launched it back up over the net. Phew.

The terrible screech of wrenching metal cut through the din of the gym. A boy in baggy blue shorts hung from the precariously bent basketball hoop. It was hard to tell from across the gym, but the boy looked like Lance Warren. The hoop canted forward under his weight, then tore out of its frame, glass blackboard and all.

The backboard exploded in a cloud of glass shrapnel as it crashed to the ground with Lance. He cried out in pain. The rest of the boys clustered around him in a tight circle.

As soon as the girls started to press toward the center line, Coach Hargrove bellowed, "Get back!"

The girls scattered, clustering on the outer rim of the Warriors logo painted on the hardwood floor.

Sanaia Morris hurried up to me. "Is that Lance?"

"I think so," I murmured.

With one leg splayed out and his back arched, Lance's face was contorted in pain. Blood spattered the glossy floor around him. The other boy's coach, Coach Lente, crouched on the ground next to him, talking quietly. He gestured to Michael, who nodded and ran out of the gym.

"Oh my God," Allie hissed as she joined us. What was I, a magnet? "Is that Lance Warren?"

"Totally," Sanaia said.

They launched into a second-by-second recap, but they sounded more excited than concerned. While they were occupied with each other, I inched away from them and closer to the bleachers for a better view. The other boys had fanned out into a half-circle, though they were creeping as close as they could without catching Coach Hargrove's attention.

What the hell had happened?

CHAPTER SIX

ALL ANYONE COULD TALK ABOUT for the rest of the day was Lance Warren's accident. People who hadn't even been there were telling the story like they'd witnessed the whole thing, down to Lance breaking his neck and being airlifted out by helicopter. False, and false.

It was even more of a relief than usual when the last bell rang. After shoving through the crowd of kids escaping school, I met Michael in the senior parking lot, where he was waiting at his white Toyota.

"Ready?" he asked. "I thought we could get something to eat while we work if that's cool."

"Sure," I said. A warm thrill rushed through me. It wasn't a date, but it was still nice to spend time with him.

We drove over to Snap, Crackle, Pop, a new shop near the mall. It served nothing but gourmet popcorn and flavored pretzels. Inside, the walls were painted in bright comic half-tones, with slick comic book style signs of *Snap! Crackle! Pop!* The rich blend of butter and caramel made it feel warn and welcoming.

I picked a corner table where we could spread out our notes while Michael went to order. For one dreamy minute, I was just a normal girl watching a boy order for her. We'd scoot close together in the booth to study, and I'd get a whiff of that cologne that Emily swore all hot guys wore. He'd even admitted that he'd been planning to ask me out before Natalie's death turned his world upside down. Since then, he'd helped me by driving me out to Wildwood State Park to find the missing kids. We texted and talked regularly, but how could you really get close to someone that you met while searching for your dead sister?

A few minutes later, Michael returned to the table with a sectioned plate heaping with popcorn and two trays of steaming pretzel sticks. He left the tray, then went back for two fountain drinks.

He set one down in front of me. "Root beer, right?"

"You remembered. Thank you," I said. God, life was unfair.

He beamed, obviously pleased with himself. "You're welcome."

After taking a bite of a garlic-butter pretzel stick, I gestured to him. "What have you got?"

He took out his phone and showed me a note file. "I started looking at the old missing persons cases for Byron County just to see how many were still open," he said. "I found some that were never resolved."

"So you were thinking…"

"We could investigate," he said. I knew what he meant, but my dumb little heart leaped into my throat at that pesky little *we*. It was nice to be part of a *we* with Michael. "Well, I guess you could investigate. But I can help you. Like a sidekick."

I chuckled. "I guess we could."

"You don't seem excited," he said, frowning. The look of disappointment on his face made me feel like the worst person in existence.

"It's not that," I said. "I'm not sure how much I can do right now and get my grades up. If I fail chemistry, Mom's going to ground me, and then I can't do anything."

"Oh," he said. "Well, I got an A in chemistry last year. I can help you with your homework, and then we can focus on the cases. Want to look at your homework?"

I handed him the papers from class. His green eyes flitted back and forth as he scanned the first few problems. Then he handed back the paper and pointed to the blanks in the first problem. "Two, then three," he said. He looked at the next one. "Hydrogen." He waited for me to write it down, but I hesitated. "What?"

"I need to know how to do it," I said. "Not just the answers."

"Oh." For a split second, his eyes narrowed, but he forced a smile. "Paper?" I handed him a piece, and he transcribed the first problem from the worksheet. "This is a two," he said. "See? There's two calcium and two oxygen here, so just make two of each on the other side. You try."

I sighed to myself. He'd said the exact same thing, only he'd written it on paper at the same time that he said it. Regular math was easy, so why was it so confusing to combine it with science? After a few minutes, I showed him my work. "Is this right?"

He glanced over it. "No, this should be a two," he said, tapping the right side of my equation. "How did you get three?"

Irritation welled up in me. "I don't know."

"It's okay," he said. "Try the next one. You'll get it."

As I puzzled through the second problem, I watched him out of the corner of my eye. He was on his phone, but he wasn't texting or checking his Facebook. The screen blurred by as he swiped, but I recognized the outline of a police shield at the top of the page.

With a quiet sigh of resignation, I scrawled random numbers in the blanks and cleared my throat. "I'm done."

"Already?"

"I only had to do the first four," I lied. It was a waste to spend all afternoon with Michael thinking I was stupid. So I'd have to find another way to get ahead in chemistry.

"Do you want me to check over it?"

"I think I've got it," I lied. "Let's look at your list."

As soon as I mentioned his list, his whole demeanor changed. He looked like a kid in line to meet Santa as he opened his notes and read the names aloud. And who could blame him? Being an undercover detective was infinitely more interesting than chemistry homework. I carefully transcribed the names on a new page in my ghost notebook.

Was this the only relationship Michael and I would ever have? Maybe it was stupid to hope for anything else.

We worked for a while, and I made a point of listening intently as Michael told me what he'd found on each of his cases. As we did, I imagined a never-ending line of spirits streaming out my bedroom door, down the stairs, and wrapping around the neighborhood. It would never stop.

I loved that Michael cared. Even if he was only doing it because it was exciting, he was trying to make a difference. But he didn't have to do the heavy lifting on top of his normal life. Was it so wrong that I wanted him to be interested in me and not helping a bunch of ghosts?

God, why did things have to be so complicated?

We spent nearly an hour and a half going through his list, stopping to look up addresses and surviving family members. I wrote everything down and promised to dispatch some of my spirit friends to investigate. When he got a text from his mom telling him to stop by the pharmacy for her prescriptions, a shadow flitted across his face. "Sorry, she's been having a rough week. I need to go."

"I understand," I said. Like many of our classmates, Michael and Natalie's mom had believed she just ran away. According to Michael, she was barely hanging on by a thread since learning the truth of Natalie's disappearance.

He was quiet as he drove me home. When he pulled into my driveway, he said, "It was nice to hang out."

"Yeah, thanks for the help," I said. His warm eyes skimmed over me. My heart thumped in anticipation. "See you tomorrow."

Once I was inside, I headed straight upstairs to my room. I flopped face-first onto the bed and groaned into the blanket.

"Why the grumpy face?" Kale asked.

The surprise of his appearance sent a shock through my system, but I didn't get up. My voice was muffled with my face pressed into the bedspread. "Boys are stupid."

"Sit up," he said. "I don't understand blanket speak."

I rolled onto my back and stared up at the ceiling. "Boys are stupid."

"Unilaterally so," Kale replied. "Is this a new discovery?"

"No," I said. "Michael."

A cool breeze chilled my feet as Kale drifted to the foot of my bed. "What did he do? Should I haunt him?" His handsome face was pulled into a menacing frown, eyes narrowed and mouth set in a thin line.

Though I appreciated his protective streak, it didn't lighten my sorrow. "Nothing. We hung out, but he just wanted to talk about missing people the whole time. I should never have asked him to help me find Diana and Corey. Now he's hooked."

"I know, what a heartless bastard he is," Kale said . "Perhaps you should find some of these friends who make inane videos for attention. Much better."

I glared at him. "Seriously. Ghost crap. That's all I am to him. Maybe I'm the stupid one for expecting anything else."

Kale smiled. "Do you want to know what I think?"

"Not really, because it's probably going to be all rational instead of agreeing that Michael is stupid," I said. "But I bet you'll tell me anyway."

He disappeared, then materialized next to me on my bed. With no substance or weight to him, his translucent form didn't sink into the mattress to shift my balance. Even so, there was something comforting about his closeness, which left a cool kiss of energy down my right side from shoulder to toe. "You and Michael have a unique relationship, considering it originated with Natalie's death."

"Can't it be more than that?"

"Of course," Kale said. "But it'll never be without that. Does that make sense? I also think Michael likes helping you because it gives him control. He was powerless to save his sister. But helping you lets him make up for it in a way. That should be a familiar feeling."

I sighed. "So do you think there will ever be anything else?"

"I don't know," he said. "But even if there's not, it doesn't make you any less special or valuable."

"You have to say that. You're my Guardian."

"No, I don't. It's not in the guidelines." Not that he would ever tell me what the guidelines were.

I smiled faintly. "Really?"

"Really." He raised one hand and narrowed his eyes in focus. His translucent skin brightened and solidified slightly. He extended his arm and brushed my hair back from my face. An electric tingle broke across my skin. "I mean, you're still a mess."

I laughed a little, then quieted as his fingers trailed down my cheek. My heart beat faster as his eyes locked on mine. My chest tightened, and I couldn't draw a full breath. There was an insane streak in me, a sudden urge to see if I could kiss him, just to find out what it would be like. Would he disintegrate at my touch? Would he suddenly be a real boy?

As if he'd sensed my thoughts going down a dangerous path, he sat up and tapped my nose in a playful gesture. "Do your homework."

"Okay, Mom." A warm flush spread along my cheeks, radiating from where he'd touched me.

"You'll thank me when you're not awake at the witching hour."

I groaned and went to my desk. Without further complaints, I got out my homework packet. After looking again at the mess of equations and my haphazard answers, I opened my laptop to search for a tutorial.

Of course, I couldn't start right away with my homework. I went to Facebook instead, and skimmed down my newsfeed. The same video thumbnail appeared multiple times, so I finally slowed down and skimmed the description.

I didn't recognize the face on the thumbnail, but the description below said:

Wanted to update you guys on Lance. We're still at the hospital…

I clicked on the video. The screen showed a grainy video of a boy sitting in a hospital waiting room, with dark blue chairs pushed against stark gray walls.

"Hey guys, Tristan here," the boy said. "Some of you guys saw my brother's crazy accident today." He pointed to his right, and a still shot of the destroyed basketball goal zoomed into place. "They brought him to the hospital, and found out he broke his hip, his wrist, and a couple of ribs. It really shows you how…"

But I tuned him out, as my attention was drawn to the sidebar that advertised Related Videos. Featuring the same yellow graphics that must have been their signature, there was a video that said *Dead Eyes Challenge.*

My eyes kept flicking back to it as I tried to refocus on Tristan's video. It cut away to a quick shot of Lance lying in a hospital bed, bandaged and trying to give a thumbs up. A nurse in blue scrubs shooed him away, and the shot cut back to the waiting room.

As Tristan promised they'd be back soon with more videos, a woman in the background scowled at him over the top of a creased People magazine. I had to agree. The whole thing was tasteless.

"So, wrapping up, AtLanTris Productions will be back soon," he said. "Until then, make sure you give us a like, share with your friends, and help my bro Lance get back on his feet."

"That happened at your school today?" Kale said.

"Yeah, I saw it," I said.

With my chest tightening in apprehension, I clicked on the *Dead Eyes* thumbnail. It had the same slick animated intro as the previous video, then it cut to Lance and Tristan sitting in a car discussing the Dead Eyes challenge. I skipped ahead to see them sitting in a graveyard with a flashlight illuminating them. Thick white candles were propped on several of the headstones. A statue cut a curving shadow against the deep blue of the twilight sky.

"What are you doing?" I murmured.

"Yo, you ready for this?" Lance said. He looked at the camera. "Remember, we're trained professionals. Don't try this at home." Tristan snickered. Lance consulted a slip of paper. "Restless spirit come to me..." He continued reading the same poem that I'd heard in the other videos.

"Another one?"

"Yep." I switched to full screen. "Would I be able to see the spirits on screen if they were there?"

"Spirit interaction with technology is unpredictable at best," he replied. "Hard to say."

The boys sat quietly for a few minutes, then Tristan whipped his head around. "You hear that?" A low sound, like a distant moan, emerged above the subtle whir of crickets and distant road noise.

"Shit, man," Lance said.

"If you're out there, show us something," Tristan said.

The candles blew out suddenly, and the screen went dark except for the harsh white beam of the flashlight against a headstone. Both boys cursed and fumbled at the camera. The flashlight whipped around. The voices were unintelligible, but whoever edited it had added subtitles.

We definitely heard something in the trees. Tristan tried to catch it on his phone but couldn't get a clear shot.

The rest of the video was a series of fast-forwarded clips spliced together with times overlaid on them. They'd stayed out in the graveyard from about seven at night until eleven, when they'd finally given up and gone in for the night. Like the first one I'd watched, they did a wrap-up, with much of the same theorizing and posturing the other guys had done.

But this one was a little different. It was uploaded yesterday, which meant they'd probably recorded it a few days ago. Was it coincidence that Lance had an accident just days after throwing out an open invitation to the spirit world?

With the image of that shattered basketball goal still burning in my mind, I checked back on Raina's page. She still hadn't responded to my message. According to her schedule, she uploaded videos every Monday and Thursday. Her last video had been Thursday. Maybe she'd gotten off schedule.

And maybe she'd had a freak accident just like Lance.

My track record told me to expect the worst. I swallowed hard and typed *Dead Eyes Challenge* into the search bar. The sheer number of results made my stomach churn. I hoped this accident was coincidence, because if it wasn't, then Lance was only the beginning.

CHAPTER SEVEN

THE NEXT DAY, Mom picked me and Colin up from school to have our teeth cleaned, and then we had to head straight to the community center for our classes. It was turning into the best day ever. Even Precious Angel Colin griped all the way there about missing his afternoon snack and game time.

"God forbid you two learn something," Mom said.

"We learn all day at school," Colin replied.

"Judging by someone's report card, I doubt that," Mom said, flicking her eyes to me.

And gosh, wasn't it the best thing for my struggling grades to take away even more of my limited extracurricular time? Not to mention that I hadn't even made a peep about the class since getting in the car.

"But—" Colin started.

"Enough complaining," Mom snapped as she parked the car. "You're doing it, and I don't want to hear about it again."

I let Colin take the brunt of Mom's ire this time, remaining quiet as we drove to Coral Park for another thrilling night of forced learning.

When I got to class, Mrs. Zapruder launched into a lesson on analogies, with sample questions projected on the board for us to discuss. I tried to follow her, nodding as she spoke. As she read a sample question and explained why we should eliminate A, Mrs. Zapruder shivered violently.

"Whew, guys," she said. "Is it cold in here to you?" She hurried over to the door and adjusted the thermostat.

Oh, come on.

I flicked my eyes from side to side, then stole a look over my shoulder. A lone male figure lurked in the back corner of the room, arms folded across his chest. Clad all in black, he might have passed for normal, except that I could see the outline of a neon yellow Food Drive poster through his translucent chest.

Not tonight. I slowly reached down toward my backpack to retrieve my necklace. Ghost Boy could wait. Maybe he didn't realize I'd seen him yet. Cold air whipped around me. My skin prickled with goosebumps as the spirit appeared next to me. I shivered and slipped my hand into the front pocket of my backpack, searching for the tiny interior pocket where I kept the dragonfly necklace.

The spirit lingered next to my desk, bending to look at me closely. As his face lowered to my eye level, my fingers closed on the fine chain. The spirit's cold hand ran down my arm, sending an icy shock down to the bone. Using all my willpower, I left it in place like I hadn't felt his touch and raised my other hand.

Mrs. Zapruder caught the motion and looked at me. "Yes, Jen—no, Bridget?"

"Can I please go to the restroom?"

"We have a break in about ten minutes. Can you wait?"

I glanced over at the spirit who was peering at me with clear gray eyes. His eyes widened in recognition. Dammit. Now he knew I could see him.

"No. Emergency." I widened my eyes and gave her a conspiratorial nod.

"Go ahead," she said. Thank goodness for unspoken period solidarity. I needed a few minutes to talk to this ghost and tell him to leave me alone.

I slammed down my pencil and hurried for the door. Pressure built in my chest until I felt like I was going to burst. I accelerated into a full sprint down the hall, sneakers pounding noisily on the tile. The spirit wasn't following me, but I couldn't slow myself down.

Just past the gym, I ducked into the ladies' room and locked myself in a stall. As I leaned against the cool metal partition, I let out a heavy sigh.

"Hey, you in here?" a female voice said.

My breath caught in my throat as I froze.

"The girl from the classroom down the hall? Green shirt," she said.

I looked down at my forest green shirt, then frowned at the door. Through the crack between the door and the wall, I had a narrow view of the back of a girl's head full of long blonde curls. Maybe Mrs. Zapruder had sent one of my classmates to check on me.

"I know you saw my friend." Without turning around, the blonde girl fiddled with her curls, piling them up high, and then releasing them to bounce over her shoulders. "You're like me, aren't you? You see things other people don't."

My eyes went wide.

Suddenly a blue eye appeared at the crack. "Boo!"

I yelped and tripped backward onto the toilet. Thank God it was too narrow for me to fall in and get soaked with toilet funk. "Who are you?"

"Open the door," she said. "Unless you're peeing, cause that would be weird."

I cautiously unlocked the door and opened it to see a blonde girl with freckles smattered across her pretty face. Her clothes were mostly black, with a stylish pink scarf looped around her neck.

"Who are you?"

"I'm Nina." She stuck out her hand. She closed her eyes, moving her lips silently. The ghostly figure I'd seen minutes earlier appeared at her shoulder. "This is Ethan. I believe you've met."

He looked me over, then gave me a little bow. "I apologize for being rude," he said in a surprisingly deep voice. "I didn't mean to frighten you."

"I'm…" I stared at Nina in disbelief. "You're like me."

She gestured to Ethan. "Obviously."

"How?"

"Well, that's a little personal for first meetings," Nina said.

"I meant how did you find me?"

"Actually, it was luck," she said. "I'm taking a photography class down the hall. Ethan gets bored and wanders. He sensed you from down the hall, so I told him to come find you." She shrugged like it was a completely normal way to meet.

I heard voices outside the door, then the creak of the bathroom door opening. One of the girls from my SAT class entered. "Oh hey," she said. "She gave us a break right after you left. We have to be back in five minutes."

"Thanks," I said.

Nina headed for the door and gestured for me to follow. I trailed after her like a puppy. Was this really happening? Her high-heeled boots clicked a sharp staccato on the tile as she walked. Ethan drifted ahead of her, apparently uninterested in our conversation.

"I should probably get back," I said, watching a cluster of kids standing outside the classroom toying with their phones. "But I can't believe this. I don't know anyone else like me. Like us."

"Here," Nina said. She took out her phone and handed it over. She had a new contact pulled up. "Put your info in, and I'll text you. Do you go to Fox Lake?"

"Yeah!" God, I sounded pathetically eager. I accepted the phone and typed my name and phone number in.

After I handed the phone back, she smiled. "Bridget. Nice to meet you."

"Oh, right," I said. "I can't tell you how nice it is to meet you."

Nina grinned. "I'll be in touch."

The rest of my class was a blur. I couldn't stop thinking about Nina. How had she ended up like me? What did she know? Was Ethan her Guardian? I had a million questions.

When Mrs. Zapruder dismissed us, I practically flew out the door. Mom and Colin were already waiting in the lobby for me.

"How was class?" Mom asked. "It must have been fun."

"Why do you say that?"

"You look like you won a million bucks," Mom said. "So it was good?"

"Fantastic." And for once, I was telling the truth.

When we got home, Mom reheated the chicken and rice she'd cooked the night before. As she pulled it out of the oven, I steeled myself.

"May I please eat upstairs tonight? I have a lot of homework and I'm already getting a late start," I said. "And I don't want to stay up all night."

Mom hesitated, looking me over. "I would rather you had dinner with us." I closed my mouth around the protest bubbling from my lips and waited it out. Her expression softened. "But if you need to do homework, I suppose that's fine. Make sure you bring your dishes down."

"Thank you!" I rushed to fix a plate and hurried upstairs. As soon as I got into my room I called for Kale.

The temperature in my room dropped as he appeared. His face was tense as he surveyed my room. "What?"

"Kale, I met someone," I said. "A girl."

He raised an eyebrow. "Well, that's not what I expected, but—"

"A friend, you dork," I interrupted. "She's like me."

He cocked his head, staring at me. "Are you sure?"

"Eyes," I said. While I changed clothes, I told him about the whole incident during class.

"Interesting."

"You don't seem happy. I'm done, by the way." I sank into my chair and opened my laptop. As soon as I logged into Facebook, I had a notification of a friend request from Nina Welles. Once I accepted the request, I investigated her profile. Her location was listed as Charlotte, North Carolina, but there were recent status updates talking about moving and missing her old friends. So she'd moved here recently.

I was in the middle of looking through pictures of a beach vacation when Kale said, "Please be careful."

His cool tone made my stomach lurch. "Why? She seemed nice."

"I'm sure she did," Kale said. "Just don't be too quick to trust. That's all. Let's get to know her."

His warning sucked the joy out of my new friendship. Deflated, I closed the page and took out my homework. After watching hours of videos last night and asking about a hundred questions in class today, I'd finally gotten the hang of balancing equations. I'd been way overthinking it before.

"Miss Bridget?" a male voice said. The drawl belonged to Jerry, an older gentleman who'd helped me search for Diana and Corey in the woods.

"Jerry!" I said as I set down my pencil. "What's up?"

"Oh," he said. "Well, I just stopped by to talk."

I glanced at the clock. It was almost nine already. Jerry liked to tell long, rambling stories about fishing and his days in the Navy, and I didn't have time to listen and get my homework done. "Oh, right. You know you're supposed to come by on Friday, right?"

"Today is Friday," Jerry said.

I shook my head. "Today is Thursday." Ghosts weren't great with time.

"Oh," he said, looking crestfallen. He bit his lip and glanced toward the window. "Should I go?"

Kale nodded silently, but Jerry looked so hopeful. "You can hang out for a while," I said. "But I have to do homework tonight, so I can't really talk for long."

"Oh, I'll be as quiet as a mouse," Jerry said. "You won't even know I'm here."

Though Jerry had a heart of gold, he took less than ninety seconds to break his promise. He talked nonstop until Kale finally cut him off at ten o'clock so I could finish my homework in sweet silence. When I went to bed, I laid awake thinking about Nina. In a completely non-creepy way. It was so strange and wonderful to think that I had a new friend that understood what this was like. Maybe she could help me with my cases and answer the questions that Kale wouldn't.

Things were finally looking up.

CHAPTER EIGHT

THE NEXT MORNING, I awoke to a text message from Nina. Well, to be fair, I awoke to the obnoxious sound of an old car horn, but when I grabbed my phone to silence the alarm, I saw the message from an unfamiliar number. Considering I hadn't given my number to anyone else recently, it had to be her.

Still half-asleep, it took me three tries to unlock my phone. My heart raced as I opened the message.

Nina: Hey girl. It's Nina! Want to hang out after school?

The prospect of a new friend who understood my world was like waking up on Christmas morning to the realization that there were full stockings and wrapped presents downstairs. I paused before I replied. I didn't want to look too desperate by replying instantly. After I had showered, put on a touch of makeup, and combed my hair, I went back for my phone. I typed my reply slowly, as if that would somehow communicate that I was cool and collected, instead of being a complete dork.

Sounds like fun! Where?

Nina: Meet me out front after last bell?

Perfect.

With my plans set, I hurried downstairs to wait for Emily.

Rain streaked the windows, blurring the golden haze of the streetlights. Despite the gloomy morning, I couldn't keep the smile off my face. I couldn't remember the last time I'd made a new friend who was both living and not related to a dead person who'd made my acquaintance first.

Headlights swept across the living room as Emily pulled into the driveway. Tugging my hood up over my hair to protect it from the rain, I hurried out to the car.

When I dropped into the passenger seat and shook the dampness off my hood, Emily gave me a quizzical look, her well-groomed brows arched. "You look way too happy for seven in the morning. What's up?"

"Just feeling good," I said as I buckled up. "Hey, I don't need you to drive me home this afternoon."

"Oh yeah?" She gave me a coy look. "Are you hanging out with Michael again?"

I froze with the words on my lips. Something in me wanted to keep Nina secret, though I wasn't sure why. "No, I'm meeting up with a friend."

"What friend?" she said. "You don't have very many."

Wow, seriously?

"Thanks a lot." Tension rose up like a wall between us.

"I'm being honest, B, not mean. I don't, either," she said. But her frankness did nothing to alleviate the tension.

"It's this girl I met at my SAT class. She goes to our school," I said. "She seemed cool."

"What's her name?"

"Nina Welles. She's new." I knew I needed to tell her, but I was afraid of how she would react. "She's like me."

"What do you mean? Oh…as in the ghost thing?"

"Yeah. It's really cool." I had hoped she might be excited, but she just raised her thin eyebrows.

"Okay. That's cool for you," she said, shrugging. "I hope you guys have fun."

Thanks to the rain, the car line of parents dropping kids off stretched out to the main road, so Emily drove past it and took the back entrance into the student lot. She had a comic book print umbrella to protect her carefully curled, purple-tipped hair from the rain.

Even in the dark gloom, I had an extra spring in my step. But my excitement was dampened by Emily's silence. Though she shared her umbrella, she didn't say a word as we slogged through puddles from the parking lot all the way to the humid foyer, which smelled like wet dog thanks to the drizzling rain and stifling heat.

I wanted to be self-assured enough not to ask, but I couldn't help speaking up as we passed the front office, where we normally went our separate ways. "Em?"

"Huh?"

"Are you mad at me?"

She shrugged. "No, why do you think that?"

"I don't know. You seem weird since I told you about Nina."

"It's all good." But her expression was neutral and cool, not the smile that would have said *you big goof, of course not*. It was a look that told me to read between the lines.

I sighed and forced a smile. "Okay. See you later."

She waved and headed down the hall toward her locker, leaving me to walk to homeroom alone.

Had I broken some unspoken rule of friendship? It was pathetic, but I'd had so few friends the last few years, I probably wouldn't know if I had. But it was hardly fair to be mad that I had a new friend. That was her problem, wasn't it?

The butterflies in my stomach didn't catch the memo that I'd decided I was in the right. One reason our friendship worked was that we actively avoided drama. We knew how to hold our tongues and overlook minor things. Maybe this would pass, too.

After homeroom, I made it to chemistry class a full minute early and watched with sympathy as Mrs. England shut the door on two tardy classmates and sent them to the office for passes. Once class started, I was happy to find that I'd gotten most of my homework correct. And I even shielded my answers from Bryce's attempts to copy. Things were finally coming up for Bridget.

My friction with Emily was a distant memory as the bell rang for PE. When I walked into the gym, all four coaches stood at the doors, directing us into the bleachers. Stacked haphazardly along the bottom row of each side of the bleachers were the battered health books that still showed the students inside carrying portable CD players. A rolling whiteboard was pushed against the wall, with instructions to read several chapters and answer questions from the textbook. The boys and girls were segregated to the home and visitors' sides of the gym respectively.

The volleyball net poles were arrayed a triangle beneath the broken hoop, with yellow caution tape stretched between them. I didn't see any more glass, but they clearly didn't want to risk any further accidents.

The accident scene reminded me of Lance and Tristan, piercing my happy haze and putting me on alert for spirits. I didn't see anything amiss, but with hundreds of people in the gym, it was a game of *Where's Dead Waldo?* And in a room this big, I wouldn't notice a temperature change unless I walked right into a cold spot.

On the visitors' side bleachers, the girls clustered into groups. Allie waved for me to join her at the top, but I pretended not to see and sat on the bottom row with some of the band girls. I didn't know them, but they were doing the bookwork with minimal chat. Allie was smart and would get the work done, but I couldn't listen to her talk for a whole class period.

Rather than reading the chapters, I flipped to the questions so I could search for the answers. After checking the index for a page number, I paused to scan the gym again. I still didn't see anything, but it made me wonder what kind of spirit could have caused the accident. Would it hang out here at the gym to keep causing trouble, or would it keep following Lance?

I was halfway done skimming the chapter on the dangers of smoking when a loud grinding noise broke my concentration. Across the gym, the home bleachers slowly retracted into their folded position against the wall. In a rising clamor of voices, the boys thundered down the bleachers or jumped clear.

Except for one.

The long plastic rows inched forward, nesting into each other with a rhythmic clank. There was a kid still sitting on one of the middle rows, pulling at his leg. Desperation sharpened his voice as he yelled, "I'm stuck!"

"Turn it off," I murmured. But the remote that operated the mechanism hung over the railing from its cord. No one was near it. The bleachers shouldn't have been moving at all.

As the boys yelled, the coaches ran out of their shared office next to the boy's locker room. "Shut it down!" Coach Hargrove bellowed, his football field voice cutting through the noise. He ran past the crowd and snatched the remote. His face went slack as he jabbed the button repeatedly to stop the movement. He smacked it against his hand, his eyes going wide as he stared up at the boy.

I squinted to make out the boy's face. I'd never met him, but I knew his face from the video last night. It was Tristan Warren, Lance's brother. A chill ran down my spine. Any doubt that there were spirits involved was gone. Two boys had climbed up to help Tristan, but the vertical wall pressed ever onward, like the high school gym version of an Indiana Jones trap.

There were three rows left. I tossed my book aside and hurried across the gym, darting around the cordoned-off area. There was nothing there.

"Help me!" Tristan screamed, shrill and desperate.

As the final row retracted, the last two boys jumped off. Tristan let out a piercing scream and fell, arms pinwheeling uselessly through open air. As he hit the bottom of the arc, he slammed into the bleachers. He screeched in pain. The gym erupted in shouts and screams in response. Feet thundered on the home side bleachers as the girls rushed forward to gawk.

Tristan tried in vain to pull himself up, but every movement made him yelp. His ankle was trapped between two of the rows. It had to be broken. Meanwhile, the mechanism was still grinding, trying to close the bleachers. A mean-sounding laugh came from behind me. *Who the hell...*

I whirled to look for the source of the sound. A shadow streaked across the court, too fast to make out any details. I backpedaled to the painted warrior helmet at center court. Like pulling open a freezer at the grocery store, there was a stark drop in the temperature here.

Definitely a ghost.

A high giggle pierced through the clamor, from farther away this time. Following the sound, I spotted the shadowy figure moving along the back wall of the gym. Crap. All of my usual protective gear—salt, holy water, sage—was in a backpack tucked under my bed at home. I didn't expect to need it at school. Even unarmed, I had to find out what this was. My heart raced in apprehension as I followed the spirit.

Everyone else in the gym was running toward the bleachers. I ignored them and followed the shadowed apparition around the corner into the boy's locker room.

My breath puffed from my lips like smoke in the glacially cold room. The locker room was strewn with backpacks and blue jeans draped over wooden benches. It smelled like sweaty socks and Axe body spray. And just barely, a hint of decay.

I froze. What was I going to do about a hostile spirit with no supplies?

"I know you're there," I said aloud. My voice echoed in the empty room. "I don't want to hurt you."

The mirrors along the wall fogged over. The spirit reappeared and dragged one grimy hand across the farthest mirror, leaving a streaked handprint that trickled condensation like rain. A few inches shorter than me, the spirit was humanoid, although it was so dark and grimy that I couldn't make out any distinct features.

"Stop!" I said. "Whatever you're here for, I can help you!"

It slowly turned, milky white eyes glowing. We stared at each other in dead silence. My heart thumped.

Then the spirit laughed again, a dissonant sound that chilled my blood. It flickered away. A faint sheen of sweat beaded on my neck as I spun around to look for it. When the next skin-crawling burst of laughter came, it was right behind me.

It shoved me forward, its hands so cold they bit into me like knives. I stumbled backward over a bench and smacked my head. A pile of discarded clothes kept me from splitting my skull open, but the impact sent a lightning shock down my spine. Black spots pulsed across my vision like an oil spill. The spirit swept through the room, rattling the lockers with a deafening clatter.

"What the he—what's going on in here?" a stern voice shouted.

Suddenly the noise stopped, leaving my ears ringing and my stomach sinking. I flailed like a flipped turtle and grabbed the bench to right myself.

Coach Lente stood in the doorway with an incredulous look on his face. "What are you doing in here?"

The only answers I could think of would sound utterly insane. "I don't know."

He shook his head. "Get out of here. You're lucky I don't give you detention."

Rubbing the back of my head, I followed him out of the locker room, looking back over my shoulder with every other step. Things had quieted down in the gym. The coaches had herded all of the students to the visitors' side. People chattered, barely able to conceal their excitement over this latest dramatic development. The school maintenance guy was working on the remote to open the bleachers, while a pair of tall boys stood under Tristan and supported his weight to alleviate the pressure on his trapped ankle.

I ignored the frantic beckoning of Allie Williams and climbed high in the home side bleachers. I ducked my head, trying to keep from attracting attention as I spoke into thin air.

"Kale." My voice was quiet, but I put every bit of willpower I had into it, picturing his beautiful face and gleaming blue eyes. "I need you here right now."

Seconds later, he appeared at the foot of the bleachers. I gestured with my head toward the top, where I took a seat and pulled out my phone.

"Are you all right?" he said. "It's school time."

"Look." I pointed across the gym. He followed my gesture and froze. In a smoky blur, he flickered across the gym, inspected Tristan, then returned moments later.

"What happened? There's dark energy lingering around there. Something was here."

"There was a spirit. It closed the bleachers on him," I said. Kale's eyes narrowed. "I chased it to the locker room, but it tried to attack me. Didn't seem interested in talking."

His expression softened as he looked me over. "Are you all right?"

"Smacked my head but I'm fine," I said. "It has to be those videos. Tristan is Lance's brother. You remember, the guy who fell from the basketball goal the other day? They made a Dead Eyes video together. This is bad."

"Okay. I'll sweep the school and see if I sense anything. Be careful."

After PE, Tristan's accident was all anyone could talk about. This time, people were speculating on who might have sabotaged the bleachers. Thanks to everyone ignoring the "no phones out during class time" rule, the rumors were flying. As of the end of fourth period, the prime suspect was James Woodward, who had gotten into it a few days ago with Tristan over a girl they both liked.

When the lunch bell rang, I considered skipping the rest of the day and walking home. But I couldn't take the risk that the spirit would show itself again. I couldn't do much with all my ghost stuff at home. It was a small comfort to know Kale was searching for signs. But if it reappeared, I wanted to try talking to it.

When I'd first encountered Natalie Fullmer after her death, she'd also been angry and aggressive, but I later discovered it was because she couldn't communicate clearly with me. Lingering spirits were emotionally unstable to begin with, and adding in a gruesome death like Natalie's only amplified that volatility. It was possible that this spirit was similar, and once I got through to it, it would calm right down and get its anger issues in check. Then again, Natalie never tried to crush someone to death, so this spirit might be on a whole different level.

That raised another concern for me. Kale had a hard time being around extremely angry spirits. When Natalie was at her worst, she was like Kale-repellent, launching him away from me whenever she appeared. And when I'd found the abandoned restaurant where the Runaway Killer took all his victims, Kale couldn't even get near it. He said all the pain and despair that had seeped into the place drove him away.

He'd tried to explain that being my Guardian didn't mean he could shield me through every reckless, dangerous thing I tried to do. Still, it was inconvenient that he couldn't be around when I needed protection the most. A spirit that was twisted enough to hurt Lance and Tristan like that would probably be the type that could push Kale away.

My stomach rolled in nervous anticipation as I shuffled along the crowded hallway toward the roar of the lunchroom. Emily and I always ate lunch together, but I was worried about her still being mad at me from this morning.

While I waited to get a limp ham sandwich from the lunch line, my phone buzzed in my pocket with a text notification.

Nina: Did u hear about kid getting crushed in bleachers?

I pondered for a moment.

I was there. Something's here in the school.

Nina: Like a dead something?

Yes

Nina: WTF! What lunch do you have?

A

Nina: Damn I have C

Nina: I'll keep my eyes open. See u after school

OK

The clacking of nails on stainless steel jolted me back to reality, where the lunch lady was staring at me from over the cash register. "You're holding up the line."

"Sorry." I shoved my phone back into my pocket as my cheeks heated with embarrassment. "Can I have the sandwich, please?"

With a little shake of her head, she handed me a tray. After I paid, I headed for my usual table. My apprehension eased a little when I saw that Emily was already sitting at our table. She looked up as I sat down. "Did you hear about Tristan?"

"I was there."

Her eyebrows perked. "Seriously? Tell me everything."

After a bite of the bland sandwich, I told her about what I'd seen, but when I got to the part about seeing the spirit, I hesitated and took a deep breath. "There's something in the school. A ghost."

Emily froze. "Like Kale?"

I shook my head. "Not a nice one. Right after Tristan got stuck, I heard it. I followed it back into the boy's locker room, but it took off."

Crossing her arms over her chest, Emily leaned forward. "So what are you doing about it?"

"Nothing right now," I said. "Kale's poking around to see what he can find, but I don't have any of my stuff here."

"So we're all sitting ducks?"

"I don't think so," I said. "I think you were on to something the other night. You know Tristan and Lance did one of those Dead Eyes videos?"

"Really?"

"Yeah," I said. "A few days ago. Then Lance gets hurt, and two days later, Tristan? Both freak accidents. You were right. It's the videos."

Her eyes widened, and her fuchsia-glossed lips curved into a faint smile. Maybe the encouragement would make up for her hurt feelings over Nina.

We chatted for a few minutes while we finished lunch, and she filled me in on all the gossip she'd heard about Tristan since that morning. Midway through her story about Tristan's girlfriend melting down in the hallway, the bell rang with a shrill tremolo. We both jumped in surprise, then looked at each other sheepishly.

"Okay, text me if you see anything weird," I told Emily. "Cold spots, weird smells—"

"I got it," she said. "Oh, have fun with your new friend."

The way her voice sank a little on the word *friend* told me all was not well in the land of friendship, even after the acknowledgement of her discovery with the Dead Eyes videos. But I had bigger, deader problems at the moment.

As I walked down the hallway to my literature class, my eyes flicked around. Just past the water fountain, the temperature plunged. I stopped in the middle of the hallway. With a shaky breath, I searched my surroundings.

The terrifying culprit? A chair was propped up against one of the outside doors, letting in a wind tunnel of icy air.

Stop it, I told myself. I'd have a nervous breakdown if I kept this up. Kale was looking into it. I didn't need to worry. At least, that's what I told myself.

In literature class, I scanned the room for my giggling ghost while Mrs. McDaniel entered her attendance. I saw nothing, and the rest of the class passed in relative normalcy.

Fifth period was US History. Before the bell rang, people clustered around desks, gossiping about what had happened in the gym. I ignored the gossip and scanned the board. Dread gripped my stomach. Written in big red letters were the words *GROUP PROJECT WORK DAY*.

I was so not a team player.

Once the bell rang, Mr. Corbin shut the door and ushered us into our seats. "Ladies and gentlemen, we'll be choosing groups today for your project," he said. I groaned inwardly. "Make sure you have a group of four, and then we'll discuss the requirements."

A commotion broke out as people started moving desks and working out bargains. Squeezing out of the mass that had suddenly turned into a cutthroat draft with groups hunting down the smartest kids in class, I approached Mr. Corbin. "Excuse me, sir? Do you think I could work on my own? Please?"

"It's a big project, Bridget," he said, frowning at me. "I'd prefer you worked with a group."

"So is that a yes or a no?"

"That's a no," he said. "There are exactly twenty-eight people in this class. I guarantee that you can find a group."

I sighed and turned back. There were already several clusters of people sitting at their desks, pushed together to make tables. There were two nerdy boys in the back that I knew got good grades. As I approached them to ask if I could join, a pair of girls swooped in like vultures to complete the group.

Damn.

I looked around the room. My stomach sank as Bryce Holloway waved at me from the back corner. Everyone else had already found groups. I'd wasted valuable time asking to work alone.

I slowly approached Bryce. "You only have three?"

"Yep," he said. "You're with us."

"Cool," I said half-heartedly. *Crap*. There was another guy in the group that I didn't know, and a girl I vaguely remembered from middle school.

"All right," the other guy said. "We're gonna split this up for the research. Candace, you do the paper. You do the Powerpoint," he said, pointing to me.

Candace wrinkled her nose. "And what are you two doing?"

"We'll make visual aids," Bryce said.

"That's what the Powerpoint is," I said drily. "We're not doing all the work for you."

"Yeah," Candace said, squaring her shoulders. "We should split it all evenly. And we can take turns talking."

"I don't do presentations," Bryce said. He didn't do anything, as far as I could tell.

"Well, you can at least help with the research," Candace said. "We can meet this weekend and work on it. How about Sunday?"

Candace looked at me, and I nodded in response. There were better things to do on a Sunday than work on a history project, but it would give me a legitimate excuse to get out of the house. Plus, Mom didn't have to know how long I was working. I could take a few extra hours for ghost work if I needed it. And based on what I'd seen today, I was going to need it.

CHAPTER NINE

I EMERGED FROM THE SCHOOL to find Nina sitting alone on one of the benches with her phone in hand. As I approached, she looked up and smiled.

"Where's Ethan?" I asked.

"After you texted me, I told him to search the school and see what he could find." As she stood, she slung a messenger bag over her shoulder and adjusted the silvery-pink scarf around her neck. "Do you like bubble tea?"

"I love it," I said.

"Then let's go," she said. "My dad got me a gift card for Christmas, so it's my treat."

We walked together to the student lot and got into her dark blue Jeep. I was used to Emily's car, which always looked like her closet had exploded into the backseat. Nina's car was spotless, and smelled so strongly of apple-cinnamon that it burned my nose.

As she drove, she filled me in on her schedule, detailing the exchange she'd had with a girl in her Spanish class about Tristan's accident. It took us about ten minutes to drive to Lovely Ice, where I'd had my meeting with Fulbright the other day. Once we'd gotten our drinks, we took a seat in the far corner.

Nina shook her blonde hair back, then twisted it and stuck a mechanical pencil through it to hold it. She still looked gorgeous. I felt like an awkward middle schooler next to her.

After a sip from her pastel blue drink, she leaned forward. "So what's your deal, Bridget? Tell me everything."

"Well…" With her intent stare on me, I felt like I was standing center stage, with a spotlight glaring down at me. "What do you want to know?"

"When did you start? Seeing them, I mean?"

"Oh," I said. "A little over two years ago. My sister and I had a car accident. She…she didn't make it. I had—" I froze as her hand covered mine. It was cold and wet from gripping her frosty drink, but there was still something oddly warm about the gesture.

"I'm so sorry." Her eyes were wide with concern. "And you were there?"

I tried not to think about the accident. That horrific moment divided my whole life into Before and After. Before was normal. After was all darkness and shattered glass and broken girls. When Valerie came to mind, I intentionally steered my brain out of its depressive rut and toward the good times we'd had. Even after her death, we had some laughs and good memories before I'd let her go on to whatever waited on the other side.

"I was there," I finally said. "My leg was wrecked, so I had to have surgery. I had a bad reaction to the anesthesia, and I flatlined for a minute. Kale, my Guardian, said that was what did it. Once I got out of the hospital and all the painkillers wore off, I saw my sister again."

"Gosh," Nina said. "I know we just met, but I'm so sorry that happened to you and your family. What a terrible loss." Maybe I just wanted her to be that nice, but she seemed genuine.

"It was." I chuckled a little to myself, despite the bleak topic.

"What's funny?"

"You know, most people say dumb stuff when they hear about Val. Like she's in a better place now, or God needed more angels. Like that makes it all okay." I could have written a book on all the well-meaning, but insensitive things people had said to us after her death.

Nina wrinkled her nose and took another sip of her bubble tea. "Even if you knew it was her time, that doesn't mean you were ready to lose her. I hate when people say that stuff."

"So I'm guessing you lost someone?"

"Yes," she said, her eyes distant. "But that's not how my ability started. I think I've always had it."

"You were born with it?"

She shook her head. "Not exactly. I had seizures when I was a baby. One night I had a bad one, and I went into cardiac arrest. Turned blue and everything. The ambulance came, and they got me breathing again, but they said my heart had stopped for a while. I don't ever remember not seeing them."

"Wow," I murmured. "Your whole life. How did you deal?"

She shrugged. "It was normal for me. I remember seeing them at my fourth birthday party."

"And you can talk to them directly?"

Nina nodded. "I've had a lot of time to practice."

"Wow," I murmured again. "I'm sorry, this is so weird. So does your family know?"

"I live with my dad. He doesn't know." She stared into her cup, fishing around in the drink for a bubble. There was more to her story, but considering we'd just met, I wouldn't pry too much too soon. She shook herself like she was waking from a daze. "Tell me about this thing in the gym."

I told her what I'd seen, from the moment I heard the bleachers moving, down to the spirit throwing a tantrum in the locker room. "You know, there was something that didn't sit right with me." I said. "I couldn't put my finger on it till just now. The handprint."

"What about it?"

"Well, I was watching it while it smacked the window and dragged its hand through the fog. Like in movies," I said, imitating the gesture on the wall behind me. "But it's like it didn't know I saw it, so it was just trying to freak me out for fun."

"Weird. What did it look like?"

"It was dark and dirty, so I couldn't make out details. Probably about my size, but I couldn't tell if it was male or female. The laugh didn't give it away."

She frowned. "Has anyone died at the school recently?"

I shook my head. "Natalie Fullmer, but that was months ago, and she moved on. I think it's related to these Dead Eyes videos."

She cocked her head quizzically. "Dead Eyes?"

"Hold on," I told her. I took out my phone to show her one of the videos, but the alerts on my lock screen stopped me cold.

Missed Call (5): Mom

Mom: Call me as soon as you get this.

Mom: Where are you??

A shiver ran down my spine. Those were the messages no one wanted to get, least of all from Mom.

"Are you okay?" Nina said.

"I just got a message from my mom," I said. "Hold on."

"Go ahead."

With dread squeezing my chest like a corset, I hurried outside and called Mom back. *Come on, pick up.* What if something had happened to Colin? Or Dad? Or even Mom? Someone at the hospital could have her phone and—

"Bridget?"

"Mom," I said. "What's wrong?"

"Oh, thank God," she said in a breathy, strained voice. "There was an accident."

My heart slammed against my ribs. "Colin?"

"Oh no, sweetie. He's fine," she said. "I saw it on the news. It was a bad wreck involving a student from Fox Lake. They saw the sticker on the car."

I let out a heavy sigh that hitched in my throat. After a moment to compose myself and temper my frustration that Mom hadn't led with *everyone is fine*, I said, "But you know I don't drive."

"I know, but I texted Kari, and she said Emily was home, but that you hadn't ridden home with her. I didn't know where you were, so I got worried. Where are you?"

"I met a new friend at my SAT class the other night," I said. "She picked me up from school today."

"Oh," she said, her tone suddenly surprised. "Well, that's nice. I wish you'd told me you weren't riding home with Emily."

"Sorry, I didn't think about it."

She sighed. "I'm sorry to freak out on you. I just got worried."

I peeked through the window to see Nina carefully folding a napkin into origami. She caught me watching and gave me a questioning look. I waved her off. "It's okay. I'm fine. Listen, Mom, I gotta go. I'm studying with my friend."

"Oh, good for you," Mom said. "Well, why don't you invite her over? I'll cook and she can study at the house with you."

"Mom, I—"

"Bridget, please," she said. "I'd feel much better if you were here."

Familiar tension crept into her voice. That was the sound of someone trying not to cry. "Okay," I said, holding back my argument. "I'll ask. See you soon."

I walked back inside to Nina.

"What was that all about?" she asked.

"My mom," I replied. "She saw an accident on the news and freaked out."

"I'm sure she thought of your sister and got worried," Nina said. She made it sound so obvious, but it hadn't even occurred to me that Mom's first thought would have been *not again*. By the time Mom found out about our accident, Val was already gone, and I was in an ambulance.

"Yeah," I said quietly. "I have to go home. You probably don't want to, but she said you can come over."

"Sounds fun," Nina said. "Let's do it."

We dropped off our trash and headed for the car. My stomach fluttered at the thought of Nina meeting my mom. If her dad didn't know about her ability, then she had to be good at keeping secrets. But with both of us in the same house, that was twice as many opportunities to get tripped up on lies.

By the time we got to my house, my heart was racing with anxiety. Mom's car was already parked in the driveway. Light glowed from the kitchen windows. A familiar silhouette passed through the glow as Mom worked in the kitchen.

Nina parked close to the curb, then took out her phone. She held the button and said, "Call Dad." The phone rang as she put it to her ear. "Hey Dad. Are you going to be home in time for dinner? Okay. My friend invited me over to study. I'll have my phone. Okay. You too."

She stuffed the phone back into her pocket. "He works all the time," she said with a shrug. "He's not home a whole lot."

That sounded nice, but I didn't say as much. I grabbed my backpack and gestured for Nina to follow me into the house. Loud action music greeted us as we walked in on Colin bombing some poor alien race on the Xbox.

We walked through a cloud of spicy-smelling steam on the way to the stairs. I poked my head into the kitchen to see my mom fussing over a frying pan on the stove. The counter was arrayed with a package of flour tortillas, shredded cheese, and a jar of salsa.

"Mom, we're home," I said. "We're going upstairs."

"Wait." She brushed her hands clean on her scrub top. Her face was etched in concern as she looked me over. There was a telltale black smudge of makeup on the inner corner of her right eye. A lump swelled in my throat as I realized how upset she'd been. I felt like a massive tool for being so annoyed with her. She let out a heavy sigh, then lightly kissed my forehead. "Hi, sweetie. Who's your friend?"

"I'm Nina Welles," she said, sticking her hand out.

My mom beamed as she shook Nina's hand. "Barbara Young. It's nice to meet you. Do you like enchiladas?"

"Mexican is my favorite," Nina replied with a bright smile. Well, she knew how to earn brownie points quickly. "It smells great."

Mom beamed. Nina was good. "You two wash your hands and help me roll these up while I go start some laundry." Nina immediately went to the sink to wash up.

"What about Colin?" I said.

"Colin has a cold, so unless you like your enchiladas with extra snot, I suggest you let him stay in there," Mom said. She slid the frying pan to another burner, and the sizzling sound quieted. On the back burner was a pot of fluffy rice. Mom pointed to each of the ingredients in turn. "Tortilla.

Handful of cheese. Cover it in chicken. Spoonful of rice. Roll it up, stick it in the pan. When they're all in, pour the salsa over it." She assembled hers, then wedged it into the glass dish on the counter. "Questions?"

"I think we got it," Nina said brightly.

"Good," Mom said. "If you're done before I am, put it in the oven for twenty minutes." She walked through the dining room and snapped her fingers over Colin's head. "You've got fifteen minutes, alien hunter, then I want to see homework."

"They're not aliens, they're cyborgs," Colin replied without looking up.

"Fifteen minutes." Mom disappeared into her room. A moment later, I heard the metallic bang of the washer door.

"Sorry you got put to work," I told Nina as we assembled enchiladas.

"Me and Dad eat a lot of takeout, so this is kind of exciting," she said. She fumbled her tortilla and dropped chicken on the floor. "Oh, crap." She looked around. "Do you have any pets?"

"I wish," I said.

She laughed. "My cat Celeste always waits in the kitchen for me to drop something." Loose rice fell on the counter as she awkwardly rolled the enchilada. "Oh, my God, I suck at this."

"We'll get it later," I said with a laugh. I finished rolling one of the enchiladas, stuck it in the pan, and started another one.

"What was the Dead Eyes thing you were trying to tell me about earlier?"

"Oh yeah," I said. Mom's urgent phone call had completely interrupted our discussion about what had happened at school. I took my phone out and started Lance and Tristan's video, propping it on the counter so we could watch it while we worked.

Nina paused with another tortilla in her hand as the video started. "What are they doing?"

"Just watch."

The bombardment in the living room went quiet. Explosions faded into the mellow background music of the Xbox main screen. Colin plodded into the dining room and sneezed.

I cringed. "Get back. I'm not getting sick from you."

"I'm not contagious." He sidled up to the pass-through window and leaned in to inspect our work.

"Where did you get your medical degree?" I replied.

"No, they're not," Nina murmured at the video. She rolled her eyes. "Seriously, guys, don't."

Tristan finished the poem right as I finished rolling the last of the enchiladas. I put the pan into the oven and set the timer.

"What are you guys watching?" Colin asked. "Is it that Dead Eyes thing?"

"No," I snapped.

He'd been suspicious ever since he figured out that I'd rescued Diana and Corey from the woods. His nerdy brain had jumped straight to *mutant*, but that probably wasn't too far off. I didn't want him catching on that I was interested in something else and trying to insert himself into it.

"I just heard it. I'm not stupid."

"Then why did you ask?"

"These guys in my gym class did it the other day while we were outside for soccer."

The fierce anger that ignited in my chest at the thought of him doing the challenge surprised me. I pointed at him with my best authoritative posture. "You are not to do one of those videos."

"Okay, Mom," he said, rolling his eyes. "It's fake, anyway."

"Don't do it, or I'm telling Mom."

He wrinkled his nose at me. "Why are you being so weird?"

Nina locked my phone, cutting off Tristan's speech mid-sentence. She pinned Colin with a stern stare. "I know this guy from Marymount who did it. The cops busted him for trespassing because he was dumb enough to post a video of where he did it. You don't want to go to juvie, do you? You know they strip-search you, right?"

Behind his glasses, Colin's green eyes went wide. "Really?"

"Hand up your butt and everything."

His jaw dropped. "Gross!"

"I'm just saying," Nina said. "Not worth it."

Colin stared at Nina like he was trying to figure out if she was lying. Heck, I wasn't even sure she was. Her expression was stony.

Finally, he broke the stalemate with a sneeze. "When's dinner?"

"Ten minutes," I said. "Mom said you have to go wash your hands first." He started to come around into the kitchen, but I blocked the door. "Upstairs. We're using this sink."

"Bridget," he whined. I stared down at him, thankful that he hadn't hit a growth spurt yet. He finally slumped and trudged up the stairs.

With the kitchen to ourselves, I spun on my heel. "Okay, obviously my mom doesn't know about me. Colin doesn't know either, but he's suspicious. And smart."

"Understood," she said.

Fifteen minutes later, we had set the table and served portions for four. Mom emerged from her bedroom with a look of delighted surprise on her face. "Girls, thank you." I'd almost forgotten what it looked like to see approval on my mother's face.

We sat down to eat. After Mom said grace, she turned to Nina. "So, Nina, what grade are you in?"

"I'm a senior," she said politely.

"Oh, how nice," Mom said. "And what are your plans after graduation?"

Nina tilted her head. "I'm probably going into the family business."

"Oh," Mom said, carefully controlling her face. "What business is that?"

A cold hand stroked my hair, and I let out a yelp of surprise. As Mom and Colin's eyes turned on me, I turned it into an overdramatic sneeze. "Excuse me."

I faked another one, turning enough to see Shirley standing behind me. I widened my eyes at her and shook my head, trying to send her the message to leave.

"Bless you. My dad works in marketing," Nina said, drawing Mom's attention back to her.

"Oh dear, I'm sorry," Shirley said. "I'll wait." The temperature returned to normal as she moved away, reappearing at the middle of the stairs.

"How nice. Have you lived here in Parkland long?" Mom said, completely oblivious to the spirit interrupting dinner.

"No," Nina said. "We moved from Charlotte over the summer, so I've been at Fox Lake all year."

"That must have been hard to move for your senior year," I said.

Nina shrugged. "I adapt quickly." She beamed. "And I met Bridget the other day, and we have a lot in common."

Mom smiled then, a genuine smile. "That's so nice. She doesn't have very many friends."

Colin snickered into his enchilada.

My cheeks went hot. "Thank you, mother."

"Bridget, did you hear about the accident already?" Kale asked.

I snapped my head up from my plate to see Kale standing between Mom and Colin, his handsome face stony. I widened my eyes at him. Nina didn't even look up, keeping her attention on my mom.

"Oh, bad time," Kale said. "I'll tell you later."

The enchiladas suddenly seemed unappetizing. If Kale was reporting an accident to me, then it had to be related to the Dead Eyes videos. Great.

"What do you do, Mrs. Young?" Nina asked.

"You can call me Barb," Mom said. "I'm an oncology nurse."

As Mom told Nina a story about a patient she'd had that morning, I marveled at the easy way Nina made conversation. She didn't seem shy or irritated with my mother. I envied her casual charm and wished it was that simple for me.

Cold air rushed around us. Mom shivered and looked around for the source of the draft, which happened to be a dark-clad spirit named Ethan. Had I missed the neon sign on the front door that said *Ghost Convention?* "Did you feel that?"

"What?" Nina asked calmly.

She flicked her eyes to Ethan. Without speaking, he nodded and disappeared.

Mom frowned. "That's strange. It was like the air kicked on for a second." She shook her head and turned to Colin. "What did you learn about in school today?"

We spent the rest of dinner hearing about Colin's science experiment where he got to test mystery liquids. I tried to look like I was listening, but I was thinking about the accident Kale mentioned. Could it have been the same one Mom got freaked out about? And if it was related, that was two incidents in one day with my laughing spirit.

When we had all finished, Nina stood and reached across the table. "May I take your plate, Mrs…Barb?"

"Oh, how sweet," Mom said. "You're my guest, I'll take it."

I practically jumped out of my seat and said, "We'll get it." Nina had already figured out how to earn points with my mom, so I was ready to follow her lead. After picking up my plate, I held out my hand for Colin's. He shot me a disbelieving stare, but handed it over without comment.

It took us another few minutes to rinse the dishes and put them in the dishwasher. By the time we'd finished, Mom had already wrapped the leftovers. For once, she seemed to be in a good mood.

"I think we need to get back to work," Nina said. "What do you think?"

"Definitely," I said. We needed answers before someone ended up dead.

Chapter Ten

I HEADED UP THE STAIRS with a string of chatty spirits trailing behind me like noisy, incorporeal ducklings. On the way up, Jerry appeared at the back of the pack like he'd just gotten word about the ghost party.

"Well, hey there," he said. "Bridget, did I ever tell you about that time I went deep-sea fishing in Key West?"

With four spirits surrounding us, it was so cold that breathing hurt my chest. I exhaled plumes of white fog. When Nina and I reached my bedroom, Shirley appeared and started talking immediately.

"Oh how lovely," she said. "I've been waiting to update you on my daughter."

Nina pointed to my door. "Is this one yours?"

"Yeah," I said. My stomach fluttered as she walked in and inspected the room.

"I love the purple," Nina said after a long, heart-pounding minute. I let out a sigh of relief and followed her inside, closing the door behind me.

Kale, Shirley, and Jerry began talking simultaneously. Ethan was still silent, still waiting patiently at the doorway. I almost felt embarrassed. I didn't want to think of them that way, but it was almost like Ethan was a well-trained dog in a pack of unruly puppies.

Nina frowned at them, then looked at me. "Can I take over for a minute?"

"By all means," I said.

She held up her hand and said, "Quiet, please." Though her voice wasn't loud, it was powerful and resonant. Unseen force pushed against me like a wave breaking on the shore. *Wow.*

The three spirits fell silent, staring at her in wonder. Jerry looked baffled, but Shirley looked sheepish, like she'd been busted talking during a test. Kale's eyes narrowed. His lips pressed together in a grim line as he appraised Nina.

"I'm sorry," Nina said. "If you all talk at once, we can't understand you. One at a time." She spoke with the authoritative air of a schoolteacher scolding a class. After waiting for a second, she turned to me. "Take it away."

Heart thumping, I turned to Shirley and Jerry. "Guys, we have a big problem to talk about tonight. Shirley, what did you want to tell me?" I wanted to help them all, but they didn't understand that even though their problems seemed monumental, they were theirs alone. If I was going to stop a violent spirit from hurting innocent people, I couldn't stop for every bit of dead-person drama along the way.

"Well, I went to my daughter Anne-Marie's house to check on her, and my older daughter Corinne was there, and—"

"Give us the quick version," Kale interrupted gently.

The older woman looked stung, but I was thankful for his interruption. "She's doing okay. Her blood pressure is a little high, but she's monitoring it. She has another month to go."

It was obvious that she wanted to talk more about it, but we didn't have the time. Behind her, Jerry was practically wiggling as he waited for his turn to talk. Seeing him gave me an idea.

"Well that's good, right?" I asked her. She smiled. "Hey, Shirley, have you met Jerry? He's also my friend. He's in a similar situation." Life-challenged, oxygen-free, and all that.

"Hey there, pleasure to meet you," Jerry said eagerly. "I was about to tell Bridget here——"

"Actually, Jerry, I was thinking you could tell Shirley about your fishing trip," I said. "And Shirley could tell you about her daughter." They looked at each other strangely, then back at me. "It'll be fun."

Jerry shrugged. "I'd certainly like to hear about your daughter, Miss Shirley," he said. "I've got three daughters myself. Seven grandbabies altogether." And I had heard about all seven of them at great length.

"Oh, how lovely," Shirley said.

"Outside," Kale said mildly.

Jerry frowned at Kale, then looked to me like he was hoping I'd change my mind. I shook my head a little, and Jerry reluctantly drifted toward the door with Shirley in tow. Their voices were audible through the door, but it was already much calmer. It was still frigid in my room, but I had blankets and hoodies galore.

"Good call," Nina said.

Their departure left Nina and me with Kale and Ethan, who waited quietly. I grabbed my laptop off the desk and plopped onto my bed. Once I was settled, I turned to them. "So did you guys find anything?"

Ethan looked to Nina before speaking, as if he needed her permission to speak. It was odd to see, considering Kale was the authority in our relationship. I mean, I'd what I thought was right, but I usually sought his approval first. What exactly was their relationship? When Nina gave him a little nod, he said, "The spirits in this area seem more agitated than I would expect."

Kale watched him, then frowned. "I was going to say the same thing."

"They're all making these videos," Nina said. She took a tablet out of her backpack, searched for Lance and Tristan's video, and held it up so Ethan could see.

While Ethan was watching the video, I opened my computer and checked Facebook. As I scrolled through my newsfeed, I came across half a dozen of the same picture, a lit votive candle glowing against a dark background, with the words *Pray for Jenna* across the bottom.

"Jenna..." I murmured. The picture was tagged with dozens of people. I skimmed through the names until I saw Jenna Nixon. Clicking on her name took me to her profile, where there were dozens of messages wishing her well and offering prayers. "Was Jenna Nixon the one in the car accident?"

"That's what I interrupted dinner for," Kale said. "There was a bad car accident near your school this afternoon."

"Yeah, Mom called me," I murmured.

"I sensed the same dark energy gathering there as I did at the school earlier today," he said. "The two incidents were definitely related."

Nina frowned. "I don't know her personally, but I think she's in my gym class."

I skimmed over Jenna's profile. Her Workplaces listed *Producer at JennaJams*. Below the title was a link to YouTube. My stomach plunged as I followed the link to the landing page for her channel. Most of her videos were about makeup looks and beauty products. But there it was, wedged between *Five Minute Smokey Eye* and *Sephora Haul*.

"JennaJams Dead Eyes Challenge," I read aloud.

I didn't want to watch the video, but I couldn't help it. After her pink and purple intro graphics, the camera cut to a pretty dark-haired girl that I recognized from the profile picture, standing in front of a stone wall with a wrought-iron arch. The sky was darkening to the muted gray-blue of twilight in winter.

"Hey Jammers," she said brightly. "Obviously, this isn't my usual video, but I got tagged, so here we go." She stepped up to the camera and fluttered her eyelashes up close. Her makeup was dramatic, with black lipstick and feathery lashes tipped in silver glitter. "Of course, I had to do it my way, so if you want to check out my *Knock 'Em Dead Eyes* tutorial, make sure you click on this link." She pointed to her right, where a little bubble had appeared with a link inside.

Like the other videos we'd watched, she walked into the graveyard and made a big point of how spooky it was. Her camera panned over the gravestones, and she ended up picking a spot under the wings of a giant angel statue. She lit half a dozen white candles and arranged them in an arc on the ground. After setting out a battery-operated lantern for light, she read the same Dead Eyes speech that Tristan had done.

After a few minutes, her head snapped to the right. "What was that? I swear I hear laughing. Can you hear that?"

An annotation appeared at the bottom of the video. *We turned up the sound to see if you can hear it.* The audio was mostly white noise. If there was a giggle, I didn't hear it.

Unlike the guys, Jenna didn't run out screaming. In fact, she showed a time-lapse video of herself at the graveyard. In fast-motion, she moved around, taking selfies, checking her lashes, occasionally flashing her phone at the camera with the current time as if to prove she wasn't faking. After a while, the video slowed again, and she stepped in front of the camera.

"Sorry, Lance and Tristan, I think you're a bunch of babies," she said. "Nothing to fear out here. JennaJams is rating this one Don't Bother!" As she said the words, she gave two thumbs down. Animated white text spelled out *Don't Bother* under her hands. "So check in with me for Friday, when I'll be sampling the new Cinemagic collection from M.A.C. If you loved what you saw, then make sure you click that cute little subscribe button. Until next time, jam on!"

When the video was over, I looked up at Nina. "It's the videos," I said. "Lance, Tristan, now Jenna?"

"How many of these videos are there?" Ethan asked.

"A lot," I said numbly, recalling my search from a few days earlier. "Thousands. How are we going to deal with thousands of these? We can't possibly find them all. We'll—"

"Slow down," Nina interrupted, breaking through my anxious rambling. "They're not all ending up with freak accidents. Or we'd have heard about a lot more."

"Not necessarily," I said. "What happened to Tristan and Lance is bad, but it's not going to end up on the national news."

"Yea, but don't you think it would be obvious if everyone who did one of those videos had a freak accident? They'd be getting even more attention for it," she said. "Is there anyone who made a video and didn't get hurt? If so, then we know it's not just the words."

"It's not just the words," Kale said.

"You said the other day that it could be," I said.

"I said it could have maybe let them see a glimpse under the right circumstances," he said. "But a bunch of kids aren't summoning spirits into the physical realm to wreak havoc just with that stupid poem. I think it's more likely you have a spirit here in town causing these incidents."

"Are you sure?" I asked.

"We could find out," Nina said. She typed on her tablet and pulled up a video. "Here's one that went up two weeks ago. The channel has posted three new videos since then." She typed again. "I've got another one from three weeks ago, and they're still updating."

My heart was still pounding at the thought of thousands of angry spirits wreaking havoc. *Calm down*, I told myself. I tried to channel my inner detective the way I had when I talked to Fulbright. On TV, they always looked for the common factors between victims. "OK, so far we know of Jenna, Tristan, and Lance. What did they have in common?"

"They're students at Fox Lake," Nina said. "But Jenna's accident wasn't at school. They both filmed in a graveyard."

"Is it the same one?" Kale asked.

"Hold on." I went back to YouTube and pulled up Lance and Tristan's video.

Watching the screen closely, I scrubbed through the video. The two boys moved in comical fast motion across my screen. But after going through the entire video, I never saw a shot that zoomed out far enough to see any identifying landmarks. I paused a few times, trying to make out the names on the headstones.

"Can you read this?" I pushed the laptop toward Nina.

She pulled it close and squinted. "Maybe Wall? Watts? Not sure." The computer chirped. "Oh, sorry! You have a call. Uh, hi." She handed the laptop back. *Sorry*, she mouthed.

When I set it in my lap, Emily's face had appeared in a Skype call window. "Hey," she said with a frown. "Uh, who's that?"

"That's my new friend I was telling you about." I turned it so Nina could see. "Emily, this is Nina. Nina, Emily."

Nina smiled and waved. "Hey, Emily!"

"Hey. I guess you must have had fun hanging out," Emily said. I turned the computer back to myself. That pointed *hey* really said it all, but the perturbed expression on Emily's face put the punctuation on it. "I was gonna tell you that I heard about an accident. Jenn—"

"Nixon," I said. "She has a YouTube channel, too."

Emily's face fell. I had stolen her thunder. Crap. "Yeah. Okay. I'll leave you guys alone."

"Wait!" I said. "Do you know anyone else at our school that does videos? Like people who might have done the Dead Eyes challenge?"

She paused. She almost hid it, but her expression slipped for a second, betraying an eager smile. "Maybe. I'll have to do some research. Call me when you're done and I'll try to have something for you."

"Okay, sounds good. Thanks!" Before I could say anything else, Emily ended the call. As the screen went dark, my shoulders slumped. So much for smoothing things over at lunch.

Nina was watching me quietly. "Everything okay?"

"Yeah, no worries," I said, trying to ignore the pit of dread sitting like a rock in my stomach.

Emily had been my best friend for years. We'd known each other since elementary school, though we hadn't gotten really close until ninth grade. She was the only one who'd stuck by me when everyone else ditched me after Valerie's death.

But it wasn't fair for her to get mad at me for making another friend. That brought my grand total up to three friends that had heartbeats. She had other friends, too, so I didn't understand why it was such a big deal. Maybe I was overreacting. I hoped so.

Nina took a deep breath, like she'd sensed the disturbance between me and Emily. "I'll look at Jenna's video again to see if I notice anything else."

"Good idea," I said, navigating back to it on my laptop. The initial shot of the stone wall and iron gate were too tight to make out any signs. As Jenna walked through the cemetery, the camera stayed close to her face. When she finally set up her candles, she was sitting in the shadow of a huge angel statue. I paused the video. "What about this?"

Nina turned her tablet around to show me the paused video a few seconds before where I'd stopped. "Angel?"

I grinned. "Great minds think alike."

"This is pretty damn distinctive," she said. "Maybe they've pissed off someone who's buried there."

Kale frowned. "Most spirits are attached to the place where they died, not their grave."

"Well, it's all we have," I said. "So what do we do? Drive all over town until we find it?"

"We could do that for you," Ethan said, speaking for the first time since Nina and I had started our research. He gestured to Kale. "Shall we?"

Kale looked at me, then back to Ethan. His eyes narrowed slightly. I might have made a good match between Jerry and Shirley, but Kale clearly didn't want to be paired up with Ethan for errands.

"Don't go running off," Kale said mildly.

"You got it," I said.

He and Ethan disappeared. When they were gone, Nina turned to me. "Don't go running off?"

I hesitated. "I may have a slight tendency to take things into my own hands."

"Oh really?" Nina's eyes gleamed as she grabbed a pillow and leaned into it. "Tell me."

"Well, there was this murderer here a few months ago."

Her jaw dropped. "Shut up!"

I told her the story of meeting Natalie and finding her grave, and eventually how I'd ended up going to rescue Emily before she met the same fate. Nina peppered my story with *dude!* and *oh my God!* When I finished, she stared at with me with an incredulous expression that made me feel oddly exposed.

Anxious for a subject change, I said, "What about you? I'm sure you've done some crazy stuff."

"Not like that," she said. "But it sounds like I might have fun hanging out with you."

I laughed. "Not that kind, I hope."

She checked her phone. "My dad's on his way home. I should get going," she said. "Let's text if we hear back from Ethan or..."

"Kale," I said.

"Kale," she said. "Like the vegetable."

"Just like the vegetable," I said. "I'll let you know."

"And maybe we can go check it out tomorrow," she said. As we walked out of my room, we passed the bathroom where Jerry and Shirley were still chatting. Laughter punctuated their chipper conversation.

Before she walked out the door, Nina approached my mom, who was watching TV in the living room. "Ms. Young, I have to go, but thank you so much for having me for dinner."

Mom looked up from her show and smiled brightly. "Oh, it was my pleasure. Come over anytime."

After I walked her out the door, I returned to the living room to find Mom wearing the strangest smile on her face. "What?"

"She seems like such a nice girl!" she gushed, like I'd just brought home a boyfriend. "I'm so glad you made a new friend."

"Okay. We talked about getting lunch and then working on a project tomorrow." It wasn't completely a lie. Finding the spirit responsible for the accidents qualified as a project.

"That's great," she said. "Keep me posted on where you go."

Yeah, right.

When I went back up to my room, my phone was glowing. I ran to the bed to snatch it up. My heart leapt into my throat when I saw I had a new text message from Michael. But when I read the preview, I froze with my thumb hovering over the screen. He'd know that I had seen it and then I'd look like a jerk for not replying.

Michael: Found something on Vivian Waller...

My heart sank into a messy little pile. Silly me. I'd thought he might have been interested in hanging out, or talking about something other than missing people.

I ignored the message. It was nine-thirty. I could pretend I'd gone to bed early, or that my phone had died. In the grand scheme of things, it was a tame lie.

Below Michael's message was a text from Detective Fulbright. It simply said:

Fulbright: Any progress?

I didn't reply to him either, but took the reminder that I needed to get back to work. After turning on some music, I dug my folded map of Parkland out of the desk drawer. Unfolding it brought an unexpected pang of sadness.

It was still marked with a rough circle in highlighter that connected several X's. I'd last used the map to pinpoint where Natalie Fullmer's body had been buried by the Runaway Killer.

After making a mental note to buy a new map with less emotional baggage, I took out Fulbright's police report and used the addresses to mark the scenes of the break-ins. My friend Sal, a former police officer, could probably investigate. Not only did he have the incorporeal thing going on, he had actual police training.

Leaning back in my chair, I closed my eyes and pictured his warm eyes and golden skin. "Sal, I've got a case for you."

In my mind, I extended a hand out the window into a dark, starry night. Cold shot up my arm as a pale hand grasped it. An unseen force pulled on me, and I opened my eyes to see Sal standing near my window.

He looked a little surprised to be there, but he smiled anyway. "Hey kid. You staying out of trouble?"

"I'm trying to," I said. "For once."

He grinned and folded his arms over his chest. In death, he still wore his police uniform, complete with silver name badge that read *Salazar*, right over the small red circle where the bullet had entered his chest. "Got something for me?"

I told him about the break-ins and spread out the police reports on the bed so he could read them. Sal was still a vibrant spirit, but he wasn't angry or overly emotional, so he could barely interact with the physical world. I left him scanning the reports while I went back to check Jenna Nixon's Facebook page for updates.

A dull sort of sadness weighed on me as I scrolled through, looking at the pictures of kids from school taking selfies at the movies, checking in at the Fly Zone, and generally doing normal teenager things.

After my sister died, I withdrew from the world. I'd realized the best way to navigate this whole mess was to keep it to myself. Maybe I couldn't stop people like Allie from gossiping about me, but I didn't have to be around them or give them more fuel for the fire. I wasn't wrong, but maybe isolation wasn't the healthiest way to go through life. Even something painfully normal like helping Mom cook dinner with Nina had been one of the best things to happen in years. How sad was that?

As if he'd sensed the pity party that was starting in my room, Kale reappeared. "So I went—Oh. Hi, Luis," he said warmly. "Good to see you."

Sal looked up from the reports and waved. "Hey, man." Without further consideration, he went back to scanning the report. This was my normal. Two ghost dudes, just hanging out in my bedroom.

"Did you find anything?" I asked Kale.

"We narrowed it down," he said. "There are three cemeteries in town with a large angel statue like the one you showed us. If I remembered the layout of the surrounding headstones correctly, I think we can rule out one of them. I couldn't refer back to the video, so I'm not sure which of the others it might be."

"That's great," I said. "Where are they?"

"Woodlawn Cemetery and Saint Teresa's Memorial Gardens."

"You weren't able to tell which one?"

"Whatever they called up wasn't in the vicinity," he said. "Both seemed unsettled, but that's normal for a cemetery."

"Cool," I said. "Sal is looking at Fulbright's reports."

Sal nodded. "I know the neighborhood. I think I can get there. How about I go check it out tonight?"

"That would be great," I said. "And maybe I ca—" My words hitched as a powerful yawn came over me. "Sorry. I found—"

"You look tired," Kale interrupted. "Why don't you get some rest? This will be here in the morning." He looked to Sal, who gave us a snappy little salute.

"I'm your guy," Sal said with his cheerful grin. "I'll let you know what I find. Could be a while." With a gust of wind, he disappeared.

After carefully collating the police reports and putting them in my notebook, I went to the bathroom to get ready for bed. Jerry and Shirley had disappeared, but the whole mirror was fogged over from the cold. Maybe they'd gone off to do the ghostly equivalent of getting coffee. As long as they were entertaining each other, I could have a little peace and quiet.

When I returned, Kale was still in my room, sitting on the end of my bed. My heart thumped, and I felt oddly self-conscious about my threadbare pajamas. "Your phone has been buzzing."

I grabbed it and found several new messages from Nina.

Nina: Ethan's back

Nina: U hear about cemeteries?

Nina: Want to go investigate tomorrow?

I quickly typed my reply.

Definitely. Can u pick me up?

Nina: 10:00 am?

Sure. See u then

Nina: ☺

I climbed into bed and propped up my head on my hand to look at Kale. He perched on the edge of my desk, looking down at me. "What do you think of Nina?"

"What do you mean?" His face didn't betray any emotion, which told me something on its own. He didn't usually hide what he thought.

"You had a strange face when she was here."

"That's rude," he said, putting one hand to his chest in mock outrage. "I'm told my face is quite handsome."

"It is," I said. His lips pursed in amusement, and my cheeks flushed. "I mean…never mind. I just couldn't tell what you were thinking."

"Well, you do know you're not psychic, right?"

"Be serious."

The playful smile evaporated into a serious expression. "I'm not sure about her yet. She's powerful. Much more in tune with her gift than you."

Ouch. "Well, she's had it longer," I said defensively.

"I don't mean it as an insult," he said. "And I don't trust Ethan. He's not a Guardian." That didn't surprise me after watching how he deferred to her.

"He's not?"

Kale shook his head. "No. I asked him what his connection to her was, but he told me it was none of my concern."

"Interesting," I said. "Do all people like us have Guardians?"

"For some duration, yes," he said. "It's possible that she's moved past needing one. That would be something for you to ask when it seems right."

"Moved past it? Does that mean you'll leave me some day?"

"Possibly," he said. "But not for a long time."

Well, that wasn't what I wanted to hear. "Besides that, you think she's okay?"

He smiled and pointed at me. "Since when do you care so much about my opinion? Your modus operandi seems to be to solicit my opinion and then inform me that you'll be doing whatever you want regardless of the answer."

"Hey," I said. "Okay, that's kind of true, but I'm trying to do better."

"I think it could be good to have a friend who shares your ability," he said. "And I prefer the idea of you two working together over you throwing yourself into danger at every opportunity that presents itself."

"Not every opportunity."

Kale rolled his eyes. "Just be cautious. People have a way of hiding their uglier sides when you first encounter them."

"Even me?"

"Some people," he said. "You're secretive and a bit too contrary for your own good, but I don't think you have a dark side."

"Neither do you," I said.

He smiled, but there was something strange about it. The faintest crease in his brow, a little flinch; what was he thinking about when I said that? "Why don't you get some sleep? If I know you, you'll probably get tangled up in something tomorrow and probably end up calling the police at some point."

"At least I'm consistent," I said.

He laughed. The shadow that had crossed his face was gone, leaving the angelic face that occupied way too much of my attention. "Good night, my sweet troublemaker."

CHAPTER ELEVEN

GETTING READY TO SPEND THE DAY with Nina felt strangely like getting ready for a date, at least based on my limited dating experience. I picked out a nice gray striped top and a new pair of dark jeans Mom had bought me for Christmas. After dabbing on some makeup, I curled my hair and put on a pair of silver earrings.

I pulled my purple backpack out. I kept all of my ghost supplies in there, then stashed it far under my bed in case Mom ever came snooping around. After checking for the usual supplies, I murmured, "Flashlight."

After a terrifying night in the woods with no light except the tiny lighter flame, I decided that I'd be adding a good flashlight to my packing list. We had plenty of daylight, but it would be smart to prepare for the unexpected. If I'd learned anything, it was that life rarely went according to plan.

I slung the bag over my shoulder and hurried downstairs. A quiet rush of water through the walls told me Mom was in the shower. Still in his flannel pajamas, Colin was sprawled on the couch watching Netflix. I ignored him and walked into the kitchen.

Next to the silverware drawer was a junk drawer stuffed to the brim with everything from ketchup packets to birthday candles to replacement batteries for the smoke detector. I took out a handful of plastic silverware packets and started rifling through the drawer.

"What are you doing?" Colin stood in the open doorway, giving me a suspicious look.

"Looking for something."

"No duh," he said. "What are you looking for?"

"None of your business, Mom," I said to him. I shoved aside a wax-smudged plastic bag filled with number candles. "Don't we have a flashlight somewhere?"

A car horn honked outside. Crap.

"Why do you need a flashlight?"

"Why are you so nosy?"

"Because you keep so many secrets," he said. My stomach flip-flopped. "I know you're up to something."

"I'm just going to study," I said.

"With a flashlight?" he said. "Besides, if you were studying every time you said you were, your grades would be better."

"Rude." Nina honked again. I shoved my hand deep into the drawer. My fingers found something sticky. Gross.

A cabinet behind me closed with a quiet thud. "Here." I took it from him silently. "Are you going off to do something dangerous?" I couldn't tell if he was concerned or frustrated that he couldn't figure out what I was up to. Neither was good.

"No," I said. "I'm just going to hang out with Nina."

He sighed and shook his head. "Whatever. I'm not going to cover for you with Mom."

"I didn't ask you to," I replied. I stashed the flashlight in my backpack and slung it onto my back. "I have permission, anyway."

Colin was smart, stubborn, and persistent. Those could be positive traits, but they were a bad mix in a suck-up of a younger sibling. If he wanted, he could make my life difficult by blabbing to Mom. I had to be more careful.

I hurried out the door to find Nina idling in the driveway. Loud metal music blared as I opened the car door and dropped into the seat. The pounding beat seemed so out of place with her perky attitude and bouncy blonde hair, but considering we were both on speaking terms with the dead, I knew better than to judge outer appearances.

Nina turned down the radio. "Ethan came back and told me that they'd narrowed it down. Did Kale tell you the details?"

"Yeah," I said. "Saint Teresa's and Woodlawn." I took out my phone. "I can look up directions on my phone."

"No need." She showed me a Post-it note with two addresses on it. "I already looked them up." She entered the first one in her GPS. "Looks like Saint Teresa's first."

As we drove across town, I felt strangely nervous, sort of like I had when I first met Michael. I fiddled with the straps on my backpack as I looked out the window.

Say something. You're being weird.

"So, have you done anything like this before?" I blurted.

"What, gone to a graveyard?"

"I guess."

"Sure," Nina said. "Have you?"

"Yeah." *Wow, great conversation, Bridget.* This was what happened when most of your social circle lacked a pulse.

"Cool," Nina said. "I told Ethan I'd call for him when we got to the first graveyard."

"I'll call Kale, too." The mention of our Guardians reminded me of my discussion with Kale last night. "Hey, is Ethan a Guardian?"

Nina cocked her head. "He watches out for me. Is that what you mean?"

"Not really," I said. "Kale is a Guardian. It's like an official thing. He won't tell me much, but I get the impression there's a whole society or something, and they get assigned to people like us. I assumed Ethan was one."

"No," Nina said. The way she said it was like this was the first she'd heard of it. She frowned. "I met him about five years ago. He got stuck here after he was killed in a drunk driving accident."

"That's awful," I said.

"Yeah. He couldn't deal with what he'd done."

Oh. My mouth went dry. "So he was…"

"Yeah. He was the driver," she said flatly. "He killed his passenger and the driver of the other car."

My blood went cold. What was I supposed to say to that? "That must have been hard for him."

Nina glanced up at the rearview mirror, then moved over to the right lane to turn into the cemetery. Her expression remained neutral as she told his story. She didn't sound angry, but she also didn't sound sympathetic. "He was such a disaster. His girlfriend was the passenger, so he was lingering around her house looking for her. Freezing their pipes, knocking things over…he was about to drive her parents insane. Her mom was on medication because they thought she had a nervous breakdown or something. So I got him to latch on to me instead."

"And you're trying to get him to move on?"

Nina shrugged. "I've suggested it a few times, but I think he's afraid of what comes after."

I paused. "Do you know what it is? After, I mean."

The true afterlife, where the ghosts went when they let go of this world was a mystery that Kale either couldn't or wouldn't reveal to me. It left me with this nagging doubt when I sent a spirit on with promises of peace and rest beyond.

She hesitated. "I have an idea, but I'm not sure," she said. "I believe there's something, and I'd like to think it's good. But it's hard for me to promise him that everything will be fine, you know? So I'm not pushing him."

"You're not worried about him staying too long?"

"So far he's been all right. I think helping me lets him feel like he's making up for what happened."

"Makes sense," I said. Though it seemed odd to let him linger for five years, I also understood not forcing him to move on. "So do you guys do stuff like this?"

"Well, we've never caught a serial killer," she said. "More stuff like your friends Shirley and Jerry. Spirits that need closure." She didn't offer any more detail.

Woodlawn Cemetery sprawled over gentle green hills, dotted with flashes of color from memorial flowers. Nina parked in the small lot at the corner of the cemetery. There was only one other car in the lot. Good. We'd be alone.

The air was cool and still, but it felt pressurized, like we were submerged underwater. My skin tingled, like fingers brushed the back of my neck.

"Let's go check it out," Nina said, heading for the smooth path that curved away into the cemetery.

"Wait," I said. "This isn't it."

She looked back at me quizzically. "How do you know?"

"At the beginning of her video, Jenna stood in front of a big iron gate under a stone archway," I said. "There's no arch." The fence enclosing the cemetery was a waist-high white wooden fence, and there was no stonework except for two thick columns on either side of the path.

"Good catch," she said. "I guess that makes it easy. Let's head to St. Teresa's."

On the way back to the car, my pocket buzzed. I took out my phone to find a message from Michael. Without thinking, I opened it.

Michael: Did you get my message? Was wondering if you wanted to do some research with your 'friends'

I sighed and got back in the car.

"What's wrong?" Nina asked as she buckled up.

"This guy I know," I said. "His name is Michael Fullmer."

"Fullmer…oh! He's in my physics class," she said. "He's super cute. You're talking to him?"

"It's a long story," I said. "Remember the serial killer? The last victim was his sister."

"Oh, crap," Nina said. She entered the new address into the GPS and turned onto the main road.

"Yeah. He knows about me."

"You told him?" she said incredulously.

"She wanted to tell him goodbye. He just seemed lost, so I told him," I said. "But now he's obsessed. He helped me find some missing kids back around Christmas. Now that's all he wants to talk about."

She raised an eyebrow. "It's okay to tell him no."

"I guess," I said.

"No, not 'I guess'," she said firmly. "It's okay."

"What if he doesn't want to spend any time with me?"

"If he didn't, then he's stupid," she said. "And also, if the only reason he's hanging out with you is for your ability, then he's a dumbass. And you deserve better."

"He's not a dumbass," I said. God, what was wrong with me? The guy had driven me out to the woods in the middle of the night to find a couple lost teenagers. He was the epitome of a good guy, and I wanted to be picky about how he chose to spend time with me?

"I doubt he is, or you wouldn't be wasting your time," she said with a laugh. "I'm just saying."

"So what do I tell him?"

"Tell him you have other things to focus on," she said. "But that you're still down to hang out if he wants to."

I hesitated, then composed a reply.

Can't today. Maybe another time.

I didn't want to disappoint him. After all, with my ability, shouldn't I have been taking every opportunity I could to help people? I'd wrestled with it when I met Natalie, and again before I stepped in dark woods on a snowy night. It wasn't particularly fair, but the fact of it was that I had the power to help someone. And if I didn't, who would? I didn't like to inflate my ego too much, but Emily would probably be dead if I hadn't intervened. Two kids might have frozen to death in the woods. Knowing they were alive made me feel good, but the inverse was that I felt like an awful person for putting myself first.

I glanced at Nina. She was watching the road and waiting to turn left at a busy intersection.

I added to my message.

I'll see what I can find and let you know next time we hang out

He responded with a series of thumbs up emojis. I sighed. I hadn't even come close to telling him no.

"Arrived," the GPS announced.

A pickup truck with a bed full of landscaping equipment was parked near the gate at St. Teresa's. As soon as I looked up, I knew we were in the right place. Black iron fence stretched away from two thick stone columns topped by a graceful archway. It was the gate we'd seen in Jenna's video.

Beyond the gates was a small, flat graveyard with dozens of headstones in neat rows. Occasionally, a taller monument broke the pattern. In the distance, filmy gray shadows moved among the stones.

"I think this is it," I said. "Kale?"

He appeared moments later, with Ethan close behind. Both of them looked unusually pale. Kale was more transparent than usual. His voice was strained when he said, "Something is here."

I reached into my backpack for the salt, then grasped the bottle of holy water in my other hand. Nina eyed me. "What's that for?"

"I don't like surprises," I said.

"You don't need all that," she said. "We'll be fine. We're just going to find out what it wants. We've both done this before." The skeptical look she gave me made me bristle defensively, but I shoved down my reaction.

A chill ran down my spine as my eyes fell on a fresh grave near the path. The sharp edges of the deep hole yawned dark in the dry brown grass. I remembered all too well standing at the edge of a grave, watching as the silver box containing my sister's body sank into the cold, damp earth. That had been a tough day, though the blow had been softened when I saw her spirit for the first time a few weeks later.

My heart thumped in anticipation as we proceeded deeper into the cemetery. What exactly were we going to do if we found it? After seeing what it had done to Tristan, Lance, and Jenna, I hoped Nina had something up her sleeve, because my trusty salt and sassy attitude might not cut it.

"It's this way," Kale said. His eyes creased in pain, and his form was more transparent than usual. A nearby headstone engraved with clasped hands was visible through his torso.

"What's wrong?" I said. *Crap.* This was what I had feared.

He grimaced. "It's been here recently. Or it could be here now. You need to be careful. If history repeats itself, I won't be able to protect you."

"What do you mean?" Nina asked.

"Some spirits that are really angry or unstable drive Kale away," I said. It wasn't his fault, but I was embarrassed as I told her, like I was telling her that he wet the bed at night.

Nina stared at him with a look that made my blood run hot for a moment. "Really? Ethan, how are you?"

"I'm fine," he said, flinging a disdainful look at Kale. I scowled at him, but he didn't flinch.

"We'll be fine," Nina said.

We pressed on. Deeper into the cemetery, the unsettled sensation intensified, like tiny invisible gnats swarming my skin. It wasn't unbearable, but it was unpleasant. It was way stronger than the usual ambience of a cemetery.

Toward the back of the cemetery was an angel monument that stood in the shadow of a cluster of pine trees. Even without getting close, I knew it had to be the one. Familiarity wrapped in apprehension washed over me when I saw its graceful wings spread wide, one hand stretched toward the heavens.

Something whispered past. There were no words, only a shushing sound at the edge of my hearing. I froze in the path and looked around. Had I imagined it? When I turned back, Nina had stopped, her head tilted like she was listening.

"Do you hear that?"

"Yeah," I murmured.

My hand was clammy, with sweat soaking into the paper label on the salt can. I could only hope that the spirit wouldn't be as angry at us as it was at the people who'd been provoking it for their videos.

Winding our way around the headstones, we walked through the dew-damp grass and approached the angel. The temperature dropped steadily as we approached. I squeezed the bottle of holy water for assurance.

The stone angel kept vigil over a neat array of eight graves. White flowers lay on the ground on a grave on the far right, opposite where we were approaching.

"What are we going to do?" I asked.

"We'll call out to it," Nina said. "But make it clear that we don't want to harm it."

"Here," I said. I shrugged off my backpack, letting it fall to the ground a few yards from the nearest grave under the angel. I pried open the can of salt and made a small ring on the ground, just big enough that we could both stand inside. "If things get hairy."

"We'll be fine," Nina said.

Kale gave me a questioning look. I hesitated, then set down salt and holy water inside the ring. What was I missing? How was Nina so confident?

"Look," Kale said, pointing at the ground. Along the row closer to us, one of the graves was littered with energy drink cans. A water-logged sheet of notebook paper was plastered to the headstone.

"They were here," I said as I crouched in front of the stone. "This is so wrong."

The headstone read *Charlene Watkins.* Soggy cigarette butts and a balled-up napkin littered the damp grass. I gathered the trash and peeled the notebook paper from her headstone. The words on the paper were lost in a smeared watercolor of blue ink.

"Charlene?" Nina said. "Are you here?"

"We're sorry they did this," I said. As I looked back over my shoulder and saw the bright flashes of flowers on other graves, I wished I had brought something to brighten up the place. If Charlene was our angry spirit, a kind gesture could go a long way to make up for her desecrated grave.

"Charlene?" Nina said again.

Barely breathing, I listened for the whispers of the dead. Blood rushed in my ears. Far away, I could still hear the dull sound of road noise and the faintest hint of a siren. This was a little backwards for me. Spirits usually demanded my attention, not the other way around.

"Nothing," Nina said. "But there's been something here for sure. Do you feel that?"

"Feel what?"

Other than the general unsettled aura of the place, I didn't notice anything out of the ordinary. I waited, heart pounding against my ribs. My jeans were damp from kneeling in the grass, and a stray hair tickled my cheek. Nina's eyes were closed, her hands reaching down toward the ground like she was running her fingers through tall grass. What did she sense?

I looked at Kale and put my hands up in a questioning gesture. His face creased. With his lips pressed thin and his blue eyes widening, he reminded me of someone who was trying not to throw up. Finally, I got up and took my phone out of my pocket. I didn't sense anything, which made me irritated that I couldn't pick up on whatever Nina did.

It was so stupid. I knew I should be glad for a friend, and doubly glad for one who shared my ability and the burden that came with it. But I was a little threatened at the fact that I couldn't do what she could.

Well, what I lacked in supernatural sense, I'd make up for with common sense. I opened my camera app and started taking pictures of each headstone in turn. *Frank Borstein. Charlene Watkins. Lois Hanners. Edward Hanners.* I tiptoed around to the back row. *Sara Workman. Travis Hillman. Charlie Hillman. Vonda Rogers.* The plaque below the angel statue read, *There is no death, only a change of worlds.* A chill swept over me as I took one last picture of the whole array.

As I swiped through the pictures to make sure they'd all come out clear, I heard a whisper. The fine hairs on my arm stood up, tingling across my skin. A figure shrouded in shadow stood beneath the angel. Its shape was human, but it had no discernible features. The shadow's translucent mass swirled and eddied, like smoke trapped inside a glass jar.

My muscles tensed as I whispered, "Kale." Without moving, I looked toward him. He was still here. "Hello." My voice was small and shaky. "I'm not here to disturb you."

Nina turned. "Oh. Hello." I envied her calm.

The shadow darkened, the faintest hints of a face emerging from the smoke. With a scratchy whisper, like dry leaves over asphalt, it slowly raised a hand. Then it gestured toward itself.

"Yes, we see you. Here," Nina said. She extended her hand.

"Nina," I said quietly.

"It's fine." There was an authoritative edge in her voice. "Quit worrying so much."

The spirit moved toward Nina. Its dark essence wrapped around her pale hand. As the shadow covered her skin, Ethan appeared next to her. His dark eyes were fixed on Nina's face, though she showed no sign of fear.

She smiled at me. "This would be easier with a little help," she said. "I won't let anything happen."

I glanced at Kale for reassurance. A grimace still contorted his face, but he moved closer and gave me a slight nod. His presence eased some of my fear; he hadn't yet been driven away, so this probably wasn't our culprit.

With trembling hands, I reached out to the spirit. As the smoky tendril touched my skin, bitter cold bit down to the bone. I gasped at the sensation, and the spirit recoiled.

"It's all right," Nina said in a soothing voice. "We're here to help."

The shadow hand reached for me again. As it drew energy from us, the dark smoke solidified. From the hazy substance came a wrinkled hand, then the cuff of a bathrobe. Color shot from the pale fingertips all the way to the spirit's face, and distinct features emerged from the blur. It was pale, with a full white beard over gaunt cheeks. Deep lines of tension around his eyes eased, like a long, stubborn pain had suddenly ceased.

My heart pounded, and I felt like I was falling away, losing touch with the world. "I need to…" I pulled my hand away. Staggering backward, I caught myself and leaned against a headstone as the world spun crazily around me.

"Are you all right?" Kale asked. *Still here.* I nodded.

As I steadied myself, Nina withdrew her hand from the spirit's grasp. He reached for her, a look of anguish on his face.

"No more," she said firmly. "That's all we can do for you right now."

"Please." His voice was only a whisper. Just in the few seconds after she broke contact, the vibrant color began receding from his face, like it was melting back to the source of warmth in his hand.

"What's your name?" Nina asked.

"I'm...I'm Ed. Ed Hanners." He pointed to the last grave on the front row, staring at the stone in confusion. "Why am I still here?"

"I'm not sure," Nina said. "I'd be happy to help you, but right now, we're trying to find out who's been hurting our friends."

Friends was pushing it, but it was easier to tell Ed "friends" than explain "YouTube personalities who made poor choices of filming location."

"I've never hurt anyone," he said.

"No, I know you didn't," Nina said. "But our friends were here before they got hurt, so we were wondering if you saw something."

"They probably had something like this," I said, holding up my phone. "They would have been reading a poem about Dead Eyes."

Ed's bushy brows furrowed, and his eyes gleamed as though lightning had struck through the filmy white cataracts.

"Shh." With his eyes going wide in terror, he checked over both shoulders before looking back to us. "It'll hear you."

"What will hear me?" I asked. Dread rolled over me like a cold mist. "What else is here?"

"Something here. Something dark."

"What do you mean?" Nina asked.

Ed winced. The healthy color had faded entirely, painting his features in shades of murky gray. "I don't see it. I feel it. I hear it. But I don't know it."

Nina looked over her shoulder, then folded her arms across her chest. "Spirit, I command you. Come to me. Show m—"

I grabbed her arm and shook her. "Are you crazy?"

"It's fine. They can't hurt us. We can see them coming." She shook off my grasp. "Restless spirit…"

"Shh," I told her.

From behind me came a cruel, teasing laugh. I whirled toward the source of the sound, but there was nothing. "Kale?"

He doubled over, his handsome face contorted into a grimace as if something was ripping him open. "Bridget, I can't. You need to…" Without a sound, his entire body simply dissipated like white smoke. Ethan was still behind Nina, but his form flickered.

Adrenaline poured into my veins. "Nina, we have to go."

Cold air rushed around us. A high-pitched laugh sounded, followed by a shout of rage. Out of the corner of my eye, I saw a quick-moving blur.

Ed's eyes went wide.

"Run," he whispered. He faded away, leaving us alone.

A biting cold wind whipped around us, filling my nose with the thick smell of decay and burnt rubber. I gagged as it clung to my throat. With my whole body trembling, I grabbed Nina's hand and started to retreat. "Let's go!"

"We're close," she said. "It's here."

"It's obviously strong," I said. "We have to go."

The next peal of cruel laughter sounded like it was right next to me. I jerked out of the way. Sharp pain stung my cheek. "Ow," I complained, pressing fingers to my face. I came away with a cockleburr and droplets of red on my fingers. Another struck the side of my head. They weren't falling naturally from the trees above, but hitting hard, like they were being thrown.

"Shit!" Nina swore, pressing her hand over her eye. Another burr struck her, tangling in her long curls.

There was another rush of cold air around us as Ethan materialized in front of Nina. His voice was deep and resonant as he bellowed, "Leave her alone!"

But the next burr passed right through him and bounced off my head. "Let's go!" I insisted. How many times did I have to say it?

She finally quit resisting and broke into a run. I stooped to grab my backpack, and then we ran for the gates. As we retreated, the spirit kept pelting us with the sharp cockleburrs. Once, there was a much harder blow that had to have been a rock.

The only sound was our heaving breaths as we sprinted out of the cemetery and jumped into Nina's car. I had barely closed my door when she stomped the gas and peeled out of the parking lot. There was no sign of Ethan or Kale. Neither of us spoke until the cemetery was well out of sight behind us.

"What the hell was that?" Nina asked. The pale skin at the outer corner of her right eye was scratched and beaded with blood.

I pulled down the mirror and checked my face. The burr had scratched the soft skin under my eye. I brushed away a dried spot of blood and closed the mirror. "It was pissed." I sighed. "We shouldn't have called it up."

"I didn't mean to make it mad," Nina said. "I didn't even say the whole thing."

Anger bubbled up in my chest. Starting a fight, even with a well-deserved *I told you so,* wouldn't help anything. Pretending to check my face again, I took a deep breath to smooth the harsh edge out of my tone. "Yeah, but maybe between me with my phone and you saying even that much of it, it could think we were like the others."

A rush of cool air filled the car. I whipped my head around to see Kale in the backseat. "You're okay. I'm so sorry."

"It's okay." The sight of him made me smile. "Just a temper tantrum. Nina, what about Ethan?"

"I'll call for him when we decide what we're doing," she said. Her wide eyes met mine in the rearview mirror. "Do you think it'll come after us like it did Jenna?"

"I don't…" I trailed off. We were on one of the busiest roads in town in the middle of Saturday afternoon traffic. My heart pounded as the image of Jenna's accident mingled with old memories of the accident that killed Val. Icy dread trickled down my spine. "Let's go to my house. We'll be safer there."

CHAPTER TWELVE

THE RIDE BACK TO MY HOUSE was uneventful, although my anxious brain spotted at least thirty-seven potential freak accidents. Mom was excited to see Nina again and offered to order Chinese. Colin was at Jeremy's house for the night, so we were safe from his nosiness.

After exchanging pleasantries with Mom and picking out what we wanted to eat, we hurried up to the safety of my room. Kale decided to patrol the perimeter of the house, figuring he'd be able to give me some warning before he got forcibly ejected again. One of these days, we had to figure out a solution to that problem.

We'd just gotten our bags spread out, notebooks and computers at the ready, when Nina cleared her throat. "Listen, I don't mean to pry, but can I ask why Kale ran off like that?"

"He didn't run off," I said defensively. "Sometimes when there's a strong spirit around, it drives him away. He says it's their pain and despair."

Nina wrinkled her nose. "Don't take this the wrong way, but that doesn't seem very helpful to you."

"He does his best," I snapped. She recoiled, and I realized my tone was hot enough to melt steel.

"I didn't mean—"

"No, I know," I said. "He protects me the best he can. The rest of the time I have to be smart and keep myself out of trouble."

It shocked me how quickly I'd gotten angry over Kale. I'd even criticized him, in much less polite terms, for the exact same thing. But he was my Kale, just like I was his Bridget, and it wasn't her place to criticize.

Still, her mention of his shortcomings did raise questions. Ethan had been unsettled by the spirit's presence, but his reaction had been nowhere near as strong as Kale's. It only made it more obvious that Ethan wasn't a Guardian, which made me wonder all over again what exactly Kale was.

"So, you think it was one of the spirits in the graves there?" Nina asked.

"I think so." It was a relief to change the subject. I took out my phone and read the names from the pictures I'd taken. Mentally, I gave myself a pat on the back for thinking ahead. "Frank Borstein. Charlene Watkins. Lois Hanners. Edward Hanners. Sara Workman. Travis Hillman. Charlie Hillman. Vonda Rogers."

"Okay," Nina said. "Two Hanners. Ed was one."

"We can take him off the list," I said. "Assuming Lois is his wife, I wouldn't think it's her. He would have recognized her."

She pondered, rubbing the stung skin next to her eye. "Maybe. That many years gone could have changed her. Let's mark them as maybes. I think it was Charlene. Her grave was trashed. And check this out."

She showed me her tablet, where she'd pulled up Lance and Tristan's video. In the corner of the shot, the *Char-* was barely visible in the dim light. "They were there too. So far, all three accidents we know about were there. If they knew each other through school, Lance and Tristan might have told Jenna that was a good place to do her video."

Though I'd never gotten a response from Raina, I wanted to go back and check her page again to see if she'd filmed at St. Teresa's too. "Okay, let's get organized," I said.

I opened my notebook and tore out eight sheets of paper. In bright purple pen, I wrote the name of one person at the top of each sheet, then handed four to Nina.

"So what are we looking for?" she asked.

"Anything that might lead to unfinished business. Violent deaths are a big one."

I opened my laptop and turned on a music channel to fill the silence. Then I began my research. Before diving into my part of the list, I checked Raina's YouTube channel. She had uploaded two new videos since her Dead Eyes video, which made it unlikely she'd had some horrific accident. With the volume muted, I skipped around in her original video. There was a towering monument surrounded by headstones, but no angel. It was early to make a definitive call, but it seemed that St. Teresa's was the common element.

With that settled in my mind, I turned to researching our potential culprits. Searching *Frank Borstein Parkland* brought up an article about Thomas Borstein, a local businessman that made a hefty donation to the children's hospital and mentioned his father, Frank in his speech. Adding *1992* to my search took to a genealogy site. I clicked around the site but immediately got a pop-up encouraging me to try the fourteen day trial. I started to sign up, but it required a credit card on the last screen. Damn. The dead didn't pay for my expert therapeutic services, so I was flat broke most of the time. Maybe I could work on Detective Fulbright to pay me in actual cash instead of ice cream or bubble teas.

The thought of Fulbright did bring up an idea. If I was going to use my supernatural skills to find leads on his cold case, then he could use his police privileges to help on mine. He could probably find the cause of death at the very least, which might help me narrow down which of these graves was home to our unsettled spirit.

I went to my next page—Charlene Watkins. I had a gut feeling about her. If she already had unfinished business keeping her here, the blatant disrespect and trash on her grave might have pushed her over the edge. According to the picture of the headstone, Charlene had died in 2013. She was only thirty-two.

Not that I was happy she was gone, but her death in the twenty-first century made her a more likely candidate than the ones who'd died in the nineties. Furthermore, her recent death meant I had a better chance of finding something about her online. I searched *Charlene Watkins Parkland Georgia.* My search returned thousands of hits. My jaw dropped as I scanned the headlines.

Mistrial declared in case of slain schoolteacher

"No justice" say parents of murdered teacher

I skimmed the first article.

In the much-watched trial of Lewis Cornell, the defense successfully moved for a mistrial, citing a mishandling of evidence in the 2013 murder of Albany kindergarten teacher Charlene Watkins. Sources called the case "open and shut," but the defense proved that the chain of custody had been broken in several key pieces of evidence, including the weapon used to shoot Ms. Watkins. The parents of Charlene Watkins refused to comment, but her fiancé spoke with us briefly, saying only, "This is injustice. The system has failed Charlene."

My stomach churned as I read the article. Charlene had been a beautiful redhead with a gentle smile that exuded warmth. I could picture her sitting on a bright-colored carpet surrounded by children, enrapt as she read them stories.

With my mouth drying up, I clicked to the next article, titled "Here's What You Missed in the Charlene Watkins Trial."

I didn't have the stomach to read all the details. Based on her credit card records, she'd made a late night trip to Wal-Mart and never it home. Her car was found the next morning in the woods a few miles from the store. Somehow, she'd survived being shot in the chest and badly burned when the guy torched the car to get rid of the evidence. She survived three days in the burn unit here in Parkland before succumbing to her injuries.

Just like that. Murdered for whatever she had in her purse and a credit card that ended up getting canceled after twenty-four hours. And her killer walked without even a slap on the wrist. A search on Lewis Cornell brought up mostly the same articles, but I found a more recent editorial, written about three months after the trial.

Lewis Cornell may be legally free, but he is certainly not free of the consequences of this trial. We must be cautious in prescribing vigilante justice, as in the case of the anonymous Craigslist poster who offered a five thousand dollar reward to whoever "took Cornell out," presumably killing him. Our legal system is built upon the idea that the prosecution must provide evidence and justification of guilt beyond a reasonable doubt. If the evidence is not there, or in this case, mishandled, we cannot press forward on a gut feeling.

Is Lewis Cornell guilty? Most likely. But the state did not do its job in collecting and handling evidence properly, and in doing so, they failed to prosecute him.

No wonder she was so angry.

I paused the music. "I think I have something."

Nina looked up from her notes. "What did you get?"

I gave her a quick run-down of what I'd read about Charlene.

"Oh, my God. That's crazy," Nina murmured. "It makes sense. Just one thing. You said she was from Albany, so why would her spirit be here?"

"The burn unit at Parkland General is really good, so they brought her here," I said. "So she died here in town."

I set my notes aside and closed my eyes. I pictured Sal and his warm smile walking through the door.

"Sal?" There was a sense of an electric current, like a tiny shock as I made contact with him. "I need you."

The temperature in my room dipped enough to make me shiver. A chill ran down my spine as Sal appeared. He smiled. "Hi Emily—wait."

"Hi," Nina said. He froze, his mouth in an *o*. "It's cool. I'm like her. Nina."

"Oh. Cool," Sal said with a shrug. "Nice to meet you. I'm Sal. I've been watching those houses you told me about, Bridget, but nothing yet."

"That's fine," I said. "I actually called you to ask about something else." I told him about finding Charlene's grave. Before I'd even finished the story, he was nodding and frowning. "You know about her?"

"Yeah," he said. "We didn't have much to do with investigating the actual case, but we helped wrangle the press while she was in the hospital here. They had us on a security detail, too, because they hadn't arrested the guy yet when she first got here." He shook his head. "Whoever did that to her was a monster."

I nodded. "So here's the question. What would she want? Like, what do you think would help her rest? Sending the guy to jail?"

"Hm," he mused. "Did she have kids? Any family?"

"Her parents," I said. "And a brother. No kids."

"Then maybe she wants to see justice," he said. "You know, a few months after I died, the man who killed me was arrested. Another stupid traffic violation, but the car was distinctive. My partner picked him out of a lineup and that was it. He went to jail for a long time. Cop-killers usually do."

"Did it help you at all?"

"A little," Sal said. "But I'm still dead. So there's that." That single fact hung between us as always. No matter how much Sal and I joked around, no matter what I did to help him be at peace or to help his family, there was the inevitable reality that he would always be dead. "And for me, my first priority, from the second I realized I was dead, was Veronica and the baby. I really didn't care if they caught the guy who killed me. But everyone's different."

"So what are the chances that he goes back on trial?" I asked.

"He can't," Nina piped up. Her voice startled me. I was so used to being alone in my conversations with the dead that I'd forgotten she was there. "Double jeopardy."

"Huh?"

"It's a law," she said. "You can't be tried twice for the same crime."

"You're not wrong," Sal said, looking impressed. "But this doesn't count. A mistrial is a little different. Theoretically they could have another trial since he wasn't found innocent or guilty in the first one. The problem is the evidence. Anything that was mishandled can't be used. They'd have to find all new evidence."

"What about a confession?" Nina asked.

Sal made a hissing sound through his teeth. "Even that's risky. You have to prove it's not obtained under duress, and if you try to record it, he has to consent to being recorded." He raised an eyebrow. "And you are not going to find a murderer and confront him. Again."

"I won't," I said. "But it's not a bad idea. The confession part, I mean."

"Why don't we just ask Charlene herself?" Nina said. "We can call her here."

"Not here in the house," I said quickly. "Not after seeing what she did to everyone else."

"I'm so proud," Sal said. "You've finally developed some common sense."

"Whatever," I replied. He smiled and leaned against my desk, crossing his wiry arms across his chest.

"So we'll go back to the cemetery," Nina said. "We'll ask her what she wants and then try to do it for her. Isn't that what you do?"

"Well, yeah," I said. She made it sound so simple. "But usually they're not this angry and violent. We might need to have a backup plan in case she catches an attitude."

"Like what?"

"I know someone," I said. "But she won't be happy about hearing from me."

'Someone' was Miss Tara, AKA Tara Lynn Bledsoe. She was a local medium, and as far as I knew, the only so-called psychic in town who wasn't a fake. When I needed help to contact the Runaway Killer's other victims, Miss Tara had summoned them for me to get their names. And it was Tara that gave me the ritual to tear down the barriers between me and the spirit world. She'd been adamant about not giving it to me, claiming I wasn't ready. But Emily had been in trouble, so Kale had terrorized Tara into teaching me. Since then, neither Kale nor I had been welcome. But under the circumstances, I figured she had a moral obligation to help me. Still, I dreaded the thought of speaking to her again worse than going back out to the cemetery.

"Two wise moves in one night," Sal said. "My little hellion is growing up."

"I'm not a hellion," I said primly. "I take calculated risks."

"I think your calculations are off," Sal said drily.

Nina held up her phone. "So should we call her tonight? I can call. I won't tell her I know you."

"Yeah, that would be best," I said.

I searched for Miss Tara's phone number online, then read the number out to Nina. She tossed her hair back as she held the phone to her ear. Her face brightened, her voice bubbly and sweet. "Hello? Miss Tara? Yes, ma'am, my name is Nina Welles. I'm—I'm sorry. Can you make an exception? It's really important, I just need—yes, ma'am. Yes, ma'am. I understand. Monday."

Nina's eyes rolled back so far she could have seen the back of her own skull. She hung up the phone. "She said she doesn't work weekends."

"You gotta be kidding me."

"She was very insistent."

"That's one word for her," I said. "Well, I'd rather have backup, but we have to do something even if she refuses. If Charlene keeps this up, more people will get hurt, and eventually, someone's going to die."

CHAPTER THIRTEEN

I TOSSED AND TURNED all night. Every sound in the shadows conjured ghosts in my imagination. Even with a bottle of holy water in arm's reach on my nightstand, my heart thumped all night. The sudden crack and clatter could have been the icemaker downstairs, or it could have been Charlene rattling in my closet. And that whooshing sound was probably the heater kicking on, but it could have been Charlene rushing around my room as she prepared to murder me in my bed.

This was the first time I'd dealt with a truly violent spirit. Plenty of them were angry, but the ones I'd encountered were angry at no one in particular. It was just upsetting to be dead. Michael's sister Natalie had been the worst I had ever encountered. And even when she'd attacked me in my bedroom, she was just trying to get my attention. She wasn't really evil or violent; more like a toddler who couldn't handle frustration yet. Once I'd promised to help her, she'd calmed down.

This was way different. Making the videos on her grave was disrespectful, but the YouTubers didn't kill Charlene. So her revenge seemed way overwrought for the offense. Had she gone after Lewis Cornell?

I gave up on sleeping around three in the morning and instead continued my research on my list of graves from St. Teresa's. Nothing on my remaining three names stood out nearly as much as Charlene's story had. Searching for Lewis only returned the same news stories I'd already read, and a Facebook search brought up dozens of Lewis Cornells across the country. And if I was a suspected murderer who'd gone free on a technicality, I probably wouldn't be on social media under my own name. That was a dead end, at least with the tools I had.

Around seven, the coffeepot broke the morning silence with its noisy burbling. Silverware clattered downstairs as Mom emptied the dishwasher and straightened up before church. I surprised her by getting showered and dressed before she came yelling at me to get out of bed.

We went to church, where I tried to listen but kept getting distracted with ideas on how I could deal with Charlene. After we ate lunch at home, Mom offered to drive me to the library to meet my group for my project. She made small talk about what her planned dinner menu for the week. I tried to keep up and feign enthusiasm, but between my worries about Charlene and the sheer exhaustion weighing me down, I was terrible company. Remembering the picture of Jenna's mangled car left me with a whole new set of concerns about Mom. Would Charlene attack Mom to get to me? It wasn't like I could warn Mom to be extra careful in case of angry spirits.

Fortunately, we made it to the library without incident. The Byron County Library was open for a few hours on Sunday afternoons. The front wall was all glass, so the afternoon sun poured in to light the whole area in a cozy natural glow. Downstairs, comfy couches and chairs were arranged all along the glass wall to create reading spots.

Kale trailed after me as I walked up the sidewalk and into the building. "Do you need me?"

I wanted him to stay, but it was probably better if I didn't have the distraction while I was trying to carry on like a normal kid. "I'll be okay."

"Call me if you need me," he said. He smiled, sending a thrill of warmth through me as he faded away.

Candace was already inside, sitting on a big leather couch in an alcove. A purple laptop sat open on the coffee table in front of her.

As I approached, she looked up and smiled. "Hey! There's another plug here if you brought your computer."

I took a deep breath. *Be normal.*

"Thanks," I said. I set up my laptop as she explained how she wanted to divide up the work.

"Now, we need to make sure we're firm. Bryce and Drew are kind of jerks, so they'll make us do all the work if we let them. We can split it up by topic and combine our notes."

"That sounds good," I said. "I'll do whatever you think is fair."

Thirteen minutes after our scheduled meeting time, Bryce and Drew arrived together with cups from Smoothie Paradise in the shopping center across the street. "Sorry, traffic," Bryce offered as an explanation.

"But you had time to get a smoothie," Candace said mildly. "Okay, let's get to work." While the boys got out tablets and laptops, Candace explained her plan for splitting the work.

"But you girls will do so much better," Bryce said. "I'm not good at PowerPoint."

Candace shook her head. "No. You're going to do your part."

"Yeah," I said quietly.

Drew sighed. "Okay, what do you want me to do?"

Candace read off the list she'd made. Our topic was law enforcement in Prohibition, and I was assigned to research Eliot Ness. While I waited for my computer to connect to the library's wi-fi network, I took out my phone and texted Nina.

Everything ok?

She didn't answer right away. Under normal circumstances, I would assume she was a normal person enjoying her weekend. But after yesterday, I immediately imagined a rapid-fire slideshow of all the horrible things Charlene could have done to Nina since seeing her last night.

I swallowed hard. Thinking like that was useless. I wiped my sweating palms against my jeans and decided to try something. I closed my eyes and visualized Kale, painting every detail of his features on the dark landscape of my mind. Nina could call Ethan without speaking, so maybe I could do it too.

A cool breeze lifted my hair as Kale appeared in front of me. Victory.

"Are you okay?" He surveyed the quiet group. "What's going on?"

I opened a new document and typed: *Can you check on Nina?*

He tilted his head and passed through me with a cold chill breaking across my skin. After reading the screen, he said, "Sure. I'll be back."

With pride swelling up in my chest at my new trick, I minimized the window and got to work. It was hard to change gears from a weekend of worrying about ghosts to focusing on school work. But I had to learn, because I was stuck in school for another year and a half, and my ghost ability wasn't going anywhere. I was about fifteen minutes into researching Eliot Ness when Kale returned. I raised my eyes to him and lifted my eyebrows.

"She's fine. She was studying and said to tell you sorry that she didn't text back."

I nodded and continued working. Emily texted me, so I paused my reading to reply.

Emily: hey, want to come over?

Guilt squirmed in my belly as I typed a reply. I hadn't seen her since lunch on Friday, and we usually hung out at least once on the weekend.

Sorry, I have a group project for history and then have to work on this dead eyes thing :(

I waited eagerly for her response, hoping she'd say *of course, you have to prioritize,* but she didn't reply. Great.

A little while later, Bryce broke my concentration by saying, "Dude, check this one out."

Over the edge of my laptop, I saw Drew leaning over Bryce's shoulder to watch. Each of wore one earbud connected to Bryce's tablet. Drew smacked Bryce's shoulder. "Shit, dude."

Candace looked up in irritation. "Shh!"

"Candace, you gotta see this," Drew said. "Take a break for a second."

She sighed and set down her laptop. After a good stretch, she walked over and perched on the edge of Bryce's chair. Her brow furrowed. "These videos are so dumb."

"What are you watching?" I asked mildly. The way they'd jumped…I had a pretty good guess.

"Have you seen this Dead Eyes thing?" Drew asked.

"Oh," I said, my chest tightening. "They're stupid, honestly."

Bryce gave me a look like I'd said something to offend him. He set his tablet aside and made a waggling motion with his fingers. "Woo," he warbled, like he was a cartoon ghost.

"Seriously?" I said. "Can we please get back to work?"

"We've been working for like two hours," Bryce said. "What, are you scared of some stupid videos?"

"No," I said. "I'm just want to get this done so we can go home."

Bryce ignored me and closed his eyes. "Restless spirit, come to me—"

"Stop it," I said, setting my laptop aside.

Drew laughed. "We should go do it out there." He pointed out the window toward the wooded area behind the library.

"Dude!" Bryce said. "Yes!"

"Don't," I said.

"It's not real, Young," Bryce said. "So what's the big deal?"

I rolled my eyes. What was I supposed to tell him? A vengeful spirit named Charlene would attack him if he tempted her? Maybe he deserved whatever accident she could cook up for him.

"I told you, it's stupid."

"That's not a good reason," Bryce said. "Restless spirit, come to me. Tell me what your dead eyes see. Unbroken and unfettered be—"

"I said stop it." My voice was sharp enough to echo, earning me a glare from the clerk behind the reference desk. Bryce's eyes narrowed.

"Guys, can we just work?" Candace said. "I have to be home soon for church."

"If you want to do stupid shit, then do it on your own time," I snapped at him. "Don't waste my time with it."

"Ohh," Bryce said, throwing up his hands defensively as a sneer twisted across his face. "I didn't realize I was working with such a VIP."

I sighed and checked my phone. I had a new text from Mom. Nothing from Nina, but Kale's visit had soothed my concerns.

Mom: *What time should I pick you up? Can't remember if you told me, sorry!*

I'd never been so glad to hear from her.

We're done now.

"As fun as this has been, I have to go," I said. "My mom's on her way."

"Your mom? Aren't you a junior? Why aren't you driving?" Bryce said.

Because my sister died in a car accident and I hate the thought of being behind the wheel?

"I haven't gotten my license yet," I said. I quickly packed up my stuff and turned to Candace. She wore a strange expression, like she wanted to apologize for the boys, but she wasn't going to defend me. "I'll email you my slides."

As I walked away, Bryce said, "Hey, Bridget?" I turned to see him standing up. "From your ancient graves be free!" Then he gasped, making a frightened face as he looked around dramatically. "Do you think something's here? Drew...did you hear that? Oh man, I'm really scared."

I groaned in disgust and walked away. Dread wove a tight knot in my stomach. Surely that wouldn't count, considering we were nowhere near Charlene's grave. But who knew what other spirits were lingering around, waiting for an invitation like the one Bryce had given?

While I waited for Mom to arrive, I sat down on one of the metal benches outside. Between the cold metal and the chill wind blowing, it was a miserable wait, but anything was better than being stuck inside with Bryce. We only had to work together a few more days, then I could go back to ignoring them. Being a normal high schooler was rapidly losing its appeal.

"What are you doing out here?" Kale asked. He drifted toward me from the night return box.

"My group was being a bunch of jerks," I told him. "I'm going home."

"Sorry," he said. He settled on the bench, balancing carefully so it looked like he was sitting. "I had an idea while you were still inside."

"Oh, yeah?"

"It bothers me that these spirits can drive me off," he said. That made two of us. "So if it comes near you, I can't warn you."

"Okay, we know that."

"So if I sense them coming and can't get to you, I'll go to Nina," he said. "And she can call you."

I nodded appreciatively. "That's a really good idea."

He smiled. "I thought so. I have them occasionally."

My phone buzzed. I checked it. "Speaking of Nina."

Nina: So far all good

Nina: Skype me when you get home?

Sounds good, should be home soon

A few minutes later, Mom's silver car pulled up to the curb. "See you at home," Kale said.

I hurried to the door and slid into the front seat. She gave me a questioning look. "What's wrong?"

"Nothing," I said instinctively. I must have been wearing my frustration like a mask.

She sighed. "Okay," she said hotly, punching the gas a little too hard as she pulled away from the curb.

I hesitated, fiddling with the strap on my backpack. For once, the problem was something I could talk to her about. "Actually. Can I talk to you?"

Her eyebrows nearly shot into her hairline in surprise. "Of course." She turned down the radio. Her eyes found mine in the rearview mirror.

"These guys in my group are jerks," I said.

"Can you specify?"

I shrugged. "They're just ass—rude," I corrected before the profanity slipped out. "They made fun of me for not driving yet."

Mom gave me a worried look. "Do you want to learn to drive?"

"Not really," I said. "It's stupid."

"Well, the best thing is to ignore that stuff. That doesn't affect the person you are. No one can take that away from you," Mom said. "Try to get along. The project is due soon, isn't it?"

"Yeah."

"See? Problem solved," she said, smiling brightly at me.

Right. Except that solved nothing.

When we got home, I hurried up to my bedroom to start a Skype call with Nina. Her wild curls were piled on top of her head in a cute blue bandana.

"Hey!" she chirped. Her smile fell. "What's wrong?"

"Nothing, just the guys in my group," I said. "They wanted to spend half the time watching Dead Eyes videos."

Nina rolled her eyes. "Ugh."

"Yeah, so now we can add them to our list of people to watch for," I said. Ugh. If Bryce was the next target, I'd have to think hard about putting myself at risk to help him. "So what did you find?"

Nina held up her sheets and put them close to her camera so I could see the lines of bubbly purple pen. "Okay, so I got some good info. First, the two Hillmans are brothers. The older one, Travis, died on Halloween. Both of them got hit by a car while they were out trick or treating. Charlie, the younger one died a couple months later."

"Oh, damn," I said. "You think it could be one of them?"

Nina shrugged. "The driver of the car wasn't found at fault, but I found a news video where she apologized publicly for it anyway. Doesn't seem like there's unfinished business there."

"Yeah," I murmured. "Seems like Charlene is still our best bet."

"I think so," she said. "I didn't get a chance to finish my research yet. I still need to look up Sara Workman, but my dad decided he wanted to have family breakfast this morning, and then I had homework, and..." She shrugged. "You know how it goes."

A notification popped up.

Incoming video call from Emily

I clicked the Ignore button. A few seconds later, a text private message popped up.

Emily: *???*

My stomach sank. I quickly typed my reply.

On another call

Just a sec

"It's cool," I said. "So what do you want to do? About the ghost, I mean."

Nina bit her lip. "I think we should deal with her sooner rather than later. Can we go out there tomorrow after school?"

"Maybe if we can get help from Miss Tara," I said. "I'm still not sure about how to handle a spirit this angry. We might make it worse if we go unprepared."

"Well, now we know what's wrong," Nina said. "If we can tell Charlene we know what happened and that we want to help her, won't that change things?"

"Maybe," I said. "I hope so. Can you try to call Miss Tara again tomorrow? I'll try, although I don't think she'll talk to me."

"You got it," Nina said.

I glanced down at the blinking notification from Emily. "Okay, I need to go talk to Emily real quick. Text me in the morning?"

"Totally," Nina said. Her screen went dark.

I started a new call with Emily. No answer. I tried again, and still got nothing. Great. I'd have to talk to her tomorrow about it. The last thing I needed on this pile of drama was for my best friend to be mad at me. The problems were piling up, and I didn't have answers for any of them.

CHAPTER FOURTEEN

MONDAY MORNING ARRIVED with a vengeance. Thanks to another sleepless night jumping at shadows, I overslept my alarm and woke up to Emily honking her horn in the driveway. In record time, I peeled off my pajamas, swiped on fresh deodorant, threw on jeans and a hoodie, and sprinted out the door to her car.

"Sorry I'm late," I said as I dropped into the passenger seat.

She looked at me skeptically. As usual, her makeup and hair looked amazing, making me feel even more haggard. "Late night?"

"Having trouble sleeping," I said. "We're working on this Dead Eyes thing, and it's got me kind of freaked."

"We," she murmured. "You and Nina?"

"Yes," I said timidly. Did she ignore my calls because of Nina?

Emily kept her eyes on the road as she spoke. "Well, if you can fit me in somehow, Mom wants to go for a mani-pedi day this Saturday. She told me to invite you." The flat tone in her voice said she didn't particularly want to.

"That sounds fun," I said, forcing enthusiasm into my voice. "Definitely."

"You don't have plans with Nina?"

"Emily," I said.

"What?"

We pulled into the school parking lot. "Is something wrong? You're acting like you're mad at me but I don't know why."

"I'm not mad," she snapped, her tone making it obvious that she was lying.

As we walked toward the school, she dug into her bag and took out a piece of paper. Written in neat blue pen on notebook paper, it was a list of what looked like screen names. "Those are all kids from Fox Lake, Marymount, and Mount Sharon High who have YouTube channels and did a Dead Eyes video in the last month. I didn't check Instagram because the time limit probably wouldn't allow for it. There could be others, but these are ones I knew about, so it's a good start."

There were at least fifteen names on the list. "Thank you," I said as I looked it over. "This is awesome. Seriously."

Her lips were tight over clenched teeth, in a forced expression that a smile in name only. "Sure." She checked her phone. "I gotta go. I'll see you after school."

"Oh," I said. Dread washed over me as I prepared to speak. "Nina's driving me so we can do some more research on—"

"Cool," Emily interrupted, dismissing me with a wave of her black-nailed hand. "Text me later if you're not too busy."

My heart sank as she disappeared into the throng of people headed in through the side door, leaving me alone on the sidewalk outside. I would have to deal with this eventually. Emily didn't have to worry about Nina. We were only spending so much time together because of the case. And besides, Emily had Heather. The two of them hung out plenty of times without me, and I didn't get my feelings hurt. Okay, I did, but I tried not to be a diva about it.

After checking in for attendance in homeroom, I headed to Chemistry class. As I walked down the hall, my eyes scanned my surroundings for signs of Charlene. Hands grabbed my shoulders and shook me roughly.

"Boo!" a voice whispered in my ear.

I screamed in surprise, flailing my arms and sending my books flying. The crowd of students around me froze, staring at me. A few people covered their mouths and laughed as I backed into a locker. I spun on my heel to see Bryce Holloway laughing to himself.

"Gotcha," he said, meeting my gaze.

"You're a jerk," I said flatly. My heart thumped, and my hands shook with adrenaline as I knelt to pick up my books. A wide, mud-caked sneaker planted on my blue ghost notebook right as I grabbed it. Emily's list peeked out from the top edge. "Move your foot."

"Ask nicely."

"Move your foot now," I said, louder this time.

He crouched so he was on eye level, elbows resting on his knees. He still didn't move his foot. I was tempted to punch him in the crotch, since he'd put it in reach. "What's your problem?"

"Right now? You are," I said. If I wasn't worried he'd hit me back, I would have swung on him. Just to see the embarrassment across his blotchy face that little Bridget Young dared to stand up to him. "Move your fat foot or I'll move it for you."

"Ooh, I'm scared," he said.

My internal alarms were ringing. *Danger. Temper is reaching critical mass.*

I gritted my teeth and yanked my notebook out from under his foot. The force of it pulled his foot hard enough to throw him back onto his butt. The jerky motion tore the front cover, leaving it hanging from the warped spiral binding. Anger shot through me like lightning. "Just leave me the hell alone."

Hadn't he gotten the message that making fun of me was so two years ago? My head rushed with sheer adrenaline as I brushed past him. The blood roaring in my ears muffled what he said, but I didn't miss the chorus of laughs behind me.

In class, I kept my books in my lap and pointedly ignored Bryce's attempts to look at my homework. It was unsympathetic, but I was grateful when Mrs. England told us she had a migraine and assigned silent work time for this week's homework packet, even giving us permission to listen to music on our phones if we wanted.

To avoid any further incident with Bryce, I went to one of the lab tables in the back of the room. I swiped a layer of dust from the corner near the window and wedged myself into the safe, tight corner. Bryce cast a sidelong glance back at me.

After plugging in my headphones, I pulled out Emily's list, already planning how to tackle my research. Then I hesitated. This was what had gotten me into such a deep hole with my grades over the last two years. I slid the list back into the spiral notebook and started reading over the homework instead.

Engrossed in chemical equations, I barely noticed when the bell rang. When I saw Bryce heading my way, I hurried out the back door of the classroom and took the shortcut across two hallways. I didn't know where he was, but I didn't want to deal with any more of him than I had to. Dread at the thought of fifth period history with him was already sinking into my stomach like bad tacos.

Halfway across the cafeteria, my feet flew out from under me. I skidded on the floor and landed on all fours. The impact jolted up my arms as I gasped in surprise. I looked around frantically any sign of spirits, for the telltale cold spot. Was it Charlene?

"Honey, didn't you see the sign?" an older woman drawled.

I looked over my shoulder to see a custodian leaning on the handle of a mop sticking out of a rolling bucket. She pointed to the yellow plastic sign that I'd knocked over in my rush to get across school.

"No, ma'am," I said. I swallowed my pride, scooped up my books, and carefully made my way out of the wet area. At least Bryce wasn't there to enjoy the scene.

The rest of the day had me on edge. After the incident with the bleachers last week, things were locked down while maintenance staff inspected every inch of the gym. The teachers took us outside to the stadium to walk laps around the track instead of playing sports inside. I took advantage of that time to watch some of the videos Emily had listed. My heart nearly burst from my chest when a deafening clang of metal broke through the noise of my headphones. A frantic search for the source led me to watch the garbage truck emptying a dumpster beside the gym.

By the time I got to lunch, I was so anxious that my hands trembled and set the green Jello on my tray shimmying all the way to the table. Relief surged through me when I saw that Emily was sitting at our usual table. She glanced up, then back down at her phone as I approached.

"Hey," she said without looking up again.

"Hey," I said. "Thanks again for the list."

"Did you find anything?"

"Not yet," I told her. "I looked at some of them, but I was trying to actually do my work for once."

A ghost of a smile played on her lips. "Suck-up."

I took out my phone and her list. "Do you want to help?"

Her gaze followed me, lips parted as she hesitated. Then the tension smoothed out. "Sure. What can I do?"

I smiled. Maybe things would be okay. "So it's not just the video part," I said. "So far all three people who had accidents made their videos in a certain graveyard. I went there this weekend."

Emily regarded me skeptically. "You went out there?" She tapped her black nails on the table. "Alone?"

"Me and Nina did."

At the mention of Nina's name, the guarded expression came back over Emily's face. Her neutral smile remained, but her nostrils flared.

"Okay," she said. "So what am I looking for?"

I cleared my throat, hoping to ease the tension. "It's at St. Teresa's Memorial Garden, near this angel statue," I said. I switched apps and opened my camera roll to show her the screenshot of the angel.

As she was examining it, her eyebrow perked. "You have a message." She handed back the phone and let out a sigh of exasperation.

On my screen was a new message from Nina.

Nina: *I talked 2 tara*

Nina: *I'll tell you after school*

Emily was watching me as I composed my reply.

Ok cool thanks for letting me know

I went back to the picture. "See that grave? It's Charlene—"

"Message," Emily said flatly.

I huffed and looked at the screen again. There was a string of thumbs up emojis from Nina. I cleared it and tried to focus. "We think it's this lady named Charlene Watkins."

Emily consulted her list. "Why don't we check my list and see who made their videos at the same cemetery? I'll start at the bottom and go up. You start at the top," she said. Then she put her bright pink headphones in her ears and pulled up the first video on her own phone.

I finished watching three of the videos before the lunch bell rang. One of them had been filmed at St. Teresa's. I made a star next to Paul Thomas, who posted under *King P Productions*. After watching me make the mark, Emily leaned over and put a mark next to *FeenixFire*. "That one didn't show the angel, but he mentioned Saint Teresa's."

"Cool, thanks," I said.

Emily nodded and shrugged her backpack up onto her shoulders. "See ya."

Her shoulders slumped as she merged into the crowd, walking away from me. I wanted to call her back and ask her how to fix this. Life was tough enough without her being mad at me, but I wasn't sure how to fix it. And honestly, I was a little mad at her for being so touchy.

I just wanted to have a friend that got me. Emily could be supportive, but she didn't know what it was like to walk through the grocery store and see a dead woman staring at her from the produce aisle. Nina did.

Would it always be like this? I could tell myself things would be back to normal after this case, but it wouldn't be long before another one came up. And another after that.

But worrying about Emily would have to wait. I had to survive the rest of the day, including fifth period with Bryce. I wasn't sure whether it would be worse to deal with him or to face off with Charlene.

Gritting my teeth, I headed to class. *Here we go.*

Chapter Fifteen

NINA WAS WAITING in her car in the senior lot when I got out of school. I heard the pounding metal from at least a hundred feet away, although she looked absolutely serene as she touched up her mascara in the mirror. I yanked open the door and slumped into the seat. She finished her eyelashes and looked over at me, reaching to turn down the music. The aggressive drums actually matched my mood.

"What's wrong with you?"

"Huh? Nothing," I said. I fiddled with my backpack straps.

She raised one eyebrow. "We're not psychic, but I'm also not stupid. It's all over your face."

I sat in silence for a while, feeling like a little kid tattling to Mommy. "This guy is being a total jerk."

"Tell me about it," Nina said.

As she pulled away from school, I told her about Bryce, beginning with him taking my homework, then the library, and finally, the laundry list of his dirty deeds that day. He'd been an obnoxious tool all through history class, kicking my desk constantly as I tried to take notes. By the time we arrived at my house, she was shaking her head and punctuating my story with *what a punk*.

"You need to tell him off," Nina said.

I shrugged. "That's just not how I am."

"And that's why he's doing it." She put up her hands defensively as I started to protest. "I'm not gonna tell you how to run your life, but people like that will keep doing it until you give them a reason not to."

I sighed. "Yeah, you're probably right. Do you want anything to eat or drink?"

She shook her head. "I'm good."

While Nina waited in the driveway, I hurried into the house. It was still dark and cool inside; Colin hadn't even gotten home yet. I hurried upstairs and traded my school bag for my ghost bag. After running back downstairs, I paused in the hallway, then went into the kitchen and raided the pantry. A handful of granola bars and some crackers went into the bag with the holy water and the salt.

When I got back to the car, Nina handed me her phone and said, "Check this out."

On her screen was a picture of a power saw, judging by the splinters of wood littered around it. And judging by the dark splatters on the silver plate surrounding the jagged blade, something had gone terribly wrong. I scanned the caption underneath.

#crazyshit went down in shop class. Swear to God this bandsaw turned on by itself and cut off this kid's fingers. Bout to get a priest up in here #yallneedjesus

"Where was this?"

"Marymount High," Nina said. "I know the kid who posted it from my photography class at the community center. I messaged him to ask who the kid was."

"You think it's connected?"

"I wouldn't be surprised," Nina said.

"So what did you hear from Miss Tara?"

Nina sighed. "She's a pain in the ass."

"Right?"

"First she didn't even want to talk to me," Nina said. "Then she said she would only talk to me at her house."

The drive to Miss Tara's took us about twenty minutes from my house. As we neared the medium's home office, my stomach danced. She had to go of her grudge if innocent people were getting hurt.

We arrived at Tara's a little after four. The sky was overcast, with a veil of hazy gray dimming the sun. If we were going to speak to Charlene today, we needed to hurry. It would be dark soon, and a cemetery after dark was high on my list of least favorite places.

The small white house didn't strike a note of cozy recognition, but instead fed a little caffeine to the squirming worms in my belly. One of Tara's companion spirits, Jeremy, had literally shoved me out the door the last time I came here.

"Stay here," Nina said. "She doesn't know we're working together."

Halfway up the driveway, she paused and glanced back at me, then threw her shoulders back and marched up to the front porch. The red door swung open before she knocked, and Miss Tara stepped out onto the porch. Easily six feet tall, Tara loomed over Nina. Miss Tara pointed to the car, then made a beckoning gesture with her hand. Even from this distance, I felt her steely glare focused on me.

Suddenly a male spirit materialized in the driver's seat. Jeremy. His cold aura overpowered the pleasant, dry heat of the car. He glared at me. "She wants you to come up too."

"How did you know?"

I didn't know it was possible for a ghost to be so snide. "Amateur hour. Inside." He disappeared again.

My chest tightened as I grabbed my backpack and let myself out of the car. I walked up Miss Tara's driveway to the porch. With hands propped on her broad hips, she looked me over and shook her head. With her long salt-and-pepper hair flowing over her shoulders, she looked like a warrior queen.

I swallowed hard. "Hi."

"No companion today?"

"He said you blocked him from your house."

I gazed at the cozy foyer beyond the open doorway. Not only did Tara's house always smell like something baking, it was well-protected from angry spirits. Given our situation, I would have much preferred to have this conversation inside.

"I did indeed," she said, stepping back to block the doorway like she'd read my mind. "Too bad the same doesn't work on idiot teenagers who won't listen to advice." She threw up her hands. "Did you think you could send your friend in and I wouldn't figure it out?"

"N-no," I said. Well, this was off to a great start.

"Didn't I warn you??" Tara said. "I told you not to stir things up, and I tried to keep you from opening that door, but you didn't listen. Sixteen years old and you know best."

"I had to," I protested. "And that has nothing to do with this." Plus, I was seventeen, but it hardly seemed worth correcting her and making her even madder.

"Miss Tara," Nina said, her voice sweet and placating. "I know you and Bridget don't get along, but could you please hear us out? You were ready to help me when you didn't know it was her."

Tara turned her sharp glare on Nina. "When I didn't know? Child, you didn't fool me for a skinny minute. I just wanted you to come here so I could try to talk some sense into you."

"Can we please come in?" I asked.

"No," she said flatly. "I told you that you weren't welcome here. Nothing's changed on my end, even if you're making a fine mess of things."

"Miss Tara, please," Nina said. "Have you heard of Dead Eyes?" Tara's brow furrowed. Nina took out her phone, cued up a video, and held it out to the older woman. "It's a video trend right now. Kids are going out to cemeteries, reciting this poem, and—"

"Lord in heaven," Tara muttered, glancing down as the video started. "And let me guess. You two did this?"

"No," I said firmly.

"Well…" Nina's curls hung like curtains around her face as she stared down at her shoes, speaking to the floor instead of meeting Tara's eyes. "I said part of it. But we were trying to find the spirit responsible."

"Jesus," Tara said.

I threw my hands up in frustration. "Can you just let go of this grudge for two seconds and listen?"

Tara's eyes narrowed and her nostrils flared as she turned her attention back to me. "This grudge? You and your Guardian threatened me. In my own sanctuary! Don't act like it's some minor disagreement. And don't forget that I told you I wouldn't be responsible for you after you did that ritual."

"I told you that this has nothing to do with what I did," I said.

Tara handed the phone back to Nina and folded her arms over her broad chest. Making a point to look directly at Nina, she asked, "So what's going on?"

"Some of the kids who've done the videos have had accidents," Nina said. "Freaky things."

"Could be coincidence."

"It's not," I said hotly. "There's been two accidents at our school, and I saw the spirit right after one of them."

"Plus, everyone who's been hurt has gone to the same cemetery and filmed near the same grave," Nina said.

"Who?"

"Charlene Watkins," I said. "She was murdered a few years ago, and her killer walked free because of a mistrial. We think it's her."

Tara shrugged. "Okay, so what do you want me to do about it? Sounds like you have it figured out."

"We already tried to talk to her, and she got pissed," Nina said.

"We need to control her or calm her down long enough to find out what she wants," I said.

Tara sighed. "You never learn, do you?"

Anger bubbled up in me. "Some of us can't just sit around and let bad things happen."

Her hand shot out and gripped my face. My cheeks went hot as her strong fingers pressed into either side of my jaw. A tingling sensation radiated from her touch, like she was carrying an electrical current. What exactly could she do?

"You watch your mouth, little girl. You don't know what you're talking about."

I swallowed and tried to mask my fear. Her grip made my speech garbled and mushy, which might have been funny if it wasn't so scary. "I know I had to scare the crap out of you to get you to help me. And if you'd had it your way, my best friend would be dead."

She released my face, almost throwing it away from her. Relief flooded through me. I squared my jaw as she stared down at me and said, "If you want to control her, you need a place of sanctuary."

"Like your house," I muttered.

Tara narrowed her eyes at me. "You're not doing it here."

"If you won't help people like her, then what do you do with your power?" I snapped.

Tara ignored me. "If you don't have such a place, then the best you can do is to protect yourself when you go to her. Prayer is a powerful protection. Call upon Saint Michael. Black salt could help, too."

"Black salt?" Nina said.

"Google it," Tara replied. She leveled her icy stare at me. "Regardless of what you think is best, Bridget, do not call this spirit to yourself, not in your home, not anywhere."

The cold steel in her voice sent a chill down my spine. "What do you mean?"

"You don't know the proper protections," Tara said. "Spirits that have become this angry can hurt you. And I don't mean accidents. I mean possession, hauntings, bad things. You let a spirit like this get in, and it can stain you."

Her words sent a shiver down my spine. "So help us. Please."

"No," Tara said. She held up her hand as I started to protest. "You're young and foolish. You'd be better off leaving this alone. Talk to your Guardian. If he's worth a damn, he'll tell you the same."

She backed up towards her door. "Now if you'll excuse me. I have an appointment."

And with that, she closed the door in our faces.

Nina gaped at me. "Seriously?"

"I told you she was difficult."

Nina spluttered all the way back to the car. "I can't believe—I mean really? Seriously?" She shook her head, then took out her phone. "I got something back from my friend. The kid who got his fingers cut off is Victor Harden."

I immediately searched Victor Harden on Facebook. Though we weren't friends, I could see his public posts. Nearly every public post was a link to a Youtube video. Sure enough, scrolling back about two weeks, there it was. "Hard V Does the Dead Eyes Challenge."

"He did it," I murmured. Halfway through the video was a clear shot of the angel statue near Charlene's grave. I saved myself the frustration and stomach-churning nausea of watching him do the invocation. "There's probably more."

Nina sighed. "Can we warn them somehow?"

"I made a fake email for when I was trying to find those missing kids over Christmas break. Could we send them a message?"

"What, and say 'watch out, you pissed off an angry spirit and now it's coming to get you?' That sounds crazy."

"Even though it's true," I said.

Nina nodded. "I guess we could. Some of them might believe it. But what about Charlene?"

"We can't shut down all the people making videos, so we have to get her to stop going after them," I said. It was already five, and the sky would darken before much longer. "Let's find about this black salt, see how we get some, and try to go tomorrow during the day."

And pray that no one got hurt tonight.

CHAPTER SIXTEEN

ON THE WAY to my house, we stopped for snacks and researched black salt. Assuming Tara wasn't recommending organic seasonings, black salt was normal salt mixed with a dark ingredient to absorb negative energy. It sounded like a serious stretch to me, but we'd found dozens of websites that referenced it. At this point, if someone told me a wall built from peanut butter and jelly sandwiches would protect us, I'd start spreading right away. Nina volunteered to find the salt while I went home and continued the search for information on Charlene.

When I walked into the house, Colin was in the living room watching an anime about orange-clad ninjas fighting and screeching about their powers. Thankfully, Mom hadn't gotten home yet.

"Where were you?" he asked as I walked in the door. He paused his show and looked at me suspiciously.

"Hanging out with Nina," I said as I walked into the kitchen for a drink.

Kale appeared behind me, then drifted toward the stairs. "I'll be upstairs."

"You spend a lot of time with her all of a sudden," Colin called from the living room.

"And?" I opened the refrigerator and took out a bottle of water. When I closed the fridge door, he was standing on the other side of the pass-through window, staring at me like a creeper. My pulse quickened as I made eye contact.

"You're up to something."

"Am not." I tried to smooth out my face and sip my water calmly.

My phone buzzed with a text from Mom, which was a welcome interruption from Colin's interrogation.

Mom: Did you get my note?

No

Mom: you need to get the ground beef out of the fridge and cook it in a sauce pan so I can start dinner when I get home

Ok

Sure enough, there was a bright pink sticky note on the refrigerator door that left the same instructions. I sighed. I had things to do that didn't involve browning beef, but I needed to be in good standing with Mom so I could continue to work on this thing with Charlene.

Like the dutiful daughter I was pretending to be, I took the package of beef out of the fridge. After staring at the mysterious empty pan and trying to picture what Mom usually did, I turned to Colin. "Does she put anything in the pan first?"

He shrugged. "I don't know."

"You're no help," I said, gesturing with the heavy pan. "Text her and ask."

"You do it."

"How about I use my mutant powers on you?"

He froze for a split second, then folded his arms over his chest. His eyes narrowed. "Do it. I want to see it."

We both held the stare for a few tense seconds. Then I flinched toward him. He yelped in surprise and recoiled. I laughed. "You're such an idiot."

I texted Mom again.

Do I just put it in the pan

Mom: put a little olive oil in first and let it get hot

I found the olive oil in a cabinet above the stove. Just as my fingers closed around the bottle, something whispered in my ear, a cold breath sighing along my neck. *Not now.* My skin pebbled with goosebumps as I startled and jerked away. Something fell from above and shattered on the stove.

My hand stung. I looked down to see a piece of glass sticking out of my left palm, with a thick rivulet of red running down my arm.

"Shit," I said. "No, no, no."

"Oh, my God," Colin said. His face went pale at the sight of the blood. "Are you okay?"

"Crap." The sharp sting was a distant runner-up to my dread. I whipped my head around, searching for a spirit. Had I imagined the cold breeze? I pinned Colin with a stare. "Go get me a towel."

He froze, still staring at the blood. "Are you…" His face was paper white.

"I'm fine. Go get me a towel from upstairs," I repeated. With wide eyes, he spun on his heel and clambered up the stairs, taking them two at a time. As soon as he was out of sight, I clamped my eyes shut. "Kale!"

But there was no response. *Oh, God.* She was here.

"Charlene," I whispered, holding my hand gingerly. "I'm trying to help you. Please don't do this."

A shadow moved in my peripheral vision. A spirit about my height hovered in the doorway. Its form was dark, like it was covered in dirty residue. But unlike Ed Hanners' dark wisp, this spirit looked solid and real. The cold emanating from it was tangible, even from a few feet away. With a raspy whisper like a sigh through a slit throat, it turned and looked toward the stairs.

Colin.

If I thought I'd been mad before, with Bryce bothering me, then I didn't know what real anger was until this moment. The thought of this ghost taking out her issues on my defenseless little brother triggered a nuclear meltdown in my chest.

"If you touch him, I'll…"

Its cloudy eyes flared bright, and the whisper turned to a wordless shout that crawled into my ears and down my spine.

I gritted my teeth against the unpleasant sensation. "I want to help you. But you can't keep doing this."

"Bridget? Should I get Band-Aids?" Colin shouted from upstairs.

The spirit snapped its attention back to the stairs.

"Yes! And find the Neosporin in the bathroom," I yelled. Hopefully that would stall him.

The spirit drifted toward the stairs, and my instincts kicked in. I ducked and grabbed for my backpack. Blood dripped off my fingers and onto the white tile. "Get back here," I muttered.

Lightning quick, I yanked the bottle of holy water from the side pocket and brandished it at the spirit. "In the name of God and all his angels, I command you to leave. And St. Michael says you have to go, too," I added, remembering Tara's instruction.

The spirit turned back to me just in time to catch a spray of holy water. The water cut a crescent through the shadowy form, and the spirit disappeared with an ominous hiss.

Colin thundered down the stairs in time to see me holding the water bottle at the ready like a weapon. He frowned. "You're bleeding on the floor." I ignored him, looking around the room slowly to see if Charlene would reappear. "Bridget? Are you okay?"

"Yeah, sorry. I'm fine." I hurried to the sink and thrust my hand under the running water to rinse it. The cold water stung against the open cut. It didn't look too deep, but it definitely hurt. My heart raced, but I wasn't worried about my hand.

Charlene had followed me home. It was one thing to seek her out, for Nina and me to risk calling her up in the cemetery. But this was my house. My safe place. This endangered Mom and Colin. The fire in my chest spread to my muscles and down into my belly. In two years, I'd never even considered that I'd have to protect them from a spirit.

"Here," I said. I wrapped my hand in a dark blue dishtowel. "Go get the broom and dustpan from the garage, and I'll get this cleaned up before Mom gets home."

He nodded rapidly. When he was outside in the garage, I called again for Kale.

"I need you now," I said quietly. "Please."

This time, he responded. He rushed into existence, his energy preceding him like a shockwave that buffeted me with cool air. I was relieved to see him, and also for the confirmation that Charlene was gone. A grimace twisted his handsome face as he scanned the room.

"Something was here," he said. "Are you all right?"

"No." I held up my towel-wrapped hand. A black rose of blood bloomed through the dark fabric. "We have to do something. Now. Can you go check on Nina and then come right back?"

"Of course," he said. He disappeared as Colin returned with the broom.

It took us a few minutes to sweep up the broken glass. Once we finished, I finally took the towel away from my hand. The glass had sliced open the fleshy pad under my left thumb. It still oozed blood, but it wasn't gushing. I reached for a Band-Aid, but Colin had already pulled one out for me.

"I'll do it," he said shyly. He dabbed the Neosporin in a thin layer over the cut, then fumbled with the Band-Aid.

As I watched him peel off the backing, I couldn't help feeling proud of him. He was annoying, but he was my little brother. Maybe it was cheesy, but there was no mistaking love welling up in my heart. And on its heels was a fresh wave of hot, chest-aching anger at the thought of Charlene Watkins taking out her death angst on my family.

"Thanks," I said, flexing my fingers after he finished. "You did good."

"You're welcome," he said, cleaning up the paper and tossing it in the trashcan.

After double-checking for glass, I poured a thin layer of oil in and dumped the beef into the pan. Colin watched me like a hawk as I cooked and drained the meat. Fortunately, there were no further incidents.

A few minutes after I moved it to a cool burner, the garage door rumbled open. In a frantic rush, I surveyed the kitchen for incriminating evidence. There were still red spots on the white tile. I raced to wet a paper towel and scrub the floor clean. Right as I tossed the evidence, Mom walked into the house.

"Hey guys," she greeted. "Smells good."

"Yep," I said brightly. "We're good cooks." When Mom walked into her bedroom to drop off her jacket, I turned to Colin and narrowed my eyes. "Don't say anything. I mean it."

He gaped at me.

She re-emerged from the bedroom and came into the kitchen. She gave Colin a hug, then gave me an awkward side hug. "Thanks, sweetie."

"You're welcome. Colin helped." I eyed Colin for any sign that he was going to spill to Mom. He clamped his lips together, though his green eyes were narrowed. "Can I go upstairs to work on homework until dinner time?"

"Sure," she said. "Should be an hour or so."

I scooped up my backpack and practically sprinted upstairs. Kale was already in my room, pacing in a tight circle on my rug. Before I did anything else, I called Nina.

She answered after the second ring, but there was a long stretch of white noise before she finally said, "Hello?"

"Hey, it's Bridget."

"Sorry, girl. Had to get you on speaker," she said. "Kale just told me something happened. Are you okay?"

"I'm fine." I told her about my encounter.

"You're sure it wasn't an accident?"

"I'm positive," I said. "You need to be careful."

"I will," she said. "I went to that organic store by the mall and asked about black salt, but they showed me this weird pink stuff. I still don't really know this town well. Where else should I go?"

"Try Madam Zanka's," I said. "She has all kinds of weird crystals and stuff. If anyone has it, she will."

Before I discovered Miss Tara, I'd gone through the phone book for psychics and mediums in Parkland. Madam Zanka billed herself as a psychic, but she was a fake. Or if she was legit, she didn't see the dead, since she'd flat out ignored my sister Valerie. I had a feeling that most of her business came from her shop, which sold crystals, jewelry, and other witchy things.

"Okay, cool. I'll call you back."

Kale was still pacing as I settled onto my bed with my laptop. "What should we do?" I asked.

"Besides stay far away?" His handsome features were tense, with worry etching deep lines around his eyes.

"Besides that."

He folded his arms over his chest. "If you want to speak directly, there's not much else you can do other than salt, holy water, the usual. A ring of protection might work."

"But what if she's too far gone? What if she won't listen?"

"There are other options," he said. "Things I haven't taught you."

"Then teach me!" I spluttered. I held up my bandaged hand. "What's the holdup?"

"I'd rather you didn't have to learn them."

"And I'd rather there wasn't an angry spirit in my house. Come on, dude," I said. "You can't protect me forever."

His head snapped up, his gaze finding mine. I wasn't sure if it was affection or pity in his eyes. A shadow seemed to darken the pretty blue shade, as if there was something hiding within their depths. "When I say other options, I don't mean some mystical herbs that calm her down. There are rituals that can bind a troublesome spirit to a physical place."

The haunted expression on his face made me shiver involuntarily. "Isn't she already bound here?"

He shook his head. "Not like this. It's possible to bind her to a specific physical location. A ritual can confine her to such a small area that she can't harm anyone unless they're right on top of her."

"So what, she'd just be stuck?"

His intense blue gaze didn't falter. "Yes, at least until she's ready to hear reason, or weakened to the point that she can't hurt anyone who tries to get close. Many supposed hauntings are in fact from spirits being bound."

"If I had to," I murmured, "I guess I would. Does it hurt?"

"Yes," he said. "Quite a lot. Both for her and for you. And most bindings last a long time. A spirit angry enough to warrant a binding isn't going to suddenly calm itself after a few days. It can take decades or centuries. That's a long time to be trapped. It's a last resort."

I swallowed hard. "So, black salt it is."

"It's a start," he said. His expression softened. "What does Google say?"

"Are you getting on board with the technology train?"

He gave me a half-smile. "I'm adaptable."

By the time Mom had yelled a second time for me to come eat, I'd collected three pages of notes on proper ghost-hunting technique from organizations that fancied themselves paranormal investigators. Many of the pointers were irrelevant, considering I knew when a spirit was around and didn't have to guess at signs. Still, there were some helpful tips that seemed fairly obvious but I'd never thought of, like prayers of protection before entering the cemetery, or simply asking the spirit to stay upon leaving.

I scarfed my dinner down, then ran back upstairs to continue my research. I had a missed call from Nina, with a text message that had arrived minutes later.

Nina: found the black salt

Under the text was a picture of a plastic bag of fine black crystals lying on her gray-upholstered seat.

Awesome. Got some info to help tomorrow.

As I continued to research, every site mentioned the same prayers to St. Michael and recommended a St. Benedict medal to protect from hauntings. I made a note to get my hands on the medal, then opened a new window and navigated to YouTube to finish checking on the list Emily had given me.

With the videos on silent, I scrubbed through the opening shots quickly to see who was in a graveyard. I eliminated anyone who was obviously in a different location. A few were on an eerie abandoned playground that had been overgrown by weeds, while another was at Wildwood State Park. There were plenty of unsettled spirits out at Wildwood. They'd been mostly benevolent, having helped in my search party to find Diana Brown and Corey Walker in the woods. But I didn't believe for a second that they were the only spirits there. I drew a star next to the user name *ChubbyUnicorn* before going to the next one.

After five videos, I had to take a break. I leaned back, watching as Kale shifted uncomfortably at my window. There was something tense in his body, like he was waiting for something to happen.

"What's wrong?" I asked him.

"I don't like this situation."

"You and me both."

"I don't like that I can't stay close enough to protect you," he said.

"Why is that?" I asked. He'd tried to explain it when we'd been searching for Diana, saying that the lingering pain of the spirits affected him so strongly that he couldn't stand it. But that had only been a step above a usual Kale non-answer. "Why does it hurt you?"

"I don't know." He answered too quickly. His averted eyes and flat tone told me he was lying. For a second, I couldn't decide if I wanted to press the issue.

"Is there a way around it? It seems a little inconvenient that you have to disappear every time I need help the most." The temperature dropped in my room, the cold rising along with his anger. I shivered, crossing my arms over my chest. He didn't often show intense emotion that way, which made it clear how upset he was.

"I'm trying." There was an unusual tremor in his voice, and I realized he wasn't angry at me for bringing it up. He was angry at himself. "This is part of why I don't want you running off into danger all the time."

"Okay," I said. My breath formed wispy plumes in the chilly air. "Is there something I can do that makes it easier?"

Like I'd flipped a switch, the cold receded. A smile tugged at his lips, though his eyes were still far away and haunted, his mind somewhere that I couldn't reach. "You can't, but I know you want to. That's why I like being your Guardian."

"You do?"

"Mm-hmm."

"I bet you say that to all the sensitives."

He laughed. "You're my one and only. I chose you, you know."

A warm feeling washed over me, like hot chocolate sliding down my throat on a frigid day. One and only. Those words were music coming from him. To be chosen, not just a random accident...

It took some effort to sneak a full breath around my racing heart. "You did?"

His eyes gleamed as he smiled. "I was drawn to you. Until you crossed over, I'd been a Guardian only to the dead."

"Wait, what?" I was so used to Kale dodging my questions that I was confused by his straightforward answer.

"Many spirits hesitate after death," he said. "It's quite rare that people are ready to accept death. Most only need a little push. I assured them that it was safe, and encouraged them to let go before they forged unhealthy ties." He held up a hand, like he knew I would interrupt him with more questions. "After death, there's a short window where the spirit is in transition. If they hang on past that window, it's like a weed taking root. And that's how you get the spirits that you see. They take a human touch, a connection to the physical world, to break free finally."

"How long did you do that?"

"A long time," he said. "Centuries."

"Centuries. You're old."

"And wise." The light returned to his eyes.

"And really old."

"Watch it," he said. "I met your sister first, but she wouldn't move on without knowing you were safe. She missed her window. Not long after she and I met, I saw your echo."

"My echo?"

"Your spirit crossed over, then was yanked back. When that happens, you leave an echo of yourself in the veil between life and death. It's like a shadow, but one made of bright light. When a sensitive is born, for lack of a better word, a Guardian like me sees the echo and goes to them. But I didn't give anyone else a chance. I saw you hours after it happened, and I knew it was my responsibility to protect you."

There it was again. I wasn't psychic, but I was pretty sure he could say *I chose you* a thousand times, and my heart would still skip a beat.

"So it wasn't my charming personality?"

He laughed a little too loud at that for my liking. "No, but I've come to appreciate that about you."

I hated to ruin the moment, but I had to. "Why are you answering my questions all of a sudden?"

"Because things are changing," he said. He hesitated, then rested his hand on mine. Without thinking, I turned my hand over so I could wrap my fingers around his. The contact sent a cool thrill up my arm. After two years without making contact, even the slightest touch of skin to skin, or whatever his glowing essence was, sent a lightning storm through my nerves. "Our connection is growing stronger as you mature."

"Our connection?"

"We have a special bond," he said. The smile faltered, and I knew there was a *but* coming to ruin the whole thing like a thunderstorm at a picnic. "And your duty will continue to grow more difficult and complicated. I want to shield you from danger, but it seems to find you even so."

"Duty?"

My breath quickened as his fingers twined with mine. His body thrummed faintly, like he was electrified. "There are those who believe you serve a higher purpose," he said. "Preserving balance and natural order."

"You don't?"

"I do, but I think you have a right to be a seventeen-year-old first," he said. He squeezed my hand.

There was an irrational part of me that wanted to fling myself toward him. If things went like they did in the movies, he'd be powerless against my feminine wiles. Those graceful hands would map the lines of my body, and I would finally feel the insistent press of his lips to mine. As if he'd sensed my brain dissolving into sappy mush, he extricated his hand from mine.

"I should go check the area," he said. "Promise you'll stay out of trouble."

"I'll try," I murmured as he disappeared.

But I was in more trouble than just with the spirits. My crush on Kale no longer qualified as a silly infatuation. I kept hearing that word *chosen* echoing in my mind, wrapping itself around my heart. The passing interest had grown into a wanting for something I had never had.

Yeah. I was in serious trouble.

CHAPTER SEVENTEEN

IT WAS THE SMALLEST of blessings that Bryce Holloway was absent from school the next day. It was hard enough to concentrate with Kale on the brain, but I also had the impending confrontation with Charlene weighing on me. Nina and I texted throughout the day to confirm our plans to contact Charlene at St. Teresa's. The prayers and rituals I'd researched the night before looked so insignificant. Every time I thought about calling her up, I broke out in a cold sweat. I needed the spiritual equivalent of a nuclear weapon, not a mass-produced religious medal.

By the time the last bell had rung, I was a nervous wreck. With my notebook clutched tight to my chest, I hurried out the main doors and toward the senior parking lot to meet Nina. She was already in the car, but it was silent.

Her wild curls were tamed into a tight bun, and she wore simple black clothing, like she was preparing for battle. After a perfunctory greeting, we rode in uncharacteristic silence, and I took the time to check my notes again.

When we reached the parking lot at Saint Teresa's, Nina parked at the spot nearest the gate, but left the car running.

"Here's what I got." I showed her my notes. The ink was smudged and smeared from my sweaty palms. "We pray before we go in. We'll put down a ring of black salt around ourselves. When we leave, we ask her to stay behind."

"So she's going to play nice because we say please?" Nina asked incredulously. "That's all we've got?"

I bristled like a territorial cat. "Do you have something better?"

Her brows arched. "I...sorry, I didn't mean it like that. I had just hoped there was something bigger we could do."

"Kale told me there's a way to bind spirits, but it's a last resort," I said.

Her eyes brightened. "You didn't get more details?"

"He didn't want to share," I said. She frowned. She seemed a little too eager to find out about it. Kale had described it as a last resort, not an easy alternative if we were scared. "For now, we've got to try something."

My heart thumped as we got out of the car. Nina carried the bags of black salt while I carried a can of regular table salt in one hand and a sports bottle full of holy water in the other. After dashing Charlene with it in the house, I was running low. Before much longer, we'd have to make a trip to St. Mary's, the Catholic church downtown, to restock. I used to worry that it was sacrilegious, but Sal was Catholic and had reassured me that it was perfectly fine to take water from the church.

The sky was overcast, throwing a hazy gray veil over the cemetery. We paused under the wrought iron archway and exchanged an awkward look. "Uh, I'm not much for praying," she said with a forced laugh.

"Me either," I said. "I guess I can try."

I went to church with Mom when she asked, but I'd never been super involved. While I wasn't all that sure about His motivations, I was pretty sure there was a God. And considering what I saw on a daily basis, I had no doubt that there was a world beyond what we saw.

"Okay, close your eyes." My heart pounded against my ribs, like I was giving a speech in front of the entire school. "Um, God, please watch over us today. We're trying to protect people from getting hurt, so um...please bless us and keep us safe. And forgive us for trespassing. Amen."

Well, it wouldn't earn me any bonus points from the pastor, but it would have to do.

"Amen," Nina echoed.

Beyond the gates, wispy shadows lingered among the graves. Some were fully manifested, looking almost like real people if not for the way I could see the dry brown grass through their bodies. Others were formless shimmers, barely more than a shadow like Ed Hanners.

We walked side-by-side on the sloping path toward the angel statue. I scanned our surroundings, looking for any sign of something moving toward us. The crawling sensation of the graveyard's energy intensified the deeper we went.

It was eerily quiet when we reached the small cluster of graves beneath the angel's spread wings. I stopped a few feet away from the foot of Charlene's grave.

"Nina," I murmured. "Back here."

I checked over my shoulder to ensure that no one was here to watch us. Further down the hill, one of the shadowy wisps had drifted our way. It remained still, but I felt its gaze on us, like it was simply interested in what we were doing.

Careful not to trample on Charlene's grave, I set down my backpack and took out the table salt. I poured a large circle of salt, big enough to let both of us stand inside. "Go over it with the black."

With shaking hands, Nina opened a plastic bag and traced my circle, speckling black particles against white. "Okay. What now?"

"Will you call for her?" I asked.

Her eyes closed, and she put both her hands out like she was waiting for someone to grasp them. "Charlene? Charlene Watkins," she said in a lilting voice. "We don't want to hurt you. We know what happened, and we want to help you rest. Please let us help you."

My muscles tensed as I waited for the response. A cool breeze picked up, startling me with a prickling down my spine. Was she here, or was that just a January wind?

"Do you feel that?"

Nina opened her eyes, then looked around. "She's not here," she murmured. She frowned, then gestured with her head. "It's only the wind."

The trees lining the outer border of the cemetery stirred, branches swaying in the gentle, natural wind.

"Try again," I said.

Nina nodded and repeated her call. She continued speaking softly to Charlene, almost like she was trying to coax a shy kitten from under the couch. Was Charlene off wreaking havoc, too busy to come to us? With the image of Charlene in mind, she should have been able to connect.

For the hundredth time, I wished Miss Tara had been more amenable to helping us. She'd been able to call dozens of the Runaway Killer's victims to herself. Charlene would have been a simple job for her.

Finally, Nina's one-sided conversation stopped. "I'm trying, but I don't sense her at all. And I reread everything we found about her, stared at her picture, everything I could do to strengthen my connection."

"So what does this mean?" I hugged my arms over my chest. "Is she off somewhere else?"

"I guess she could be."

On the one hand, if we just sat here waiting, she could be off terrorizing someone else. There were at least five people that we knew of who'd done the Dead Eyes challenge here. Any one of them could get hurt next. If we sat here waiting, they were sitting ducks.

Then again, what could we do about it? If she didn't come, she didn't come. Basic probability said if we guessed at who she was targeting next, we only had a twenty percent chance of being correct. "Can you call Miss Tara?" I asked. "She won't come out here, but maybe she can tell us something."

"Yeah, she's gonna tell us to go to hell," Nina said. She shook her head and took out her phone. "But I'll try."

Another quick scan of the cemetery showed no sign of Charlene. It should have been a relief to be alone, but something wasn't right. Maybe I was paranoid. Maybe not.

"Hello? Miss Tara, this is Nina Welles." Long pause. "Yes, ma'am. I know. I was wondering if you had any more advice on—" Another long pause. "Okay, you can't even tell me something else? Yeah, I did the black salt. Seriously?" I looked over to see her staring at her phone in disgust. She looked at me. "She hung up on me. She said she'd told me once already to not interfere, and that I shouldn't let you drag me down with you."

I sighed. How was it even remotely fair that trying to save lives had earned me such a bad reputation with the only person around who could help us? And what would it take for her to get over it?

"Forget her. Let's give it a few minutes, then try again." I glanced at my phone. It was already four-fifteen. I had to be at my SAT class by six, or Mom would bypass Charlene and take the number one spot on my most dangerous list.

By five o'clock, I was officially freaked out. We'd wait a few minutes, Nina would call Charlene, and then we'd listen and watch. Nothing. Rinse and repeat for forty-five minutes. Charlene was a no-show, although we gathered an audience of a dozen spirits that hung back and watched us silently. The sight of them was sobering; each one probably had a sad story that kept them here. If Charlene ever showed up, I was going to point at the other spirits and say, "They can behave themselves while lingering in limbo, why can't you?"

Finally, Nina looked at me and shook her head. "I don't think it's going to work," she said. "Do you think she saw us setting up and thought we wanted to hurt her?"

"No, that would—" I hesitated. After she'd shown up at the house, I'd used the holy water on her. She might have figured out that we had the ability to send her away, even hurt her, if she came too close. "Maybe." I looked down at the ground, tracing the curve of white against the winter-dry grass.

Salt created a powerful barrier that spirits couldn't cross. Maybe she couldn't hear us from within its protection. The only other time I'd blocked a spirit with salt was with Natalie, and that was before I could talk openly with her. I didn't really know the particulars of how it worked, but it couldn't hurt to try. With my heart racing, I took a tentative step out of the circle. "Stay there."

"What are you doing?"

I stepped all the way out of the circle and walked forward, legs trembling as I approached Charlene's headstone.

"Charlene, it's safe to come speak to us," I said, surveying the quiet cemetery. "We only want to talk to you. I know you're there. Please come speak to me."

The words had barely crossed my lips when the ambient whispers rose in intensity. "Go away," a rough voice said. Like smoke coalescing, a hulking shadow materialized on the other side of Charlene's headstone. I couldn't make out features, but it was small, like the one I'd seen in the house last night.

"Charlene?" I asked, my voice shaking. Without breaking visual contact, I inched backward toward the safety of the circle. "I think we all got off to a bad start. We just want to talk to you and find out how we can help you. Doesn't that sound good?"

A laugh sounded from behind me, then icy hands shoved me.

"Bridget!" Nina shouted.

My hands slid uselessly along the dew-slick tombstone, and I slammed into the edge of the stone face first. An explosion ignited in my head, turning my field of vision white. When the white had cleared, the pain retracted into an insistent pounding over my left eye.

"Stop!" the spirit shouted at me.

My vision blurred as I turned to look up at the shadowy figure. It was in front of me now. Were there two, or was that just my shaken brain seeing double?

"We're trying to help you," I replied. Using the tombstone to pull myself up, I put up one hand in a *stop* motion. "Please, let us help. Tell us what you want."

But the spirit threw its head back, letting out a fearsome shout. It split open, revealing the feathery gray sky. When the remains of its spectral form had dissipated, I saw Nina standing just outside the circle with the holy water in her hand, eyes wide and frightened.

"Oh, my God," she said. "Oh, God." With a quick glance over her shoulder, she darted out, grabbed my outstretched hand, and dragged me back into the circle. I tripped over my feet and went down on my knees inside the circle. A wave of nausea crawled through me. "Are you okay?"

"Umm," I said, clapping my hand over my mouth. My head was still swimming, and I could barely see out of my left eye. I gingerly touched my cheekbone, sending a sharp pain into my skull. "Ouch."

"I heard it," Nina said. "We should go. We're not ready for this."

"I agree," I said.

I reached for my bag, but she batted my hand away and threw the holy water and salt into my backpack. Without me asking, she shouldered both of our bags, then hauled me to my feet. We hurried onto the path, leaving the angel and the graves behind.

The gathered spirits along the path scattered as we approached. All I could think about was how much my face hurt. When face met granite, granite always won.

At the car, Nina opened the door for me and pushed me in. She tossed both bags into my lap, then hurried around to the driver side. With wild eyes, she looked around us, then started the car and peeled out of the parking lot. She was at the traffic light before I realized I hadn't said the prayer to ask Charlene to stay behind. Clearly, she wasn't listening to reason.

I pulled down the visor mirror. "Oh, crap." Blood oozed from a cut in my eyebrow, streaking across my eyelid. The pale skin over my cheekbone was already darkening. "Shit," I whimpered. "I gotta cover this up."

"How about we get somewhere safe first?"

Somewhere safe turned out to be the first gas station Nina saw. Parked close to the curb, the neon lottery and beer signs cast a comforting rainbow glow across the hood. Looking through the glass windows at the stacked cases of soda anchored me, assuring me that we'd left behind the nightmare world of the cemetery and returned to reality.

We sat in the parking lot in silence. I couldn't stop checking the mirror. In the short time we'd been driving, the area around my eye had begun to swell. "I have to go to class tonight," I said. "Everyone's gonna notice."

"It's not that—oh shit, that's bad," Nina said. "Hold on."

She left the car running, grabbed her purse, and hurried into the store, leaving me alone.

"Kale?" I asked, my voice pitiful.

He appeared in the back seat a few moments later. I turned to see him, and his jaw dropped.

"What the hell happened?"

I told him what had gone down, from laying down the circle up to Nina banishing her. "I don't want to hurt her, but she's dangerous."

His jaw clenched as he held my gaze. "I want you to go home where it's safer. I'm going to my superiors for help. You go home, and I'll let you know what I find out."

I shook my head. "I have my class tonight."

"You can get out of it just this once."

"Mom will kill me."

"She's going to kill you when she sees your face."

The car door opened. I yelped in surprise, but it was just Nina. She had a plastic bag with two sodas in one hand, and a cup full of ice in the other. After depositing the drinks into the cup holders, she dumped the ice into the bag to make an icepack.

"Oh, my gosh, thank you," I said as I pressed it to my face. The pressure hurt, but the cool sensation made up for it as it sank into the throbbing lump.

"No problem," she said. She peeked back. "Hey, Kale."

"Hi," he said. "Nina, I want you and Bridget both to lay low. I'll seek help where I can, but until then, stay out of harm's way. Stay home if you can."

"We have to go to school," Nina said. "Not that I would mind staying home, but unless you can write us a doctor's note…"

He sighed. "I'll be back to check on you as soon as I can." He disappeared, leaving a cool wind in his wake.

"What now?" Nina asked.

I glanced at the clock. It was already five-thirty. "Crap. I have my SAT class tonight. And my mom will be expecting to pick me up there. I have to go."

"Move it." She touched the back of my hand, and I pulled the ice pack away from my face. She winced. "Can I fix your face?"

"Unless you have magic Band-Aids, I don't think you can."

"Next best thing." She rifled through her purse. After a noisy rattle, she came up with a small tube of concealer and a powder compact. "Do you want me to do it?"

"Yeah," I said. "I'm terrible at makeup."

I closed my eyes while she dabbed the concealer onto my face. Once, her finger patted the makeup on a little too hard, and I involuntarily gasped in pain.

"I'm so sorry."

"It's okay," I said. A powder puff patted across my cheekbone.

"Okay," she said. "You can still see the swelling, but the color is better."

I checked the mirror again. It was obvious that I had on a ton of makeup. The already pale skin on my face was alabaster, with an obvious powdery texture around my eye. But it blended well enough that someone might not notice the swelling unless they were close enough to kiss. And in that case, I had bigger problems. After more consideration, I pulled the elastic out of my hair and let it hang down around my face. It didn't fully cover it, but it was a little less obvious. It would have to do.

The only benefit of my SAT class that night was staying out of trouble with Mom for a few hours longer. Mrs. Zapruder might as well have been speaking Chinese for as much as I actually comprehended. From the minute I walked in the door, my mind was stuck on one of two things: Charlene Watkins, and Kale's attempts to get help from his superiors, whatever that meant.

Why hadn't Charlene come when we first called? I replayed it over and over in my head. Suddenly something struck me, something odd that I hadn't been able to really consider while a spirit was knocking the daylights out of me.

It didn't seem to be an iron-clad rule, but most spirits appeared in the clothes they'd died in. I would have expected a knee-length hospital gown on Charlene. Though its dark, grimy appearance made it hard to pick out details, the spirit's ill-fitting garment was long, almost to the ground. Furthermore, Charlene had shouted at me to go away and to stop. But that didn't make sense, not after she'd come into my house on the attack.

What if the spirit wasn't Charlene Watkins?

My eyes widened, and I swapped my SAT workbook out for my ghost notebook. In a noisy rush, I frantically flipped through pages until I found the list of names on the graves around the angel statute. Maybe the reason Charlene hadn't answered was because she was already on the other side where she belonged. Maybe we'd been calling the wrong name all this time.

"Bridget?"

I yelped in surprise, snapping my head up to see Mrs. Zapruder looking at me, eyebrows raised. The SAT workbook lay open in her hand. Her brow was furrowed in disapproval.

"Yes, ma'am?"

She frowned. "Can you answer number fourteen for us?"

I scrambled to hide my list under the SAT workbook. Crap, it was still open to the table of contents. "I lost my page."

She gave a long-suffering sigh. "Thirty-seven. Please pay attention."

With my cheeks burning, I skimmed the question. It was something about missing angles in parallel lines. One of the smart girls in the front of the room shifted uncomfortably in her seat, one hand creeping up. My heart pounded.

"Does anyone else—"

"It's C," I said loudly. "Forty-five degrees." I didn't have to be paying attention to answer a basic question about supplementary angles.

Mrs. Zapruder looked at me skeptically, then checked her answer key. Her brow furrowed. "That's…that's right. Would you like to explain?"

You're darn right. I didn't like the look of utter surprise on her face at the fact that I could do a simple problem. Then again, my performance thus far hadn't been particularly impressive.

"Um…" The girl in the front row practically leaped out of her seat as she thrust her hand in the air. "She can do it."

The teacher looked like she wanted to protest, but probably figured it wasn't worth the stress. She turned and said, "Go ahead, Ellie."

As Ellie launched into a description of solving the problem, I tuned out again. Keeping the book out, I slid my notebook to the side and poised my pencil alongside the list of names so it looked like I was keeping notes.

The eight graves had belonged to Frank Borstein, Charlene Watkins, Lois Hanners, Edward Hanners, Sara Workman, Travis Hillman, Charlie Hillman, and Vonda Rogers.

We'd already figured Ed and Lois were out. Nothing I'd seen in Frank Borstein's history would have made him linger, although those things weren't always obvious. Like I'd seen with Shirley, sometimes it was the little things that kept people hanging on. But this spirit was doing a lot more than moping. And if it wasn't Charlene, that left us with Sara, Travis, Charlie, or Vonda. I narrowed my eyes at the list. All of those names had been Nina's.

I slid my phone out of my pocket and sent Nina a message.

Can you get 2 bathroom

A few seconds later, the reply came.

Nina: OMW

I raised my hand.

Mrs. Zapruder pointed to me. "Did you want to explain number fifteen?"

"Well…" The look on her face was the same one that Mom always wore, an expression that needed no words to express exactly what she was thinking. Just once, I wanted to defy expectations instead of being a disappointment. I scanned the problem. It was a rectangle with a labeled point inside, then a bunch of similar figures below. The question asked about rotating, then reflecting the figure. "It's B and D."

"A, too," Ellie piped up from across the room.

My cheeks flushed as I scanned the page. No, Girl Genius was wrong this time.

I looked at Mrs. Zapruder expectantly. She smiled at me. "Bridget was right. B and D. See what happens with A," she said as she began sketching on the board.

My pleasure at being right was short-lived. I raised my hand again. "May I go to the restroom? It's an emergency."

"Go ahead."

As I hurried down the hall, passing the loud music in the Zumba room and the shouts of the karate kids, Nina stuck her head out the door on the far end of the hall. We met outside the bathroom door and slipped in together. Through the thin walls, I could hear a teacher calling out Spanish words from one side, and the bouncing rhythm of basketballs on the other.

"What's up? Did you see something?" she asked. She bent down to check for feet in the other stalls, then shook her head.

"No, nothing here," I said. "I was just wondering if the reason our plan didn't work is that Charlene Watkins isn't our ghost."

Nina tilted her head. "She seemed the most obvious."

"What about Sara Workman and Vonda Rogers?" I asked. "What did you find out about them?"

Nina frowned at me. "Well, we decided it was Charlene."

"So you don't know anything about them?"

Her eyes narrowed slightly, and there was a subtle shift in her body language. It wasn't fear wiring all her bones together anymore. She went stiff, like she was making herself into a stone wall to protect herself from my questions. "Well, you seemed to think it was Charlene, so I didn't keep researching. After that, I found the black salt like you told me to."

My stomach did a loop-the-loop around my spine. There was definitely accusation in her tone. Suddenly *our* theory about Charlene had become *my* theory. It wasn't worth arguing over. "I'm not accusing you of anything. I'm sorry if it sounded like that." To my relief, her stiff posture loosened a little, though her face was still stony as I continued. "You're right, I was pretty sure it was Charlene. Now I'm not sure."

She took out her phone. "You look up Sara, and I'll look up Vonda. What was it?"

"Rogers," I said. I quickly typed *Sara Workman* into my search bar. It brought up hundreds of results, so I added *Parkland Georgia* to my search. The search brought up an obituary as the top result. I tapped the title, then skimmed it.

Sara Workman entered into rest on October 14, 2014. She is preceded in death by her sons Travis and Charlie Hillman, and her grandmother Hazel Toombs. She is survived by her parents, Max and Margie Workman of Albany, her sister Carolyn McIntosh of Atlanta, and her brother Robert Workman of Orlando, Florida. In lieu of flowers, the family requests that donations be made to the Compassionate Friends in honor of Sara's work with bereaved parents.

"Holy crap," I murmured. "This is insane."

"What?"

"Sara Workman is the mother of Travis and Charlie Hillman. All three of them are dead."

Nina's eyes went wide. "You think it's her?"

"Maybe. It could be one of the kids. Or even all three." The memory of our encounter at the graveyard flashed through my mind. "Did you see two spirits? I thought I was just confused and freaked out, but I could swear there was one behind me and one in front of me."

She shrugged. "Maybe. It happened so fast. "

How was it that getting closer to the answer made things exponentially more complicated? I glanced at my phone again. It had already been nearly ten minutes since I left. They were either going to think I had crazy diarrhea or that I was skipping class. "I gotta go."

"What do we do?"

"Tonight we research Sara Workman and her kids. See if Ethan can find anything, and I'll send Kale out. We've got to crack this."

Chapter Eighteen

THE REST OF MY CLASS passed without incident, although if someone had asked, I couldn't have told them a single thing we'd talked about. When class was over, I walked out to meet Mom and Colin in the lobby. As I passed a mirrored trophy case, I caught a glimpse of my bruised face. The swollen area under my eye was worse now, showing the dark color even through the heavy makeup. Crap. I fixed my hair, tossing it over dramatically so it covered the side of my face better.

Mom was standing in the lobby already, her neon orange top sweaty in a heart pattern across her back. When she saw me, she did a double take. "You look different."

"What do you mean?" I asked innocently. *Don't look too close.*

"Your hair," she said. "You never wear it down. It's pretty."

I shrugged. "I thought I'd try something different." One of her eyebrows perked, like she'd noticed something else. I quickly turned, looking down the hall. "There's Colin!" I said, hoping he would distract her.

My brother scurried toward us with his karate belt held high. There was a piece of yellow tape wrapped around one end. "Look! I got a stripe!"

"Good job, sweetie," Mom said as we headed toward the doors. "How did you get that?"

"So I had to do all the kicks," he said. "And I almost fell when I did my roundhouse but he let me go again."

Thankfully, my brother got along fine with my mom, and they kept each other entertained the whole way home. While Colin prattled about the minutiae of getting his new belt, I was watching Mom and seeing her in a different light. She'd lost Valerie in an accident. If something had happened to her too, would she linger, still bitter and bound by her loss? How much worse would it be for her if she'd lost all three of us?

It was already dark by the time we got home. While Mom and Colin went to change out of sweaty clothes, I took a Tupperware full of leftover spaghetti out of the refrigerator and started making plates. I had just finished microwaving the third one when Mom came out. A look of surprise took over her face.

"Well, thank you," she said. Her smile made me feel surprisingly proud. "That was so helpful."

"No problem," I said.

If she'd picked up on my ulterior motives, she didn't let on. I wanted to eat in my room and find out what Sara Workman's deal was. And the sooner I got upstairs, the sooner I could call for Kale and see if he'd gotten any more help.

She joined me in the kitchen, working around behind me to get glasses and fill them with ice. "Water or tea?"

"Water is fine," I said, turning to look at her.

She squinted and leaned closer. "Bridget, are you wearing makeup?"

"Nina and I were just experimenting," I said. Crap, I'd almost forgotten. "I was—"

"What happened?"

"What do you mean?" I asked innocently. My heart thumped.

"Don't. Your face." I jumped a little as she brushed my hair out of the way. Her thumb gently traced the swollen lump, sending a sharp pang through my face. "Honey, what happened?"

Cornered and exposed, I felt like Spiderman getting his mask pulled off. "I…um…" My mind spun in manic circles. What was I supposed to tell her? "I did it at school," I stammered. "In gym."

"In gym? Were you boxing?" she spluttered.

"Basketball," I blurted as the image of Lance falling from the shattered basketball goal flashed through my mind. "I got hit with a basketball."

She pursed her lips, staring at me skeptically. "A basketball."

"Uh-huh. One of the boys tried to pass it and it hit me."

"You're sure? If you got in a fight, you need to tell me so we can deal with it," she said. Her right eyebrow arched, as if she was getting a spike on her internal lie detector. "Was it Allie again?"

"Mom, no," I said. Although that would have been satisfying. "Besides, I didn't really get in a fight with Allie the first time. It was basically over after I gave her a black eye. She never hit me back." *Because she was too busy crying.*

"Bridget," she said in an exasperated tone. "Did you at least go see the nurse at school?"

"No, but I put ice on it."

"Does your head hurt?"

"Yes."

"Do you feel dizzy?" She was going into nurse mode. And after my experience with Natalie's killer, I knew she was trying to determine if I had a concussion.

"No," I said. "I didn't hit my head."

"Your face is your head, Bridget. Any blow to the face shakes up your brain. And the gym teacher didn't even check on you? They should know better. I should call and—"

"You don't have to," I interrupted. "I didn't think it was too bad, so I didn't tell the coach."

"Well, now people are going to think I beat you," she said, her mouth tugging up in a half smile. "After you eat, you need to get ice on it and take some ibuprofen."

"Okay. Can I still eat upstairs?"

"Go ahead." But her voice was still strained. Hopefully she didn't get suspicious and call the school anyway.

Carefully balancing my plate, I hurried up the stairs to my bedroom. It was empty, and for just a second, I wondered what it would be like to sit and watch dumb TV shows on my laptop until I was too tired to keep my eyes open. I had hours of research ahead of me, and beyond that, the stress of knowing that a super pissed-off spirit was out there hurting people.

I sat down at my desk and called for Kale, then started twirling spaghetti around my fork. My mouth was full of noodles when he appeared at my window. My stomach still wasn't quite settled after the excitement of the day, but my appetite won out.

"Hrmm," I said around my food.

"You don't say."

I swallowed the half-chewed lump and dabbed at my mouth with a napkin. "Mom saw my eye."

"A blind man could see your eye."

"Very funny."

"I wasn't trying to be," he said. "It looks awful."

I ignored him. "What did you find out? Are they sending a SWAT team?"

He sighed a little. "I requested an audience with my immediate superior." The look of distaste on his face told me that things hadn't gone particularly well.

"An audience? What is he, a king?"

Kale perked an eyebrow. "One would think. He told me that he would contact another Guardian to assist us. I'm to meet him later tonight to discuss our options."

"What, like at the Waffle House?" The thought of Kale and another mysterious and annoyingly vague spirit conferring over greasy bacon and butter-soaked waffles made me smile.

He chuckled. "Not quite. I'll let you know as soon as I know something."

"I was hoping you would come back with answers. And a ghost-proof bubble."

"So was I," he said.

I crossed my arms. "You'd think there would be some kind of manual," I said. "If they care enough to send a Guardian to watch out for me, shouldn't they be preparing me for this kind of thing?"

He hesitated. "That may be coming."

The odd answer gave me pause, and I laid down my fork to process it. "What does that mean?"

"There's a sort of training for people like you," he said. "I've told them for years that you weren't ready. But my asking for help may draw their attention. It may not be my decision to delay any longer."

"Training? Kale, what the hell?"

His blue eyes were downturned, like a guilty puppy who'd gotten busted for chewing my shoes. "I don't want you to worry about it for now," he said. "We can continue to defer until you're an adult."

"Well, maybe we can defer, but you don't get to keep me in suspense until then," I said hotly. "What do you mean, training?"

I suddenly pictured a mental montage of myself sword-fighting against a squad of ninja spirits. Maybe the head injury was worse than I thought.

"All of your questions have answers," he said.

I'd had more than enough of his cryptic crap. "Are you saying there are people who can teach me to deal with this and not depend on Google to protect me? Stuff like Miss Tara knows?"

"Yes."

A ferocious wave of anger ignited in my belly. My accident was twenty-six months ago. Why was this the first I'd heard of it? I slammed my fork down. "Kale! What the—"

"But you're young," he said firmly. "Once you involve yourself with them, you're committed. And you have to follow their rules. I think we both know how well you deal with that."

"I could deal with it if it meant knowing no one would come and hurt my mom and my brother," I said, my voice cracking.

"You say that now…" His condescending tone only intensified my anger, like blowing on the embers of a campfire. "Just stay out of trouble for now and try not to worry about it."

"How? If I sit here and tell the spirits 'sorry, I can't play,' will they just go away? Is that how it works now?"

"Bridget."

"It came into my house," I said. "But next time I'll just ask it politely to go."

"I'm looking for answers, I promise."

With a surprising ferocity, I shoved my plate aside and pulled out my laptop. "Well, maybe you can ask your secret ghost trainer how I can protect my freaking house. If you think I can handle that kind of delicate information."

"Bridget, don't be that way," he said. The temperature dropped as he approached me.

For once, I didn't want him closer. "Did it occur to you to ask me if I wanted to learn? Maybe I didn't want to be fumbling my way through all this crap alone for two years."

The word *alone* sent him reeling, his eyes going wide like I'd slapped him.

"Do you remember the first year after your sister died? Because I do. You were in no state to undergo training then," he said sharply. "And you're not alone. I have always been and will always be here to protect you."

"Except when a homicidal ghost comes after me, in which case, you can watch from afar as it rips me to shreds," I spat. "But at least you'll be there to help me make the transition when I'm dead, right?"

My chest heaved with anger. Tears stung my eyes. *Don't you dare*, I told myself, clenching my fists until my short fingernails cut crescents into my palms.

"You're being irrational," he said.

I glared at him. "I haven't slept in days. A spirit came to my house and threatened me. And the person, or whatever you are, who I trust most in the entire world has been keeping things from me. Again! Oh, I know. When you meet your superior, ask them if they can also teach me about being rational. I obviously missed that class, too."

"Bridget…" His shoulders slumped. "I understand that you're upset, so I'll leave you alone and let you cool off, rather than argue with you. Call if you need me."

"I won't," I said flatly.

He disappeared, leaving my room unusually warm as the cold air followed him. My breath hitched as I sniffled. I was not going to cry, dammit.

It had only been in the last few months that I'd begun to think of Kale as a real friend, and possibly more. He'd given me cryptic answers and half-truths as long as I'd known him, parceling out information when he felt I was ready. And after he'd led me on to think I could get rid of my ability, only to trick me into letting go of Valerie, it shouldn't have surprised me that he was hiding more secrets. Why had I deluded myself into thinking he was a person like me? Because I'd gotten a case of the tingles when he touched me? *Stupid*, I scolded myself.

I scrubbed the tears away from my eyes and muttered curses as I reawakened the pain in my eye. With my head throbbing, I typed *how to protect your house from ghosts* into the search bar. I considered adding *because your Guardian won't tell you jack shit*.

There was a lot of hippie-sounding stuff about visualizing white light and positive energy. Screw that. I wanted concrete solutions, tangible barriers that would let me sleep easily knowing that my family and I were all safe.

After a few minutes of reading, I found a page of natural remedies and folklore about protecting a dwelling from haunting. That was more like it. I turned to a fresh page in my notebook, labeled it *Protective Stuff*, and started taking notes. Some I'd heard of, like coriander, dandelion, and even blackberry, but others were utterly foreign, like asphodel and styrax. That sounded like an alien from a bad movie.

Finally I found something I could use. One website recommended vinegar, claiming that it would disrupt a demon or ghost for days. Just reading the word *demon* sent a chill down my spine. I didn't think those were real either, but maybe it was yet another in Kale's massive backlog of secrets.

My instinct was to call for him and ask if vinegar would really work, but for the first time since we'd met, I didn't want to see his face. Unless I got to punch it.

Instead, I set aside my notebook and hurried downstairs with my plate. Researching Sara Workman would have to wait until I made sure the house was safe.

Mom was curled up on the couch with a blanket over her legs, her tablet propped against her knees. Reading glasses perched on the end of her nose as she swiped through the pages. Colin was on the other end of the couch, playing video games with his headphones on.

Mom looked up as I came down the stairs. "Are you feeling okay?"

"I'm great," I lied. It felt like the entire Fox Lake drumline was conducting rehearsal inside my skull. "The ibuprofen made me feel a lot better."

"Good," she said. "Make sure you get some more ice on it before bed."

I was about to put my plate in the sink, then looked up at Mom again. For once, I was on her good side, and it was easy enough to keep it up. I rinsed my dishes and loaded them into the dishwasher. Resisting the urge to point out my diligence, I tiptoed toward the pantry.

A quick search of the cabinets yielded a glass bottle of vinegar. In my research, I'd found recommendations to mop the floors or even bathe with the vinegar. Mom would definitely notice if I decided randomly to mop the floors at nine in the evening. Another article recommended leaving out dishes of vinegar to evaporate overnight.

I stood up to peek through the pass-through window. Mom was engrossed in her book. Moving quietly, I pulled a few Tupperware containers out of the cabinet and hid them under my hoodie.

After surveying the kitchen for a good hiding spot, I poured an inch of vinegar into one of the dishes and put it on top of the fridge behind a decorative basket. The sharp smell made my nose wrinkle. I hoped it wouldn't permeate the kitchen and leave the whole house smelling like sweaty feet.

A lot of my research had recommended protecting the front door to the house, so my next stop was the front porch. I wasn't certain that ghosts followed the rules about entering through the front door instead of materializing wherever the heck they wanted, but it couldn't hurt. With my heart racing, I carefully unlocked the front door, then turned the handle. As I pulled it toward me, the door seal let out a cracking sound and ruined my attempt to be stealthy. I froze.

"Bridget?" Mom called from the living room.

"Yeah?"

"What are you doing?" Mom asked.

"I...uh...I think I dropped my favorite pen outside when I got home from school," I said. "Be right back."

I didn't turn back to see if she was buying it. Cold air bit at my bare feet as I stepped outside. I breathed deeply, but I didn't smell anything off. There were no glowing eyes watching me from the shadows.

An oversized terra cotta planter sat next to the front door. The flowers inside had shriveled to withered stalks in the harsh cold. Digging my hands into the dry, crumbly soil, I made a small crater and deposited one of the

Tupperware containers in the hole so the lip was flush with the soil. I filled it with vinegar, then hid the bottle in my hoodie again.

When I came back inside, Mom called, "Don't forget to lock it."

Too bad the deadbolt wouldn't keep ghosts out. After locking the door, I hurried upstairs with the vinegar sloshing noisily in the bottle.

I set another dish on the top shelf of the laundry room, which was between Colin's bedroom and mine. Once I was back in my room, I put another dish on my desk. There was enough vinegar left to put a finger's width in the container.

My faith in Kale had been shaken, but I wasn't sure I had much more faith in a couple of disposable Tupperware containers and generic brand vinegar. Still, I had to try.

I continued my research into the night. It occurred to me that my work to block the angry spirit might keep out benign spirits like Shirley and Jerry. Well, they'd have to go without their Bridget fix until all of this settled down.

After I heard Colin brushing his teeth, I tried to sleep. Despite snuggling into my cozy new pajamas from Christmas, I was wide awake, staring at the ceiling in the dark and wondering if the creaking downstairs was Mom sneaking ice cream or a ghost coming to kill me.

After half an hour of tensing at every tiny noise, I sat up, put a pillow in the crack of my door to keep the light from spilling into the hallway, and got my computer out to continue researching Sara Workman and the Hillmans.

As Nina had told me, the Hillman boys had been young when they died. Both had been struck by a car on Halloween night. According to an article, a bystander said the older boy, Travis, threw himself into the road and shoved his younger brother, Charlie, out of the path of the car.

Unfortunately, Charlie had still been critically injured, and both boys were taken to the hospital. Travis died within hours of arriving at Parkland General. That was the hospital where Charlene Watkins had died, and where my mom had started her nursing career.

Charlie had lingered for over a month on life support, showing minimal brain activity. An infection in his brain ended up killing him.

After reading the first few articles about Travis and Charlie's deaths, I was convinced Sara was our angry spirit. Losing both her children to a senseless accident would make anyone snap. But my research didn't support that theory.

In the articles, their mother—who was still Sara Hillman then—said on record that she didn't blame the driver. The police did toxicology screens, tire mark analysis, and collected numerous eyewitness reports to confirm that the driver wasn't at fault. Both boys had light-up necklaces, but they were hidden under their costumes.

Witnesses said that both boys had been wearing dark Grim Reaper costumes, rendering them invisible in the dark of night. The irony of it sent chills down my spine. And as I tried to picture the shadowy spirits that had attacked me in the house and the cemetery, the clothing made sense. What had looked like a shapeless dress could have been a loose black robe.

With the clock ticking away into the wee hours of the night, it gave me plenty of time to think. Maybe Sara had felt like she needed to say something nice to the media. After all, you didn't always tell the whole world what you really thought. Maybe she'd held onto some kind of bitterness that festered into a violent rampage after her death.

After rereading Sara's obituary, I'd looked up *Sara Workman Compassionate Friends* and found a website for a local support group for bereaved parents.

There was a memorial post to Sara, describing the work she'd done for the organization.

We are sad to announce the passing of one of our local leaders, Sara Workman, who recently lost her battle with an aggressive form of pancreatic cancer. Many would have been destroyed by the kind of loss Sara experienced. But Sara chose to bring healing from her tragedy. In addition to leading support groups for bereaved parents, she organized a local safety drive called Healthy Halloween, and issued the annual Charlie's Challenge to fill the shelves at the local food bank.

There were links to some of the events she'd organized. As I read through them, I found short statements from Sara saying that she'd chosen to honor her boys through giving back to the community. As I continued down the rabbit hole of Internet searches, I found a guest post on a blog about grief recovery. Again, Sara stated that she didn't blame the car's driver. Not only was there no evidence of anger, but there was a mountain of proof that she'd coped surprisingly well.

So maybe she wasn't our spirit. Maybe it was one of the boys, or even both. I could understand their anger; they were dead and separated from their mother. But it didn't make sense that they would lash out at people who came to their graves. Most spirits didn't linger near their graves, so why was that so important to them?

None of it made sense, but I had to get answers soon.

Chapter Nineteen

I BARELY SLEPT. Kale stopped in to check on me during the night, but I pretended to be asleep. His cool aura swept over me, then disappeared as quickly as it had come. Even in my anger, there was something comforting about him keeping watch.

When my alarm went off at five forty-five, I didn't even snooze. I tumbled out of bed and headed for the shower in a lurching zombie walk. My face was a ghastly sight. The dark bruise around my eye had spread into a purple crescent along my cheekbone. I would have to wear makeup or field questions about it all day.

I took out my seldom-used makeup and applied foundation to even out my skin. Gritting my teeth, I smeared concealer over the tender spot around my eye. By the time I was done, I was as pale as one of my ghostly visitors. My dark eyes looked tiny and beady in the expanse of white. I sighed and added blush, hoping I looked alive without evoking a circus clown. Emboldened, I even tried to add liquid eyeliner. Emily could apply a perfect wing in twenty seconds at a red light, but I struggled just to get one side straight.

When I finally finished, I looked halfway normal. It was way more makeup than my usual mascara and Chapstick, but I'd managed to hide the discoloration.

After getting dressed, I headed downstairs. I froze halfway down the stairs when I noticed all the lights were on. There was noise in the kitchen. Clenching the bottle of holy water in my backpack, I tiptoed down and tried to be stealthy as I slid along the wall.

Relief surged through me when I peeked around the corner. Mom was going through the fridge and humming to herself.

"What are you doing up?" I asked, sauntering in the kitchen like I hadn't been expecting a murderous spirit.

"Colin's sick again." She took a coffee cup out of the microwave, tested the water inside with one finger, then dumped powdered creamer into it. "He's running a fever, so I'm keeping him home and take him to the doctor later." Looking me at over her coffee cup, she frowned. "You look pretty, but it's a little much for school, don't you think?"

Always a critic. "Well, it was this or answering questions about my eye all day," I said. "So I'd rather people think I'm trying too hard than have to answer all day."

"Okay," she said, stifling a yawn. Her brow creased as she sniffed. "Do you smell something funny? I'd swear it was vinegar." She leaned over the sink and gave it a long sniff. "Must be something in the fridge."

"Nope," I said, my gaze drifting to the cabinet over the fridge.

Emily honked her horn as she pulled into the driveway.

"Bye, Mom, love you," I said, hoping to distract her from the smell.

"Love you too," she said absently, still sniffing quietly.

I hurried outside and climbed into Emily's car. She took one look at me and said, "Whoa."

"Do I look like crap?"

She tilted her head and inspected my face. "The blush is too orange for you. But your eyeliner is on point. What's the occasion?"

I froze, my tongue stuck to the roof of my mouth as I considered. This was Emily, and since she'd been abducted by the Runaway Killer, I'd told her virtually everything. Why was it even a question of whether to tell her?

I leaned a little closer, brushing my hair away from my face. "Can you see it?"

She cocked her head. "Holy crap. What did you do?"

"Nina and I went out to the graveyard yesterday to deal with the Dead Eyes thing," I said.

As soon as Nina's name crossed my tongue, something in her expression changed. It went from concerned to suspicious in a split second. "Since when do you get your ass kicked by ghosts? I thought it was all go into the light sort of stuff."

I grimaced. "Not this time. There's something really angry out there."

"And you're the best person to deal with it?" she said.

"What are you saying?"

"I'm not saying you can't," she said. "But it seems kind of screwed up that a seventeen-year-old girl is trying to take on a pissed-off ghost."

After my argument with Kale the previous evening, I definitely agreed. "Kale's trying to find out what to do."

She gave me a stern look. "B, you need to be careful. You don't have to solve all the world's problems."

I sighed. "I don't want to, believe me. This one kind of got dumped in my lap. What am I supposed to do?"

Her brow furrowed. "Are you blaming me?"

"Huh?"

"Well, I sent you the videos," she said. "So are you blaming me?"

"Emily, really?" My voice was more heated than I'd intended. "I didn't say that."

She shook her head. "Sorry. I guess I'm just worried."

"It's okay," I said. "If anything, I'm glad you did. People are getting hurt, and I wouldn't have known to look for the connection if you didn't tell me."

I had hoped my words would be a healing balm to the rift between us, and we'd have one of those sappy sitcom moments where everything was magically right between us. Cue the happy music and knowing smiles.

Unfortunately, things didn't go that way. I did get a faint, purple-glossed smile, but it was fleeting.

As we walked into school, she checked her phone and asked, "So are you and Nina hanging out again today?" Her casual tone faltered when she said *Nina.*

"Actually, no," I said. "Do you want to ride home together?"

She shrugged. "I guess."

That same uneasy tension hung between us all the way to school, like a thick cloud of steam. There were so many bigger things on my plate, but I didn't want to be at odds with all my friends. I didn't have many to begin with.

As I walked into the school, I kept my head down and headed for homeroom. During the morning announcements, I texted Nina under my desk.

Lots of research on sara last night. Doesn't seem like she was angry

I didn't get a response right away. When I reached the science hall and walked up to Mrs. England's door, I found a hand-written sign directing us to the computer lab on the math wing. The detour made me a minute late, but the door was still open when I arrived. Glancing behind me, I saw half a dozen other students meandering toward the computer lab.

Inside the lab was an unfamiliar teacher wearing a *Substitute* badge on a lanyard around her neck. The blonde-haired woman wrote instructions on the whiteboard in neat red letters that reminded me of a kindergarten teacher's precise handwriting. According to the board, her name was Miss Mead, and we were to watch review videos and take notes about balancing equations.

While I hoped Mrs. England wasn't deathly ill, I couldn't have been happier that she was gone. A class period at the computer was a welcome break, and the math lab was perfect. Set up with short rows that faced the board and the teacher's desk in the front corner, it was easy to do some side work without getting busted.

I hurried toward a seat in the back, right against the wall. As I put my binder down next to the keyboard, Bryce headed my way. Heat rose from my chest and up my neck.

"That's my seat," he said, standing in front of me. He folded his arms across his chest, and I was reminded of a cat arching its back and turning sideways to look bigger and scarier.

I squared off with a ghost with a vendetta last night. You're nothing.

"I got here first."

"Don't be a loser," he said. "Just move."

"Get here faster next time," I snapped.

His incredulous sneer lingered as I sank into the seat, but I ignored him. He went to the next row and sat at the computer directly in front of mine. I scanned the instructions on the board. We would have a quiz when Mrs. England returned, but there was nothing about turning the notes in.

I set my phone next to the keyboard. With the substitute all the way at the front, she couldn't see the phone. Nina had responded.

Nina: I'll send Ethan to talk to you, got a test next period

"Yes, sir?" the substitute said.

I looked up to see Bryce with his hand in the air. "Miss Mead? Are we allowed to have our phones out?"

Oh, you enormous tool.

Miss Mead frowned. "No, sir," she said. "Mrs. England left that in her notes."

Bryce turned to me. "Yeah, Bridget. Put your phone away."

The sub looked back at me. She looked like she was barely older than me, but her sleek bun seemed to be an attempt to make her appear older and more stern. "Are you texting?"

"No, ma'am," I lied. I hid the phone under my binder and glared at Bryce. He shot me a nasty smile and turned back to his computer.

After considering my options, I realized I wouldn't find much more about Sara and the boys than I'd already found. I wanted to find out where to buy some of the herbs I'd read about, but it wasn't like I could shop right now. So I decided to actually do the assignment.

My screen went dark three minutes into the first video. I frowned, checked the power switch, then stared at the dark screen blankly. Bryce's shoulders shook with silent laughter as he whispered to the guy next to him. I stood up and peered over the edge of my monitor. The power cord dangled from the back of the monitor. jammed it back into place, bringing my screen back to life.

A cool breeze blew across my hands. I looked up and jumped in surprise. Ethan stood next to me, directly between me and the quiet girl to my left.

"Nina sent me. She has a test," he said in his deep, flat voice. "She found out that Sara Workman was married before she died. To Jeff Hillman. He still lives in the area. She has his phone number."

I nodded at him, not speaking. He looked at me expectantly. I sighed, then opened a new Word document. I typed *anything else?* in an oversized font.

"She had to study last night," he said. "That was all she found."

I stared at him blankly. She had to study? So I stayed up all night and guarded my damn house with vinegar, and she took the night off to study? I was shocked at how quickly my temper flared again. It had to be the exhaustion talking.

Suddenly my screen went dark again. I rolled my eyes and turned forward again.

"Seriously?" I whispered. I stood up and looked over the edge of the monitor, but the cables were all in place.

"He pulled the plug," Ethan said. "From the wall."

Planting my hand against the cool cinderblock, I leaned over and found the plug pulled out of the socket.

"Stop," I hissed. I pushed the plug back in and got the *Would you like to start in safe mode?* message.

"Miss Mead?" Bryce said. "Could you please ask Bridget to stop distracting me? I'm trying to focus on my notes and she's talking."

"He unplugged my computer," I said.

"No I didn't. She bumped it with her chair," Bryce replied.

"Enough. Both of you, please keep quiet and do your work. People are trying to learn," Miss Mead said. "I will assign you detention if you continue to be disruptive."

I was going to kill him. While I waited for my browser to start again, I looked over my screen to see Bryce looking up videos on YouTube. He'd gotten around the school's filter somehow, because there was a whole lot of barely-clad booty bouncing on his screen.

"Would you like me to handle it?" Ethan said.

I turned to him and stared quizzically. How exactly was he going to handle Bryce?

Unlike many of the spirits I encountered, Ethan didn't always bother with putting on appearances of being alive. He passed right through the furniture and crept up behind Bryce. As he did, Bryce shivered, pulling down the sleeves of his hoodie to cover his thick forearms. Ethan put his hand on the computer tower. The screen wavered, and then a loud squall of music broke the silence in the lab.

"Y'all know I like that ass fat," Bryce's computer blasted. Everyone in the lab froze as Bryce fumbled at the volume, then yanked one of his earbuds out. He threw up his hands, as if trying to express his anguish over the betrayal of technology.

Laughter broke out among my classmates as the song continued lauding the virtues of big butts, with plenty of descriptive profanity. The substitute launched herself out of the seat and headed our way. At first her eyes were on me, but I shook my head.

She hurried down the aisle. "Young man, that is completely inappropriate! What is your name?"

"It's not my fault," he spluttered. "It was a pop-up."

"Name!"

"Bryce Holloway," he muttered.

"You can expect a detention, young man."

Suddenly, I liked Ethan a whole lot better.

The lack of sleep caught up with me by lunchtime. Even with the dull roar of the lunchroom, I was pretty sure I could lay my head on the table and be asleep in seconds. Maybe I could lobby for the school to serve espresso along with the milk cartons in the line.

Emily hadn't arrived at the table, so I took out my notebook and ran through a mental agenda of what I needed to do. A lot of my hope depended on Kale having answers when he came back from his meeting.

The table shifted, and I looked up with a smile, ready to greet Emily. Instead, it was Bryce and two boys I didn't recognize.

"Are you lost?" I asked calmly.

"Whatcha working on?" Bryce asked.

He snatched my notebook before I could react. The spiral rings scraped against my palms as he pulled it away. My heart thumped. "Give it back."

He twisted in the seat to keep it away from me. "Protection stuff? Asphodel, dandelion, holly," he read, his pockmarked brow furrowing. "What the hell is this? Are you into witchcraft or something?"

"It's none of your business," I said. "Give it back."

He folded one thick arm over his chest, trapping my notebook against his body. With his other hand, he pulled out his phone. "I'll make a trade," he said. "You do the Dead Eyes thing, and I'll give it back."

The notebook in his arms held my entire ghost-whispering life. It was more personal than a diary, more thorough than any project I'd done for school. Not to mention, it would make me look crazy as hell if they opened it and read it. And this pile of human garbage was taunting me with it.

"Just give it back," I said, tempering my voice. Why couldn't our angry spirit show up and mess with Bryce instead of me? "Please."

"Do it," he said, holding up his phone. "Whenever you're ready."

"Why are you so obsessed with me doing this?"

"Come on, it's just a stupid video," he said. "Quit being such a freak."

I glared at the case in his hand, my eyes meeting the tiny glass lens. Suddenly, the roiling storm inside me stilled. I knew what I had to do. Playing nice hadn't worked. Now it was time for a different tactic.

"You win," I said. "Are you recording?"

"Yep," he said, not looking away from the phone.

I stood up, then tossed my hair back over my shoulder. With a heavy sigh, I mumbled, "Restless spirit, come to me." His chapped lips widened into a nasty smile. I darted forward, ninja-quick, and snatched the phone clean out of his hand. "Give me back my notebook," I said as he stared at me with his eyes wide in shock.

"Bitch, you better give me back my phone," he said.

"Notebook."

He sneered and slung the notebook across the table. Several folded sheets of paper fell out and fluttered to the ground. I bent down and shoved the notebook into my backpack roughly.

"What the hell is your problem? You can't take a joke," he said. "Guess the crazy never went away. Maybe you should get that checked out."

The smug look on his face put the last bit of pressure on the thin fiber that remained of my composure. I'd planned to hand the phone back, but he'd pushed me too far now. I grabbed my backpack so he couldn't mess with it and slung it onto my shoulder.

"You're my problem. You're an asshole," I said, holding his phone hostage behind my back. "I've literally never done anything to you, but for some reason, you won't leave me alone."

"Because—"

"Shut your stupid mouth," I snapped. His eyes went wide. "You wanna know why I won't do that stupid video? Because my sister died. Because

Natalie Fullmer died. Because I'm not a piece of garbage, and I'm not going to go stand in a graveyard where people's loved ones are buried to make a stupid video so other stupid people will like me."

"It's not that serious."

"Oh yeah? How about this?" I said, my voice rising. "You watch one of your friends die in front of you, and then see how funny you think that crap is."

"Jesus," he muttered. "Give me back my phone, psycho."

Psycho? You asked for it.

Instead of handing it over, I turned on my heel and marched toward the disposal where we dumped our trays. My hands shook from the sheer adrenaline coursing through my veins. I knew I needed to let it go. I just couldn't. Not anymore.

A hush fell over the tables in my wake. Bryce yelled after me as he tried to keep up. His fat hand brushed against my backpack, but I kept going.

"Don't you dare," he yelled.

Between the dish window and the exit for the lunch line was a big ice-filled tub, where students who didn't want the milk that came with lunch could leave it for students who wanted extra. Half-melted ice bobbed in a good eight inches of dingy water.

"Bridget—"

"Screw you and your video," I said without looking back. I held the phone high for dramatic effect and dropped it into the ice water. Cold droplets splashed onto my hands. Then I turned to face him, blocking the bin with my body. "What are you going to do?"

The look of shock on his face was almost as good as the one Allie Williams had worn when I punched her in ninth grade. "You bitch," he breathed.

"Maybe next time you'll listen when I tell you to leave me the hell alone," I said, narrowing my eyes.

He took a tentative step toward me, his fist clenching at his side. The way his eyes narrowed, his jaw set; I knew he wanted to hit me. Instead he grabbed my arm and pulled me out of the way. He stuck his hand into the ice and grabbed the phone, then jogged toward the office, which was on the opposite side of the lunchroom.

Shit.

With my heart still pounding, I slunk back toward my table with the weight of hundreds of eyes following me. Heat bloomed in my cheeks as the scared little part of me, freshman Bridget who'd been wrecked by Valerie's death and the ensuing social chaos, started wailing in the corner of my mind. We were right back to freshman year, with people staring and talking.

But by the time I reached my usual seat, the noise had returned to normal as people resumed their conversations. Emily had since arrived, and she was staring at me like she had when I told her for the first time that I saw ghosts. The look made me squirm as I sat down across from her.

"Uh…what the hell was that?" she asked incredulously.

"I had enough of him," I replied.

My foot slipped on a piece of paper as I settled into the seat. I looked under the table to find a printout of an article I'd found for another ghost case a few weeks ago. Reddish taco meat was squished into the paper. The sight of the greasy stain made me angry all over again.

Not to mention the look on Emily's face. I'd have expected her to be applauding, not staring at me like I'd grown an extra cranium. I jammed the paper into my backpack.

"Is everything okay?" she asked.

"No, it's not," I said. "I'm trying to do the right thing and everyone is giving me crap about it."

Emily frowned, laying down half of her sandwich and fiddling with the curled ends of her hair. "Do you want to talk about it? I kind of feel like you're shutting me out."

"I'm not." She recoiled, and I realized my voice had come out hot and acidic.

"Okay," she said sharply. "Look, I know I'm not special like you and Nina. But I'm still your friend. You don't have to be mean."

"I'm not being mean!" Couldn't I just get a break from my best friend?

She glared at me. "I'm trying to help you, and you're yelling at me."

"What do you mean, I'm not acting like myself? This is me. And I'm not yelling."

"We used to talk and text every single day, and I've barely heard from you since you met her," she said.

"Emily, I've got a ghost that's doing its best to kill people. That's more a little more important right now." Her dark-lined eyes went wide as she recoiled. My stomach sank as my own words echoed in my head. "I'm not saying you're not—"

"No, I get what you're saying. Loud and clear," she said. She forced a smile that cut through my anger and found that tender place that knew I was wrong. "Sorry I brought it up."

"No, that's not—"

"Miss Young?"

The deep male voice sent dread squirming into my belly. I turned to see Mr. Macklin, one of the assistant principals, standing beside me. His thick arms and huge chest strained against his embroidered polo shirt, making him look like a wrestler masquerading as a school official.

"Yes, sir?" I said, trying to soften the edge that had crept into my tone.

"I need to see you in my office," he said politely. "You can bring your lunch."

Emily stared down at her lunch as I got up. It felt like everyone was staring, but I didn't look back as I followed Mr. Macklin into the office. Inside, Bryce sat in a leather chair with a wad of paper towels in one hand and his phone in the other. He scowled at me as I passed.

With my heart pounding and hands trembling, I walked into Mr. Macklin's office. The lights were off, blinds open to let in the soothing natural light. The blue walls were mostly bare, except for a framed college diploma and a collage of pictures of a baby with ridiculously fat but adorable cheeks. Standing next to the computer was another picture of Mr. Macklin, his wife, and the baby with pink icing all over her face.

"Cute baby," I said, trying to sound casual. Maybe he would lecture me and let me off with a warning.

His lips twitched into a smile for a second, then smoothed again as he put on his serious face. He gestured to the chair across the desk. "Sit down, please."

I usually stayed out of trouble. The only other time I'd been written up was when I'd punched Allie in ninth grade. Back then, they'd still been giving me special treatment because of my sister's death. After telling them what Allie had been saying, and Mom telling them about the medication I'd supposedly been taking, they'd resolved the issue with counseling and a stern warning about handling my problems appropriately.

Mr. Macklin was hard to read, so I couldn't tell if he was angry or wearing an all-purpose stern expression. I knew what my file would say—average to poor student, no one special. Maybe a note about being associated with Emily King's abduction.

I waited for him to start lecturing, but instead he handed me a piece of paper. Block letters read *Incident Report* across the top, and the rest of the paper was covered in blank lines. "I want you to write a statement about what happened."

"A statement?"

"Stick to the facts," he said. He gestured to a cup of pens and pencils on his desk. "Do you need a pen?"

I sighed. "No, sir."

I took a purple pen out of my bag and bent my head down to write. I couldn't tell him about Charlene and the Hillmans and being so sleep-deprived that I was about to have a nervous breakdown.

Bryce has been bothering me in class and in the halls for a few days. Today he took my personal journal and wouldn't give it back unless I said something inappropriate on video. I took his phone to make him give me back the notebook.

I paused, the tip of the pen hovering over the paper. Was I ballsy enough to say *yeah, I did it, and I'm not sorry?* Cause I wasn't. Even if they said I could avoid the consequences by apologizing to him, it'd be a hard choice. Bryce was lucky that a wet phone was the worst thing that had happened to him.

This was stupid. I handed the paper back. Mr. Macklin scanned it, then gave me a stern look over the edge of the paper. "That's all? I think you left something out." He handed it back.

I sighed and added: *He said I was crazy and I dropped his phone in the water.*

He read it again, then steepled his hands and looked at me. "So what happened?"

"I…" I gestured to the paper. "That."

"You don't come here often," he said gently. "What really happened?"

"Bryce has been bothering me for days."

"I'm not asking about Bryce," he said. "I'm asking about you."

"Well, considering the circumstances, you can't not ask about him," I said. "He is the one who came up and told on me, right?"

Mr. Macklin's eyebrows went up.

Rein it in. Don't make it worse. I rubbed my sweaty palms against the legs of my jeans.

He set aside my statement and held up another one. With the sunlight shining from behind, I could see an entire page filled with blue ink. Good Lord. For someone who couldn't do his chemistry homework, he'd gone all in to get me in trouble.

"According to Bryce, you've been harassing him over the last few days. He indicated that he felt bullied and threatened by your behavior. It says you threatened him in the hall, among other things. He also claims you called him some very inappropriate names, such as an 'a-hole' and a jerk."

I barked a laugh. "Are you kidding me?"

Mr. Macklin lowered the paper. His expression was stern. "This is very serious."

I clenched my hand into a fist under my bag where he couldn't see. "He's been harassing me," I said. "He keeps trying to copy my homework and take my stuff. Every chance he gets, he messes with me. Literally this morning in the computer lab he was pulling out my cords so I couldn't do my work. I mean, that's tampering with school computers, right?"

Mr. Macklin regarded me, then glanced toward the door like he was trying to read Bryce's mind from down the hall. "Did you inform the teacher?"

I went silent. "Yes, and she yelled at both of us for being disruptive even though I didn't do anything wrong."

He sighed. "And what's this about a video?"

"He was trying to make me say that Dead Eyes thing on video," I said. A brilliant idea struck me. "It's this stupid viral thing, kind of like Bloody Mary. He wanted me to say it, but it bothers me. Because of what happened to my sister."

At the mention of *sister*, his expression faltered. Then he shook his head. "Believe me, I'm very sympathetic to your loss, but I think the time has passed where you can use that as an excuse."

My jaw dropped. "I'm not." Yeah, I kind of was. "But can't you understand why I'd be upset that he keeps saying crap about dead spirits and graves to me?"

He sighed. "I understand why you find it upsetting, but that still doesn't give you a right to destroy his property." He shook his head, then turned to his computer screen. "I'm going to have to give you a day of in-school suspension."

At the mere mention, my determination to keep myself in check went right out the window. "Seriously?"

"Sweetheart, it's the rules," he said. "You destroyed his property."

"Fine," I said. "Then I want to write a report too. He grabbed me and called me a bitch. I feel both physically and verbally threatened."

"And you can certainly do that," he said, face reddening at my use of profanity. "And it will be dealt with, I assure you."

I sat back in the chair, seething as his fingers flew across the keyboard. The dark thought crossed my mind, to wipe off the caked-on makeup around my eye and tell him a tearful story about Bryce cornering me and punching me. My ability had forced me to get good at lying. I could sell the story, and Bryce was enough of a jerk to deserve it. But I did my best to stay on the right side of that line, even if my line sank into an ever-blurring gray area.

Well, at least I wouldn't have to worry about Sara or her sons anymore, because Mom was going to murder me. So much for all my brownie points over the last few days. Maybe I could avoid telling her. In-school suspension just meant I had to go sit in a room at the far end of the science hallway and work silently all day. It wasn't the end of the world.

After another minute or two of typing and clicking through menus, he pushed back from the computer. The printer whirred to life and spit out a sheet of paper. He handed the paper to me, then picked up his phone. After consulting the screen, he dialed. Each keystroke was like a nail in the coffin.

While he was waiting for it to ring, he nestled the phone against his shoulder and said, "Read it and sign, please." He smiled. "Hi, Mrs. Young? This is Ray Macklin from Fox Lake High School." His voice was more animated, warm as he talked to my mother. My heart sank. "No ma'am, she's fine. We had a little incident that resulted in an office referral. Uh-huh."

As he told Mom about me dumping the phone in the water, I started picturing my life for the next few days. It was going to be back to the Stone Age for me, because she'd take my phone and my laptop. As I pictured her taking everything, I instantly remembered Valerie's old computer, tucked away in my closet.

"Bridget?"

I was startled by the sound of my own name. "Huh?"

"Your mother wants to speak to you."

My mouth went dry as I held my hand out for the phone. "Yes?"

"I am so disappointed in your behavior." What else was new? "I don't know what's going on with you, but we are going to have a serious talk when I get home. You are not to go anywhere after school. You go straight home. Do you understand me?"

"Yes," I said flatly. She'd ground me, and it would be hard to stop rampaging spirits from the confines of my room. I'd snuck out at night before, and I might have to do it again. The last thing I wanted to do was deal with two unhinged spirits in the middle of the night in a graveyard, but my mother might leave me no choice.

Fantastic.

CHAPTER TWENTY

AFTER MY MOTHER FINISHED scolding me, Mr. Macklin sent me for an awkward session with one of the guidance counselors who'd obviously been interrupted from the stack of files on her desk. After promising I'd let them know in the future instead of taking matters—or people's phones—into my own hands, I went to the library to work for the rest of the afternoon so Bryce and I didn't get into it again in history class.

Finally, the last bell rang, and I hurried to the student parking lot where Emily was waiting for me. "Well?" she asked.

"I got a day of in-school," I said as I handed her the slip. Despite her bluster, Emily had never gotten in any real trouble. She'd gotten plenty of detentions for being tardy to class and the occasional dress code violation, but I'd officially surpassed her in the Bad Girls Club.

After she got into the car and cranked the ignition, she read it. She handed it back and said grimly, "Your mom is going to kill you."

"Yep."

As soon as I got home, I dashed upstairs to check the hall closet for Valerie's computer. Still in its monogrammed bag with the bright green initials, it was a reminder of all the lost time and lost potential. She'd gotten it a few weeks before she died, and it had gone into a closet, virtually untouched after the accident. Mom had apparently forgotten about it. I'd used it to talk to Natalie, back when I couldn't speak openly to the spirits and relied on their interference with electronic devices.

After checking that the power cord was still in the bag, I stashed it on the top shelf of my closet and arranged a dusty quilt over it. Then I took out my laptop and phone, cleared the browser history on both devices, and took them downstairs to wait my inevitable doom at Mom's hands. In the time since I'd gotten home, Colin had gotten off the bus and started playing games with his friends. With the oversized headset over his ears, he didn't even notice when I came in and flopped onto the couch opposite him.

Mom got home an hour early, making me glad I'd hurried to erase my electronic tracks. The anticipation of yelling at me must have been too much to resist. The car door slammed, and a minute later, she stormed into the house. Her keys clattered across the counter. "Bridget?"

"In here," I said.

She entered the room, then dropped her tote bag on the floor next to the couch and crossed her arms. My pulse quickened as she glared down at me.

Colin paused his game and looked up at her, moving one side of headset so he could hear. "You're home early."

"I need to speak to your sister. Go upstairs and do your homework."

"I already did it."

"Then go up and read for a while," she said.

"Mom—"

"Colin!"

He sighed and resumed the game. "Sorry guys, I gotta go. No. Probably tomorrow." Glaring at me the whole time, he shut the game down and took off his headset. On his way upstairs, he threw an irritated glance at me.

Silence, thick and uncomfortable, settled over the living room. Mom maintained an even stare as she sat on the couch. She almost looked disappointed that I didn't start explaining myself so she could jump in. She would have to break the ice.

When I didn't crack, she finally said, "What the heck is going on with you lately?"

"This guy wouldn't quit bothering me," I said. "I told you about him the other day."

"The one from the library? What do you mean?"

"Stupid stuff," I said. "Trying to copy my homework, taking my stuff. We were supposed to be doing a project, and he kept watching these dumb Dead Eyes videos."

She sighed. "I told you to just ignore him. You don't have to let it get to you."

"I tried," I said. "So he just did more and more until he got a reaction. I told you ignoring him wouldn't work."

"But you can't let people like that win, sweetie."

"And I'm not going to let him walk on me, either," I said. "I don't care. I'll do the suspension. And I bet he'll leave me alone now."

"That is not how we solve our problems," she said sharply. As if *we* were a team all of a sudden. The unspoken rule of the Young household was that we never discussed problems. Everything could be solved by ignoring it until it went away. "I've been thinking, and I want you to start seeing Dr. Rankin again."

"No." I'd seen the therapist for a while after Valerie died because of my 'difficulty adjusting.' Considering my problem was seeing dead people, there wasn't a whole lot he could do to help.

She froze, her mouth hanging open. "I'm not—It's not…"

"You're welcome to drop me off at his office," I said evenly. "But I'm not talking to him. So you'll just be wasting your money. If it'll make you feel better, give me the eighty-five bucks every week and I'll watch Dr. Phil here on the couch."

"Bridget! Where is this attitude coming from?"

To my surprise, tears pricked my eyes. Why couldn't people leave me alone? Why was doing the right thing so hard lately? And why couldn't I be a normal person who spent her evenings taking dumb selfies instead of trying to find local sellers of obscure herbs to protect my house from angry spirits?

"Are we done?" I said, blinking back the tears of frustration.

She looked like I'd slapped her. "Honey, I want you to talk to me. Something's going on with you, and I want to help, but you won't let me."

"I do talk to you. I told you I was trying to get my grades up, and you put me in more school. I told you Bryce was giving me a hard time, and you told me to ignore it."

"But—"

"Just leave me alone. That's how you can help me," I said. "I want everyone to leave me the hell alone."

The shocked expression on her face turned to anger. "You want to be left alone? Fine." Her eyes narrowed. "You're grounded for the next two weeks. I want your phone and your laptop. Maybe you can use your alone time to get your grades up and think about better choices."

"Great." I made a sweeping gesture to the laptop and phone stacked on the couch next to me. "I called it. They're all yours. Can I go now?"

She sucked a sharp breath through her teeth. "Please do."

I hadn't even made it halfway up the stairs before the tears started streaming down my face. Something invaded me, squirming down my throat and burying hot roots into my belly. I didn't know if I was more angry at her, myself, or the whole damn world for being so unfair. Colin poked his head out the door, then darted back inside as I passed. I slammed the door and paced across my purple rug.

As if he'd sensed the perfect opportunity to pile more on the garbage heap that this day had become, Kale appeared near the window. "What's wrong?"

"Everything," I said. There was a gentle breeze as Kale drew near. "What did you find out?"

He hesitated. "You probably don't want to know."

"Can we not?" I snapped. "Just tell me."

"First tell me why you're so upset," he said. "Are you still angry with me?"

"Yes. I don't know," I said. "It's everything. Everything's wrong."

"Do you want to talk about it?"

"Not really." I wanted to be righteously angry with him. I wanted to tell him to get the hell out. But he was my lifeline, even if I was still pissed. So I told him about my crappy day, right up to my argument with Mom.

His face creased with concern. "I'm sorry all that happened."

I tilted my head. "Huh?"

"What?"

"I expected you to tell me I should have handled it better," I said. "I should have ignored Bryce, and I should played nice with Mom. I have to be a mature person so I can uphold my duty and all that."

He shrugged. "Maybe, but sometimes our emotions get the best of us," he said. "And you're under a lot of stress."

"Why are you being so understanding? You're warming me up for bad news, aren't you?"

He hesitated again. "I spoke to the other Guardian. He told me he would call in a sensitive from Atlanta who's dealt with a similar issue. A very angry spirit that didn't respond to his attempts to calm it."

My stomach plunged. "And?"

"What I feared," he said, a shadow passing over his face. "They did a binding. They confined it to a secluded area so it couldn't venture away to hurt anyone."

"And they went back and fixed things, right?" I asked, fearing his answer. His long pause was all the answer I needed. "Kale, I can't do that." I'd never hurt a spirit, not even the ones who'd lashed out at me. I'd protected myself with holy water if I had to, but in the end I'd helped them. This would hurt them, trapping them alone with nothing but their own anguish.

"It may be the only way to protect the living," he said. "I don't want you to do it. He'll do it so you don't have to."

"That doesn't make it better. What if someone did that to you?" I said. He flinched, his lips moving silently. Realization dawned on me. "Did someone do that to you?"

"I...that's..." He let out a sigh. I'd never seen him get tongue-tied, so I knew I was onto something. "I know it's distasteful, but you have to consider the people who could be hurt or killed if we allow this spirit to remain unbound."

"Kale, please don't change the subject."

"Do you want to deal with this or not?" he said harshly. The temperature dipped, and goosebumps broke across my arms. "Or would you rather keep flinging yourself at it until something works or it kills you?"

My mouth was still hanging open, my cheeks burning with anger and embarrassment at his sharp tone, when my bedroom door swung open. Mom stood in the doorway, her face set in a stony expression. She held out a plastic bag from Walmart. I trudged toward her and took it.

"What's this?" I peeked inside to see a sliced open clamshell package with a cheap prepaid phone inside. "Seriously?"

"I put my numbers in it already," she said. "For the next two weeks, you are to come home immediately after school. Do you understand?"

My face burned, and I held the bag for a long time before responding. There was a part of me that wanted to shout at her, and throw the phone back in her face.

From behind me, Kale said sternly, "Smile and agree. This time I'm telling you to be mature."

"I understand," I said, spitting the words out like shards of glass. She looked at me expectantly, but I just stared back without flinching.

"I don't know what to do with you," she said, shaking her head.

I stared back at her, holding back the biting response on the tip of my tongue. Finally, she left, closing the door behind her.

With a heavy sigh, I flopped back onto my bed. Going horizontal reminded me that I had barely slept in days. I felt like I was filled with sand, sinking through the mattress as exhaustion weighed me down. The soothing refuge of my room felt like a prison. "Everything sucks."

"I understand the sentiment," he said. "But I need an answer. Either you do it, or someone else does. That's the risk of involving them."

I reluctantly sat up, resting my elbow on my knees and staring at him. "Tell me your deal."

"It's irrelevant."

"Please stop dodging my questions for once. You think you're helping, but you're making it harder," I said. He recoiled from the heat in my tone. "I saw how you reacted. Did you bind someone? Or…did they bind you?"

To my surprise, he drifted toward me and reappeared sitting backwards in my desk chair, his arms folded across the back. "I don't want you to think of me differently."

"I won't."

He tilted his head. "Bridget. I'm centuries old. I know that's not true."

The thought of it made me pause. What was it that he was worried about? Part of me wanted to stop, to let him remain my quasi-angelic and infuriating dreamboat of a Guardian, but I was consumed by curiosity. "Please tell me."

"Okay," he said. "But you're going to have to make a decision afterward. What I choose to tell you is my decision. You don't get to pry for details. My past is mine to tell, and you're not entitled to it simply because you're curious. And for the record, you don't get to be self-righteous about lying with anyone. We've both done what we had to."

"Okay." My throat went dry as his harsh words sank into me like bruising fists.

He hesitated, staring at the ceiling for a long stretch. If he was alive, he'd have taken a deep breath. Finally, he looked down, his blue eyes fixed on me.

"I was human once. You always ask if I'm an angel. I'm not," he said. "I was human like you once. And then I died. Quite violently." My chest ached to think of something bad happening to Kale. The question was on my lips, but I remembered his terms. "I lingered in my ancestral home. I was angry, and it didn't take long for me to turn."

"To turn?"

"I was like Natalie when you first met her, like this spirit you've been facing," he said. "Honestly, much worse." He looked away from me, shame pulling his eyes down to the floor. "I caused a great deal of harm. My despair drove people away from my home, believing it to be cursed and haunted. Many years passed. By the time they came for me, I was barely a wisp of a person."

"Who came for you?"

His shoulders slumped. I'd never seen him look so resigned. "Someone like you," he said to the floor. "They attempted to reason with me, but I was too far gone. Every word sounded like curses and lies. Even kind gestures sent me into a rage. So they performed a binding to seal me in my family's home, long since abandoned to the 'demon' that lived there."

"Oh, my God," I murmured.

"I lost track of time, of myself. It was like being trapped in a glass cage deep underwater. Cold, alone, and silent." He finally looked up at me, and though he was looking my direction, his gaze was far away, and his mind was somewhere distant. "But looking back, it was the only way. Had they not bound me, I would have gone on as I was, harming anyone who came near."

"What did you do?"

He raised an eyebrow. "What did I say about asking questions?"

I swallowed hard. "So how are you here, then?"

"That's a story for another day," he said. "I know you better than you think I do. I know that you don't want to hurt anyone, and that you'd rather take the blow yourself than cause harm to someone innocent. But I can tell you that binding may be the only way to prevent others from getting hurt. Living people. Trust me when I say I would not wish that fate on anyone, but it appears to be the only choice left."

236

"But…"

I lost my words, my tongue thick and useless in my mouth as I stared at Kale. I'd always known there was more to Kale than the pretty face and the vague hints. But though he'd always been adamant that he wasn't an angel, I'd harbored the notion that he was something pretty darn close. Now he was telling me he was basically a lucky promotion away from being one of the angry spirits I dealt with on the regular.

He winced, his lips pulling into a tense smile while his eyes were still wide and haunted. "That's why I didn't want to tell you. That look on your face. I'm not what you thought I was. I wish I was."

"I…I'm sorry," I said. "I'm just trying to process it. I'm sorry all of that happened to you."

The tension in his jaw smoothed out. "I know you are. Thank you." Running one hand through his dark hair, he sighed. "I didn't tell you to elicit sympathy, but because it's reality. You want everything to work out, but sometimes you have to do hard things. Now I need to know what you choose. The other sensitive, Marcus, will be here Saturday. If you won't do it, he will."

"Don't we have other options?"

"We've been through this," he said. "You wanted the help of the other Guardians, this is how it comes. They care about the big picture. They know you will continue to endanger yourself, and that other living souls are at risk as long as this spirit goes unchecked. Those are unacceptable risks, so this is their solution."

"What if I can reason with the spirits before then?"

"No," he said. "I forbid it."

"You…you what?"

"You heard me. I forbid it," he said firmly. "All you need to do is stay safe until Marcus arrives."

I nodded, and he gave me a solemn nod in return.

But I still had to try. And I had to believe I would find something. If I could reach them, then everything would be fine. People had gotten hurt, including me. They had threatened my family. That should have made it easy, but it didn't. After all the pain Sara and her sons had been through, I understood why they would lash out. I couldn't bear the thought of sentencing them to even more suffering. What if someone had bound Valerie like they had Kale? I could picture my sister in a tiny cage, pounding uselessly on the bars as she cried for help. The thought tied my stomach into a burning knot of anguish.

One way or another, this ended Saturday. I had four days to stay alive and save a murderous spirit from an even worse fate.

Chapter Twenty-One

MY DELINQUENT DAY got off to a great start. I got up before sunrise and pulled out Valerie's laptop. I had new Facebook messages from Nina, Michael, and Emily. Michael had asked where I was, and Emily asked for an update on what Mom had done. I ignored the messages in favor of Nina's, since it was likely to be about our spirit situation.

Nina: did you get my text?

Nina: I texted you but no answer. I saw this. Her name is Kassie Jarrell. Is she on your list?

She'd sent me a link to a news story from last night. The headline read: *Freak accident at local gymnastics tournament.* A video clip showed a girl in a blue leotard walking to a gymnastics vault. My stomach churned as she began her run. Her feet hit the springboard, then the table simply collapsed under her hands. Her legs flailed overhead, and she ended up in a heap of limbs on the ground. The video shook as coaches and teammates surrounded her. The video cut back to the reporter.

"The young woman was rushed to the hospital, where her condition is reported as good," she said. "Officials said that the equipment may have been faulty, but the hosting gym insists that their equipment is well maintained, and multiple competitors had vaulted before the accident occurred."

I didn't even have to look at the list to recognize Kassie's name.

She's on the list. Mom took my phone. Can you drive me home after school? I have news but I have to go straight home so we can talk then.

Nina: Sure, meet me at the Coke machine

On the way to school, the conversation with Emily was clipped and cool, making it clear that things were not okay between us. It didn't even seem to faze her when I said I was riding home with Nina that afternoon. As soon as we got to the school, she headed in the side door and left me to walk to the front office alone to get my work.

The discipline secretary looked me over with a scowl, then searched through the plastic basket of files. "Young?"

"Yes, ma'am," I said.

"Here's your work," she said, handing me a manila folder. "Make sure you have all your materials, and then report to the classroom. Do you know where to go?"

"Yes, ma'am," I said again, tucking the file under my arm. As I walked down the hall, I scanned my surroundings for any sign of a spirit.

In-school suspension was in a stark white classroom at the end of the science hall. It smelled like eggs and gym socks, and all the desks were turned toward the wall so all we could see was cinderblocks.

My heart thumped as I walked in. The teacher, Mr. Karnes, gave me a skeptical look, then said, "Go find an empty seat."

I hurried to the back corner. The pencil-stained desk was shoved right up against the dingy cinderblock wall. I stowed my books in the rack underneath and sank into the hard seat.

After the morning announcements, Mr. Karnes printed a list from his computer and took the roll. I expected chaos, something like one of those movies about the "bad class" where everyone threw paper and teased the teacher, but everyone stayed in their seats and got to work. Mr. Karnes put on quiet piano music, and other than the occasional sniffle or scraping chair, it was quiet. It was actually nice to work in peace, without Bryce turning around to steal my paper or kicking my desk. Ugh. It still wasn't fair that I was in trouble while he'd gotten off with a detention.

At the end of the day, I met Nina in the commons area. Ethan flanked her, although the stream of students passing around us obviously didn't notice him. "How was it being a bad kid today?"

"It was great," I said. "Nice and quiet."

We walked out of the building side-by-side. "I think it's kind of awesome," Nina said. "People were saying how cool it was that you stood up to Bryce."

I paused. "Really?"

"Yeah, totally," she said. It was a welcome change from Emily and Mom's disapproval. "Okay, so what's your big news?"

"Let's get to the car," I said. Once we were safely inside, I told her about Marcus. "I don't want him to interfere."

"Why? If he can help, I say let him come. Plus, Marcus is a hot name."

I laughed. All of that, and her takeaway was that he was probably hot. "I'm guessing he's older if he's been trained to do this. Kale said there's training for people like us. Do you know anything about that?"

Nina's eyebrows perked as she shook her head. "Nope. I kind of figured it out on my own. Why are you so worried about him coming? If we don't have the power to help, then this is a good thing."

"But he's not really coming to help the spirit. He's going to seal it up so it's not a problem anymore."

Nina hesitated. "And that's bad?"

I gaped at her. "Of course that's bad," I said. "We're supposed to help the spirits."

"Are we?"

I stared at her incredulously. "Yes?" But she was so matter of fact that I couldn't help but question it.

She shrugged. "Honestly, I'm not sure the spirits are the priority. I think we're supposed to do the right thing," she said. "You gotta think big picture, girl. I made a list. Kassie Jarrell's accident makes six that we know about. At what point do you draw the line? They're alive. They deserve a chance."

"Yeah, and the spirits deserve peace," I snapped back. She sounded like Kale. Maybe I was the one who had things backwards.

"I don't like it either," Nina said, putting up her hands in a gesture of surrender. "I'm just saying. Besides, we've exhausted everything we know how to do."

"I don't know," I said. "Maybe when Marcus gets here, we can talk him into helping."

"Maybe," she said. But she didn't seem convinced. It looked more and more like I was going to be alone on Team Ghost. I only hoped I could figure out something in time.

As ordered, I went directly home after school. When Mom got home to pick us up for our classes, I was ready on the couch with my backpack. She barely spoke to me on the ride there. Colin filled the fraught silence with nervous chattering.

Mrs. Zapruder gave us a practice writing assignment. We had to read an essay about the importance of literacy and write our own essay in response. With my head lowered to read the essay, I almost missed the flicker of movement out of the corner of my eye.

Adrenaline jolted through my muscles like lightning. A shadowy figure darted around the room. There was a squeak, then a metallic *ping* from above.

The spirit was clinging to the projector on the ceiling a few feet above my head.

With a cracking sound, the projector broke out of the brackets. I darted out of my seat right as the projector shattered on the desk below. Shards of glass and plastic exploded from it.

The classroom erupted in chaos as people started talking and moving their desks around. I stared in horror at the spot where I'd been sitting, then scanned the room for the spirit. The shadowy figure stood in the doorway, its eyes glowing white from the dark-stained face. When I met its eyes, it tilted its head in recognition. I narrowed my eyes, hoping it got my message.

I see you.

Then it backed away, passing through the door. I made a face and raised my hand. "Mrs. Zapruder, I think I cut my hand. Can I go wash up?"

Mrs. Zapruder looked frazzled as she surveyed the damage. Tendrils of smoke drifted up from the broken projector, and high above, a bundle of wires dangled from the ceiling.

"Go ahead," she said, waving me off.

I snagged my backpack and hurried out toward the door.

"Kale," I said insistently as I stepped out into the dim hallway. Lights flickered outside the classroom, creating a disconcerting strobing effect. He didn't respond. I knew he would want me to stay put. Stay safe.

But I was so close.

Pausing long enough to dig the bottle of holy water and can of salt from my backpack, I pictured the name *Sara Workman* across a plain white surface in my mind. I tried to picture her smiling face from the obituary, reaching out to her mentally the way I did with Sal and Kale. There was no response, but the lights still flickered overhead. I changed tactics, visualizing the older brother, Travis's face. *Travis Hillman.*

This time I connected. Something brushed my mind, like it was reaching for my hand, then thought better of it.

"Travis," I murmured. So it wasn't Sara. It was her son. "It's okay."

Icy cold shot down my spine. My eyes flew open to a dark silhouette further down the hall.

"Go away." His voice was like sandpaper scraping over stone. As I stepped forward, he retreated. "Stop!"

"Travis, I just want to help you," I said. "Please. Is Charlie here, too?"

He didn't answer as he moved away from me. Even as my feet pounded down the hallway, I knew I should go back to the relative safety of the light, of the four walls filled with normal kids.

But I didn't. Some part of me knew if I could just tell Travis I understood, that I cared, that he would listen. He would stop hurting innocent people. He had to. I could do this.

With my heart racing, I ran after the quick-moving spirit. He disappeared around a corner. A plastic sign on the corner pointed the direction to the natatorium. The smell of chlorine was thick in the air as I ran down the glass-windowed hallway along the enclosed swimming pool.

The pool area was empty for the night. "Travis? Charlie?" I said hesitantly. My hands were clammy around the water bottle and the can of salt. "I know what happened to you. I just want to help you rest. It's okay now. You don't have to be afraid of me. I'm on your side."

Travis lingered on the opposite side of the pool. He was much less solid than I'd remembered from our previous encounters. The light glowing from the pool shimmered through his translucent form. He didn't speak.

My heart beat harder. "Look, I want to help you," I said. "But if you won't talk to me, someone is going to come and seal you in. And then you'll be stuck where I can't help you anymore."

"Charlie," he murmured, the syllables long and whispered.

"Is Charlie here too?" I said. "Please. Let me help you."

"Charlie!" he said again, this time urgent.

Then I understood, but it was too late. A foot swept across my ankles, sending me headfirst into the deep end of the pool. The water was warm, but the shock of it made me gasp, sucking a mouthful of water down the wrong way. A vise-like grip tightened around my ponytail and pushed me underwater. I tried to look up, but the chlorine stung my eyes. All I could see was a blurry shadow above me.

Panic threatened to overwhelm me. Pounding heart, burning chest, everything beating like drums. All I could think of was Kale saying *I told you so.*

My fingers scraped the concrete ledge, and I tried to pull myself up. The force on my head was relentless. Spots pulsed in the blackness behind my eyes as my body screamed for oxygen.

Then a miracle happened. The pressure on my head vanished. A hand closed around my flailing arm and yanked me up. My head broke the surface of the water, and I sucked in a ragged breath.

"Bridget!" Nina stood over me, struggling to haul me out of the water. I caught the edge with my elbow and pulled myself clear.

Kneeling on the rough concrete, I coughed violently and spat out a mouthful of chlorinated water. It felt like I would vomit from coughing. My throat and chest burned. Finally, I managed to squeeze out, "Where'd they go?"

"I think the more important question is what the hell you were doing in here."

"One of them tried to take me out with falling office equipment." I coughed again. "I followed Travis here."

"Wait, Travis?" she asked. "Not Sara?"

"It's the boys. I was talking to Travis, trying to reason with him, and he kept saying Charlie. Then something knocked me into the water."

"You think they both stayed?"

"Yeah," I said, my voice still ragged. "I thought he was trying to say he was worried about Charlie or something, but he was talking to Charlie. Telling him to stop. I think Sara moved on, but the kids didn't." Now it made sense. Travis must have been the one who yelled *stop* at the cemetery when Charlie attacked me. I hadn't seen double after all.

"Shit. So they can be in two places at once?"

I nodded. This was exponentially worse than I had expected. And to top it off it, I was soaking wet and had been out of class for way too long. I sighed heavily and got to my feet. I wanted to sit and cry until things magically fixed themselves, but I wasn't a Disney princess, and the real world wouldn't right itself because of my magical tears. "What am I going to do?"

"Um, let this Marcus dude do his job?"

"I mean about this." I wrung out the hem of my shirt, watching water drip to the wet concrete.

"Oh. I have gym clothes in my car," she said. "Come on."

Ten minutes later, I had changed into a wrinkled Myrtle Beach t-shirt and a pair of gym shorts. My shoes and underwear were damp, but it was still a drastic improvement. Nina quickly braided my hair and pinned it up to keep it from soaking through the dry shirt. Improvising with her powder and mascara, we touched up my partially melted makeup. Mom would have questions, but that was nothing new.

"We need to make sure we stay out of their way until Saturday," Nina said. "Promise me you'll be safe. No more going off on your own."

"I will," I said.

"I'm serious. What would have happened if I didn't come find you?"

A shiver wracked my body, as much from her words as the cold. "I know."

Mom was already waiting in the lobby when I got out of class. I was still halfway down the hall when she wrinkled her nose and frowned. When I got to her, she asked, "What are you wearing?"

"There was an accident in class," I said. Not a lie. "The projector fell and I cut my hand." I showed her the cut from the broken glass the other night. "It got on my clothes, so I borrowed gym clothes from Nina."

Please don't notice the wet hair.

Mom sighed heavily. "Make sure you give me the clothes when we get home so I can get some stain remover on it."

"Okay," I said. I looked down at the grocery bag, with the clothes stuck to the surface. "I tried to clean it a little myself but it didn't work."

On the way home, I let Colin sit in the front seat to act as a buffer. "Mom, can Jeremy come over and spend the night tomorrow?"

"Did he ask his parents already?"

"I think so," Colin said.

"I want to talk to his mother or father first, but it's all right with me, honey."

The way she talked to Colin was a stark contrast to the way she spoke to me. It wasn't only the words she used, but her tone was sweeter, and her whole face was more relaxed. She didn't arm up for battle every time she spoke to him.

I missed those days. I hadn't always been an epic pain in her ass. Back when I was a normal kid before Val died, I'd gotten the softer side of Mom, too. We all had. Coincidentally, that was when I didn't have a care in the world except what I was wearing the next day at school.

Life was unfair that way.

Mom stopped for fast food on the way home, which was promising for my chances of eating in my room. But when we pulled into the driveway, Kale was already standing on the porch like an angry dad ready to shout at me for a missed curfew. I ignored him as I picked out my salad from the bag and grabbed my soda, and then took my wet clothes up to the laundry room. When I arrived in my room, he was already waiting.

I didn't even manage to close the door before he went off, his voice dripping with anger. "What did I tell you? Were you even listening?"

"I knew you would do this," I said, calmly sitting at my desk and putting my straw into my drink. "How did you even know?"

"I saw you go after it," he said. "And by the time I realized what you were doing, you were too close for me to do anything."

"You saw?"

"I saw the whole thing," he said. "And I went for Nina like we discussed. I told you—"

"I know what you told me," I interrupted. "I thought I could help."

"You could have gotten hurt," he said. "What if she hadn't gotten to you?"

"I know," I said quietly.

The concern in his voice wore away the sharp edges of anger. He let out a heavy sigh. "Please, let me be your Guardian. You know what the word means, right? It's my job to protect you. Sometimes from yourself."

"Why?"

He froze. "What do you mean?"

"The question is pretty self-explanatory," I said. "Why is it your job? Is it to make up for what you did before they bound you?"

He stared at me, his face shocked as if I had slapped him. "In part," he finally said. He drifted toward me, then knelt so he was almost on eye level with me. "That's how I became a Guardian."

"So if I cause trouble, you don't get your brownie points." I knew it sounded mean, but I didn't understand how he could so easily leave the Hillman boys to the same fate he'd suffered.

He shook his head. "It's not like that."

"What is it like?"

He held out his hands. I hesitated, then let my hands rest over his. As I watched, the color flowed into his translucent form, till he looked almost solid. His fingers closed around mine, the contact sending a warm thrill through me.

He looked up at me, his eyes searching my face. "I chose you. And I know you think I'm difficult, but I do care for you. Sometimes that caring means telling you when you're being foolish so you don't get yourself killed."

Something hid behind his words. I wanted it come out, to show itself. "You care for me?"

"I do," he said. "You're important to me. And that's why I have to protect you. I know I've kept things from you, but I need you to trust me. Leave these spirits alone. Let Marcus handle it when he comes."

"Okay," I said absently. My mind was adrift, caught on that blue gaze.

I withdrew my hand from his, emboldened by the closeness of him. With my hand trembling, I reached out, my fingers hovering a breath away from his cheek. He leaned ever so slightly, pressing his cheek into my touch. I gasped in surprise at the tingle of contact, yanking my hand away. His hand went up to meet mine, bringing it back to his face. As his eyes closed, his glowing pale features took on a rosier color. With my touch, he became solid. Real. Mine.

My mind howled in confusion. What the hell was I doing?

What I've wanted for a long time.

A sharp knock cut through the beautiful chaos. I nearly jumped out of my skin when my mom stuck her head in the door. Panic washed over me, until I remembered that she couldn't see Kale.

Mom's expression was creased in worry. "Your phone has been going off." She held it out. "You're still grounded, but you have a bunch of missed messages from Nina. I thought it might be important."

My stomach plunged through my shoes and into the ground as I accepted the phone. I swiped it open and read through the messages.

Nina: this is nina's dad

Nina: she had a car accident

Nina: she had to have surgery but she wanted me to tell you about it

Nina: you can come visit tomorrow if you want

My throat closed up, and I scrambled around my room to find my shoes. "We have to go." My vision blurred as the tears came, hot and unwelcome. "Nina had an accident."

With my fingers trembling, I called her phone. After three rings, a male voice answered. "Hello?"

"Hi, Mr. Welles?" I said. "This is Bridget. Nina's friend."

"Yeah, I saw." His voice was hoarse and strained by exhaustion.

"I just wanted to check on her," I said. My heart pounded. Was Ethan watching out for her? How much could he really do if the Hillmans showed up? "Is she okay?"

"She's out of surgery now," he said. "She tore up her arm pretty good, but no head injuries, nothing internal. She should be fine."

"Okay," I said. My voice shook, but I kept it together. "Do you think I could come see her?"

He hesitated. "Listen, she's going to be knocked out for a while still. Why don't you check in on her tomorrow after school? Visiting hours go till seven. I'll be here, so just call her phone."

"Yes, sir," I said. "If she wakes up, tell her I said I hope she feels better."

"Thanks," he said. He hung up, and I slowly handed the phone back to Mom.

"What did he say?" Mom asked, her expression frozen in horror.

"She broke her arm and they had to do surgery," I said, sniffling to keep from breaking into a full-on sob. "No head injuries."

Mom let out a shaky sigh. It surprised me that she was so concerned, considering how new our friendship was. "That's good. I'm so glad."

"He said I can come visit tomorrow," I said. "Can I?"

She hesitated. "I'm on call tomorrow. Maybe we can go Saturday."

"She's my friend," I said. "I'm sure Emily will give me a ride."

Mom shook her head. "You're still grounded. You can call her tomorrow, and as long as I don't get called in, I'll run you there myself on Saturday." I started to protest. "End of discussion. It's getting late. You should get to sleep."

It was hard not to laugh. I hadn't been to bed before ten in a long time. "I will."

She closed my door, but I lingered near the doorway and listened to the creaking rhythm of footfalls down the stairs. When I heard the ice dispenser on the refrigerator, I was reasonably satisfied that she was out of earshot. I closed my door and turned back to Kale.

"Well?" I said to him. "What do I do?"

"Nothing," he said. Whatever magical glow had surrounded us minutes before was gone, dissipated like smoke in the aftermath of the news about Nina. His jaw was set in determination, his eyes narrowed. "I'll go check on her and get back to you. I'm sure Ethan will try to protect her."

"Okay," I said.

"Make sure you protect the house," he said. "And then stay put. I mean it."

CHAPTER TWENTY~TWO

AFTER COLIN BRUSHED HIS TEETH in our shared bathroom and closed his bedroom door, I listened for Mom's nightly routine. After rattling around downstairs for a bit, she closed the bedroom door. When her soft snores started, I got back to work.

After checking that there was still vinegar in each of the dishes I'd placed yesterday, I tossed salt into the corners of the living room and along the front and back doors. Finally, I sprinkled holy water at the doors and windows. If I wasn't worried that I'd set off the smoke detector, I would have smudged sage as well. But Mom would definitely notice me burning bundles of pungent herbs through her house.

Once I was done, I retrieved Valerie's laptop from the closet, set it up on my desk next to my bottle of holy water, and got back to work. I found the contact information for the driver who had struck Travis and Charlie. Ashley Crewes, a young mother with a spotless driving record, had hit them. Even though she was found to have no fault in the accident, it might be worth talking to her anyway. Would it take an apology from her for the Hillmans to move on?

In addition to Ashley's info, I found a mention of a high school student named Sam Tucker who'd been quoted in several articles about the incident. He'd also been interviewed in a TV news story the next day. Since then, he'd graduated and gone to UGA, according to my Facebook stalking.

Claiming to have seen the whole thing, Sam was emphatic that the Hillmans had been out in the road, and that it wasn't the driver's fault. But there was something off. In the TV interview, he said, "People were just playing around, and one of them fell down in the street." The newspaper article didn't mention anyone 'playing around,' and said that the boys had been walking down the street together. Maybe it was nothing, but I'd take anything I could find.

I'd received another Facebook message from Michael around midnight.

Hey, just checking on you, hadn't heard from you for a while

Everything ok? Do you need help with something?

I hesitated before I replied. The fact that he'd checked on me spread a goofy smile on my face. If I asked for his help, he'd probably come running. He'd even be excited about it, because he was that nice of a guy. But I wouldn't put a target on him for the Hillmans. I sighed and typed my reply.

Sorry, I got grounded and lost my phone – sneaking my sister's old computer. Everything is cool. Maybe we can hang out when I'm ungrounded? :)

It was nice to think that things might be normal enough soon to hang out with Michael. Even if he wanted to talk about missing people, it would be a welcome change from the stress of dealing with the Hillmans.

Sheer exhaustion overwhelmed me, and I fell asleep at my desk. A sharp ache in my neck woke me up around four, and I flopped into bed to sleep a little longer. After my second alarm, I got dressed and applied makeup over the spreading bruise around my eye.

When I got into Emily's car to ride to school, she took one look at me and said, "You look like crap. No offense."

"None taken," I said. "I've barely slept in days."

She frowned as she backed out of the driveway. "Still the Dead Eyes thing?"

"Yeah," I murmured.

"Can I help?"

"Not really," I said.

"Right," she said. "Because I'm not like you. I get it."

"It's not that. I don't want you to get hurt. They did this to me, and I can see them coming. You can't." I tried to inject a little more enthusiasm into my voice. "Kale found another sensitive from Atlanta that's going to help. He's got it under control."

"Sensitive?"

"That's what he calls us," I said. "I just have to stay out of trouble till then."

"Oh," Emily said, still looking at me skeptically. "Well, I hope that works out."

"If you don't mind, I do need to stock up on supplies," I said. "Could you take me shopping after school? I need some salt and a couple other basics."

"I thought you were grounded," she said, arching her eyebrows.

"We can make it quick," I said. "Mom doesn't have to know."

A mischievous grin pulled at her lips, hinting at the Emily I was used to. "We can go to Target on the way home from school."

Mom could say what she wanted about me making bad choices, but there was something to be said for taking matters into my own hands. In chemistry class, Bryce changed seats and sat two rows away, then gave me a wide berth as I left the room. Most of the morning passed without incident.

When it was time for lunch, I skipped the line and stepped outside with the flip phone Mom had bought me. I sat on the picnic table on a seldom-used patio next to the art room. The garbage can near the door mixed with the kiln vent from the art room, giving this area a particular odor that could kill the appetite in an instant. No one ate here, so it was the perfect spot to have a private conversation.

I dialed Sam Tucker's number.

"Hello?" a male voice said.

My nerves lit up, sending my stomach into a frenetic whirlwind. "Hey, is this Sam Tucker?"

Long pause. "Yes. Who's this?"

"Hi, I'm following up on a story about the young boys who died on Halloween a few years ago in Parkland," I said. "I was wondering if I could ask you some questions."

He hesitated. "Look, it's been a really long time, and I told my story a thousand times to the papers, and the cops, and everyone else. I don't want to talk about it anymore. Please don't—"

"Wait," I interrupted. Crap. What was I going to tell him to keep him on the line? I took the phone away from my ear, then took a deep breath as I put it back. "I'm going to tell you something crazy. Please don't hang up." He was silent. "The Hillmans are ghosts and they're haunting people. There's some reason that they can't pass on, and I need your help to figure out why. I know you were there and you may be the only person who can help me."

White noise filled my ear. I waited for him to tell me I was insane or to hang up. Finally he inhaled sharply and asked, "How did you know about that?"

I was stunned. "What do...wait, you believe me?"

"Who is this?"

"My name is Natalie," I lied. "What do you know?"

"One of the other guys that was there, James Rucker, swore that those kids were haunting him. He told me once that he probably deserved it."

My heart practically skipped out of my chest. "Why?"

"That night, me and James and this other guy Logan were all hanging out at Logan's house. We were just messing with the kids. You know, scaring them when they came up to get candy. So those two kids came up, and the little one got freaked out. He was kinda weird, and he started threatening to use his ninja powers on us and yelling random Japanese stuff. James kept messing with him, saying he's going to eat him and stuff. I took off my mask so he would stop, but then Logan came out of the house carrying a fake body, and the kid lost it. He took off toward the street, and James chased him. Right at the curb, the kid tripped over the bottom of his costume and completely ate it. All his candy went flying, so he was on the ground trying to pick it up. His brother tried to go get him out of the road, and then a car came. Me and the guys yelled and tried to get to them, but Logan's yard was huge. The older kid shoved the little one out of the way but the car still hit both of them. They were both in black, and down on the ground, there was no way the driver could have seen them."

"Oh, my God," I murmured. "Did you tell the police?"

"Of course," he said. "Nobody meant for them to get hurt. My parents told me if anyone asked me to keep the story simple so no one looked bad." So that was why he'd said 'playing around' in the interview. "I held the little one's hand until the ambulance got there. I have a little brother, and I kept thinking it could have been him."

"I'm sorry," I said. "That must have been awful to see."

He was quiet. "We would never have hurt a little kid on purpose. We were just having fun with them. If we'd known…" I heard a distant sniffle, like he'd moved the phone away from his face.

"So why did James think he was haunted?"

"A couple weeks after the accident, weird stuff was happening at his house. Lights going on and off, cold breezes when the heat was on…He swore he heard voices at night. It got bad enough that his parents took him to one of those institutions for a while. They ended up moving up to Atlanta."

"Did it ever happen to you?"

"Maybe," he said. "I always figured it was a dream until James told me what happened to him. One night a few months after it happened, I saw those kids, still wearing those creepy Grim Reaper costumes. They just stood at the end of my bed staring at me, so I told them I was really sorry that we scared them and that I wished I could have got to them in time."

"What did they say?"

"Nothing," he said. "They just disappeared. But it never happened again."

"Did James ever say he was sorry?"

"I don't know," he said. "I haven't really talked to him since he moved away. No one really has."

Then maybe James was the answer. If he'd been the one to scare Charlie into the street, the boys could blame him for what happened. But Sam had apologized years ago, right after the boys died. It had been years, and an apology might fall on deaf ears after this long. "Do you have his information?"

"We're friends on Facebook," he said. "I don't have his number, though. That whole thing really messed him up. Most of the people he knew haven't been in contact with him either."

"Okay," I said. "Thanks, I know it's hard to talk about."

"So are you going to fix it? What are you going to do? Can I come help you?"

"No," I said. "But thanks for your help."

Tucking the flip phone back into my bag, I trudged back into the building and joined Emily at the lunch table. After filling her in on my conversation with Sam, she shook her head. "That's crazy."

"I know, right?" I said.

"But I thought you weren't going to get involved," she said. "That guy Matthe—"

"Marcus."

"Marcus is coming," she said. She raised her eyebrow and gave me an authoritative look that she must have learned in private lessons with my mother. "You are staying out of it, right?"

I swallowed. "Of course," I lied. "I just wanted to find out what I could about the spirits. To make it easier for Marcus. And maybe he won't have to seal them away."

Her brow furrowed as she stared at me. Then she softened. "I can't imagine what those guys feel like," she said. "You remember the year Mom built the haunted house in our garage and we scared all the kids who came through?"

"Yeah," I murmured.

"It was just fun," she said.

"I think that's all it was to them too," I said. "Sometimes things just go bad."

After school, Emily drove me to Target for supplies. With Mom's rule about going straight home, I didn't have long to shop. I also didn't have the luxury of discretionary income. Currently I was operating on a budget of twenty dollars in birthday money from my grandmother. At this rate, I'd have to get creative with sneaking supplies onto Mom's grocery list, or get a real job.

Inside the store, the bright lights and long expanses of white tile were comforting, although a glimpse in the mirror on a sunglasses display showed me that the fluorescents weren't doing my haggard face any favors.

A middle-aged woman in a ballcap nearly walked into me. I quickly side-stepped her and said, "Excuse me."

As I passed her, a cold chill spilled down my back. Under the smell of floor cleaner, I caught a whiff of death, of rotting meat and grave dirt. I snapped my head around to see the woman staring back at me. The hat cast a shadow over her face, but her eyes gleamed dead white from the darkness. Any doubt of what she was evaporated when a woman pushed a buggy overflowing with toddlers and toilet paper right through her.

The spirit woman's lips parted as she took a step toward me.

I shook my head a little. "Not today," I said quietly. "Sorry."

With guilt tugging at my heart, I turned away and hurried toward the grocery section. Winding haphazardly through the aisles, I picked up three cans of salt, a big jug of vinegar, and two boxes of garlic cloves. My shopping list was fragrant, to say the least.

I was perusing the fancy mixes of chocolate bars when I felt a cold breeze on my neck. I tried not to look, hoping she'd go away.

But the breeze intensified right before I heard, "Bridget!" Kale stood next to me, glowing bright. "What are you doing here?"

"I'm getting supplies," I said. I glanced over my shoulder to make sure there was no one on the aisle to hear me talking to thin air.

His wide blue eyes glowed. "Something's happening at your house. I went to make sure that Marcus was still coming tomorrow, and then I went to tell you, but I couldn't get anywhere close." His eyes narrowed as his voice took on a sharp edge. "Did you do something?"

"No!" I hesitated. "Well, I called someone that was there when the Hillmans died."

"Bridget!"

"But I didn't do anything. I didn't summon them or anything. I swear," I protested. I froze, peering around Kale to see a little girl standing at the end of the aisle with a bag of M&Ms in her hand, gaping at me. "Hi."

She raised the bag of M&Ms at me. "Who you talk to?" After the week I'd had, I couldn't tell if she was real or just another spirit.

"My friend," I said. "Where's your mommy?"

"Is your brother home?" Kale asked.

My mouth went dry. I turned back to the little girl, who was toddling off toward a woman balancing a stack of towels on her arm. The toddler grasped her mother's hand, looked back at me, then followed as her mother circled to the next aisle.

I turned back to Kale. "Why would they hurt him? He hasn't done anything."

"I don't know," he said. "Call him."

"I can't, I don't have his number." Mom still had my phone, and I didn't have his cell number memorized. And Mom had gotten rid of the landline when we moved to the new house since we never used it. "Emily has it."

Dread bubbled up in me, turning my guts into churning acid. A dozen scenarios, each progressively more awful, flashed through my mind. Colin with his hand down the garbage disposal. Colin electrocuted by the Xbox.

With my basket bouncing in my hand, I ran down the main aisle of the store and found Emily trying on scarves and preening in the mirror.

"Something's wrong," I blurted. "I need to check on Colin."

Her eyes flew open, and she immediately threw the scarf over the nearest rack and grabbed her purse. "Okay," she said. "Leave your stuff. Let's go."

I hesitated as I looked at my basket. "I may need it." I hurried to the first check out, cutting off the lady I'd seen earlier with the cart full of toilet paper. She made an irritated tsk sound as I cut around her.

Slinging my basket onto the counter, I bounced nervously on the balls of my feet as the cashier slowly scanned each item. "Would you like to save five percent with—"

"No!" I exclaimed as I shoved my twenty dollar bill at her.

Her lips pursed as she counted out my change. Before I'd even picked up my bag, she was greeting the next customer with a pleasant smile.

"It's gonna be okay," Emily said as we hurried out. "He's a smart kid."

"He's helpless. He doesn't know this stuff exists," I said. My hands were sweaty and shaking around the handles of the plastic bag. "Can I use your phone?" She unlocked her phone and handed it over. When Emily had first started driving me around, Mom had made us all exchange numbers. In exchange for the occasional gas gift card, Emily picked Colin up from school if he stayed late for book club.

We jogged across the parking lot and jumped into Emily's car. My call rang four times, then went to Colin's voicemail.

"Nothing?" she said.

"No," I murmured.

"Try again. Text him, too." As she stomped the gas, I quickly typed a text.

It's bridget. Answer your phone. where are you

Kale appeared in the backseat. "Bridget..."

"If you tell me not to go to him, then you can save it," I said. "I know what you said, but this is Colin. Unless Marcus can teleport, then I have to."

Kale sighed. "I know you're going to."

"I won't engage them if I don't have to," I said. "Minimal risk. But he's my brother. If they hurt him, it's gonna be bad."

I tried calling again. As I listened to the long, unanswered rings, my heart raced and my blood roared in my ears. Panic overwhelmed me. It felt like I was detached from my body, watching myself ride in Emily's car.

This was my fault. Colin was in danger, maybe hurt, maybe...

Think. Panicking wouldn't help anyone. "Take me to the house," I said.

"Should we call the police?"

I gave Emily an incredulous look. "And tell them what? That we need the Ghostbusters?" It figured that now I had Fulbright's trust, and he couldn't do a thing to help me.

Emily recoiled from my sharp tone. "I don't know, I'm just thinking out loud!"

Emily sped through a few questionable red lights to get me home in record time. Kale disappeared when we reached the neighbor's house, which showed how intense and dark the Hillmans' presence was.

I slung my backpack over my shoulder and looked at Emily. She was unbuckling her seatbelt. "Stay here," I said.

She looked at me incredulously. "I'm coming to help you."

"You can't help."

"Why, cause I'm not Nina?"

"Oh, my God," I muttered. "You can't see them, Emily! I don't want you to get hurt, too. Jesus, I'm sorry for caring about your safety!"

Emily's mouth dropped open, her eyes glistening with tears. She leaned back in the seat and frowned. "Okay. Just be careful. Get him out safe. I'll wait here."

CHAPTER TWENTY-THREE

HALFWAY UP THE DRIVEWAY, the atmosphere changed. Like the crawling sensation in the cemetery, the air felt charged. An unseen energy prickled all over my skin like tiny needles.

I hurried to the front door and found it unlocked. When I opened it, I was buffeted by a gust of cold air. The house felt like a deep freezer, and it reeked of decay. It wasn't the faint smell that surrounded Shirley, either. Thick and cloying, the smell was like someone had slapped me in the face with a slab of rotten meat. My stomach heaved as I stepped over the threshold.

"Colin!" I shouted. "Where are you?"

Heavy thumps rattled the floor from upstairs. I headed for the stairs and froze as something crunched under my foot. I looked down to see a picture frame holding a picture of Colin and me smashed to pieces. The pictures from the wall were crooked, with several strewn across the stairs.

Colin shouted, "Oh my God!" in a shrill voice that would have been funny if it wasn't dripping with fear.

I reached the bottom of the stairs in time to see him fall. A cruel laugh scraped at my ears as he tumbled down the stairs in a rolling knot of flailing limbs. I tried to catch him, but his momentum bowled me over, and we hit the wall together. Picture frames banged to the ground. His head slammed into my belly and knocked the wind out of me, but it kept him from busting his skull on the tile floor. He groaned in pain, cradling one arm.

"Colin!" I said. "What the hell?"

He stared at me in confusion. His glasses were crooked and hanging from his face. Blood oozed from tiny cuts on his cheeks.

"Are you okay?" I asked.

"My arm," he moaned. "I don't know what's happening. My room got cold, and then things just started flying off the shelves. I tried to get out of there, but it shoved me down the stairs and..." His voice broke as he dissolved into tears.

"It's okay. I won't let it hurt you anymore," I said. Untangling myself from him, I got up and helped him to his feet. "Come on, we're getting out of here."

We only took one step before he collapsed and whined, "My ankle."

"Can you get on my back?" I wasn't super strong, but he was small for his age. The adrenaline would let me piggy-back him out of the house and to the safety of Emily's car.

"We gotta get Jeremy, too," he said. "He's still up there."

"Who?"

"Jeremy's upstairs," he said. "My friend."

As if on cue, there was another scream from upstairs.

"Jeremy!" I yelled, running up the first few stairs. My feet crunched on broken glass. "Come down here!"

"Help me!" he shrieked. "It won't let me!"

I looked at Colin, then back at the stairs. My breath plumed into the frigid air. Bracing my legs to give him more support, I hauled him up and half-carried him to the kitchen.

"Sit down," I said. "What happened?"

He shook his head rapidly as he sat down on the floor. "I don't know. We were working on his video and then—"

"Video? You didn't…" I murmured. His gazed dropped to the floor. "Colin, seriously? Did you make a Dead Eyes video?"

"It's not real!" he protested.

"Don't say a word," I said. "You sit there and don't move."

He looked at me, tears still streaming down his cheeks. "Why?"

"Just do it," I barked. With one of the new cans of salt, I poured a protective ring around him. He never broke his gaze as I poured the white granules on the floor.

"What are you doing?"

"Don't ask," I said. "Don't move. I don't care what you hear or see."

With my heart still pounding, I started up the stairs.

"Travis! Charlie!" I called. "They're not the ones you're mad at!"

At the sound of their names, I felt a whispering sensation. The quiet sound was in my ears, but it was also a dry, cold finger running down my spine. Something had noticed me. A picture frame bounced off my chest and clattered to my feet. It was the single picture of Valerie that Mom had hung in the new house. Cracks spider-webbed across her bright smile.

A hulking black shape stood at the top of the stairs. Its white eyes glowed as bright as spotlights in the smoky face.

"I know what happened to you," I said. The wind suddenly picked up. This time I threw my arms in front of my face. Another picture bounced off my blocking arms. "But these two didn't do anything to hurt you. I only want to help you," I said in my most soothing voice. *Or banish you the hell out of here, whichever is easier.*

"Help me!" Jeremy screamed. The sound came from the hallway, probably from Colin's room. I tried not to let the fearful cry rattle my nerves. My fingers clamped on the bottle of holy water.

"I understand, guys," I said loudly, hoping both of them could hear. "I know that those boys picked on you. It's partially their fault that you got hurt."

I was nearly on eye level with the spirit at the top of the stairs. My heart thrummed in my chest. The smell of death and rotting things was even stronger up here, thick enough to make my stomach churn. I didn't want to rush right through the spirit, for fear that it would shove me backwards down the stairs like it had Colin.

"Are you Travis?"

The spirit cocked its head, as if it was surprised that I recognized it.

"I see you," I said. "I want to help you. That's all I want."

As I stepped up to the top, the spirit lunged at me. But I was ready for it. Pressing myself tight to the wall so it couldn't push me down the stairs, I sprayed an arc of holy water at it. Its smoky form separated, like passing a hand through a cloud of smoke. Sprinting past the swirling darkness, I barreled through Colin's door.

Icy hands shoved me as I cleared the frame. I tripped over a toppled chair and slammed into Colin's dresser with my shoulder, sending a sharp bolt of pain down my arm. Shoving myself upright, I tried to get my bearings.

It looked like a bomb had gone off in Colin's room. Books and action figures were strewn everywhere, bodies contorted among the wreckage. And there was a kid who had to be Jeremy, hiding in the corner with his hands over his head as a second spirit, presumably Charlie, swiped at him. Each blow left a long, bleeding scratch along his bare arms.

"Hey!" I snapped. Both the spirit and Jeremy looked at me. "Leave him alone."

Jeremy was wide-eyed as I stood in the doorway. Tears brimmed over his puffy, red eyes.

"Charlie?" I asked, stepping toward the spirit with my free hand extended. "It's okay."

For a second, the shadowy figure resolved into distinct features, as if the sound of his name had yanked him closer to physical reality. Boyish features emerged from the charcoal gray mass. The dark, grimy clothes faded for a moment, giving me a glimpse of a bloodied t-shirt neck sticking up from a baggy Grim Reaper robe. He let out a low moan, and his features darkened again.

"Wait," I said. "I know what happened to you. I'm so sorry. But this won't change it. They didn't hurt you."

"Stay," Charlie whispered, a sound that scraped along my skin and sent a chill down my spine.

I glanced at Jeremy, then back to Charlie. "Go downstairs to Colin."

Jeremy nodded rapidly and stumbled toward the door. Charlie let out a wail and grabbed the back of Jeremy's ripped shirt, dragging him back into the room.

Putting all my force into it, I shouted, "Let him go!" and sprayed the holy water at him. With a hissing sound, Charlie released him, his fist passing harmlessly through the living boy. Jeremy yelped as he stumbled forward, then careened into the hall. His thundering footsteps shook the house as he ran downstairs.

Charlie whipped around, fixing his baleful gaze on me. I extended my shaking hand to Charlie. I knew how to scare him off temporarily, but sending him running would only leave them to hurt someone else tonight. With the brothers riled up like this, there was no telling what would happen.

"Let me help you," I said, trying to soften my voice.

Charlie's form darkened as he whispered, "No."

"Show me what you want. I can make you feel better." I held out my hand, pushing my palm out toward him. "Aren't you cold? I can help you be warm and safe again."

He hesitated. My heart beat faster, my skin going clammy as he took a tentative step toward me. With his glowing eyes searching me, he took my hand. I gasped involuntarily at his icy touch, biting down into my bones.

"Show me what you need," I said through clenched jaws.

Color spread from his fingers, up his arm and across his body like someone was sloughing away a thick layer of encrusted grime. But under the hazy gray, I now saw the terrible injuries left by the accident in lurid detail. The right side of Charlie's face was misshapen, as if the whole thing had inverted. Blood trickled from his ear. His right eye was a blue iris floating in bright, angry red blood spots.

"Show me," I said again, pushing away the instinctive revulsion. "I won't hurt you."

Something pushed behind my eyes with a pressure that verged on painful. Then he pulled me down into his memories. A female voice spoke, echoing in my brain and leaving my ears ringing.

Stay with me, angel. Stay with me. Her voice was like a warm summer breeze in that cold, dark place.

I experienced his memories in flashes. First, he was approaching the dark house for candy. He was afraid, tightening his sweaty grip around his candy bucket as he tiptoed across the long yard. The yard seemed to go on forever. Halfway across the dark landscape, the scarecrow on the porch lurched forward and bellowed at him. His tummy tied in a knot. His legs tangled as he tried to run back to the safe glow of the street lights.

Then he saw red anger as the scarecrow rushed him again. His little fist balled up, and he threw a wild punch as he shouted his ninja jutsu. The scarecrow shoved him down. His candy went flying. He was just trying to clean it up when everything went blinding white.

Then there was pain everywhere. Flashes of light, shouts all around him. Someone touched his head. Then it was dark. He kept running from the scarecrow. Sometimes he heard Mommy speak.

Stay with me, angel. Stay with me.

He could never run fast enough from the scarecrow. His feet pounded over uneven ground, his little heart thumping until it felt like it would explode from his chest. But it always caught him, shoving him onto the hard ground. A nightmare that would never end, it loomed over him, leering and laughing as squirming black bugs and thick blood spilled from its mouth and onto his skin.

Then everything changed. He was awake again, but the world was gray, and everyone around him was sad. Mommy cried, and Daddy yelled. Travis was there, in bright color against the faded, shadowy world. He promised it would be okay, that he would protect him. Then there were boxes going into the ground and big bundles of white flowers.

He waited. He heard her say *stay with me, stay with me,* over and over. So he stayed. He tried to talk to Mommy, but she didn't listen. No matter how loud he shouted, she didn't hear.

The thought of Sara Workman jolted me into awareness. I was so cold that my teeth chattered, and every muscle felt weak and tired. Charlie was literally sucking the life out of me.

"Charlie, what can I do?" I croaked. "Why are you hurting people?"

At that, a cascade of images went through his mind, and into mine. I saw him and Travis sitting, forlorn, under the angel statue. Then came the YouTubers. As each of the older kids stood near his grave, near Mommy's grave, their faces distorted into the scarecrow, eyes dark and squirming. They laughed and tried to scare each other. This was his place, where he was waiting for Mommy like she told him to. Their voices broke through the quiet and made his head hurt. If they wanted to see a scary ghost, then they would see one.

My heart pounded so hard I was shaking in my shoes. Darkness pressed in around the edge of my vision. I wouldn't last much longer with this kind of connection. "Charlie, what can I do? How can I fix it?"

I saw the scarecrow, this time lying on the ground with a thick wooden stake through its heart. Travis and Charlie stood behind it, looking grim.

"We need to kill the scarecrow," I said. "Let's figure out how to do that. Can you promise me to not hurt anyone?"

He recoiled, but I clamped down to keep our connection. I didn't want to hurt him, but he had left me no choice. With my free hand, I reached for the salt. Holding him firmly in place, I poured a circle of salt around us to close him in. He finally caught on to what I was doing and tried to pull away.

"No!" he screeched. The sound was like an icepick stabbing into my eardrum. He gave up trying to pull away from me, and instead swiped at me with his other hand. I'd given him more physical substance, and he took advantage by digging his icy fingers into my ponytail and twisting it hard against my scalp.

I squealed in pain, twisting in his grasp so I could complete the circle. The pressure around us spiked as the circle closed. "Let go!" I commanded

Charlie. He resisted, pulling harder on my hair. I gathered up the energy I had left and pushed it out with my voice. "Let go of me!"

Something rushed out of me and into Charlie. He staggered and released me. Reality slammed back in around me, painting the world bright and vivid again. I leaped backwards out of the circle, tripped over a pile of books, and caught myself on the edge of Colin's bed.

The salt circle was maybe three feet in diameter, right in front of Colin's desk. Inside the circle, Charlie spun frantically and pounded his little fists against an invisible wall, like he was pressing against glass. The salt kept him in, but it didn't block his awful, screeching cries.

My respite was short-lived as Travis appeared in the doorway. He looked at Charlie, then at me. His form darkened as his eyes glowed brighter. Maybe he was the calm one, but he didn't like me threatening Charlie. Inspiration struck through my exhaustion.

I flung another arc of holy water at him. He dodged it, and I sprinted past him. My legs were heavy and clumsy as I ran down the hall to my bedroom and threw open the door. I poured the remains of the salt in a circle on my bedroom rug, leaving a small section of its perimeter open.

Travis appeared at the doorway. Anger radiated off him in waves of cold. Extending my hand toward him, I tapped that same force that had commanded Charlie.

"Come here," I ordered. As the words rolled off my tongue, my legs went wobbly and threatened to give out from under me.

The milky white eyes widened in surprise as he rushed toward me. I was too tired to be excited that the command had worked. In seconds, he was in my face, bathing me in a cloud of stinking cold. Like Charlie, he swung at me, but I was ready for it.

"Stay here!" I commanded. I dodged his next swing, stumbled out of the circle, and closed it behind me.

It was hard to enjoy the satisfaction at my own cleverness when I saw the way Travis glared at me from within the salt line. How in the world was I going to break through that much rage and pain to get them to move on?

"Bridget?" Colin called. "Are you okay?"

Crap. I hurried downstairs to find Jeremy huddled next to Colin inside the circle of salt downstairs.

"What's going on?" Colin asked.

"What was all that?" Jeremy said, his body trembling with fear.

I ignored him and gestured to Colin. "How's your leg?"

Colin winced and pulled up the edge of his jeans. Swollen over the edge of his sock, his ankle was already turning purple. "Bridget, is this part of your mutant thing?"

"Your sister's a mutant?" Jeremy asked.

"Quit being nerds," I said. "We have to get you to the hospital."

"Mom's gonna freak," Colin said.

"You'll be lucky if I don't kill you first. I told you not to do that video, you idiot," I snapped at him.

"It's not real," Jeremy blurted. "It's not real."

"Really? Then explain what just happened to you," I said. He stared at me blankly. "Yeah, that's what I thought."

"Where did it go?" Colin asked. "The ghost."

"It's trapped upstairs," I said. Both of them squawked in protest. They didn't need to know there were two spirits hell-bent on hurting them. "Jeremy, help me get him up. Emily's outside, and she can drive us to the doctor."

With Jeremy's help, I got Colin to his feet and let him hop along between us. The salt would hold the Hillmans upstairs for a while, giving me time to take care of Colin.

I emerged from the front door to find Emily standing in the front yard with her arms over her chest. When she saw us coming, she rushed toward us. "What the hell happened?"

"I'll tell you later," I said. "Can you drive us to the hospital? He fell down the stairs and busted his ankle."

"Yeah, of course," she said, helping me get Colin into the car. "Are you okay?"

"I'm tired, but I'm okay," I said. Tired was a massive understatement. My body felt impossibly heavy. Turning my head made me dizzy; even once my head stopped, the world kept spinning around me.

"Do you want to call your mom?"

"Yeah," I said. "I'll call her." I took the flip phone out and selected *Mom*. It was the only number in the phone. As the phone rang, I scrambled for a story that made sense.

"Hello?"

"Mom, it's me," I said.

"Hi sweetie," she said. "What's up?"

"Um, so there was an accident." As she gasped sharply, I said, "Everyone's fine."

"Jesus," she breathed.

"Sorry. Everyone's fine. Colin fell down the stairs. I think he busted his ankle. Emily is still here, so we can take him to the hospital if you want."

"Hold on." I heard her cover the phone, and then a muffled voice like she was talking to someone else in the office. "Don't go to the ER. You'll be there for hours. Take him to the urgent care near my office. You know how to get there?"

"I think so," I said.

"Make sure you give them your insurance card. Oh, and give them his medical information. He has an allergy…you know what, all the emergency info is in his phone. Make sure he has it."

"Okay," I said. "Are you going to come?"

"I'll be there as quick as I can," she said. "I just started a treatment and I have to finish it, but it shouldn't be long. I'll probably get there the same time you do. Let me talk to him."

I handed the phone to him. "Yeah, it hurts. No. No. Uh-huh. Okay. I love you too," he said. He handed my phone back.

"Where's your phone?" I asked him. "Mom said we need it for your allergies."

"It's on my desk," he said.

I hurried back into the house and was instantly bombarded by the furious shouts of two spirits. I passed Colin's door first and peeked into my bedroom. The salt circle held strong. Inside, Travis glared at me, his milky eyes glowing in a steady pulse. I hurried back to Colin's room. The circle around Charlie was still solid, but part of the line was uneven where it crossed over a pile of books. I took the nearly empty can from my bag and worked the circle further inward, tightening the cage around Charlie. He screamed in rage.

"Okay, phone," I muttered, ignoring the ghostly temper tantrum going on three feet away.

Fortunately for Colin's impressive computer setup, his desk had dodged most of the destruction. I searched the surface for his phone, but I froze when the paused frame on the monitor caught my eye. On the paused video, Jeremy stood in front of a tombstone. With my mouth going dry, I pressed *play* on the screen.

"How's this?" Jeremy asked, positioning himself in front of Charlene's headstone. The swooping curve of the angel wing cut across the pale blue sky behind him.

Off-screen, Colin said, "That's good. Go when you're ready."

I scrubbed it forward a few seconds to hear Jeremy say, "Tell what your dead eyes see."

"Oh, you little jerks." How could they be so stupid? Never mind that it could have happened without this, but this made it even worse. I stopped the video and searched the desk. Under a half-eaten bag of Doritos was Colin's phone. I grabbed it, then turned to Charlie. "I'm so sorry about this. I promise I'm doing this to help you. Try to calm down, and think about what I can do to help you. I'll do anything I can. I mean it."

Had I really just put a spirit in time out?

"No!" Charlie screamed back at me. There was a slight puff of cold air as he pounded the barrier with his tiny fists. My eyes were drawn to the ground. Had the line of salt moved? No, it couldn't have.

"Right," I said, backing away slowly. "So, just sit tight. Maybe we can talk this out later."

I hurried back downstairs and slid into the passenger seat.

"Did you get—" Colin started.

I cut him off. "Don't talk to me. You don't know what I've been through to help these spirits, and you disturbed them for a stupid video. Like I told you not to."

"So all of it's real? We really called something from the grave?" Jeremy almost looked excited. "I knew I felt something and—"

"Shut up. I don't know you, and I already don't like you. You didn't actually call anything. They were already there, and you painted a target on yourself," I said. I sighed and squeezed the bridge of my nose. "Okay, here's the deal. When Mom asks what happened, this is what you're going to tell her. You two were horsing around, and Jeremy accidentally pushed you. You tripped and fell down the stairs."

"But then I'll be in trouble," Jeremy complained.

"You should be," I shouted. Emily yelped in surprise, jerking the wheel. "Getting grounded is a whole lot better than what would have happened if I hadn't come home when I did. Tell it back to me. What happened?"

Colin stared at me blankly. "But why can't we just tell Mom? She'll think it's cool."

"Have you met Mom? If you tell her, she'll have both of us committed."

"No she won't," he protested.

"I'm serious. Don't you dare tell her."

"Bridget, this would be like the video to end all videos," Jeremy protested. "If people saw ours worked, we could…"

"Unbelievable," I muttered. "After the week I've had, I'd be happy to take out my frustration on Colin's computer."

"You wouldn't," Colin said, his jaw dropping.

"Try me."

CHAPTER TWENTY-FOUR

FROM THE MINUTE I helped Colin hobble into the waiting room, I handled everything. I filled out his forms with his input, gave them my insurance card, and made sure to meticulously write down the allergies and warnings from his phone. While we sat in the waiting room, Jeremy called his mother to pick him up. I hoped she'd ground him into next year.

They called us back to an exam room about ten minutes later. We left Emily and Jeremy in the waiting room, both pointedly ignoring each other and messing with their phones.

After checking Colin's blood pressure and heart rate, the nurse started quizzing him about what happened. With his eyes downcast, he said, "Me and my friend were horsing around and I fell down the stairs." Jeez. He couldn't have looked more guilty if he tried.

"And you are…" the nurse said.

"I'm his sister," I said. "I came home and found him and his friend hurt."

There was a suspicious glint in her eye as she looked me over. Did she think I'd done something to him? After seeing that video, I was tempted to. Maybe I should have gotten a solid hit in while I could still blame it on Jeremy.

She made a note on her chart, then stood up. "One of the PAs will be in to see you soon, okay, honey?"

"Okay," he said miserably. As soon as the nurse had left he stared at me. "Bridget, what happened? I mean for real. Are there really ghosts?"

"Yes," I said. What was the point of lying? I could lie about the cold spots, but there was no easy explanation for him getting thrown down the stairs by an invisible force. "You remember when you thought I was a mutant?"

"Oh, my God, I knew it," he said, looking almost delighted. "I knew it!"

I shook my head. "I'm not a mutant. But I can see ghosts. And talk to them."

"Oh, my God." As he contemplated the implications, he gave me a frantic look. "And they're in our house?"

"Sometimes," I said. "Most of them are friendly. You and your stupid friend gave an open invitation to a couple of nasty ones. What were you thinking?"

"I didn't know," he murmured. "I didn't really think it would work. We were just trying to get more subscribers for Jeremy's channel."

"I know," I said. "But you did it near the graves of a couple of kids who were killed a few years ago. And they're pissed."

"So what did you do?"

"I sealed them in for now," I said. "I'm trying to help them move on."

"How long have you been like this?"

"You remember after Valerie's accident? When I had that surgery on my leg? You were little, but—"

"I was in fifth grade," he said primly. "Not that little."

"Okay, big boy," I said. "During the surgery, my heart stopped for a little while. Mom and Dad probably didn't tell you since I was fine afterward. But that's when it started."

"Holy crap." Then like it had just struck him, his whole face went still, his eyes wide and mouth open. "What about Valerie? Did you ever see her?"

The thought of her sent a hot spear of grief through my chest and down into my gut. "Yeah," I said, trying to keep my composure. "For a while."

"Is she…is she still here?" he said. The hope in his voice was so sweet that it made tears spring to my eyes. Sometimes I forgot that he'd lost her too.

"Not anymore," I said. "She moved on."

"But did she—"

"Hey there," a friendly female voice said. The PA swept into the room, scanning Colin's chart. "What happened, buddy?"

Colin kept to the story. The PA was securing the thick bandage around Colin's ankle when Mom rushed into the room. Tears streamed down her cheeks as she wrapped her arms around Colin. "I'm so glad you're okay," she said. She pulled away and held him by the shoulders. "You boys have to be careful. You're lucky your sister was home."

Colin shot me a look over Mom's shoulder. "Yeah."

Mom gave me a quick hug and kissed the top of my head. "Thank you for handling things."

"You're welcome," I said. "Is it okay if Emily drives me home? I left some of my stuff in her car in our hurry."

Mom nodded. "That's fine. I'll have to go by the pharmacy, but I'll take him with me. Thanks again, sweetheart."

Emily drove me home in silence. When we arrived, we sat quietly in the driveway for a few minutes. I didn't want to go in the house and deal with the mess the Hillmans had made, but I had to.

"Is it safe for you to be here alone?" Emily asked. "You could come to my house."

"They made a mess. I have to clean it up before Mom sees it," I replied.

"Do you want help?"

I did, but I also wanted some time on my own to regroup. And if the Hillmans got free somehow, I didn't want Emily anywhere near them.

"I should be fine," I said. "But thank you."

She looked a little stung, but I was too tired to worry much about it. "Okay," she said. "Message me later? If you can do it without getting busted."

"I will," I said.

With my body still aching and exhausted, I trudged up the front lawn. As I walked, I pictured Kale in my mind. "Kale? Can you come this way?"

"Here." I turned on my heel and saw him standing at the edge of the yard. He gestured to the house. "It's still dark here. Are they inside?"

I nodded. "I locked them up. Good old sodium chloride."

He didn't seem to appreciate my humor. "I told you not to—"

"I know. You were right," I said. "Can you come with me?"

"I'll try."

I hurried up the front steps and into the house. It was still uncomfortably cold, but Travis and Charlie were quiet. What if they'd gotten out somehow? No, Kale would have sensed if they were gone. Wouldn't he?

I sighed. My brain was a steel trap. Once a worry snuck in, it would never shake loose on its own. I hurried upstairs to make sure the boys were still there. Halfway up the stairs, one of the spirits started shouting again. I peeked into Colin's room. Charlie glared at me from inside his salt prison. I startled at the intensity of his gaze and backed away.

After closing the door, I hurried down the hall to my room. Travis was still there, but something was amiss. My salt circle hadn't been perfect, thanks to my panic-driven work, but there was a definite wonky spot now, like someone had been blowing on it from inside. I ran back downstairs for another can of salt, then returned to my room to reinforce the circle. Travis's stare was a heavy weight on my back as I laid another layer around the circle. Once I was satisfied, I went back in to check Charlie's circle. Like Travis's circle, his was warped into a teardrop shape.

"You guys are really making this difficult," I said.

I poured another line of salt around it. Halfway around the circle, it occurred to me that Colin and I were going to be hard-pressed to explain to Mom why there was enough salt on the floor to kill the world's biggest slug. Unlike the broken picture frames, that wasn't explained by a little immature wrestling.

Think, Bridget.

My mind raced as I ran back downstairs. Out of habit, I scanned the living room. I jumped at the sight of a silhouette at the sliding glass doors to the back patio.

"It's just me," Kale said. "This is as far as I can go."

"Okay, give me a minute," I said.

It took me a few minutes to sweep up the salt from the kitchen floor. Then I had to clean up the smashed picture frames, sweep up the glass, and vacuum just to be safe. By the time I finished, I was sweating and exhausted. It had been a rough couple of days.

I couldn't vacuum the salt from upstairs, or I'd release Charlie and Travis to wreak havoc again. So I had to keep Mom downstairs, which meant keeping Colin downstairs.

Doing my best to ignore Charlie's cries of outrage, I took the pillows and heavy quilt off Colin's bed. I carried them downstairs and made up a bed for him on the couch. Hopefully Mom would think it was thoughtful instead of being suspicious of my motives. I went back up and cleaned up the worst of the mess, shoving books back onto the shelves haphazardly and stowing his fallen action figures in the closet. When I was done, the room was still messy but looked more like the work of a middle school boy than a poltergeist.

Finally, I could catch my breath. I opened the glass door and walked onto the back porch. The automatic lights flicked on, casting a warm yellow glow over the backyard. Outside, I couldn't hear the Hillmans yelling and pounding, though I still sensed their anger like an itch at the back of my mind.

Kale joined me as I sank into one of the patio chairs and let out a sigh. He paced in front of me, his bare feet moving silently over the carpet of dead leaves on the patio. "Are you okay?"

"I'm okay. I connected with Charlie. Tried to understand what he wanted, but he's so angry." I sighed. "This whole thing is such a mess."

"It is," Kale said. "I don't have to tell you how dangerous it was to make that connection."

"No, you don't." I swallowed hard and looked out over the backyard. A gentle wind stirred the mounds of dead leaves, whispering and rustling. Compared to the icy presence of the Hillman boys, the winter breeze was downright warm. "They were just kids."

Kale's hand rested on my shoulder. While the rest of him was still translucent, his hand had taken on solidity as he focused his energy. Without thinking, I put my own hand over it, relishing the feel of it. Though there was no real body there, I still felt velvety-soft skin on the back of his hand. Beneath my fingertips was a thrumming energy where a pulse might have been in a living human.

"Please don't be mad at me." I couldn't bear to see disapproval on his face. Not tonight. "They were so young. Those boys scared them, hurt them, and then everyone who went out there using their graves for a stupid video set them off over and over again. It's not fair."

"I'm not mad." His touch shifted. Longing panged in my chest as he broke contact, but he reappeared, kneeling in front of me. Hesitating with his hand in the open air between us, he looked up at me, then let his hand rest lightly on my knee. It sent a shock through me, like lightning breaking across a summer sky. "It's in your nature."

"To be a screw-up?"

"To care so much that it hurts." His lips curved into a gentle smile. "I like that about you. Even if it makes me absolutely insane."

I swallowed, my eyes flitting from his hand to his bright eyes. "I've tried everything I know. I don't want to hurt them any more than they've already been hurt."

"You haven't done anything to hurt them," he said. "None of this is your fault."

His other hand rested on my leg. Almost instinctively, I leaned down to be closer. Here, I could smell his clean, growing-green smell. That was the smell of safety and familiarity, of things that were undeniably good.

"But we will hurt them," I said. "When Marcus gets here."

His eyes creased. "Sometimes we have to do difficult things for the greater good. I know it's not fair."

Something broke open in my chest. Charlie was already half-unhinged with his constant nightmares of the scarecrow. If we sealed him away, he would have nothing but the worst moments of his short life cycling forever in his head. The thought of someone I loved, like Valerie or Colin, or if I was being honest, Kale, trapped like that? My throat closed up, and tears spilled over my cheeks.

"It's okay," he said, his cool hand squeezing my knee. "You have to think of the big picture. How many people have they already hurt? Even if it's not their fault, you can't let them go on doing as they please. How long until someone dies? You could have drowned. Colin could have broken his neck. And how would you feel then?"

His hands closed lightly around my wrists, pulling my hands away from my face. I looked at him, painfully aware of how bad I looked between the scuffle with the Hillmans and now crying like a baby. "It's not fair."

His eyes were kind and gentle as he tilted his head. "Sometimes life is unfair that way. Sometimes there are no easy answers."

I sniffled, blinking to clear the tears from my eyes. Before I could wipe them away, Kale reached forward, his fingers cool on my cheek as he brushed at the tears. His touch left a tingle in its wake. But instead of withdrawing to his usual distance, his fingers lingered on my cheek.

"I know you struggle under this burden," he said, "but you are such a beautiful soul."

My heart thumped. There was something welling up inside me, something dangerously like hope tinged with a fervent desire. How many times had I fantasized about Kale being like this, close enough that it would take nothing at all to erase the distance between us?

He leaned toward me, slowly at first, then all at once. His soft lips found mine. My senses exploded. There was the electric touch of his lips, the clean smell of him all around me, an effervescent sensation like plunging into a cool bath of bubbles that burst against my skin. I forgot how to breathe.

Then he broke away, leaving me feeling like the sun had been blotted from the sky. "I'm sorry, I shouldn't have."

"You shouldn't?" I asked, trying not to let the tremble of impending tears shake my voice. *Don't take this away from me. Let me have this one good thing.*

"It's not appropriate. I'm your Guardian."

He still hadn't broken his gaze, although seeing him so close but feeling so far away didn't alleviate the feeling of loss. The inches between us felt like miles.

"Since when do I care about the rules? If you want to, then do it."

A light gleamed in his eyes. We both leaned forward that time, partners in crime. Fireworks exploded in my brain as our lips met again. One cool hand caressed my cheek, then slid into my hair, sending a delicious thrill down my spine. I'd never really kissed a boy, but if this was what it was like, I'd been missing out.

For once, there were no thoughts and worries battling for my attention. My whole existence seemed to hang in this moment. I was complete and content, which was such a new sensation that I didn't realize its absence from my life until just then. There was only me and this beautiful spirit who inexplicably thought I was something wonderful.

My heart thumped, and I felt woozy.

Suddenly Kale pulled away from me. "Are you all right?"

"I just…whew," I said. My vision rippled, a mirage-like blur pressing around the edges. "Either you're really good at that, or I'm exhausted."

He looked down at his hands. They were brilliant, like he'd turned on the juice to bring himself into the physical world. And with a blush heating my cheeks, I noticed his face, particularly his full lips, was vibrant and real.

"I must be drawing from you. I didn't mean to," he said. "You can't afford that right now."

"It's a risk I can take," I said dreamily.

He laughed. "And your mother would wonder why you were passed out on the back porch. Come on."

Much to my dismay, he didn't kiss me again, instead tracing the back of my hand with one graceful finger. I watched him for a while, the way he concentrated so intently on that slow, hypnotic touch. With his contact, I noticed a subtle sensation of pulling from my core, like someone was suctioning something from me.

The dreamy sensation passed, and my worrying brain reactivated itself. "Kale, what does this mean? For us?" I hesitated to even use the word *us*. It had been me and Kale for a long time, but I'd never thought of *us* in this way. It frightened me, to be honest.

"I don't know." He continued tracing my hand. "I don't mean to change the subject, but we may not have much time if your mother comes home soon. Marcus will be here tomorrow."

Like that, the magic was gone. "You know I'm grounded."

"Maybe with your unusually good behavior, your mother will let you off the hook for a day. If you're going to study."

"With as much studying as I do lately, she's going to expect straight As," I said.

"He can do it with or without you there," he said. "I'll explain the circumstances."

"I want to be there," I said.

I wanted one last chance to try to reason with the boys. I wanted to give them a chance to be at peace. And I wanted to be at peace, not having to live with the idea of them trapped and more alone than ever.

CHAPTER TWENTY~FIVE

AFTER CLEANING UP and leaving Kale to check on final details with Marcus, I'd sat downstairs at the dining room table with Valerie's laptop to research, but it was hard to focus with Charlie and Travis still raising hell from inside the salt circles. I'd already had to reinforce them again after an hour, which had me wondering what would happen if I fell asleep and quit checking them. I gave up on researching and turned on the TV to drown out the ruckus from upstairs.

Solitude gave me time to think about Kale. Where I'd mostly had pleasant associations with him in the past, things had been amplified. Now thinking about his gorgeous blue eyes was different; his beautiful eyes were on me, looking at me as more than his troublesome charge. And I no longer had to wonder about those lips. I could still feel the cool, electric intensity of them pressed to mine. Had he wanted to do that for as long as I had?

The mere thought of the kiss—*kisses, plural*—made my cheeks flush again. I'd never even kissed a boy before. Technically, I still hadn't. I'd skipped over teenage boys and gone straight to centuries-old incorporeal spirits.

But what would it mean? As much as I'd dreamed about it, I almost wished it hadn't happened. Because I couldn't imagine how anything could ever happen with Kale. Weird as my life was, it wasn't a freaking fairy tale, where my magic kiss would bring him back to life.

The grinding sound of the garage door opening startled me from fantasizing about a certain dreamy spirit. I turned off the TV and hurried to the door just in time to spare Mom from opening it with her full hands. In one hand she carried a paper bag from the pharmacy, and in the other, a big shopping bag from Giavino's.

"Here. Colin wanted Italian," she said breathlessly, handing me the food.

I peeked inside and found a stack of Styrofoam takeout boxes, with a grease-spotted bag of what could only be garlic bread on top. The rich smell of marinara and garlic butter hit me in a delicious wave that made my stomach growl.

At the sound of our voices, Travis and Charlie resumed their noise-making. It startled me, and I instinctively looked at Mom. For a second, I couldn't believe that she was carrying on like normal. But she couldn't hear a thing, despite the angry shouting that scraped my senses. I'd assumed the salt circles would silence them, since I hadn't gotten a response until stepping out of the circle in the graveyard. Maybe they could sense somehow that I was protected in the circle and waited for me to come out where they could attack.

"Did you bring all that down for him?" she asked, pointing to the couch.

"Yeah, I thought it would be easier for Colin to stay down here if his ankle was hurt," I said.

"That was so thoughtful," she said, smiling at me. "Let me go help him in."

She rushed back into the garage, and walked Colin from the car into the house. He wasn't on crutches, but his lower leg was encased in a clunky black orthopedic boot. His green eyes narrowed behind his glasses as he scanned the living room, like he was looking for the ghosts I'd told him about. When he met my eyes, he raised his eyebrows a little.

Mom was oblivious to his worry. She hustled him to the table, prattling on about what the doctor had said, what kind of medicine he'd been prescribed, the long line at the pharmacy, and Friday night traffic. As she bustled around the house, Colin's eyes never left me. Even when Mom delivered the forbidden treat of a Coke to his seat, he still watched me, his eyes narrowed in a mix of suspicion and fear. She was still in the kitchen going on about something when his eyes found mine.

"Is it gone?" he whispered.

I shook my head a little. "But everything's fine for right now."

Mom finally finished her mad rush around the house and flopped into her seat with a big sigh. "Goodness," she said. "You two look very serious."

"Just tired," Colin said quickly.

"Tell me about it," Mom said.

We passed the rest of the meal in awkward conversation. For once, Mom peppered the conversation with admonitions to Colin about being careful and not horseplaying in the house. Although I felt a little guilty, considering he'd been blindsided by a couple of pissed-off spirits—mostly his fault—it was nice to not be the target of Mom's irritation for once. After we finished eating, I cleared the table and put on my best Good Girl smile.

"Mom, I'll get this. Why don't you go take a hot bath and relax?" I said.

She looked at me strangely. Maybe that had been a little too out of character for me. But if she thought it was weird, she didn't care enough to call me on it.

"That's not a bad idea." She shook her head. "I'm still on call for the weekend. Some rest would be good." She turned to Colin. "Get comfortable on the couch and I'll get some PJs for you." She started to head for the stairs.

"I'll get them!" I said, a little too loudly. She gave me a strange look. "Go enjoy your bath."

"Don't go in my room," Colin whined at me. I shot him my best death stare, hoping it effectively conveyed *I will destroy you.* He shrank back. "Thanks, Bridget."

I hurried upstairs. The ghosts had quieted somewhat, which made me even more nervous. I stopped in Colin's room first, where the salt barrier was still solid. Though he was still yelling, Charlie wasn't quite as energetic as he had been. Maybe he'd finally settle down and take a nap, letting me get some sleep. I retrieved a set of pajamas, then headed back into the hallway.

With a sense of dread growing in my stomach, I approached my room. Travis Hillman's dark form was pooled on the ground, still trapped in the salt circle. He didn't move, but his piercing white stare followed me as I circled the room and inspected the salt line. Satisfied with my traps, I hurried back downstairs.

Mom was in the kitchen fiddling with pill bottles. She took Colin a handful of tablets. Colin grimaced as he washed them down with his Coke.

"Don't stay up all night playing games," she said. "You need to rest."

After she checked the doors, she went into her room and closed the door. A few minutes later, I heard the bathtub running.

Colin leaned forward, giving me an insistent stare. "Are you serious? It's still here?"

"They, and yes," I said. "That's why you're sleeping down here."

"I'm not sleeping anywhere," he muttered. "Why are they here?"

"Because if they're here, they can't hurt anyone else," I said. "You'll be fine."

"So are you gonna kill them?"

I gaped at him. "They're already dead, dummy."

"I mean like…get rid of them, or banish them, or whatever. They're evil, right?"

There was an arrogant, self-righteous cast to his expression, a little curl to his lip that I didn't like. I got it. I'd been angry, too. But somehow seeing Colin react that way set me off.

"They're not evil. They only bothered you because you provoked them," I snapped. "You literally asked them to appear to you."

"I didn't know anything would happen!"

"That doesn't make it a good idea!" I retorted. "Look, just try to get some sleep. I'm handling it."

"What can you do about it?"

I quirked an eyebrow at him. For a seventh grader, he managed to sound awfully condescending. "What do you mean, what can I do?"

"I didn't mean—"

"No, I know what you meant. News flash, Colin. I'm not stupid. I only suck at school because I have this crap going on all the time. And every time I get a break, another one shows up. So you can shut up about things you don't understand."

His jaw dropped, eyes wide like I'd slapped him. "I…I'm sorry." He was quiet for a while, and his tone was meek when he spoke again. "So what are you going to do?"

"I don't know," I said. "I want to help them, but I'm afraid I can't this time."

"What happened to them?"

I told him about the accident that had killed Charlie and Travis, and how they'd lingered. His eyes welled over with tears when I told him about their mother leaving them behind when she died.

He sat in stunned silence for several long heartbeats. Finally, he murmured, "I'm sorry."

"Huh?"

"I'm sorry we made the video," he said. "I wish I could apologize to them. We weren't trying to be mean to anyone."

"I don't think they're really upset at you," I said. "They're just really sad and confused."

But the word *apologize* echoed in my mind. Sam had apologized, and the Hillmans never bothered him again. I'd thought before they might need closure from the car's driver, but she wasn't at fault. And even if they somehow blamed her anyway, Charlie wasn't fixated on the driver. He was angry at the kids who'd made videos, but the primary target of his rage was James Rucker, who'd chased Charlie and became the scarecrow haunting his never-ending nightmare.

If an apology from James was the solution, how was I going to make it happen with less than twenty-four hours until Marcus arrived?

"Colin, let me use your phone," I said suddenly.

"For what?"

I glared at him. He fumbled it out of his pocket and handed it over.

An hour later, I had tracked down James Rucker on Facebook, found three possible phone numbers, and located his apartment. For once, luck was on my side, and the address was for an apartment complex in Macon, only about two hours away. It was past eleven, so I'd have to wait until morning to call. Never mind if it sounded crazy; it might be the key to giving Travis and Charlie a chance at peace instead of a silent, cold existence even further from their mother.

When I'd first started researching James Rucker, Colin had ignored me in favor of watching anime on Netflix, but after a while, he'd turned his attention to me. After I added the address to my list, he leaned over to see what I was doing.

"You're like a detective or something," he said.

"Too bad I can't get paid," I said. "Salt gets expensive."

The thought of salt reminded me of my unwilling guests. The noise from the TV had dulled my senses. I excused myself and hurried upstairs. It was too quiet. My heart thumped, and I tried to tell myself, *It's fine, they just got tired.*

Like an idiot, I believed that right up until the point I pushed Colin's door open. The salt line had turned into a blast radius. White petals spread out from the center where Charlie had been trapped, like he'd exploded out of the barrier. Tensing for the incoming attack, I searched the room, but I was alone.

"No, no," I murmured.

I ran to my room, throwing the door open hard enough that it banged against the wall. The circle inside my room was broken, though not blown open like the other one. Both of the Hillmans were gone. And my room was a disaster. The clothes had been ripped out of my closet, strewn all over the room. My nightstand had been cleared, with my lamp hanging awkwardly over the edge by its cord, the shade crooked. There was no reason for that except sheer spite.

"Oh, God," I said. What the hell was I supposed to do now? "Kale?"

He appeared seconds after I called. At least I knew the Hillmans weren't lurking right around the corner waiting to jump me. Despite my thumping heart and growing sense of dread, a dumb little part of me reared up and squealed *kiss him again!*

So not the time.

I didn't even have to tell him what had happened. I expected him to be upset, but he only stared in shock at the broken circle on my floor. "How?"

"I don't know," I said. "Go look in Colin's room."

He faded away, then returned a few minutes later looking odd. He winced, then shook his head violently. It was like he'd gotten dizzy and was trying to shake it off.

"I've never seen anything like that," he said.

"What was it?"

"It's like a bomb went off," he said. "There's so much dark, negative energy in there."

"What should I do?"

"Nothing," he said. "I'll check on Nina and let Ethan know he needs to watch over her. Just stay put. If you want to be there for the binding, then Marcus will pick you up at noon at the front of your neighborhood. Be ready."

CHAPTER TWENTY-SIX

ONCE COLIN WAS KNOCKED OUT, snoring quietly on the couch, I crept around the house to lay down salt as I had the previous nights. Though it hadn't kept the Hillmans away, it felt wrong to do nothing. I ended up laying on the short loveseat across from Colin, where I could see him and hear Mom snoring through her door.

Kale took the opportunity to search around town for any sign of Travis and Charlie. There were still a handful of people who'd done videos that we knew of. Thanks to my fear-induced insomnia and my ever-present anxious tendencies, I'd had the sobering thought around three in the morning that our list was nowhere near complete. Colin was proof. Emily's list was helpful, but it covered only high schoolers from our area who she knew had YouTube channels. How many more people had done the challenge for fun without posting videos? I knew it was out of my control, but it didn't keep me from worrying.

Finally, eight o'clock seemed like an acceptable hour to make a phone call. I'd have been pissed if someone woke me up at eight on a Saturday, but this was an extreme situation. Our family generally observed Sleep-In Saturday, which often worked in my favor. Colin and Mom were both asleep as I crept outside to the back porch to call James Rucker.

I dialed the first number on my list. After two rings, a gruff female voice answered. "Hello?"

"Um, hi, I'm looking for James?"

"Ain't no James." She hung up.

Okay, then.

On my second number, I got an automated message saying *The number you have dialed is no longer in service.* Well, here was hoping the last one was his number. I dialed the number, toying with the paper as I listened to the rings.

On the fourth ring, a sleepy male voice answered. "Uh, yeah?"

I took a deep breath. "Hello, I'm looking for James."

"This is James."

"Is this the James Rucker that used to live in Parkland, Georgia?"

Long pause. "Yeah. Who is this?"

"You don't know me, but I have to talk to you about something important."

He doesn't know you. It doesn't matter if you sound crazy.

"Look, I'm not interested," he said. "Please don't—"

"It's about the accident on Halloween," I blurted. He was silent for so long that I thought he might have hung up. "Are you there?"

"Please don't call again."

He hung up on me.

I called again.

"Look, I said not to—"

"I'm a ghost whisperer and I need you to come talk to the boys that died that night," I said. Might as well get it all out at once, like puking. Better out than in.

"This is ridiculous. Don't call—"

"I'm serious," I interrupted. "Look, I know you experienced something weird before you moved. Your house was cold, things were moving around, maybe you even heard something? Am I right?"

He was quiet enough that I didn't wait for an answer.

"Those boys have stayed around for some reason, and they're hurting people," I said. "I think if you speak to them, it may help them move on."

"I don't believe in ghosts," he said.

"Yes, you do. I know that's part of why you moved," I said. "I know it sounds crazy, but I'm telling you the truth. Please. And I know what it's like to feel guilty about something. This is a chance to help."

I'd carried the guilt of Valerie's death for years, feeling like my insistence on her driving me to the mall that night had caused her death. Before she moved on, she'd insisted it wasn't my fault, but on my darker days, I still felt the crushing weight of guilt for that night.

He was quiet for a long time. Finally, he said, "Don't call again." He hung up.

I stared at the phone, then dialed again. It went straight to voicemail. I tried twice more, and still got no answer. Tears stung my eyes. It was almost eight-thirty. Marcus would be here soon, and I had no way to help the Hillmans.

At eleven thirty in the morning, hope broke through the gloom. I was sitting at the dining room table, catching up on *A Tale of Two Cities* for school and silently panicking. Mom had been reading on her tablet, but a phone call interrupted her. When she hung up, she sighed and said, "I have to go into work for a few hours."

"Oh, man," I murmured, hoping my mouth wasn't betraying me with a smile. "On Saturday? That's terrible."

"I should be back around two-thirty," Mom said. "I'll call you guys if it looks like I'll be any later." She looked at Colin. "And you stay off your foot."

"I will," Colin said.

I managed to contain myself, watching with what I hoped passed for detached apathy, until she left.

Once her car started, I leaped into action. I sprinted upstairs for my backpack and double-checked all my supplies. Hurrying back downstairs, I found Mom's gym water bottle in the drying rack and filled it half way with holy water. When I delivered it to Colin, he stared at it like I'd handed him a steaming pile of dog crap.

"What is this?"

"It's holy water," I said.

"Where did you get holy water?"

"At St. Mary's."

"You stole it?"

"You can't steal it," I said. "It's supposed to be for people. Dude, never mind. If something weird happens, use this."

"Wait, you're leaving me here?"

"I have to go finish this," I said. "You'll be fine."

"But…" he trailed off, eyes going wide in fear.

As I looked at him, he suddenly looked tiny and defenseless. We weren't so far apart in age, but I still remembered him being a baby and staring down in wonder at the tiny screaming creature Mom was so infatuated with.

And someone had hurt him.

I closed my eyes and envisioned Sal's smile and the sharp blue of his uniform. Without speaking, I reached for him, sending his name through my mind like an arrow. It soared out into the black behind my eyes. Cool air stirred around me, prickling the pale hairs along my arm.

"Hey kiddo, what's up?" Sal said.

"Sal, this is my brother. He knows about me now," I said.

Colin yelped. "Who are you talking to?"

"My friend," I said. Oh, right. He might have known now, but he still couldn't see spirits. Now he just got to watch me talking to myself.

"There's a g-ghost here?" His eyes were so wide that he looked like one of the anime characters from his show.

Sal looked at me quizzically, then to Colin, then back. "Uh…Bridget?"

"I need you to watch him. If something comes, come find me. Kale can tell you where I'm going," I said.

"No!" Colin protested.

"You're fine," I said. "Sal's a good guy. He's a cop."

My brother narrowed his eyes, looking back and forth as if he would find Sal if he looked hard enough.

"Thank you," I told Sal.

"Be careful," he replied, giving me a nod.

And with that, I left to meet Marcus. With my backpack bouncing against my back, I hurried down my street. The sun was high in a cloudless sky, but I still felt as though a dark cloud hung over me. Worry and dread clung to me like a sticky film as I approached the main road.

A dark blue SUV idled on the side of the road, just inside the neighborhood entrance. I paused for a moment on my approach, trying to get a closer look at the man behind the wheel. Through the windshield, all I could see was the top of his head, lowered like he was looking down at a phone in his lap.

As if he'd felt my attention on him, his head popped up. His eyebrows lifted as he saw me. He was young. And attractive. I guess I'd assumed he would be older and dad-like, but I was wrong. I suddenly felt extra self-conscious about my messy bun and the dark circles under my eyes.

I realized I'd been staring for far too long when he gave a *come here* gesture. It occurred to me that I was about to break one of the cardinal rules of kindergarten: *Don't get in cars with strangers.* Surely Kale's approval was enough to guarantee my safety. Even so, my heart thumped as I approached the car and opened the passenger door.

Cool air and quiet guitar music greeted me. The white paper coffee cup in the cupholder was the only sign of anyone having used the car before. There were even visible vacuum lines in the floormats.

"You must be Bridget," he said. He extended his hand.

I accepted it. His grip was strong. "I am."

"It's nice to meet you." The warmth of his skin didn't make it to his brown eyes. He was handsome, but there was something cold and distant about his demeanor. His smile was an afterthought, a fleeting expression that was more out of politeness than any actual pleasure. "Where is your sanctuary?"

"My what?"

He gave me an odd look. "Guardian."

The sound of his voice reminded me of when Nina had shushed all the spirits in my room. An odd resonance filled the air, like the last reverberations of a heavy church bell.

Kale snapped from his vantage point outside the car into the backseat. He looked as surprised as I felt. "Yes?"

"Has she been trained?"

"She's only seventeen," Kale said.

"That's not what I asked."

"No," Kale said. "I was giving her time to adapt. That's why I asked you here."

Marcus sighed and reached for the gearshift. He made a tight turn in the street and pulled onto the main road. "You might have mentioned that when we spoke before," he said. I frowned. What had Kale said about me?

As we merged into traffic, I toyed with my hands. "Listen, I know Kale asked you here to seal up the spirits, but I want to help them if we can."

"Bridget," Kale said in a warning tone.

"They're just little kids."

"Not anymore," Marcus said. "They're incorporeal spirits, ones that have already harmed the living on multiple occasions, according to your Guardian. And you, judging by the state of your eye."

"That doesn't make them any less human," I said.

"If you don't want my help, I'm happy to leave," Marcus said. "You asked me here. Not the other way around. Trust me, I have better things to do on a Saturday."

"No!" Kale said. "We're doing this."

"Is there a church nearby? Older would be better," Marcus asked.

I frowned and oriented myself by the familiar landmarks: the Kwik-Stop on one corner and an overgrown vacant house on the other.

"Turn left up here," I said. I guided him through the next few turns, until he pulled into the lot of the old Creekview Baptist Church, or what remained of it after the fire. The old sign out front was in disrepair, with its marquee panels hanging askew from a rusted black frame.

Years after the fire, the church was little more than a charred husk that still hadn't been knocked down. The outer walls were broken away, like something had taken huge bites from them. I'd been to the burned church many times before. Months ago, I'd come here to send off the wistful spirit of Anna Cole, who'd been killed by her jerk husband in a jealous rage.

I had just placed my hand on the door to get out when the flip phone rang. I answered it quickly. Only three people would have this number.

"Colin?" I asked, my heart racing in anticipation.

The deep male voice on the other end said, "No. Uh, this is James. I talked to you earlier."

The response stunned me into silence.

"Are you there?"

"Y-yeah, I'm here." I glanced over at Marcus, who was watching me with a questioning look on his face. "Just a second." I got out of the car, pressing the phone to my ear. The cold breeze at my back told me Kale was close behind me. "Why are you calling?"

"I'm almost to Parkland," James said, like he'd been holding his breath and couldn't handle it anymore. "I got on the road after you called. This is crazy, but—"

"No, it's not," I said. "This is good. Can you come meet me?"

"Where?"

"We're at the old Creekview Baptist Church," I said. "Call me when you get here."

"Okay," he said, voice shaky.

As soon as I hung up, Kale spluttered, "Bridget. What part of letting Marcus handle this did you not get?"

"Well, he already thinks I'm an idiot. Why disappoint him now?" I folded my arms and leveled a stare at Kale. Even though I wanted to be mature and serious, I was distracted by his lips. A flush heated my cheeks. I squared my shoulders and said, "This is the last resort, right? So we have to try everything we can. If this doesn't work, I won't fight you on it anymore. I promise."

Kale sighed, his eyes downturned. "Let's go."

It wasn't the indulgent sigh I so often heard from him. There was genuine disappointment there, maybe even a hint of anger. But I had to give the Hillmans one last opportunity. If it failed, then I'd at least know I tried.

When we got back to the car, Marcus was pulling a large backpack out of the trunk. After situating it on his shoulders, he gave me an appraising look. "Are you done? I hate to keep you from more important things."

"You don't have to be so rude," I said.

"Bridget," Kale said sternly.

Oh, no. He was not going to give me the dad treatment so he could show Marcus how he was in charge here.

"And yes, I'm done," I said sweetly. "Thanks for being so patient."

Marcus closed his eyes, as if he was listening for something far away. When he opened his eyes, he nodded. "This place is suitable. Divinity still holds."

What the heck did that even mean? I looked back at Kale, who gave me a stern look and shook his head as if to tell me not to question Marcus.

Marcus inched around the exterior of the church, looking it up and down like he was considering buying it. I couldn't help noticing that the looks didn't stop with a nice face. He wasn't a supermodel, but he was good-looking in a way that made him approachable, rather than melting unsuspecting girls into useless puddles. It was too bad about the personality.

We circled around to the graveyard along the side of the church, enclosed in a low brick wall. The Bradford pear tree that usually shaded the tiny cemetery was bare for the winter, its branches dry and gnarled. White petals congealed into brown-stained splotches on the ground below.

"In the graveyard?" I suggested.

"No," Marcus said sharply. He sighed and looked at Kale again. "What have you been teaching her?"

"Hey," I said. "Don't talk to him like that. Or about me like that."

Never mind that I'd been pestering Kale for over two years to answer my questions. It wasn't this jerk's place to criticize him.

Marcus gave me an incredulous look. "You're nearly an adult, and you apparently don't know the first thing about your ability or your function in this world."

"Then tell me," I said. "What don't I know?"

Marcus sighed, squeezing the bridge of his nose like he'd been struck by a headache. "We don't have time for this."

"But you have plenty of time to criticize me for it," I said. "Isn't it easier just to answer me?"

He turned and climbed over the back wall of the cemetery. I followed, struggling to get my legs up over the brick. Behind the burned chapel was a stretch of overgrown grassy field that pushed into dense woods. Marcus hurried toward the woods, his strides long and purposeful.

As I scurried after him, he finally spoke. "You would never seal an angry spirit inside a cemetery," he said, like it was the most obvious thing in the world. His demeanor reminded me of when I asked Mrs. England for help on a problem she'd already done in our notes. "On the chance that any other spirits still lingered, they might be influenced by the negative energy and emotion. Moreover, they might cause harm to any mourners who happened by."

"I thought the seal kept them from hurting anyone," I said.

Knee-high grass whispered as it swished around our legs. Morning dew painted my legs with cool, damp brushstrokes.

"It should, but if someone was very close and was vulnerable to a spiritual attack because of their grief, then it's possible," he said. "It's better to isolate them and reduce the risk of collateral damage."

Collateral damage was such a clean, sterile way to talk about an imprisoned soul. As I absorbed his answers, I had to wonder about the training he and Kale kept referring to. If I ever did it, would I become cold and detached like Marcus? The thought made me shiver.

We continued into the shaded cover of the woods. My heart beat faster as I followed, our feet rustling through a dense carpet of pine straw and dead leaves. The last time I'd ventured into the woods, I'd gotten up close and personal with the anguished spirit of a long-dead hiker and discovered how cold one could get without actually getting frostbite.

Fortunately, we didn't go far. After a minute or so of walking, Marcus stopped to survey the trees around him. Sunlight was still visible through the trees behind us, and I could pick out the jagged silhouette of the church. If things went badly, I could sprint out of the woods. Knowing I had an exit alleviated some of the fear weighing on me.

I didn't know what he was looking for, but he seemed to find it in an old tree a few yards from where he'd stopped. Gnarled roots rose from the ground like small islands around the wide trunk.

He braced one hand against the trunk, looked up, then back to me. "Let's get this over with."

Even though his attitude needed work, it was fascinating to watch Marcus. He pulled a smaller bag from his backpack and opened it to reveal a dozen neatly organized pockets. It looked like a first aid kit, but instead of pulling out Band-Aids and ointment, he took out assorted items to conduct a ritual.

Some I recognized, like salt and the pale, papery sage leaves. As for some of the others, I could only guess what their function was. The whole time he worked, he spoke quietly to himself. When he bent over to clear a pile of dead leaves, a small gold pendant dangled from his neck.

He pushed the stakes into the ground, forming a rough circle around the base of the tree.

"Iron," he said. After making a hole with the final stake, he twisted it around to widen the opening, then pulled it back out. He tossed it to me, and I fumbled to catch it. The heavy, cold stake felt like a vicious weapon. "This is your responsibility. When I tell you to, you close the circle."

I didn't like his tone. "I got it."

He stared at me. "I'm serious. Don't hesitate."

"I got it," I said hotly. I was stubborn, not stupid.

He took another bag from his backpack, this one narrow and about as long as his forearm. He unzipped it to reveal a steely glint. His shoulders slumped a little as he examined it, then set it reverently just outside the circle. Inside the case was a sharp knife with symbols etched on the blade.

I froze at the sight of it. "What's that for?" *Oh God.* Kale didn't say anything about knives. Knives meant cutting, and cutting meant blood. I didn't sign up for this.

"This is not a simple ritual," he said cryptically. "Let's get this over with."

Preparing myself for a scornful response, I asked, "Can we please try to talk to them first?"

To my surprise, he didn't snap at me. Instead, he nodded and said, "Of course. But prepare yourself. It's been my experience that a spirit this far gone won't change its ways because someone asks nicely."

I glanced back to Kale. What had changed his mind? Then I took a deep breath. "What if I bring someone who can help them rest?"

Marcus cocked his head. "I'm already here."

"Not you," I said.

"Bridget…" Kale said.

I ignored him, though the rising warning in his voice wormed into my gut and made me squirm a little. "I think they're angry at this boy who scared them before they died. He's coming here."

"You've got to be kidding me," Marcus said, pinching the bridge of his nose. "You realize this looks crazy to an outsider."

"So? Does it matter if we help them? Isn't that the point?" I said, toying with the finger-thick metal in my hand.

"The whole point is to keep the balance," Marcus said. "It's to do good. This isn't a Lifetime movie where you can make everything work out magically."

"Trust me, I get that," I said.

"Do you?" Marcus said. He took several steps toward me, until he was close enough that I could smell the sage on his hands. He loomed a good six inches taller than me, and his very presence was tangible, like there was a force field around him. I set my jaw and stared up at him. His eyes narrowed as he continued. "You obviously haven't had to deal with any of this going badly. Not really. And you've never had to make this decision that you've asked me to make so you can keep your hands clean."

"You don't know what I've had to do," I snapped.

"And I don't care," Marcus said. He stepped into his circle. "You can speak to them, but before I leave here, this situation will be resolved one way or the other."

CHAPTER TWENTY-SEVEN

"LET'S SEE WHAT YOU HAVE," Marcus said. "Names?"

"Travis and Charlie Hillman," I said, still unsteady from his admonition.

"Pictures?"

"I don't have any," I said.

Marcus looked pained. "Then look it up."

I took out the flip phone and showed it to him. "This is all I've got. You'll have to do it."

His eyes rolled back in irritation as he dug his phone out of his bag and handed it to me.

"Why are you so hostile?"

"I'm not hostile," he said. "I just want to get the job done, and this has not been the simple process your Guardian promised me."

I thumbed through the menus on his phone and opened a browser window, then typed in the boys' names. While I waited for Charlie's obituary to load, I looked up at Marcus. "These are people, not a job."

"It's a job," he said flatly.

"I guess you've never had to see someone you love this way, then," I said.

He narrowed his eyes. "Now who's assuming? Don't presume to know my history. This is simple math. Two spirits who are already dead, versus dozens of potential victims of their rage. The needs of the many—"

"Ugh," I interrupted. "Spare me." I handed him the phone with Charlie's picture pulled up. "That's the younger one. He's the dangerous one."

Marcus stared at the picture, zoomed in, then nodded as he handed it back. I repeated the process with Travis's picture and gave it to him.

He looked it over, then put the phone in his pocket and said, "I'm ready. You know what to do?"

"I'm good."

Marcus reached into the neck of his shirt and pulled out the thin gold chain there. A small shield-shaped medal lay against his chest. He closed his eyes, murmuring quietly to himself. After a few moments of what must have been prayer, he opened his eyes and held his hands palm up like he was waiting to feel raindrops fall.

His voice was deep and resonant as he said, "St. Michael the archangel, give us your protection. Send your soldiers to guard us from above and below, and to battle all who would do us harm. Travis Hillman. I command you to come to me. Charlie Hillman, I command you to come to me. You will show yourself to me. Travis Hillman…" He continued to repeat it over and over, interspersing it with prayers to Saint Michael.

For as much as he'd irritated me, it was certainly something to behold as he conducted the ritual. He was stoic, as if he was in complete control. His voice never faltered.

"Be careful," Kale murmured in my ear. His hand solidified and rested on my shoulder. The cool rushing sensation of energy pulled at my chest. "When they come, I'll go."

As he spoke, the air cooled around us. The crawling sensation I'd felt in the graveyard was here again, like ragged fingernails running over my skin. Maybe it was all in my head, but it even seemed to get darker. The shadows of the woods deepened.

Marcus startled suddenly, and his hands balled into fists like he was pulling something to him. There was a raucous screech as two dark figures appeared on either side of Marcus, close enough to him that his hands disappeared within their shadowy bodies.

Holy crap.

"Now," Marcus said through clenched teeth.

I darted forward and drove my iron stake into the hole to close the circle. Then as if they were no more than stubborn cobwebs clinging to his hands, Marcus shook off Travis and Charlie and stepped out of the circle, leaving them pressed against an invisible barrier.

Color me impressed. I looked around, and there was no sign of Kale. Well, that wasn't as bad as I expected.

"Well, have at it," he said. "Let's talk about our feelings. They're temporarily trapped, but this will not hold them permanently. Spirits this strong can wear down physical protections."

"They're not sealed yet?"

Marcus shook his head. "I didn't drive three hours to get here to poke some metal stakes into the ground," he said. "This is better than salt, but they can escape eventually if they try hard enough. Time is ticking."

"Let's wait a minute," I pleaded.

The Hillmans showed me what they thought of my plan by slamming into the barrier. But the iron held firm, much better than my lines of salt had. Their dead white eyes glowed, and their forms dissipated as they swirled like smoke in a glass jar. But it was to no avail. The iron kept them imprisoned, though like before, they shouted their rage. Their voices were muffled, like I was hearing them through a wall.

"Marcus, why can we still hear them?"

He shrugged. "You just can. Why do you ask?"

"When we tried to speak to them before, I had to leave a salt circle before they would appear," I said. "I thought they couldn't hear me."

He shook his head. "Protective barriers give off a certain energy that spirits can detect. That's why I made you wait to close the circle until they were here. They would have resisted much harder if they'd seen it closed. In your case, they probably knew they couldn't get to you inside the circle, so they waited for you to come out."

Then my instincts weren't as bad as he seemed to think. "Good to know," I said. With a deep breath to steady myself, I pulled out the flip phone and called James. It rang twice before he answered.

"Yeah?" he said.

"It's Bridget," I said. "Where are you?"

"Walking out back," he said. "You meant the old burned up church, right?"

"Yeah," I said. "Go through the field and into the woods. We're not far in."

"In the woods?"

"Yes. Hurry," I said, then hung up and shoved the phone back into my pocket.

Marcus glared at me as I joined him at the edge of the circle. "This is not how things are done," he said sharply. He turned his icy stare on the spirits in the circle. "Control yourself," he ordered. The smoky substance shuddered, then coalesced into two bodies once more. "You will obey. Your presence here is unnatural and unwelcome." Well, way to start off the conversation. He put up his hands as if he was touching the smooth surface of the barrier. Then he grimaced and pulled away. "Bridget, there is nothing you can say. They're too far gone to hear reason."

"Bridget?" a gruff voice called from behind me.

"Please give us a chance," I said. I turned toward the sound of James' voice. A skinny figure stood in silhouette at the edge of the woods. I approached and called, "We're here."

I walked back and met James on the path. If I didn't know better, I'd have thought James was a ghost himself. A few inches taller than me, he was gaunt and pale, with dark circles under his eyes that told me he didn't sleep much.

"Are you James?" I asked.

He nodded, but didn't speak. His hand was behind his back. My blood went cold. I knew what had to be there. Suddenly, I had a vision of him pulling out a gun and shooting me where I stood. My heart shuddered, beating so fast that it made me dizzy.

"You don't have to be afraid," I said, my voice trembling as I spoke. "I called you because you can help." I slowly showed him my hands.

His bloodshot eyes froze. He appeared to be on the brink of bolting. It was just like speaking with a spirit, trapped by pain and the memories of things long past.

"What do I have to do?" he finally said. His hand slowly dropped to his side. It was empty.

I let out a shaky breath as relief rushed through me. "Come with me and talk to them."

With James following me, I returned to the circle. Marcus shifted uncomfortably, squaring his shoulders as if to send the message that he was the alpha here. It was an unnecessary move. Though they were about the same height, James' hunched posture and skinny frame made him look fragile next to the other man.

"You have five minutes."

I ignored Marcus and turned to James. "I know you don't see anything, but they're here."

His head whipped around frantically.

"It's okay," I said. "You're safe from them. Just talk."

"Uh, hi," James said. "You probably don't remember me, but—"

Deafening wails exploded from inside the barrier. The sound echoed in my head, so loud and piercing I cried out in pain. Even Marcus grunted, pressing one hand to his temple. It sounded like a dozen children crying and screaming at the same time. The only word I could make out was *no*.

"Boys, please," I said. "You have to listen." This was their last chance.

"What's happening?" James asked.

At the sound of his voice, the Hillmans cried out again, but the fearful shouting turned to guttural, rage-filled screams. They slammed against the barrier, and this time I actually felt the impact, like someone shoved me in the chest.

We couldn't do anything like this.

"James, wait," I said. "Let me try something."

I took a step forward, but Marcus seized my arm. His large hand closed completely around my elbow and hauled me backward. "Unacceptable," he said. "You're not going in."

"They just need to know it's safe," I protested. "I can stabilize them." Like this, they were the embodiment of anguish, nothing but frayed memories stitched together by threads of fear. The touch of something living and real would knit them back together, bringing those raging memories into check so they could hear reason. At least I hoped it would.

I shook off Marcus' grasp and stepped into the circle on shaking legs. This was so stupid. But I had to try. Stepping beyond the protective circle was like surfacing from deep water into a hurricane. I'd thought it was bad before, but the noise inside the circle was deafening, scraping down my eardrums and into my bones. The air was so cold it sliced into my lungs as I breathed, and I coughed at the thick reek of decay.

A deep voice shook the barrier.

"Get out," Marcus commanded. The barrier actually vibrated with the power of his voice, but he didn't have the same compulsion effect on me as the spirits.

"Travis. Charlie," I pleaded. "You have to listen. I want to help you. I understand what happened. And I don't think you want to hurt anyone."

Even though I knew Kale would disapprove, I put my hands out like Marcus had done. One of the Hillmans reached for it, making contact. Cold shot up my arm, turning my bones to brittle ice. I gritted my teeth and tried not to flinch at the bleeding sensation as warmth, my life energy, poured into the spirit. The color spread from his fingertips, across the tattered remains of his Grim Reaper costume, and up to his face. It was Travis. Charlie still pounded on the barrier, screaming incoherently.

"Please help us." His voice was like dead leaves blown across stone, barely more than a hoarse whisper. "I can't stop him from hurting people."

Without taking my hand from Travis, I reached for Charlie. He tried to pull away, but I seized his arm. Though I'd been the one to initiate contact, it still had the same effect. Color bloomed from my grasp, spreading over him and up to his small face. Trying to stabilize both of them was exhausting, but I had to do it.

Connecting with both boys sheared my vision down the middle. On one side, I saw the bloody-mouthed scarecrow chasing Charlie. On the other, I saw Charlie himself lying in a hospital bed, barely visible under a tangled mat of tubes and wires. I recognized Sara Workman in a chair next to him, whispering as she stroked his hand.

Stay with me. Stay with me.

And when the monitors finally went flat, nurses with sad eyes gently removed the tubes from Charlie's lifeless body. They were in no particular hurry. The need for urgency had passed. Sara brushed a light kiss on his forehead, then walked away with her husband supporting her.

And there stood Charlie, baffled as he watched his mother walking away from him, even as he and Travis called *Mommy! Right here!*

They had stayed. Just like she told them.

They'd watched her waste away in the hospital. They'd been there to hear her say to the empty room, "Travis and Charlie, I'm coming to be with you soon. We'll be together," and it was the happiest moment of their existence, a bright spot in what had been a dark misery for so long.

When her spirit left her body, this beautiful golden glowing thing, it was like sunrise after an endless night. But their joy turned to despair as it faded away, dissolving into nothingness. She couldn't hear them or see them. She left them alone in the gray place. They screamed after her, begging her to stay, but there was nothing left of her spirit here.

And so they waited.

The vision broke as strong hands grabbed my shoulders and pulled me backward hard enough to sweep me off my feet. As the world came rushing back, a sharp pain bolted between my temples, ahead of a monstrous headache that squeezed my head in a vise.

The world was hazy, and my ears were ringing. After a few seconds, I opened my eyes to see tree branches overhead. The light was blocked by a face. Through bleary eyes, I recognized Marcus standing over me.

"Are you all right?" he said.

"I think so," I said, squinting against the light. "I know what they need."

I held my hand out. Marcus took it and hauled me to my feet. His stern look of disapproval had softened into concern. Wet heat trickled over my lip. My tongue darted out and caught the metallic taste of blood. I frowned and pressed my fingers to my nose.

They came away dripping with fresh blood. "Crap."

Pressing the sleeve of my shirt to staunch the flow from my nose, I turned to James, who recoiled at the sight of me. I must have looked rough as hell. "Don't say anything yet."

I started toward the barrier, but Marcus grabbed my arm again to hold me back. "I'll duct tape you to that tree if I have to. You're not going back in."

"That's the sweetest thing you've said yet. I won't," I said. "Let go, please."

Instead, I gazed at the Hillmans. After drawing from me, they were both solid. I forced myself to look at them, knowing I'd have nightmares about the ruin of what had been Travis's face.

"I know you're scared," I said. "And you miss her, don't you? You miss your mommy."

A faint whisper broke through the barrier. *Mommy.*

"She misses you, too," I said. "What happened to you was so unfair, but it was an accident. He didn't mean to hurt you, just like you didn't meant to hurt any of the people here. Right?"

Charlie's narrowed as he looked from me, then to James. Then he looked back at me and hung his head.

"Sometimes when we get hurt, we do things we don't mean," I said. "But it's okay. Can my friend James talk to you?"

I turned to James, who was watching me with wide, frozen eyes. He took a hesitant step forward and shivered. The temperature plunged again.

"It's okay," I said, as much for James as for the spirits.

"Um, hi," he said. His gaze was focused on the dead grass. Even if he could have seen Travis and Charlie, I doubted he would have been able to look into their eyes. "I wanted to tell you I'm so sorry about what happened that night. You know, we just thought we would have fun messing with the little kids. And I should have realized you guys were scared and stopped. If I could go back right now, I would. Hell, I'd let that car hit me instead of you if that would bring you back. I always wanted to go talk to your mom and apologize, but I was too chicken."

As he spoke, the two brothers looked at each other, then back to James. I still sensed the whispering, but it was blessedly quiet compared to their primal screaming.

"I swear to God, I never meant to hurt you guys," James said. His voice broke as tears spilled over his cheeks. "But I did. And I can't ever forgive myself for it. And I understand if you can't either. But I wanted to tell you I was sorry. I truly am, and I—" His voice cracked.

Charlie looked up and pressed his hand toward the barrier. I gently put mine against it, and without waiting for Marcus to shout at me, I pushed it through to touch him.

With his icy hand in mine, Charlie spoke clearly. "I'm scared."

"I know, sweetie," I said. "It can be really scary here. But I've seen a lot of spirits go to a better place. Isn't it lonely and dark here?"

"Yeah," Travis said. He looked at me gratefully, then took Charlie's other hand. "We can go together."

"She told us to stay," Charlie said.

"She wanted you to live and be here with her," I said. "I wish you could have. But she wouldn't have wanted you to stay here all alone. She would want you to be wherever she was."

Charlie looked up over my shoulder at James. His eyes narrowed, and his grasp on my hand tightened, sending icy needles up my arm. "He's the scarecrow."

"He was," I said. "But he's not anymore. He wouldn't have scared you if he knew what would happen."

"It was an accident," Travis said. The words came slowly, like he'd been digging forever to finally uncover the realization like hidden treasure.

"Just an accident," I said.

"We'll see Mommy?" Charlie said.

God, I hoped so. If there was any good in the world, that was exactly what would happen. "It's going to be okay," I told them. "Think about your mother."

Travis held his hand out to Charlie. The younger boy took it, and they both looked at me expectantly. I took a step back, then knelt and pulled one of the stakes out of the ground to break the circle.

"No," Marcus spat.

"Just wait," I snapped at him. Despite their calm, I stayed close to the circle so I could jam the stake back into the ground if I had to. "She's waiting for you. Think about how beautiful she is. Her smile. How nice her hugs were."

The air around us stirred, sending a chill down my spine. A small voice whispered *no* in my ear, but Travis said, "It's okay, Charlie. I'll make sure you're okay."

Then their dark forms lightened, like the sun had broken through after a long storm. Their fading wasn't a quick process, as I'd seen in the past. They'd fade for a few seconds, and then darken again like they were trying their best to hold on. Fear held them here. They were miserable here, but a familiar misery could be easier than the fear of the unknown.

"You can let go," I said. "She's waiting for you. She loves you so much."

Leaves skittered across the ground as the icy breeze picked up. Gentle whispers rose on the wind. As they both looked upward, their mangled faces relaxed. The brutal injuries melted away to reveal smooth, pale cheeks and bright eyes. The dirt and grime simply faded away from their bodies as the pain relented. Light filtered through their dissipating forms. A prickling tingle ran down my spine.

They were shadows of themselves, and then only the vaguest shimmering outlines remained. Finally, they faded into nothingness. There was an unmistakable sigh of relief on the wind. I turned slowly to see James gaping at me. I'd hoped for some kind of approval, but Marcus crossed his arms over his chest and narrowed his eyes.

Within seconds, Kale reappeared. "What did you do?" he murmured.

I ignored him as James composed himself and looked around. "I...did they...this is insane."

"They've gone on," I said.

He stared in my direction, though his gaze was far away. "I can't believe this."

"Thank you for coming," I said. "I think that's what set them free."

He nodded quietly, although he didn't look convinced. I glanced at Kale, then back to James. "Before they went, they said they forgave you."

James' head snapped up. Out of the corner of my eye, I saw Marcus shift suddenly, his head tilting. "Really?" James asked in a quavering voice.

Liar, liar, pants on fire. "They were angry before, but they understood you didn't mean to hurt them," I said. "It's okay."

James let out a sigh that turned into a sob. He put his hands over his face and sank to his knees. His shoulders shook as he released years of guilt. Marcus stared at me evenly, shaking his head slightly. I ignored him and checked the flip phone. I had two missed calls from a mystery number. Mom's number was programmed, and James was here, which left only Colin.

I called him back. "What's wrong?"

"Mom got off early and she's on her way home. She's stopping to get lunch, but you probably only have thirty minutes," he said.

"Thanks," I said. I hung up and gestured to Marcus. "I have to go."

Marcus frowned. "We still need to purify this place."

"Then let's get purifying."

CHAPTER TWENTY-EIGHT

IT TOOK US ANOTHER ten minutes to clean up. I picked up the stakes, and Marcus spent the next few minutes praying quietly instead of scolding me. While he packed his supplies, I used a burning bundle of sage to waft cleansing smoke around the whole area. James watched with skeptical fascination. Once Marcus had inspected it one last time and declared it safe, we started back toward the church.

When we reached the parking lot, James paused near a beat-up red car. "So what now?"

"Live your life," I said.

"I just don't know how to get past this," he said.

"Try therapy," Marcus said sharply. "Let's go."

James hesitated, then put out his hand. I shook it. "Thank you."

We left him and headed for Marcus's car. James watched us go, an expression of confused wonder still on his face. As soon as I climbed into the passenger seat, Marcus fixed me with a stern look. "What the hell was that?"

"What?"

"All of that," he retorted. "Jumping in the circle. Lying to him about the whole forgiveness thing."

"He needed it," I said. "You guys say our job is to protect the living."

"They didn't offer it."

"Well, they're not here to argue with me, are they?"

Marcus sighed. "I don't like how you do things, Bridget."

"That makes two of you," I said.

I looked over my shoulder at Kale in the back seat. He was quiet, his gaze far away.

Marcus shook his head. "It's reckless. And it'll get you killed if you're not careful."

We spent the rest of the drive in silence, which was a nice change. When we reached my neighborhood, Marcus parked at the curb in front of the first house on the street. He pulled out a plain leather wallet and withdrew an ivory business card. It simply said *Marcus Alder*, with a phone number and an email printed below, all in plain black text. "I'm guessing you don't know many other sensitives. If you decide you're ready to get your training, contact me and I'll put you in touch with the right people. But I'll warn you that we don't like reckless behavior. We have rules that have kept us safe for many generations. So if you want to keep doing things your own way, then lose that number."

"Right," I said, slowly turning the card over in my hands. He'd given me plenty to chew on for the moment. "Well, thanks for coming."

"It's my job," he said. "Even if I didn't get to do it."

"Okay, good talk," I said.

Our neighborhood was small, so it only took a few minutes of brisk walking to reach the driveway. My stomach plunged to the ground at the sight of Mom's car in the driveway. Considering I was already grounded, she'd have to get creative with her punishment.

I paused in the driveway and looked back to Kale. "Are you angry at me?"

"I'm frustrated with you," he said, lingering at the foot of the driveway without following me.

"It was the right thing to do," I said.

"I know that's how you feel. And you got lucky this time with James coming to talk to them," he said. "But Marcus wasn't wrong. You take risks because you think everything has to work out if you're doing the right thing. One of these times, it's not going to work out, and you're going to get killed. And I can't bring you back."

The thought was sobering. "That won't happen. You won't let it."

He gave me sad smile. "If all it took was my willpower to protect you, it'd never be a problem. But that's not how things work." He shook his head. "You should go. Your mom is going to be upset."

That was an understatement, but I didn't turn to go into the house yet. "Kale? About yesterday…"

"I'm sorry," he said. "I let my emotions carry me away."

"Oh," I said. So that was what it felt like for hope to shatter into a thousand pieces. It felt strangely like dying, which I knew from experience. A sick feeling sank into my stomach. "That's it?"

"That's all it can be," he said, not meeting my eyes.

"I see," I said. It was a good thing he wasn't looking, because the welling tears in my eyes threatened to betray me at any moment.

He nodded. "Be good. I'll be back soon."

And with that, he vanished, like he hadn't just shattered me. *Be good?* The tiny, precious bloom of hope that had sprouted in the wake of his kiss was crushed under his foot, as if it was no more than a piece of garbage.

As if things weren't already bad enough, I heard the front door swing open. "Bridget? Explain to me why you're out on a little trip when you're grounded."

CHAPTER TWENTY-NINE

"SO THINGS ARE COOL NOW?" Emily asked.

I settled down with my tray. I peeked over her shoulder to see Bryce and his idiot friends sneaking looks at me. Kale might have called me a beautiful soul, but there was a mean soul in me too, and that mean little soul was sort of regretting not trying to turn the Hillmans on Bryce.

"I guess," I said. "Back to normal, at least."

Well, normal for me, considering my house was the hottest spot in town for the life-challenged. On Saturday night, Sal had organized a bunch of spirits in an afterlife neighborhood watch, eventually catching a couple of teenagers breaking into a house in the same neighborhood as Fulbright's other break-ins. Two of Sal's phantom deputies followed the kids back to their Jeep and memorized the license plate, which I promptly passed on to Fulbright. He didn't question it, just thanked me and said he'd look into it.

Over the last week, Shirley and Jerry had become fast friends, and had stopped by my room on Sunday to fill me in at great length on the baby shower for Shirley's daughter. Hearing about every detail of the finger foods and gifts was a nice change from worrying about tragic deaths and supernatural protection.

Emily took a bite of her PB&J and gestured with it. "Have you seen Nina?"

"She's home now. Mom took me to see her yesterday afternoon," I said. "She's good. They said she can come back to school in another week or so."

Other than a mild infection that kept her in the hospital a few days longer, Nina had been recovering well, though she'd been disappointed to miss out on the final goodbye to the Hillmans. She confirmed that she'd seen one of the boys right before her accident, most likely Charlie. He'd materialized in her car and tangled around her feet so she couldn't hit the brakes. But she'd been much more interested in hearing about the mysterious Marcus. Considering his less-than-personable attitude, I didn't think she'd missed much.

There was a subtle lift to her eyebrows and the hint of a frown on her lips, both of which told me she was in no hurry for Nina to come back.

"Are we cool?" I finally asked.

She hesitated, which gave me my answer. "I miss hanging out with you."

"Me too."

"I was kind of hoping you'd show up for mani-pedi day on Saturday," she said, showing me her glitter-tipped nails.

Dread rolled through my stomach. I had completely forgotten. "I had to deal with the Hillmans, and then Mom was so mad that I went out without permission, I couldn't—"

"I know. You don't have to make excuses," she said. "But you didn't even message me or anything. You didn't say anything after I took your brother to the doctor, and I was really worried about you guys. In fact, the only time you've wanted anything to do with me since Nina showed up was when she got hurt and you needed a ride. And I did it, didn't I?"

"Emily, I'm—"

"Let me finish. I'm sorry if I sound mean. I'm actually not mad anymore," she said. "I know you think I don't get it, but I do. You have really important, scary stuff going on in your life. And I understand that helping people is more important than getting your nails done. I know." She sighed. I wanted her to stop, because every bit of it was true, and I couldn't defend it. It was never fun to hear a laundry list of ways you'd screwed up. I didn't want to have to acknowledge that I'd hurt her. "I just don't want you to forget that I'm your friend, too. And even with all this going on, I hope our friendship still matters to you, even if it's not the most important thing in your world. Because it matters to me." She raised her eyes, and I was shocked to see the glisten of tears there. Emily never cried.

My throat clenched, and I had to sit quietly for a minute to process and let the tension pass. The immature part of me wanted to lash out. But she was my best friend and had stood by me when literally no one else had. Saving lives was important, but my ability didn't give me the right to treat her like crap. "I'm sorry," I said quietly. "I'm sorry I made you feel unimportant. You're still important to me. And I would much rather hang out with you than ghosts."

Her lips quirked. "I know," she said. "I'm a lot more fun."

"Seriously. I'm sorry," I said. "And I'll do better. I promise."

"Okay," she said. "Thank you."

"Can I tell you something crazy?" I asked her, hoping my news would make her smile. "I haven't told anyone and I might die if I don't." I hadn't even told Nina about Kale, too afraid of what she'd say.

"Of course. I love crazy."

"Kale kissed me. Or I kissed him. Both? I don't really know."

Emily gaped at me and leaned across the table. "You kissed a ghost?"

"Yep," I said.

Emily's eyes went wide. "How?"

"I don't know," I said. "It's kind of…I hate to say magical, but that's kind of it. When I touch him, he becomes real, I guess."

"That might be the weirdest and yet coolest thing ever," she said. "What was it like?"

I smiled, although the memory was tinged with sadness that it couldn't be anything more. "It was nice. Really nice, actually."

"So what does that mean for you? Are you like…a thing? More than you already are?"

"No," I said, recalling his stony expression with an ache in my chest. "He said he let his emotions carry him away. And that was all."

"Bullshit," Emily said. "He totally likes you."

God, how I wanted that to be true. "It doesn't matter. It's not like we could ever be together."

She sighed. "Star-crossed lovers. Like Romeo and Juliet."

"Did you actually read the play? They're so not relationship goal material."

"No, but my teacher keeps saying it," Emily said.

I laughed aloud. "We also met up with this guy who helped me with the spirits. He made it sound like there's all this stuff I've missed out on. He gave me a number to get in contact with him."

"Are you gonna do it?"

"Maybe," I said.

After getting a blistering earful from Mom about breaking her trust—yet again—I'd been sent to my room with an extra two weeks added to my sentence. I'd toyed with Marcus's card, daydreaming about what there might be in store for me. Was there some fancy school for people like me, all X-Men style? Or would I get a grumpy teacher like Marcus to tell me to follow all the rules? He and Kale both made it sound like I'd have to toe the line pretty hard if I went that way.

But trapped in my room with no electronics and no pressing cases, I'd thought over and over about what they'd both said. For more than two years, I'd ignored the dangers and tried to help people, no matter the cost. But what Kale had said about getting myself killed had stuck in my brain, like a stubborn splinter in the pad of my finger.

Things had gotten progressively more complicated and dangerous since I'd first developed my ability. For one, I'd gotten myself involved in police business. Second, now that I could see all kinds of spirits, I risked attracting dangerous ones like Travis and Charlie.

I'd laid awake for hours last night thinking about the boys. I'd been able to reason with them, but only because James had come. If he hadn't stepped up, would I have kept trying until I literally died, leaving Marcus to deal with the aftermath?

Under the dark haze of insomnia, I'd realized something deeply troubling and sobering. Just as Marcus and Kale had both said, there would come a time when I had to make the hard decision. Sheer willpower wouldn't prevent it. I'd been lucky, at least by a generous definition of the word.

My power wasn't going away, and neither were the spirits. If I had to deal with this for the rest of my life, then it was time to understand it. I might have grown older, and maybe a bit wiser at least by my standards, if not Kale's. But my power was still immature. I was a white belt…maybe a yellow.

"So what's next?" Emily asked. "Are you already onto something new?"

"I'm onto trying to pass Spanish," I said. "And try to convince Mom to unground me."

"I think you're probably better off with the ghosts."

"You're probably right," I said.

Big things were on the horizon, and I had a lot of growing up to do. But for today, I wanted to be a normal girl. Bring on the homework and the petty drama. If I could handle an overprotective mother, a Guardian spirit toying with my heart, and two vengeful spirits wreaking havoc, then I could handle fifth period.

Bring it on.

WHAT NOW?

If you enjoyed getting to know Bridget and the ghost gang, then please let your friends, family, and the whole world know by sharing on social media and leaving reviews on the platform of your choice. Just a few minutes can help another reader find a story they may love. Thank you!

To learn more about upcoming books, short stories, and giveaways, make sure you find me online at:

www.jessicahawke.com

There you can sign up for my mailing list and get your free copy of *Phantom Light*, the spooky prequel to the *Phantoms* series!

Here are some of the places you can find me online!

Facebook: https://www.facebook.com/AuthorJessicaHawke/
Twitter: @JJHawke
Instagram: @writerjessicahawke
Website: https://www.jessicahawke.com

Acknowledgements

Writing may seem like a lonely business, but it takes more of a community than most people realize.

Thanks to…

The Tuesday Sushi Club—Hildie and Olivia, my writer BFFs, for encouragement, tough love, a never-ending wellspring of wisdom, and stickers, because we all need a sticker once in a while.

Rainy Kaye—for keen editing and a sharp eye for story

Melanie Kemp—for beta reading and providing the loving but necessary feedback

Clarissa Yeo—for a gorgeous cover

Carmen—my BFF, who pushes me to do my best with every new project.

Facebook Tribe—for suggestions on titles. This makes two in a row that you've named!

AAYAA—for a great community of authors working to make each other better!

My Family—for always being there to remind me to chase my dreams.

Finally, thank you, generous readers, for sticking around for Book Three. I hope you enjoy this one, and that we can share this journey of story for years to come.

About the Author

Jessica Hawke's first stories were painstakingly scrawled on notebook paper in second grade. While the story of the Three Little Fish will never again see the light of day, her parents felt this was a sign, and as usual, they turned out to be right. She enjoys writing paranormal and fantasy novels, since reality is overrated.

www.ingramcontent.com/pod-product-compliance
Lightning Source LLC
Chambersburg PA
CBHW030558180626
46816CB00005B/1593